WHISPERS IN THE NIGHT

"God help me, you're beautiful." Kincaid reached out with one broad hand to caress Meg's cheek. "You know I could protect you from whomever you're running from. Your husband—"

"Not my husband," she said firmly. "I already told you more than once, he's dead."

"Whomever." He massaged her shoulder.

Meg stood there, trembling inside. It was like this every time Kincaid grew near her. Every time he touched her.

He took her into his arms and she made no protest. He ran his hand down her arm. "Meg, love, I could make you happy if you'd let me try."

Meg closed her eyes as he brushed his mouth against hers. His offer was so tempting. She wanted so desperately for someone to care for her, love her. "I have to go away from here," she whispered. "If the one who's looking for me finds me, he'll kill me."

"Then I'll go, too. I'll finish my business here and I'll go. We'll go together, anywhere you want."

"Let's not talk about this anymore," she murmured in his ear. She wrapped her arms around his waist. "Let's do this, instead." She lifted up on her toes to press her lips to his.

"Ah, Meg, you do this to me time and time again." He kissed her full on the mouth with a groan. "And this is how the argument always ends. This is always how you win."

"Hush and kiss me," she answered. "Kiss me while I'm still here to be kissed."

Books by Colleen Faulkner

Published by Zebra Books

TO LOVE
A DARK
STRANGER

Colleen Faulkner

Zebra Books
Kensington Publishing Corp.
http://www.zebrabooks.com

ZEBRA BOOKS are published by

Kensington Publishing Corp.
850 Third Avenue
New York, NY 10022

First Printing: April, 1997
10 9 8 7 6 5 4 3 2 1

Printed in the United States of America

One

January, 1662
Rutledge Castle
Kent County, England

The knife fell from Margaret's hand, hit the wood floor, and slid under the tapestry-draped bed. She stared in shock at her blood-stained hands. The heat of the bedchamber was unbearable. The scent of the blood, his and hers, cloistering. Slowly, her gaze drifted to the dead man at her feet . . . her husband.

"Baby . . ." she whispered. "My baby . . ."

Margaret lifted the infant from the edge of the bed. Swaddled in linens, he too was covered with blood.

Tears ran down Margaret's cheeks as she raised the babe to her breast as if she could somehow comfort him. He was dead. She knew he was dead—the poor thing with his misshapen little mouth and his throat slit.

A sob wracked Margaret's body as she sank to her knees, hugging the lifeless infant, wishing desperately that she could have saved him. She knew she should pray, but no words would come. She was filled with nothing but regret for that which she could not change.

"M'lady Surrey . . ." A voice came, barely audible, yet insistent. "Lady Surrey!"

Margaret looked up to see the midwife. She held out her newborn son. "Mavis, can . . . can you help him?"

Gently, the old hag took Margaret's first born from her arms and laid him on the great bed. She stepped over the body of Lord Randall as if dead men commonly attended lying-ins.

Smelling of cloves, the midwife leaned over the tiny, still body. She listened for breath. She felt for a pulse.

Another sob rose up in Margaret's throat as she came to her feet, reaching for her infant. "No . . ."

Mavis covered the child's deformed face with the corner of the bloody blanket. "You must run, m'lady," she insisted in her crackly voice. "Run before I have to summon the earl."

Margaret looked at her husband. He was an ugly man with a flared pig's nose and bristly blond hair. Sprawled unnaturally on the floor, his club foot lay exposed, its linen wrapping undone. It was said that a sense of peace came over a man at his death bed, but she saw no such peace. All she saw was years of bitterness and hatred. How odd it was that a man's cruel deeds had a way of showing on his wrinkled face.

"But why must I run?" Margaret whispered, too numb to comprehend. "He killed my child."

"A father's right . . ." the old woman intoned. She was moving about the bedchamber now with the same efficiency with which she had attended the birth only hours before.

"He . . . he turned on me. First my child, then me when I tried to save my son. It . . . it was self-defense." Margaret wrung her blood-sticky hands. "Surely no man would condemn me for—"

"No man?" Mavis yanked Margaret's bloody robe from her shoulders and dropped a clean day gown over her trembling, naked body. "Ha! Any man would condemn ye! Yer husband sought to rid himself of an abomination and you killed him for it!"

"No. Not an abomination. A child . . . my child."

"I only say what they'll say, m'lady."

Margaret accepted the rough leather shoes and patched stockings the old woman thrust into her arms. "Surely the courts will—"

The midwife gave her a push. "Don't ye hear my words? No one will believe ye! Ye just killed the Earl of Rutledge's youngest brother! Run, child! Run into the night and let it swallow ye up!"

Margaret took a stumbling step backward, clutching the shoes and stockings to her aching, milk-swollen breasts. "Run? Run where?"

"London! London is the only place to hide!"

"But my baby. He must be buried." Margaret reached out with one hand toward the bundle on the bed. "He must have a decent burial!"

Mavis ushered Margaret to the door, pinning a maid's cap to her dark, tumbled hair. "I'll see 'im buried in the church-yard, same as I seen all the others."

Margaret stared at the woman's craggy face. "I cannot run," she whispered desperately. "I'm afraid. I haven't the courage."

"Ha! Men's words!" The old woman's gray eyes narrowed. "Ye had the courage to kill the bastard to save yerself, didn't ye?"

Margaret leaned against the door and slipped her feet into the stockings, not bothering to pull them up. "Which way shall I go?" She stepped into the leather shoes. "I . . . I've never even been to London."

"Take the road east, only stay to the woods line." The mid-wife removed the mended woolen cloak from her own shoul-ders and covered Margaret's. "Flag down the first coach ye see and say yer Lady Surrey's handmaid. Claim yer headed to London to see yer dyin' mother. By the time the earl gets the high sheriff from his bed and in his boots, you'll be lost to 'im in Londontown."

Margaret rested her hand on the doorknob. She was so numb that all she could do was follow the woman's orders. "Say I'm Lady Surrey's maid, gone to London . . . dying mother," she repeated. She stared at the bloody bundle at the end of the bed she had shared with her husband.

The midwife reached out to stop her, but Margaret couldn't

leave her son without saying goodbye. She stepped around Philip's body and leaned over the bed. She lifted the corner of the fleece blanket, and with the love born of a mother, she kissed her infant's not-so-perfect little mouth. "Goodbye, my love," she whispered, letting the blanket fall. Then, with resignation, she turned to go.

"Wait!" Mavis grabbed her arm. "You'll not get a mile looking like that." She hurried across the room, and came back with a clean rag dipped in the wash basin. She wiped Margaret's teary cheeks. Then she took Margaret's hands and scrubbed them vigorously.

The wash towel turned crimson.

"Go, now . . ." the midwife encouraged, done with her. "Run from the Randall curse! Run for your life!"

Margaret took one last look at the little bundle on the bed and then stumbled out of her bedchamber and into the cold, drafty hallway. No light illuminated the narrow stone corridor, but she knew it all too well. For fifteen years she had walked these hallways, alone in the darkness. Fifteen years she had been imprisoned.

Margaret followed the corridor from the east wing into the main house. All was silent, but for her own muffled footsteps. In the main hall, she caught a glimpse of pale light from a doorway. The earl's private library . . .

Her breath caught in her throat as she pressed her back to the wall. She had to pass the earl's library to escape the castle.

She stole a glance into the lit room. There was the earl, her dead husband's elder brother, seated at his desk. He was sipping a glass of claret, making that odd sucking sound that he did. Seeing the earl's deformed mouth brought tears to her eyes. It was the same mouth her son had been born with. It was strange, she thought, that looking at the Earl of Rutledge's deformity, revolted her, and yet the first glance at her newborn son had brought about none of those same feelings of repulsion. Then Margaret knew that it was not the deformity of the earl's palate that disgusted her, but the deformity of his cruel heart.

As Margaret stared at the earl in the feeble light she came to the practical realization of what the murder she had just committed meant. If she could escape, it meant freedom. Freedom from her brutal husband, Philip. Freedom from the earl's twisted words and sexual innuendoes. Freedom from his threats. Freedom from her fear.

How ironic it was that the death of her son could bring her the release she had lost hope of so many years ago. But then, her grandmother had always said that even in the darkest moments, God shed light upon his children.

Suddenly feeling stronger, Margaret reached down and slipped out of her shoes. Picking them up, she tiptoed past the earl's open door. She walked down the corridor and out the front hallway. She stepped into the dark, cold night and into freedom.

Captain Scarlet rode low in his saddle, fighting the bitter wind in his face. It was a damned dreary night to be about business. He'd have preferred to spend the hours at the Cock and Crow ordinary with a jack of ale in one hand and a piece of the seductive Mrs. Caine in the other. He almost wished he'd let his friend Monti talk him into remaining in London tonight, but a man had a duty to his work and Kincaid understood that duty, even if Monti didn't.

Monti pulled in his mount to ride beside Kincaid. He was a short man, with a broad face like a shovel and protruding ears. He wasn't a handsome fellow, but he was as devoted to their friendship as any man could be. "I don't like the looks of this, Captain," he hollered against the wind. "I told you I should have checked with my astrologer first. The snow's a bad omen. I can feel it in my bones."

"What snow?" Kincaid scoffed, amused by Monti's usual litany. Monti was a superstitious man who saw ill-luck at every turn. "I see no snow, and your bones are always telling you to stay home when it's cold out." His words were no sooner out of his mouth than the first wet snowflakes hit his cheekbones. By the light of the pale, silvered moon he could see the 'I told you so,' look on his companion's face.

"There's still time to turn back," Monti offered. "No one will be the wiser." He wiped his runny nose with a green handkerchief he extracted from inside his cloak. "We can catch this stinking cuttlefish another night."

Kincaid frowned. No. He'd not turn back, not tonight. He wanted this one, and he wanted him badly. Nearly six months he'd waited for dear Edmund Tolliger to depart the city at a convenient time and circumstance. "Excellent try," he called good-naturedly to Monti. "But I'll not bite."

Both men ducked to avoid a low-hanging branch as the road, barely more than a trail in places, made a sharp bend to the right. The horses' hooves sank in the rutted road, splattering horse and rider with mud.

Just as Kincaid rounded the bend, he spotted something beside the road. He immediately whirled his mount around to go back.

"What are you doing?" The brutal wind tore at Monti's cloak as he attempted to turn his mount. "You know it's imperative that we stick to our schedule!"

Kincaid held up one gloved finger, signaling to his friend to wait but a moment. He rode his horse back to the spot where he had seen the bundle. Sure enough, there it was, a heap of blankets lying in the dead grass. No . . . a cloak.

Kincaid dismounted, turning his back to the wind to see what he'd found. He pulled at the edge of the wet, mud-caked cloak and, to his surprise, found a tumble of curls.

A dead woman lying beside the road? He thrust his hand beneath the cloak to feel warmth. No, not dead at all.

"Madame?" Kincaid crouched beside her. "Madame, could I assist you?" He tugged back a bit more of the wool cape. She was a tearing beauty, whoever she was. Not a beauty like the ladies of the court with their bleached hair and moleskin face patches, but a natural beauty . . . an innocent.

She was as pale as milk glass. "Madame?" He touched her shoulder.

She stirred, her dark lashes fluttering open. The moment her eyes focused, she sought to fight him off. "No!" she screamed, hitting him with surprising force. She kicked him in the chest, knocking him into the mud, and then scrambled up the wet bank off the road. "You'll not take me alive! I'll not go back!"

"I mean you no harm," Kincaid hollered, fascinated by the sound of the woman's voice, by her haunting eyes. He didn't know what color they were, though. *He couldn't let her go without knowing what color they were.*

He chased her up the grassy bank, taking care of his footing. The falling snow made it slippery. "Stop! I only want to aid you!"

She nearly reached the top of the bank before she slid in the wet snow that was fast turning to sleet. "No!" she called one last time before she slid into him.

"God's bowels, what have you found? A woman?" Monti called from the road where his mount pranced back and forth nervously. "We've no time for wenches tonight, man! Come along!"

Kincaid reached down and picked her up. This time she didn't fight him. "Where are you taking me?" she whispered, her head rolling onto his shoulder. "Not Newgate."

Kincaid carefully placed one boot in front of the other, fearful he would slip carrying her down the bank to the road. "I sure as hell hope not, sweetheart," he crooned.

"What are you doing?" Monti demanded as Kincaid reached the road and pursed his cold lips to whistle for his horse.

"Taking her with us."

"Bloody hell you are!"

How could Kincaid explain this to his friend? Yes, he'd

always had a weakness for females, but the moment he had seen this woman's face, he knew she was different from the others. He knew he had to protect her, shield her, though from what, he was unsure. "She'll freeze to death on a night like this."

"Who is she?" Monti badgered. "Where did she come from? Whose wife do you carry off tonight, Captain Scarlet?"

Kincaid attempted to sit her on his horse, ignoring Monti. "Come on, sweetheart," he murmured into her muddy, tangled hair. "You're going to have to help me a little here. I have to mount behind you."

Either she heard him, or in her state of unconsciousness she merely reacted. She grabbed the silver pommel of his saddle and leaned forward, resting her head on the horse's braided mane.

Kincaid swung into the saddle behind her and, opening his cloak, pulled her close to his own body for warmth.

Monti reined in beside him. "So now we go home?"

Kincaid took up the reins in his gloved hands. "No. Our plans stand."

"Are you mad?" Monti urged his mount forward to keep up with Kincaid. "You can't bring a woman along! She'll surely vex our luck and we'll be hanging from the triple tree of Tyburn before the month's end."

"Nonsense. We're invincible and luck has nothing to do with it." Kincaid slid one hand inside his cloak to wrap his arm around her waist. She was dirty and shivering, but, sweet heaven, she smelled good. "Skill. Skill and charm is all it is." Then he sank his heels into his mount's flanks and the horse leaped forward, breaking into a gallop. Kincaid knew he'd have to make up for lost time now, or miss Tolliger. He'd waited too long for the Puritan bastard to let him go.

Captain Scarlet and his companion, Montigue Kern, thundered down the center of the road from Kent to London. Ahead lay a copse of trees and if Kincaid was correct in his mathematical calculation, as he usually was, Tolliger and his mistress would be passing through in a matter of moments.

As the men grew closer to their destination, Kincaid was forced to remove his arm from the warmth of the woman's body to draw his blunderbuss. Out of the corner of his eye, he spotted Monti unsheathing his musket. Firepower was Monti's trademark. Every man on the highway had a trademark these days.

"What's your fancy this fine night?" Kincaid asked, wiping the freezing rain from his mouth. "The fallen log, or the drunken jig—your choice, my friend."

Monti scowled. "If you think I'm dismounting—"

Kincaid hushed him with a wave of his broad hand. "The fallen log it is."

Shortly they reached the designated spot. Kincaid dismounted and led his horse behind a giant, leaning oak tree. He tucked the woman's cloak tighter around her. "Listen, sweetheart," he whispered, trying to better shield her from the driving snow and sleet. "This will take but a few moments and then we can be on our way. A warm bed and a bit of hot porridge is all you need."

When he touched her, the woman lifted her head from the saddle's pommel. She looked at him, dull-eyed, as if she saw him, but did not see.

He couldn't resist reaching out to catch a lock of hair between his fingers. "What's your name, sweet, can you tell me that?"

"Lady S—M . . . Meg," she whispered in the same haunting voice. Then she laid her head down again.

"Meg," Kincaid repeated, pulling a second pistol from his saddle bag. "Meg." He liked the name. It suited her heart-shaped face, rosy lips, and nut-brown hair.

"Captain!"

"Coming," Kincaid answered in a carefree tone.

"I hear the coach," came Monti's anxious voice.

"I'm coming, I'm coming." Kincaid secured his horse's

reins to a tree limb and then walked back to the road. Tucking his pistols into his breeches, he caught the line Monti tossed him. The two had followed the routine so often that there was no need to speak as they worked.

Kincaid tied one end of the rope to a decent-sized fallen tree and Monti used his horse to drag the log into the middle of the roadway.

"Approaching," Monti warned as he backed his horse into the cover of the tree line.

Kincaid stepped behind a tree just as he spotted the coach rounding the bend. It was snowing harder now, the snow mixing with sleet, driving sideways. It was a foul night for business. Dangerous. He wiped the wet snow from his eyes and drew his primed pistol. In the dim light of the moon, his gaze met Monti's worried one and he winked. Then he swathed his face in a scarf of red silk drawn from his cloak, and turned to face the approaching vehicle.

The coach rolled down the center of the guttered road and came to a halt at the log that blocked its advance. In the sleet, Kincaid couldn't make out the crest on the coach door, but it had to be Tolliger. What other fool would be out on such a dreary night?

Kincaid took a deep breath, drew a cocky smile, and stepped out of the trees. Rumor had it, it was his laughing eyes that made the ladies swoon. "Stand and Deliver!" he boomed in his best highwayman's voice.

But the moment the words passed his lips, he knew something was wrong. The driver leapt to his feet, swinging a musket from beneath his cloak.

A trap.

The coach door burst open and Kincaid found himself staring down the flared barrel of another musket.

Behind him, Monti gave a cry. Musket fire exploded into the night and the driver fell from his perch into the mud. The coach horses shied, and the vehicle began to roll backwards as more men poured from its door.

Soldiers. Blast them to hell!

Kincaid spun on the balls of his feet.

"Coming for you!" Monti shouted, barreling at a full gallop toward him.

"Alive! I want them alive!" ordered one of the king's soldiers.

Everything was happening so quickly. The wink of an eye. Yet in Kincaid's head, all seemed to move at quarter speed. He saw the frightened whites of the soldiers' eyes as they lunged for the infamous highwayman known as Captain Scarlet. He heard the pounding of hoofbeats as Monti approached.

Kincaid knew all he need do was reach up as his companion rode by and they would be able to escape two astride.

But then he remembered the woman hidden in the trees. He couldn't abandon her. The soldiers would surely arrest her as an accomplice. It would be his fault. She'd be in Newgate and he'd be drinking in the ordinary by dawn.

"Go on without me!" Kincaid shouted to Monti, turning to run in the opposite direction.

"Captain!"

"Go!" Kincaid signaled as Monti galloped by.

Kincaid fired in the direction of the oncoming soldiers as he rushed into the woods, heading straight for his Meg. Out of the corner of his eye he saw the stock of the musket as it swung down and cracked him soundly in the head.

The ground rushed up and Kincaid sank in darkness.

Two

"Meg? Meg, can you hear me, sweetheart?"

Margaret heard the voice from a distance, as if she were in a well. The sound echoed hollowly off the walls. *Meg?* Was the voice talking to her? No one ever called her Meg. No one but Grandmama, and that had been a long time ago.

"Meg. Open your eyes, sweetheart. You're beginning to worry me. *Meg, I know you can hear me.*"

Whose voice was that? Margaret wondered. A man's, but not her husband's and not the earl's. No, this was a kind voice. Besides, Philip was dead, wasn't he?

Frightening memories flooded Margaret's mind. The baby. Philip's rage. The knife. Then blood.

She fought the emotions that overcame her, threatening to drag her down. *He killed my baby. He tried to kill me.* She was glad he was dead, God save her soul.

"Meg, please. Open your eyes. Let me see the color of those beautiful eyes." The voice was insistent. Someone was stroking her hair.

Margaret felt like she'd been heavily drugged. Either she'd been drugged, or given birth and then run miles in the snow and sleet. She attempted to open her eyes. For some reason the voice sounded familiar. It beckoned her from the well of unconsciousness.

Was she dreaming, or had someone picked her up from the road and put her on his horse?

She remembered the warmth of his broad frame, the sound

of his husky voice. He had smelled of ale and tobacco and shaving soap. The voice had rescued her. She remembered now.

But where had the soldiers come from? She remembered the sounds of men shouting and musket fire. Her horse had shied. . . . Surely they had not tracked her from Rutledge Castle so quickly. Surely the earl hadn't—

Margaret's eyelids flew open.

"Green. Of course. I should have known your eyes would be as green as summer grass."

Slowly she focused on a broad, handsome face. He was smiling, smiling at her in a way no man ever had before.

"Who . . . who are you?" she whispered, her voice as dry and cracked as the old midwife's had been. She saw no sign of the earl or his retainer with the limpid eyes.

The man brought a tankard to her parched lips and she sipped the cool water.

He was smiling at her still, as if welcoming a long lost friend . . . or lover. "The name's Captain Scarlet. Your servant . . . Meg."

"I . . . I told you my name was Meg?"

He lifted a dark brow. His shining crown of sleek black hair hung freely about his shoulders, still damp from bathing. "Aye. Is that not your name, mystery woman?"

Margaret knew she had to think quickly. She tried to sit up in the bed. "Yes . . . yes of course. Meg."

He sat down on the edge of the bed so that the blanket tightened about her waist. "You don't sound certain." He was testing the credence of her words, but he didn't seem hostile, only inquisitive.

She lifted the coverlet, glancing beneath it. Sweet heaven, someone had removed the ragged clothing the midwife had provided and put a fresh sleeping gown on her. Her gaze darted about the small room. Suddenly she was frightened. Where was she and who was this man?

The room was small compared to those of Rutledge Castle,

perhaps three paces by five. Worn tapestries covered portions of the stone and mortar walls. The space was furnished with pieces that were of good making, but had seen years of hard use. The draperies that covered the windows were nearly threadbare. The tabletops were scarred, the crimson seat cushions tawdry.

"Are we in an inn, sir?" She clutched the blanket tightly to her chin.

He looked away. "I wish it were so, dear." He rose to fill the tankard with water again and she saw that he was a tall man. A giant of a man, more than eighteen hands. "But I fear in my well-meaning, I've put us in a bit of misfortune."

The sound of a woman's cry in the distance made Margaret start. The shriek echoed off the walls. They were in some large building. As she listened harder, she heard more voices, more movement. Somewhere below chains rattled. She looked with frightened eyes at the man called Captain Scarlet. *"Where am I, sir?"*

It was in that moment of his hesitation that Margaret spotted the bars on the windows, nearly hidden by the draperies. "No," she whispered.

He looked at the window. "I'm sorry. Truly I am. I meant only to take you from the cold." He shrugged. "But then I ran into a bit of trouble with the king's soldiers."

Margaret tried to think clearly. She knew that the next words she spoke might mean her life or death. Was he saying that they were here because of him and not her? Did he truly not know who she was or what heinous crime she had committed?

"Where are we?" she repeated, her voice stronger.

"London."

"London? How?" She looked at his kind face, confused.

"You've been unconscious . . . asleep more than a day. They brought us here—the soldiers. I cared for you myself."

"Where in London?"

He glanced at the tankard in his hand. "Newgate. We're in

Newgate, Meg. Thanks to me." He looked up at her. "But I'll get us out. I swear I will."

Margaret nearly laughed out loud. She was in Newgate Prison, the very place she had run from Rutledge Castle to avoid. So the joke was on her . . . no, on the earl, for surely he would never look here for her, would he?

"Could I get you something to eat? Bread? Cheese? There's a bit of goose and a few oysters still left." He pointed to a small table strewn with bowls and platters. Oyster shells were stacked haphazardly on the corner. "Perhaps a little sack posset to clear your head?"

Margaret . . . Meg ran her fingers through her clean hair. She was Meg now. She made the decision in an instant. A new life. She would put the past behind her and begin anew this moment. "How did I get here? Who changed my clothing?" She looked at her bare hands, then her arms. The blood was gone. "Who bathed me?"

"I apologize for my forwardness, but a maid couldn't be hired at the time of day we arrived. I looked the other way when I changed your clothing, I swear I did."

Meg knew her cheeks colored. No man had ever seen her naked, but Philip, and even then it was in the shadows of darkness and candlelight. She knew she should be angry, but instead she felt an odd sense of gratefulness. This Captain Scarlet, this stranger, had done more to care for her than Philip had in fifteen years.

Then a thought came to her, and she felt the heat in her cheeks. If he had stripped her, surely he knew she had only recently given birth. She would still be bleeding. Then she realized she could feel clean rags between her legs. She looked up at him, knowing he knew what had crossed her mind.

Captain Scarlet smiled gently, not in the least embarrassed. "I will not pry, but I feel it necessary to ask. The child—"

Meg looked away. She refused to cry because if she started, she feared she'd never stop. "Dead, sir. Buried in the church-yard." *She hoped, she prayed.*

"I'm sorry."

She looked at his broad, striking face, into his soft brown eyes with flecks of green, and she knew that he was truly sorry.

Meg laid back down in the bed, her head spinning. She closed her eyes. "We're in Newgate, you say, but not a cell?"

"All is bought and paid for here, sweet. Nothing free. Even those tossed here for debt must pay their way. I rented this room. You'd not be safe below with the commoners, a lady like yourself."

"And how do you know I'm a lady? I was dressed in rags when you found me."

"There's more to a lady than her clothing. I can bear witness to that."

She let her hand fall limply at her side, choosing to change the subject for now. "Might I ask what our crime is? Why did the soldiers bring us here, you and I?"

He came to her with the tankard in his large hand. She was fascinated by his height and breadth. He had a sweeping frame and shoulders like a stable blacksmith's. "Highway robbery, I fear."

Her eyes widened. "You're a highwayman?"

He flashed a charming grin that she intuitively knew could make a woman wilt in her slippers.

"Not exactly."

"You do not rob, sir? The soldiers were mistaken?"

He frowned, his sparkling eyes crinkling at the corners. " 'Tis a difficult matter to explain. Rather complicated."

She closed her eyes to fight off waves of nausea. She felt weak, as if she were barely in control. "It looks as if I have the time. I'm not going anywhere anytime soon, I suspect."

She heard him sigh. A chair scraped wood against wood as he dragged it to the bedside. He sat. "I do halt coaches and request *a donation.*"

"So these men give of their jewels and coin voluntarily?"

"After I strip 'em and tie 'em to a tree they do." He slapped his knee, laughing at his own jest.

Meg opened her eyes. Something in what he said rang familiar. Only last week at the dining table Philip and the earl had been discussing an infamous highwayman the soldiers had been unable to capture. The bold highwayman was said to be swathed in red silk. Not only did he rob the rich, but he stripped the gentlemen and their female companions down to their undergarments and tied them to trees at the roadside for passersby to see. Philip had said the rumor was that the swaggering jade always kissed the women before he departed.

Now she remembered. Philip said his name was Captain Scarlet. "You . . . you're the one I've heard of! You rob a man not only of his purse, but his clothing, as well!"

He chuckled as if she'd paid him a steep compliment. "Aye. That's me. A man must make his mark on the highway these days, else he'll gain no reputation at all."

Meg closed her eyes, genuinely shocked. A highwayman. It was only her luck that the man who would save her would be a common criminal!

"Listen, darling," he said after a moment. "There's really more to the story than meets the common eye. I'm a good man at heart. A Godly man."

This was all too much for Meg to fathom. She had killed her husband who murdered her baby and tried to murder her. She had fled her home. A man had saved her along the roadside from death, a highwayman, and now she was imprisoned alongside him. She drew a deep breath. "Am I imprisoned as a thief, as well?"

His tone lost its amusement. "An accomplice."

"But I did nothing." She thought hard. The last forty-eight hours were a blur in her mind. "At least not that I can recall. But then I can recall very little," she finished lamely.

He propped one black-heeled boot on his knee. "You were with me when I was apprehended. Astride my horse. That makes you an accomplice, sorry I am to say."

She turned her head to stare at the wall beside the bed. The initials R.L.G. and the date 1642 were carved in the stone. "I'll be tried on these false charges?"

"Eventually you would be, but we'll not be behind bars long enough to have our day in court."

"What do you mean?" She looked back at him. "Surely not escape?"

He shrugged his blacksmith's shoulders, grinning. "It's easier than you think." He rubbed his thumb and index finger together. She noticed that his hands were clean, his nails neatly trimmed and polished like a gentleman's. "It takes but the right coin to grease the wheels of justice—or injustice as in our case."

Meg closed her eyes again. "I can't believe this is happening."

There was silence from Captain Scarlet.

After a moment she opened her eyes to look at him, knowing he looked at her. He obviously wanted something. "What?"

"Well, I've told you about myself. Is there anything you want to tell me? We're going to be together awhile. 'Twould make it easier, getting to know you."

"It's not necessary that you get to know me, sir." She bit down on her lower lip, averting her eyes. "I've nothing to say. My past is my past and my affair alone."

"I must ask if you're another man's wife."

"Dead," she answered. "As dead as my babe."

He watched with concern in his gaze. "All right then," he said softly after a moment. "I'll not ask. I've certain matters I wish to share with no one but my Maker." He tucked her blanket beneath the mattress to ward off the chill in the room. "I only want to say I'm sorry for who has hurt you, for what they've done."

Meg looked away, a lump rising in her throat. What an odd thing for a man to say, a stranger. . . . "What makes you think I've been hurt, sir?"

He brushed the back of his hand against her palm, lying open on the blanket. It was an odd gesture, but strangely intimate coming from a man she didn't know. "I can see it in your eyes, Meg. I hear it in your voice."

She looked away, not knowing how to respond. No man, nor woman for that matter, had spoken to her so tenderly in many years.

When she made no reply, he seemed compelled to speak again. "I just want you to know that I won't hurt you. I want to protect you, Meg. Care for you."

She gave a look of skepticism. "You don't know me. You don't know what I've done."

"So tell me. I'll forgive you."

"No."

"Then I forgive you anyway." Before she could respond, he got up from his chair and dragged it back across the plank floor. "I'm going down to the tap room for an ale. I'm mighty dry. Would you like me to bring something when I return? Clean clothing? A bath? Something to eat?"

"No." She turned to the wall, her back to him. Suddenly she was tired. Exhausted! The man didn't make any sense. None of what had happened—was happening—made any sense to her. It was all beyond belief.

"All right, then," he said at the door. "I won't leave you long." He paused. "Rest."

She heard the door open before she called to him. "Wait."

He was at her bedside in an instant.

She didn't turn to face him. "Your name. I don't know your name."

"I told you, Captain Scarlet. It's what everyone calls me."

She frowned, rolling over to face him. "That's ridiculous. You and I are sharing sleeping quarters, for sweet heaven's sake! I'll not call you anything of the sort. Don't you have a Christian name?"

He grinned. "Feeling better, already, I see. Yes, I have a name. My friends call me Kincaid."

"Kincaid." She rolled over presenting her back to him. "Kincaid," she repeated, liking the sound of it. "Bring me some wine when you return, Kincaid. I prefer claret."

"Yes, Meg. Anything else, sweetheart?"

"Yes. Don't call me that. I'm not your sweetheart."

She heard him chuckling as he closed the door behind him.

Three

Meg pushed the piece of blood sausage around her pewter plate, circumnavigating her peas and onions.

"Sweetheart, you have to eat."

She looked up from the plate at Kincaid. He'd barely left her side for the last week, God bless his soul. Without him, Meg didn't know what she'd have done.

The world of Newgate Gaol was so different from that of Rutledge Castle. It wasn't that Meg had ever been tenderly cared for in Philip's home, but at least the servants had provided a warm hearth and food on the table. Even here, in the privileged rented rooms of the Press Yard, Kincaid had explained patiently, common needs had to be sought out and paid for. Inside the walls, a prisoner was at the mercy of the corrupt men and women employed there. Through bribery, anything could be obtained, but at an exorbitant cost.

There was the laundress who kept the fire lit and brought fresh candles and bedding each day. There were meals to be brought in from a tavern on Holborn Street by the turnkey. There was the daily rent on the room to be paid to the jailer, plus a long list of fees like easement that Meg still didn't quite understand. But Kincaid had been here for her. He had provided the knowledge and the coin to keep her safe and in relative comfort.

Meg glanced up at Kincaid, who was still waiting for her response. She sighed. A part of her wanted to please him because he'd been so kind to her. But she'd spent a lifetime pleasing men: her stoic father, then Philip and his brother, the Earl of Rutledge. "I'm just not hungry."

"I spoke with Mrs. Chandler, a woman on the common debtors' side. She's a midwife. She says you must eat red meat, plenty of liver and blood sausage to replace what your body's lost."

Meg set the fork on the edge of her plate and dabbed her lips with her napkin. "I don't like blood sausage or liver. Never did."

"Then what do you like? Lamb? Partridge? I'll get it for you. I can order from the tavern whatever you crave."

Meg shook her head in disbelief, glancing away toward the barred windows. The man sounded so sincere that it scared her. She wasn't used to such honest giving of one's self. At Rutledge Castle there was always a motive behind any good deed or pleasant word. "I just don't understand you, Kincaid. Why are you doing this? I'm nothing to you. No one."

He slathered butter on his warm bread and took a bite. He ate with the same enthusiasm with which he seemed to meet every aspect of life. "I told you. I like you."

Her gaze moved to the fire on the hearth. Though the wind was blowing harshly beyond the walls of Newgate Prison, their rented cell was as cozy as a Duke's withdrawing room. "You don't know me."

"So help me get to know you better. Tell me your childhood nursemaid's name." He took another bite of his bread. "Tell me what gift you received last Christmas Eve. How many freckles do you have on the back of your right knee?"

Meg swung her head around to look at him with shock at his outrageousness. "Sir, I hardly think—"

Kincaid was grinning—as usual. He pointed. "Touché."

Meg sighed. She was trying hard not to like him, not to get too attached. After all, the man was a highwayman, a common criminal. He was liable to be hanged before long. And what future was there in a friendship she would only have to break? As soon as she managed her release, she would follow through with her plan to become a ladies' maid. Her key to survival, she knew, was anonymity. "I really wish you would not speak to me in such intimate ways, sir."

"Kincaid," he corrected, washing his bread down with his ale. "I'm no gentleman. I'll be called by a Christian name."

"Kincaid," she conceded impatiently. She rose to walk to the hearth, her skirts brushing the floor. Somehow he had managed to acquire all the trappings of a lady's attire. The gown, underclothing, and shoes were unadorned, but well made. Inside the gaol walls, they must have cost him the price of a seeded pearl gown fit for an audience with King Charles himself.

She put out her hands to the fire to warm them. "As I was saying, *Kincaid,* I wish you wouldn't speak to me with such familiarity. It's not appropriate."

He chuckled. "Meg, we sleep and eat together. I know it embarrasses you, but I've attended to your personal needs. Like it or not, we've become as familiar as most men and their wives, more familiar than many I know."

He had a point. She knew he did. That was one of the things she immediately liked about him. Kincaid was a practical man, seemingly unencumbered by society's rules. "You claim you're not a gentleman and yet you speak like one." She stared into the flickering fire. "You act like one."

"Me? A gentleman?" He made an event of folding his linen napkin, his movements exaggerated and effeminate. "Are you calling me a fop, madame?"

She laughed at his antics. Sweet God, how long had it been since she'd had cause to laugh? "I didn't say fop, I said gentleman. A man of refinement, of education," she eyed him over her shoulder, "perhaps title."

Kincaid tossed the napkin into the air and it floated downward until it settled over a serving dish of congealed raisin pudding. *"I am what I am."*

His tone had changed so that there was an edge to his voice. Meg realized immediately that she'd struck a nerve in her highwayman. "I wasn't prying. We agreed there'd be no discussion of our pasts, yours or mine. I only meant to say—"

"I'm going to the taproom for a pottle of wine."

This was the first time in the week she had known him that he had showed this side of his personality. So Kincaid could be as moody as any man if pushed to the point.

He caught his wool cloak from a hook near the door and tossed it over his broad shoulders. It was so cold in the gaol this time of year that men and women without proper covering or the coin to pay for a fire froze to death daily. "Lock the door behind me. I'll be but an hour or so."

Meg followed him to the door, sorry that she had angered him. "Kincaid—"

His face was stony. "Let it go, Meg."

Then he was gone, closing the door behind him. "The lock." His voice echoed off the stone walls of the corridor Meg had not passed through since her arrival.

Meg turned the heavy iron key and the door mechanism caught. She stood listening to his heavy footfall until it dissipated. With a sigh, she went back to the fireplace to pour herself a cup of tea the laundress had left brewing for her. Warm cup in hand, she pulled a chair to the hearth and sat down, hiking her silk brocade skirts to her knees to warm herself. She sipped the sweet cinnamon brew.

"Meg," she whispered. Then louder, "Meg." She liked the sound of her new name. She liked what it represented. Gone was Margaret Hannibal, Daughter of John Hannibal. Gone was Lady Surrey, wife of the Viscount of Surrey. Gone were the Randalls and their hideous curse of deformities. Meg was a new woman now. A woman without a past, with only a future. In time she would forget the loneliness, the despair of her past. She would seek what happiness there was in the world for her, the happiness her grandmama had always promised her darling Meg.

Meg's thoughts turned to Kincaid . . . all too easily for her comfort. So where did Kincaid fit into this new life? He had saved her on the road to London. Of course, he had saved her from Rutledge's pursuit only to have her tossed into gaol for a crime she didn't commit.

But he had given her the time she needed to heal, both physically and mentally. Even not knowing what had happened to her, he'd found a way these last few days to ease the ache she felt in her heart for her lost babe. Somehow, without knowing the pain she suffered, or the crime she'd committed, Kincaid had a way of placing her past in perspective. He claimed not to be a Godly man, and yet his philosophies of life helped Meg restore her faith, not just in God, but in herself. Looking back at the life she had led at Rutledge Castle, she couldn't honestly say now which loss had been the greatest, that of her child's life or her confidence in God and therefore herself.

Meg smoothed the bodice of her gown where her breasts were bound. They still ached with milk meant for a child, but they were better. She was better. She took another sip of her tea.

So, she had successfully escaped the earl and the law for her crime of killing her husband. But now, how did she escape this crime for which she was completely innocent? Highway robbery was a serious felony. Men and women were hanged weekly at Tyburn for the offense.

Kincaid swore he would get her out of Newgate. He said it would take but a few days, a few weeks at the most. He said his man, Monti, was working on the necessary bribes, by the time Kincaid and Meg had reached the vaulted walls of the gaol.

Meg knew she had little choice but to trust Kincaid. After all, she couldn't well explain to the sheriff that she was actually innocent of the crime of aiding a highwayman. What would she say? *I murdered my husband, fled my home, fell unconscious, and this kind highwayman picked me up along the road? I did kill my husband, but I was merely an unconscious bystander to the coach robbery, kind sheriff?*

Meg laughed to herself. She was stuck, stuck with Kincaid at least for the time-being. Once they were released, they would go their separate ways. She would seek her happiness in the city, as a ladies' maid, or perhaps a clerk at the 'Change selling ribbons or cloth. Maybe she would even dare to find a way to go to the American colonies.

Philip and the earl had once had a guest stay at the castle, a ship's captain. Night after night he had entertained her with tales of the sea and even more intriguing, tales of the American wilderness. Listening to his stories of red Indians, lush forests, and salty bays, she had longed to see the land she knew she would never see. Now, suddenly there was the possibility. Despite the dangers of a woman without chaperone, alone in Londontown, there were possibilities—possibilities that had never existed for her at Rutledge.

The sound of a knock at the door startled Meg. "Kincaid?" She rose, turning to face the door. It was too soon for him to return from the taproom. Perhaps it was the laundress. "Mrs. Kohn? Is that you?"

The knock came again, firm and echoing.

"Who . . . who is it?"

"Turnkey for the woman, Meg," came a grating voice.

She recognized the voice immediately. It was the filthy little man with the bulging eyes that came to the door each day for his payment. He brought their meals from the tavern and carried messages beyond the walls of Newgate. Kincaid never let him inside their room, but dealt with him in the taproom or the corridor.

"What do you want?"

"Open the door, Meggy"

Kincaid had told her to open the door for no one. He said she was not safe anywhere within Newgate, except locked here in their room, or at his side. "Tell me what you want. C . . . Captain Scarlet doesn't wish to be disturbed."

"I seen your man go down the hall, so don't play the sly with me. I know 'e ain't there, Meggy."

She set her tea mug on the rough-hewn mantel over the hearth. "Go away." She hugged herself, wishing Kincaid were there. She didn't know what to do.

"Cain't. You been summoned."

"Summoned?" Her heart skipped a beat. Had someone realized who she was? Had they come for her? "Summoned by whom?"

"Summoned by whom?" the turnkey mocked. "The Lord Chief Justice 'imself, that's *whom!* So get yer lily-white ass out 'ere!"

Harsh words had no effect on Meg. She'd listened to them a lifetime. She steadied her voice. "Why? Why does he want me?" she asked through the door.

"Questionin'." He rattled the doorknob impatiently. "Open up, Meggy. He ain't a man to be set waitin'."

She took a step toward the door. "Doesn't he want to speak with . . . with Captain Scarlet, as well?"

"Said just you. Just the highwayman's woman."

So I've become the highwayman's woman, have I? She rested her hand on the key to the lock.

The turnkey rattled the knob again. "It ain't like you got a choice, Miss High and Mighty. Ye been summoned. Either you come to the Lord Justice on yer own two precious feet, or I call the guard, they busts the door, and haul you outta there."

After a moment of indecision, Meg turned the lock. The door swung open immediately and she stood face-to-face with the Deputy Turnkey. He held up a sputtering candle to illuminate her doorway. He was a short man with a protruding stomach, the ragged cloth that covered it stained with the likes of gravy and mashed turnips. He wore a cheap, ill-fitting wig that must have once been white, but had turned a dull gray with time and lack of upkeep.

The disgusting little man picked at his teeth with a long, grimy fingernail as he stared up at her. Extracting a shred of beef, he wiped it on his coat. "Even', missy. It's no wonder the cap'ain keeps you to 'imself. Comely bitch you is, for certain."

Meg pulled the cloak Kincaid had procured for her from the nail on the wall. *Words, nothing but words, and words couldn't hurt unless a woman let them, that was what Grandmama always said.* "Well, let's go. Let's be done with it."

"This way m'laidy." The turnkey gave a sweep of his fat hand.

Meg passed the creature, taking care not to let her skirts brush against him. The man smelled of a sewer. "Which way?"

He held the candle high so that pale light cast over the stone floor and walls. Meg felt like she was inside a tomb.

"This way, missy." He pushed past her, touching her hip purposefully with one hand as he went by.

Meg shrank back against the wall and a rat screeched, caught between her and the stone. She gave a jump, stifling a cry as the rodent scurried over her slipper and disappeared into the darkness.

The turnkey hocked and spat on the floor. "Stay with Archie, 'ere, missy. I'll protect ye from the vermin." Chuckling, he started down the dark hallway again, leaving Meg with no choice but to follow or be left behind in the pitch darkness.

The turnkey led her through the catacombs of the prison, said to be built early in the thirteenth century during the reign of King John. For hundreds of year the gaol had been the abode of suffering and sorrow for the likes of debtors, felons, religious martyrs, and committers of treason.

Meg followed Archie down steps and up through the fetid passageways that stank of stale air, human excrement, and hopelessness. Above and below her and on all sides, she heard the sounds that would haunt her in her dreams forever. Some men laughed, others cried. Sobs reverberated off the cold stone walls, neither male nor female, only voices floating. Somewhere a woman screamed in the agony of the last stage of childbirth, and Meg, remembering her own delivery, wondered if the mother cried in anguish because of the pain, or because of the wretched circumstances of her child's birth.

The turnkey went around another corner and Meg hurried to catch up. In the gloom of the madness, even this creature was a comfort. "How much farther?" she asked, hoping he didn't hear the uneasiness in her voice.

"Not much, missy."

They walked to the end of the corridor and Archie rapped on a wooden and iron door and then flung it open. "The girl, Meg, to see you, m'lord."

Meg stepped into the chamber, very similar to the one she shared with Kincaid. Only here there was no bed, but instead, a desk and a chair on each side.

A tall, bewigged man in a gold cloak turned from the fireplace to face her. He had a long nose and high cheekbones, an honest face.

Meg dipped a curtsy as one of her own maids would have. "M'lord."

Archie stood in the arched doorway scratching furiously beneath his wig. Catching a plump louse between his thumb and finger, he cracked it enthusiastically.

Meg's stomach churned.

"Get out," the Lord Justice ordered with a wave of his ringed finger. "Out, you malodorous Papist!" He brought an embroidery-edged handkerchief to his nose. "In God's name, man. You stink! Have they no running water inside these walls?"

Archie bowed and backed out of the room, grinning.

Meg stood just in front of the door the turnkey closed. She could still hear him outside in the passageway. He must have been told to wait.

The Lord Justice walked to a Spartan table and poured himself a portion of sack posset. "A warm drink on a cold night, madame?" He lifted the bottle.

Meg shook her head. She kept her hands folded neatly, her eyes averted.

"I suppose you wonder why I've called you here."

She looked up, but made no reply.

The middle-aged man sighed. He appeared both tired and overworked.

"I sent for you because I need your help. All of England needs your help, madame." He sipped from his glass, letting his words sink in. "It seems that since the return of His Highness, we have been overrun with highway robberies. The mails are not safe from these thieves. Innocent men and women are being assaulted."

Still, Meg said nothing.

The man sighed. "If you were to provide the courts with information—"

"I don't know anything."

". . . you could easily be pardoned."

So that was his game. Pardon. Release. Of course she couldn't give any information, because she didn't know any. And even if she did, how could she betray Kincaid, criminal or not? He had risked his life to save her on the muddy road. He had a chance to escape the king's soldiers that night, but he had chosen to return for her.

"I told you," she said, her voice without emotion. "I don't know anything."

He swished the liquor in his glass, watching it slosh up the sides and run down into the pool again. "How can you not know anything? You were caught with the bandits that night."

"A mistake," she said softly. Then she looked at him with a defiance in her eyes. "I was simply in the wrong place at the wrong time." A smile played in the corners of her mouth. This felt good, this new strength of hers. It felt good to defy authority. It felt good to be alive.

The Lord Chief Justice set his glass down impatiently. "Come, madame. This could mean your life. Don't you understand, you could be hanged beside this man!"

Again, she dropped her gaze to the stone floor at her feet. "I'm sorry, sir, but I've nothing to offer you. I came upon the gentleman in a tavern." She was amazed how easily the lie rolled off her tongue. It was as if she was creating her own past as she went along. "We but shared a little wine and laughter."

"You're telling me he was taking you home to his bed, when on his way he decided to rob a coach?" The man laughed, but it was obvious he saw no humor in her explanation. "Come, child, surely you don't think me *that* old and foolish."

She lifted one shoulder in a shrug as she often saw Kincaid do. So let the Lord Justice think she was a whore, better than a murderess, was it not? " 'Tis the truth. I cannot change it, not even for my own release."

He exhaled, blowing from his cheeks. "Heaven help my soul, I've been at this too long. I almost believe you."

They stared at each other for another moment. Then he waved his hand. "Well, go with you. But if ye have a change of heart, call for me. I'm the only man in all of England save our good king himself who can get you out of this hell hole, and it's not likely he'll come calling, I can promise you that."

Meg only nodded.

After another moment the Lord Justice turned away, dismissing her. "Deputy Turnkey!"

The door opened so quickly that Meg knew Archie must have been listening at the door. "M'lord?"

"Take her back to her cell and see she's not harmed on the way." He tossed a coin into the air and Archie put out his dirty hand to catch it.

Meg heard the turnkey add the coin to a pouch on his waist before he lifted the candle to light the way. "Come along with ye, miss."

She followed him back the way they'd come, through the dark tunnels, thankful he was there. Otherwise she'd never have found her way back to the Press Yard where she and Kincaid shared their cell. After five minutes of walking, Meg began to grow uneasy. Was Archie leading her the same way they'd come? The darkness and the stench were making her nervous. "Archie, is it far, now?"

"Not much," he cackled. But then he halted in the middle of the narrow passageway and turned to face her. Meg had only to look at his face to see his intention.

She took a step back, lifting her hands in defense. "No. Get back," she whispered. "The Lord Justice said to return me safely. He paid you to return me to my quarters safely."

"Ye tellin' me what to do, Miss High and Mighty!" Archie lunged forward, grabbing a handful of her cloak.

Meg screamed, striking him on the side of the head with her closed fist. She knocked the candle out of his hand, launching them into darkness.

Four

"In for a little sport are ye?"

Meg felt the turnkey's hand on her breast as he groped in the darkness. She could hear him panting.

"No!" Meg screamed. Thoughts of Philip flashed through her head. She remembered him pushing her onto their bed. She remembered him lifting her sleeping gown, despite her protests. How many times had that happened in the last few years as he tried desperately to plant his seed inside her? She squeezed her eyes shut, fighting her panic. She could still smell Philip's fishy breath on her face. *No.* She had wanted to tell him no so many times. So why hadn't she?

Suddenly Meg reacted. "Son of a malodorous whore!" she shouted, giving Archie a hard shove.

"Aye!" he cackled. "I like it with a fight just as well as the next man, I do!" He caught her by one wrist, then the other, pushing her backwards.

In the darkness Meg could see nothing but the outline of his form. Her attempt to fight him off seemed only to be adding to his sexual excitement. He pushed her against the stone wall and she jerked up her leg, catching him squarely in the groin with her knee.

"Owlll!" Archie screeched. "Bitch!" He reached out to slap her, but she ducked, and dove beneath his arm.

"Where ye think yer goin', missy?" He grasped her by the back of her cloak and jerked it so hard that her neck snapped back.

"Help!" Meg screamed, swinging her fists. "Help me! Someone!"

The Deputy Turnkey grabbed her around the neck and pulled her against him. Through the thick cloth of her cloak and gown she could feel his hand on her buttocks as he squeezed viciously.

"What's the matter, Missy? Ain't I good enough for ye? I'm only askin' for a piece of what yer givin' that highwayman."

"You do this and he'll come after you." She panted, trying to catch her breath, trying to keep her head about her. "You do this and he'll slit your throat!"

"Shut up before I shut you up!"

When he clamped his hand over her mouth, she sank her teeth into the flesh of his palm.

"Bitch!" he shouted, immediately loosening his grip to nurse his wounded hand.

Meg ducked and lunged forward. She could taste his blood in her mouth, metallic and sickening.

Archie grabbed her again and she jabbed him in the chest with her elbow. He grabbed a hank of her hair and Meg reached up instinctively to her head.

She gritted her teeth, her mind spinning. She'd been a victim too long. She'd not give in to this man and his lust. She'd not do it. Not for this man or any other. Not ever again.

With a vindictive scream, Meg turned to face her attacker, taking him by surprise. Fingers flexed, she sank her fingernails into his eyes.

Archie squealed like a hog at slaughter, letting go of her hair. He stumbled backwards.

But instead of fleeing as she should have, Meg flung herself against him. "How dare you?" she ranted, sinking her fist into his soft middle. "How dare you try to take advantage of me," she emphasized each word with a well-placed punch, "you . . . sniveling . . . leech!"

When Archie doubled over, she brought her knee up, striking him in the mouth.

"Sweet God, you're mad!" he blubbered.

Meg knocked off his wig. She ripped his cloak from his shoulders.

"Help me!" Archie cried as he cowered against the wall, trying to protect his face. "Someone help me, please!"

"What's about, down there?" came a voice out the darkness.

"Help!" Archie screamed. "Mad woman! Mad woman! Call the guards!"

Meg didn't know what had come over her, but she couldn't stop herself. She couldn't stop swinging her fists. She couldn't stop screaming.

"What the devil?" The hallway filled with feeble light. "What's going on? Let her go!" came a vaguely familiar voice.

"Let her go?" moaned the turnkey. "She's the one assaultin' me! Call the guards!"

"Shut up!" Meg shouted at Archie, drawing back her fist threateningly. "You hear me! Keep your filthy mouth shut."

"Meg?"

She took a step back. Her heart was pounding, her breath rapid. She was shaking from head to foot.

"Meg, is that you?"

She took another step back from the wall and the turnkey, who was still huddled on the floor, his hands covering his head. She could see blood on his face. She must have split his lip. Blood was running from one nostril, too.

"Oh . . . what have I done?" Meg said aloud, staring in horror.

The man with the lantern came up behind, putting his hand on her shoulder. It was Kincaid, of course. Her savior. Her highwayman.

"Meg," he said gently. "What's happened here?"

Meg stared numbly at her hand, still balled in a fist. She didn't know what was wrong with her. She didn't feel like herself. Whose feelings were these? She had never gotten so angry before. She had always tried to placate Philip and his brother. Whose hands were these that had assaulted the turnkey? Never once in all those years had she turned her hand to Philip, not until the night she had killed him . . .

Meg was so confused. She turned to look at Kincaid. Then, before she knew what she was doing, she found herself placing her arms on his chest, pressing her body against his. She needed the warmth of this man, the assurance of his touch. "He attacked me," she whispered.

"Liar!" Archie accused, stumbling to his feet. "She went mad. I was takin' her back to her room, like the Lord Chief Justice done said, and she went wild on me." He grabbed up his wig from the floor and dropped it sideways onto his bristly-haired head.

Meg shook her head emphatically as she looked into Kincaid's eyes. "No." She didn't know why, but she needed desperately for him to believe her. "It wasn't like that. He touched me. He was going to rape me." Her lower lip trembled. "If you hadn't come, he'd have taken what wasn't his to take."

Kincaid's handsome mouth turned up slowly into a lopsided grin. "If I hadn't come, hell, sweetheart! Looked to me like you were doing just fine defending yourself. Remind me not to ever make you angry. I saw that right fist of yours." He touched his chin. "Ouch."

Then he rested his hand on her shoulder and for a moment nothing mattered for her but his smile. How was it that Kincaid could always turn anything into a joke? How could he always make the best of a terrible situation? She smiled back, her gaze lost in his.

"There'll be charges!" Archie shouted, retrieving his cloak from the stone floor. "I'll see you pay."

Kincaid swung Meg around into one arm so that he could face the Deputy Turnkey, but still held tightly to her. "No you won't, Archie," he said, his voice calm, yet his anger obvious. "You'll not speak a word of this incident."

The filthy man wiped his bloody nose with the back of his hand. "Why not? She coulda kilt me!"

"You won't." He moved so fast that he startled both her and Archie. He grasped the turnkey by his armpits and lifted him straight in the air until his rotting boots hung a hand above the floor.

Meg watched Kincaid in amazement. She knew he was so angry he could have killed the turnkey, and yet he remained in control of himself and the situation. The soft steel of his voice was more intimidating than any shouting she had heard from Philip.

"You won't," he explained evenly, "because you want to continue to live your pathetic existence, that's why, Archie. You won't because if you do, you'll die. Poisoned pudding. Armed robbery. An angry whore with a blade!"

Archie stared gape-mouthed at Kincaid, his feet still dangling in the air.

"There's really a myriad of ways to send you to hell, Archie," Kincaid went on, calmly. "And I quite like the idea of choosing one best suited to a maggot like yourself." With his last words he dropped the turnkey onto the floor in a heap.

Archie scrambled to his feet. Tightening his cloak around his shoulders, he took a cautious step back. He was visibly shaking. "You . . . you couldn't. You wouldn't dare."

Kincaid stared at the man with a gaze that would have intimidated a braver fellow. "I can do anything or get anything I wish within these walls, and you know it. So go with you." He dismissed him with a wave of his hand as if swatting at a gnat. "Go before I really lose my patience and kill you here and be done with you."

Archie turned on his worn heels and hurried down the passageway into the pitch darkness.

"And from now on you'll work for me for half wages!" Kincaid called after him.

Meg heard nothing but the echo of Archie's fading footsteps as he broke into a run.

After a moment, Kincaid turned his gaze to her again.

She took half a step back, staring at him. The only evidence left of his anger was his narrowed eyes that still burned with his fury.

When he came toward her, she stood perfectly still, prepared to bolt if his fury was directed toward her. Just in case . . . That was the way Philip and the earl had always been. When they were angry with someone or over something, they always took it out on her.

But Kincaid's face changed the moment he looked at her. His anger was gone as suddenly as it had come and he was smiling. In barely a second's time, he was the Kincaid she knew once again.

He took her in his arms and she let him. "So, sweet, since you're up and about, would you care to share a drink with me in the taproom?"

She couldn't resist a smile, though she was still wary. She didn't know what to make of him. How could a man turn so angry so quickly and then change back again to such a gentle fellow? She was amazed. "I . . . I'd be honored, sir."

Kincaid ushered her through the catacomb of hallways and landings toward the sound of laughter and music. At a closed doorway at the bottom of a worn stone step, he offered a man his candle and a coin. The man took the coin, bit into it, smiled, and pushed open the door.

The taproom was filled with pinpricks of light cast from punched tin lanterns that hung from the rafters overhead. It was a bright place in the darkness of the gaol. The room was filled with patrons, like any common taproom on any evening in Londontown. To look at the faces, one would not have guessed that these men were criminals of one ilk or another. They looked like any man one would see on the street behind an ox cart or selling milk at a country market. Here, like in any tavern, the men laughed. Dice tumbled across the tables and coin passed hands. In the far corner of the room, a man played a lute and a woman with long red tresses sang a bawdy tune.

Kincaid ushered Meg through the crowd of men and a few women patrons. Several men glanced up at Meg in interest, but the look her protector gave them made them look away in fear.

Kincaid indicated a table and Meg slid across the bench seat. He sat across from her, facing the room, and waved to the woman behind the bar. "Dame Watson! Ale for myself, claret for the lady."

Then Kincaid folded his clean, big hands on the table and peered at Meg. "You all right?"

"I'm all right."

"I can have him killed. If he touched you—"

"No. I'm all right." Though she thought he had over-reacted, she appreciated Kincaid's concern. She didn't dare tell him that his loss of temper had frightened her almost as much as the turnkey's attack. "Archie's crime wasn't great enough to die for." She took a deep breath. Her hands had ceased shaking. Her head was clear again. "He just scared me, that's all. I don't want any retaliation."

Kincaid nodded. "As you wish." He slowly traced a heart carved into the worn trestle table. There had once been names inside the heart, but they were now too worn to read. "So what did he want with you, love? The Lord Chief Justice?"

Meg couldn't take her eyes off the highwayman. She was mesmerized by his high cheekbones, his twinkling eyes, the kindness in his half smile. Heavens, but she was infatuated. She looked away, suddenly feeling shy. "Questioning."

"About me?"

The dame brought Meg her wine and Kincaid his ale. Meg waited until he had paid the bar mistress and she had gone before she responded. "Aye."

"What did he offer you? Coin?"

Meg sipped her claret. "Pardon."

"Muckworm. He should have at least offered you a few

pounds with your pardon. Something for your trouble." He took a long pull of ale from his leather jack. "So what did you tell our man of the court?"

"Everything." Meg didn't know what made her say it, it just came out of her mouth. It was as if she was suddenly bedeviled.

He raised an eyebrow, looking entirely too serious for himself. "Everything, Madame?"

Meg couldn't help herself. *"Everything.* I told him where the infamous Captain Scarlet hides out, who his accomplices are, which robberies he was responsible for." She had to drink from her glass to keep from giggling. "What choice did I have? I had to save myself, sir."

He leaned across the table. "But Meg, you don't know anything."

She looked over the rim of her glass and gave an exaggerated frown. "No, I don't suppose I do, do I, Captain Scarlet?"

He stared at her for a moment perplexed, then broke into hearty laughter. He slapped his hand so hard on the table that ale sloshed over the side of his jack.

Meg laughed, too.

"You didn't tell him anything, did you sweetheart?" He was still laughing.

"How could I?" Tears ran down her cheeks, she was laughing so hard. The look on Kincaid's face there for a moment; it had been so funny. "How . . . how could I when I was unconscious?"

"Good point!"

As their laughter finally subsided, Kincaid reached across the table to take her hand. Meg let him.

"Ah, Meg. It's so good to hear you laugh. I feared you hadn't a lick of humor in that serious heart of yours." He turned her hand in his, studying it. "I feared that whatever happened to you in the past left you with no laughter."

Meg's gaze met Kincaid's. She knew she had to be careful. She knew she was emotionally vulnerable right now. With all that had happened, he was the first man who had ever been kind. It was only natural, she knew, that she would react to him this way. But she couldn't help herself. After all these years of loneliness, she craved affection. She craved Kincaid's affection. "Please don't ask me how I got on that road," she whispered. "Please don't, Kincaid, because I can't tell you. I won't."

He brought her hand to his lips and kissed her knuckles. "I could kill the bastard who did this to you, Meg, for surely it was a man. I can see it in your eyes." He studied her face carefully. "I can see it when you watch me, always fearing I'm going to lash out at you." He shook his head ever so gently. "But I won't. I would never hurt you. I will only protect you. I will only love you."

Meg could feel her heart pounding, her pulse racing. For the first time in her life she was physically attracted to a man, and it felt wonderful. Scary, but wonderful.

She looked away. "Love? You don't know me, Kincaid. You don't know what you're saying. You don't love me."

"Don't tell me what's in my heart." He pressed her hand beneath his cloak to the place where she could feel his heart beating. "Feel that? That's for you."

She laughed, withdrawing her hand from his. "How silly do you think I am, Kincaid, that I can't see a man playing me for a fool. Love, indeed. You want nothing but what every man wants of a woman." She knew it was true, but she wasn't offended. In fact, she was flattered. Kincaid was the first man in her life who had ever expressed a desire for her who didn't repulse her.

"That's not true." He reached for his ale. He was still flirting with her, but in a way that wasn't threatening. He lowered his voice until it was husky. "Well it *is* true. I can think of nothing I'd like to do more right now than to cradle you in my arms and make love to you all night."

Make love. Meg liked the sound of that. Certainly what she and Philip had done in their marriage bed had nothing to do with love.

"But I'd be willing to make you an honest woman."

Meg's breath caught in her throat. Suddenly the playfulness was gone. "What did you say?"

"I said, I want to make love to you, but I'd make you an honest woman." He leaned back against the bench, crossing his arms over his chest. He was entirely serious. "I would marry you, Meg. I'd make you my wife and I'd take care of you the rest of your days. I'd give you more babies if that was what you wanted," he said softly.

A tear gathered in the corner of Meg's eye. Suddenly her breasts ached for her dead son. "Don't say that."

"It's true. I'm in love with you. Have been since the night I found you on that muddy road."

Meg leaned back, wrapping herself tightly in her cloak, withdrawing into herself. "Please don't say that again. You don't know what kind of person I am. You don't know what I did."

"I bet I know you better than you think." He was watching her, watching her with eyes that seemed to see through to her very soul.

Suddenly Meg was short of breath. She slid off the bench. She had let this innocent flirtation go too far. "Take me back, Kincaid."

He was at her side in an instant. "Meg—"

She took a step back, avoiding his touch, for if she let him touch her right now, she feared she wouldn't be able to control her emotions. She feared she would break into tears, tears that would never stop. All she could think of was why, why had she met Kincaid now and not eight years ago when she was forced to marry Philip?

"Please, Kincaid," she whispered, keeping her eyes downcast. "Just take me to the room. I'm . . . I'm tired. I need rest."

He stood there for a moment, looking at her. Then he reached

out and gently took her arm. "Certainly. Whatever you want.
But this won't be the end of this conversation. I won't give
up on you."

Meg didn't answer. She didn't know what to say.

Kincaid paced the length of the yard, stretching his long
legs. It was so cold out tonight that his lungs ached with each
breath he took, but he needed the time alone, the time to
think. It was a clear night, illuminated by a three-quarters
moon that hung in the sky above the city. The stars twinkled
overhead, their beauty reminding him that there was indeed a
God in the heavens.

"I want to marry you? I'll give you babies," Kincaid muttered aloud. "I can't believe I said that!" He struck himself
in the forehead with the heel of his hand. "Fool!" That was
no way to woo a woman like Meg.

Although she would admit to nothing, he knew she was a
highborn lady. He could hear it in her speech. He could see
it in the way she carried herself. And ladies didn't want to
hear of such domestic drivel. Kincaid had enough experience
to know they wanted to be told how beautiful they were, how
sexually alluring.

Kincaid gave a snort. He didn't know what was wrong with
him. No woman had ever affected him like this before. No
woman had ever made him say and do such foolish things.
Of all the women he had known in his lifetime, from common
whores to duchesses, no one had ever made him feel like this
inside.

Meg . . . Meg. She had him rattled. She was so feminine
and yet she had the strength Kincaid had thought possible
only in a man. She was bright; she was strong-willed.

Kincaid reached the high stone wall of the gaol yard and
turned on his heels to go the other way.

Meg led him to believe she had committed some terrible
sin, yet he could not imagine it possible. The truth was, he

didn't care. He saw the woman she was. He saw the tenderness, the intelligence, and that was all that mattered to him. Monti had always warned him he would fall in love one day and that when he did it would hit him like a lead weight. He would give Monti credit where credit was due. Be damned if Meg hadn't hit him hard.

"This is madness," Kincaid said gruffly, throwing up his hands. He startled a pigeon on its roost on the wall and it took flight, its wings beating in the frigid air. "I can't love this woman." *She could never love you,* whispered a voice inside his head. *No one could.* Wasn't that what his father said?

Kincaid stopped in the center of the small walled yard and stared up at the moon. His father. The sick bastard. What kind of man would say that to a six-year-old boy?

What kind of man would still remember thirty years later . . . still half believe it?

He sighed, rubbing his arms briskly for warmth as he headed toward the door where some turnkey waited to let him inside the gaol again . . . for a price of course.

Tomorrow Monti would be coming to visit him and Meg. Hopefully, the bribes would be taken care of and he would have word of their release. Once Kincaid was outside the walls of Newgate, he would be able to think with a clearer head. Outside these walls his feelings for Meg would make more sense to him. He rapped on the outside door with his cold knuckles. He hoped they would make more sense . . . he prayed.

Five

Percival Randall, the Earl of Rutledge, stood in the library doorway, tapping the toe of his slipper. He was dressed for bed in a flannel banyon and a skull cap to keep his balding head warm. "Hurry, men," he ordered through clenched teeth.

The two servants came barreling down the dark hallway, one dressed in stockings and breeches, the other, barefoot in his holey nightgown.

The earl pointed into the well-lit library, shrieking. *"Who dusted today?"*

"I . . . I did, my Lord." Tom came to halt before his master and lowered his head subserviently.

"And . . . and I," Sam admitted, stopping beside the other servant. Neither man made eye contact with the earl.

Rutledge plucked at the callused deformity on his upper lip. "What are the rules?"

"Gl . . . gloves," answered one man.

"She . . . sheep's wool rags on . . . only," responded the other.

The earl glanced over the servants' heads, his hand aching to slap them both. Why was it that for the sum of money he paid these two donkey's asses, they could not follow simple directions? "And how far from the end of the shelf must the spines be!" His voice echoed off the walls.

"One—"

"One Rutledge knuckle," Tom finished for Sam.

The earl curled his finger, beckoning the servants into his

library. The room was wall to wall, floor to ceiling bookshelves, and on those shelves was displayed one of the finest collections of leather-bound books in the world. Hundreds of tomes lined the walls, writings by Sir Thomas Malory, Machiavelli, Sir Thomas More, Michael Drayton, and John Milton.

Rutledge led them to the far wall, near the window. He pointed.

Both men leaned to stare.

"Do you see that?" the earl snapped, indicating the spine of a copy of Chaucer's *Book of the Duchess*.

When the servants made no response but to gawk tongue-tied at the book, the earl thrust his finger onto the dusted shelf. "One Rutledge knuckle!" he shouted. *"One Rutledge knuckle! Does that look like one Rutledge knuckle to you?"* He was shouting so loudly, with such force, that spittle ran from the hole in his palate, over his lower lip, and down his chin. "Does that look like a Rutledge knuckle to you?" he repeated, slapping Sam in the face.

Sam's cheek reddened, but he didn't flinch. He didn't dare. "No . . . no, my Lord."

Tom, the braver of the two, reached out with one finger and pushed Chaucer back a hair. "No, my Lord."

"No, my Lord. No, my Lord," Rutledge mimicked, walking away. He was so angry that he could have broken bones. "Do you think Mister Chaucer would appreciate his life's works set askew on a shelf?"

The servants stood at the shelf designated for fourteenth-century poets, still staring at the book. Somehow, despite their lack of intelligence, they seemed to sense it was a rhetorical question.

The earl tapped his foot. "Show me one Rutledge knuckle."

The servants held up their index fingers, each marked with a thin, deep burn line.

"Excellent." Rutledge took a deep breath, pleased that he was able to remain so calm, considering the severity of the crime. "Now," he went on, his voice placid. "How shall we repair the damage done?" He lifted his hands toward the domed ceiling painted in fresco by an Italian artist. "What if another tome is amiss? I haven't drawn too close for fear that if I find another blunder, I'll lose my forbearance."

The two men just stared at the earl, too frightened or lack-witted to move.

Rutledge made a sweeping gesture with his hand. "Check the books! *Check the books!* Measure them again!"

"A . . . all of them, my Lord?"

"Yes, all of them!" Rutledge sprayed Tom with spittle.

Tom whispered something to Sam beneath his breath and Sam dashed out of the library. Not three minutes later, the servant reappeared, carrying white cotton gloves, each pair with the right index finger missing. The two donned the gloves and moved to the far wall. Hands trembling, they began to measure the distance between the edge of the bookshelf and the spine of each book, book by book.

The Earl of Rutledge tucked his hands behind his back and walked to the window to stare out at the night. Behind him, on the mantel, a case clock chimed three in the morning. He looked out at the bright three-quarters moon low in the sky. It was a cold night, so cold that when his breath hit the window, it frosted the Italian glass panes.

"So where the Christ are you, Margaret, *dear?"* he muttered, staring into the abyss beyond the window. "Where do you hide, you clever little witch?"

It was because of Margaret that he was awake at three in the morning. It was because of his sister-in-law that he couldn't sleep at night, or concentrate on his business during the day.

Rutledge pulled on the tie of his flannel robe, giving it a snap. His little brother Philip was dead and his murderess was still free. That was why he couldn't think, he couldn't sleep, he couldn't enjoy what he ate.

It was her fault, that perfect little bitch with her creamy unblemished skin, silken waves of hair, and perfect rosy mouth. He closed his eyes thinking of the fullness of her breasts, a fullness pregnancy had brought on. He thought of the curve of her hips and the length of her legs that he had caught a glimpse of whenever she climbed the grand staircase.

Rutledge made a fist with one hand, squeezing so tightly that he felt the sharp bite of his own polished fingernails. God above, how he hated her perfection. He sighed. How he had loved it . . .

He opened his eyes, staring at the window that caught his own reflection from the candlelight behind him. He stared at his twisted mouth, so ugly, so abominated.

It wasn't fair. He, a man of education, of title, of royal blood by marriage some generations ago, should not be so cursed. It wasn't right, he, a man who so appreciated perfection in art, in music, in literature, should be so devil-cursed.

Cursed. That was what the yeomen down in the village whispered, though they didn't dare say it aloud. *The Rutledge Curse* was what they called it. The cottars down the hill were having their perfect mealy-mouthed children while up on the hill, every child born of the Rutledge name, save one, in the last one hundred years had been deformed in some manner or another. He himself had been born with a harelip, Philip with his club foot. Their brother, Morris, had been born with part of his brain exposed. Dear little Jacob, who had lived nearly ten years, had entered this cruel world without legs, but instead, tadpole-like flippers.

The earl continued to stare at his own hideous reflection. He had never attempted to wed. Women found him abhorrent. But Philip, Philip had been the charming one, his deformity more easily hidden. He'd had three pretty young wives in a row. Mary had given birth to James, a perfect son, but then others had followed, limbs twisted, holes in their faces where mouths should have been. Mary followed her last three children to the grave. Then there had been Ånne. Anne had only lasted through two births. She, too, lay beside her deformed children in the graveyard.

But lastly, lastly had come sweet Margaret. A child. She was here even before Anne met her untimely death on the stairs to the tower. Margaret had grown into such a lovely woman. So perfect. Surely such an icon of perfection would have spawned perfection. But that child had been born hare-lipped like himself, and when Philip had done away with the abhorrence, as he had with the others, sweet Margaret had killed him.

Rutledge drew his mouth back tightly in anger. Then the bitch had fled. She had actually thought she could escape him. She thought she would not have to pay for what she had done.

There was another Rutledge who had fled, a long time ago. James had been perfect, too. Perhaps it was impossible for perfection to survive here at Rutledge Castle . . .

The earl turned away, passing the two servants, one on a ladder, the other on the floor. Both were still measuring furiously.

"Put out the light when you're done," he called as he passed them.

"Yes, my lord."

"Yes, my lord."

The earl went down the pitch black passageway, a candle unnecessary, for he had been born in this house. He had spent a lifetime walking these hallways alone and in the darkness. He would go to bed. He would sleep with the aid of a draught. And in the morning he would call his men together and begin a search of his own. He'd not leave it up to the authorities to find her. James had managed to escape. He could do nothing about that now. But Margaret, sweet Margaret would not escape. He would find her and he would punish her. He would punish her for the crime she committed . . . and for her perfection.

"No, let me stay." Meg hung back. "You go to the gigger, meet with your friend, and I'll just stay here."

"I'm not leaving you alone, not with Archie breathing on the door." Kincaid pulled her cloak off the wall and held it out for her. "Besides, I want you to meet Monti. He's as good a friend as a man can have."

Meg remained near the window in indecision. After nearly a month inside these walls, she was ready to move on. Her body physically healed from the birth and her mind stronger, she was anxious to go into the city and seek her fortune. She was also anxious to put a distance between herself and Kincaid. She was growing too comfortable with him, too dependent upon him emotionally. She needed to be on her own and Monti, it seemed, was the key to her release.

"He's bringing sweets from the bakery," Kincaid said, in an attempt at bribery.

She laughed at his boyishness. "Kincaid, I'm not a child that I can be bought with cakes."

"I like cake." He grinned handsomely. "I especially like cake when I can share it with you."

She rolled her eyes, walking toward him, knowing she had to give in. The flattery he heaped upon her was embarrassing, and yet in some strange way it was very healing. For the first time in her adult life, here was someone who liked her, who thought she was pretty, who was interested in her opinion. At times, it was intoxicating.

"All right, I'll go."

He dropped her cloak over her shoulders. "Good, because if you didn't come voluntarily, I'd have had to drag you out."

She tied the ribbon of the cloak at her throat. "Hah! I made short work of the turnkey, what makes you think I couldn't do the same with you?"

He laughed as he opened the door and let her pass. "Excellent point, my dearest. Why do you think I sleep on my pallet by the hearth with a blade clutched to my breast. In fear, of course." He locked the door behind him and reached for her arm.

Meg allowed him to be so familiar with her because it was

all part of the farce. She had to play the highwayman's woman if she was to convince others she was indeed Meg Drummond, lady's maid, of the Press Yard as of late. It was all a ploy, she kept telling herself . . . she tried to convince herself.

Kincaid led Meg through the hallways he was as familiar with as a man would be in his own castle. As they passed other prisoners in the chilled, fetid hallways, both men and women greeted him, speaking with a mixture of awe and admiration. It seemed that Captain Scarlet had quite the reputation among the commoners. For reasons that eluded Meg, they all saw him as some sort of hero, despite the fact that he was a thief.

"This way," Kincaid intoned, passing a guard to whom he slipped a coin. "Just through these doors, sweet."

Side by side, her hand in his, the two entered the public visiting room of Newgate, known as the gigger. Here, prisoners were able to meet with friends and loved ones. Food and embraces were shared. Good news and bad news crossed the beaten tables where prisoners and free men sat across from each other.

The large room was an assault to Meg's senses. It was loud and bright and filled with confusion. It stank of unwashed bodies and despair. Prisoners called out to friends and loved ones, waving. Baskets of food and sometimes coin passed hands. Some couples kissed. Children crawled over the tables to touch their fathers, many of whom had no chance of release.

Here was also where contraband entered the prison. Kincaid had informed Meg that anything could be had for a price inside the walls of the gaol: clothing, medicine, weapons, drugs to ease pain, poisons to murder. Professional criminals such as pickpockets, clippers, and coiners carried on business from here, ordering employees and collecting fees. It was rumored that somewhere between the walls of Newgate, counterfeit money was being produced to the tune of six thousand pounds per month.

Meg scanned the room, her heart going out to the men and women on both sides of the tables.

A woman at a table against a barred window wailed as she held her imprisoned husband's hand. Meg recognized the man as Pete, from the debtors side. Pete owed two pounds to a fishmonger and until he met his debt, he would remain behind the walls of Newgate. Of course, imprisoned, Pete could not earn a wage to repay the fishmonger. Now his eldest son, only nine, worked in a hatter's loft in an attempt to earn enough to keep his mother and four brothers and sisters from starving. To add to their troubles, food had to be brought into the prison to Pete daily, else he would starve. It was an unjust system, Meg saw, that discriminated vastly against the poor.

"There he is!" Kincaid gave a wave and pulled her along. "Monti!"

Meg took the chipped, painted stool Kincaid offered her. He sat beside her, stretching his broad hand out. "Good to see you, friend."

Monti was a short man with a broad, ruddy face and bright blue eyes. He wore a long mustache and a pointed goatee on his chin. He was certainly not an ugly man, but nor was he handsome. Of course in Meg's eyes, no one could compare to Kincaid.

Monti clasped Kincaid's hand, but looked toward Meg.

"And this is my Meg." Kincaid released Monti's hand and took Meg's again. "A tearing beauty isn't she, Monti?"

She offered her hand.

He stood to accept it. "Tearing." His smile was genuine, his grip on her hand firm but gentle.

Another kind man! Meg couldn't believe her luck. "It's good to meet you, sir," she said shyly. "Kincaid speaks often of you."

"Not too badly, I hope." He was still smiling.

"God's teeth," Kincaid muttered, pulling Meg's hand from Monti's. "Could you stop drooling on my wench, Monti, and take your seat?"

Monti reluctantly turned his attention back to his partner. "How are your accommodations? Are the meals coming from the tavern?"

"The accommodations are fine. The meat is fine," Kincaid said impatiently. "Now what news have you," he lowered his voice, "of our leave of this fine establishment?"

"I'm working on the matter. But it takes time." Monti and Kincaid spoke in hushed whispers.

"I thought you'd have us out by now," Kincaid murmured, glancing at the guard that passed. "I'm itching for a decent bed and a home-cooked meal."

Monti kept looking at Meg as he spoke. He was obviously taken with her and she couldn't help wondering how Kincaid would handle the matter. Kincaid obviously considered her his property. Philip's jealous rages had been frightening. Were all men the same in the matter of their women?

"As I said, it's not been easy, seeking your release," Monti went on. "It seems there's been a rise in crime on the highways and some jackanapes has decided something needs to be done about it."

"You couldn't get a pardon for us? Not with the amount of coin you received from my goldsmith?"

Monti frowned. "I will get the pardon, but I tell you, it's going to take time. This is quite a *coup d'état* for the Lord Chief Justice, catching Captain Scarlet."

Kincaid sat back on his stool, letting Meg's hand go. He ran his fingers through his sleek, dark hair, He looked this way and that, the carefree grin gone from his face. "I'm ready to take my leave of these vermin, friend."

"Don't get hot with me." Monti leaned over the table. "Remember, I was the one who suggested we abort that night. I told you the luck was bad."

Meg looked away, pretending to be interested in the young woman who had just sat down at the table beside them. She felt like she was intruding between Kincaid and Monti.

She watched as a man with a mop of blond curls, her hus-

band Meg guessed, handed an infant to her over the table and
the woman put the baby to her breast to nurse. Meg felt a
lump rise in her throat.

"I don't think this is the time or the place to harp on the
matter," Kincaid said. "Get me out of here and then chastise
me."

"I will. But if you're not willing to wait on the pardon, it
will have to be an escape." Monti was quiet for a moment as
a dirty-faced guard passed their table.

"Fine. Give me the details."

"They're not completely laid out." Monti pulled impatiently
on his goatee. "I'll have to come back tomorrow or the next."

"All right. What of coin?" Kincaid slid his hand across the
table. "I hope you brought more. This brief stay is going to
cost me a year of profits at the gambling tables."

The men went on talking as Meg glanced from one table
to the next, trying to occupy her mind, wishing she could stop
from thinking of her son and envying the mother beside her.

Meg's gaze wandered to the next table, then the next. Suddenly she stiffened. Not three tables down, seated across from
a middle-aged man with a drooping mustache and tobacco
juice dried on his chin, was the vicar from Rutledge Castle.

Meg averted her eyes, but not before her gaze met the
vicar's. She froze with fear. Surely he had recognized her.

"Meg, are you all right?"

She felt Kincaid take her trembling hand.

"Sweetheart, you're as pale as whitewash. What's wrong?"

"I have to go." Meg bolted upright off her stool.

Kincaid leaped to his feet. "I'll take you back to the chamber."

Monti jumped up, too. "What's wrong? Is she ill?"

"No." Meg shook her head emphatically, turning away,
keeping her back to the vicar. "I can find the way myself."
She hurried away, not taking the time to say goodbye to Monti
or thank him for his attempts to set her free.

Meg's heart was pounding in her chest, her palms cold and clammy.

"Meg." Kincaid was at her side, his gaze searching her face for understanding. "What is it? Are you ill? Shall I have Monti fetch a surgeon?"

When he tried to take her hand, she pulled away from him. In the last weeks, Meg had allowed herself to pretend the Earl of Rutledge was far away in Kent, too far to ever touch her. But she had been fooling herself and she knew it. She had been indulging herself, allowing herself to enjoy Kincaid's company, even toying with the thought of staying with him for a while once they were released.

But the sight of the vicar brought her past crashing back again.

Kincaid attempted to seize her hand again.

"Let me go," she insisted in a hushed whisper, snatching the key that dangled from a string on his waist. "I don't need you. I don't want you!"

He let go of her. "I'm sorry. I only meant to help." He sounded hurt.

"Just let me go," she whispered, "and make no scene." Then she hurried away. The guard at the door admitted her to the prison hallway and she fled at a run, not stopping until she reached the safety of her prison cell in the Press Yard.

Six

"I have to get out of here." Meg covered her face with her hands. She was shaking uncontrollably.

Kincaid tried to reach out and take her shoulders, but she pulled away. "What's wrong, sweetheart? You look as if you've seen a ghost."

Meg turned from him. At this moment she was even more frightened than she had been the night she killed Philip. That night she ran because the midwife told her to. She ran out of instinct, but she didn't know if she had really cared if she escaped. But now that she had met Kincaid she felt differently. Meg wanted desperately to live. Kincaid had made her realize that.

"Meg . . ." He stood behind her.

"Please," she whispered. She feared that if she let him touch her, she would crumble. "Just help me get out of here . . . before it's too late."

Kincaid sighed. She heard him begin to pace the floor. "Meg, I don't know how much longer I can stand this secrecy." There was an edge to his voice. "Who did you see in the gigger?"

"No one."

"What did you hear, then?"

She shook her head.

"Damn it, Meg." His temper flared. "I can't protect you if I don't know what I'm protecting you against!"

When he shouted, she didn't flinch as she always had with

Philip and the earl. For some reason, she was not afraid of
Kincaid, despite his physical brawn. She knew instinctively
that he wouldn't strike her, no matter how angry he became.
She was only irritated with him that he would try to use his
anger to bully her into answering him. "Don't shout at me!
You are not my husband!" She pointed at him, amazed by her
own assertiveness. "And you don't have to protect me." She
took a deep breath, knowing hysterics would get her nowhere.
"You just have to get me out of here. I have no coin to pay
you now, but I'll return every tuppence, I swear I will."

"Meg," he muttered, softening his tone. "I don't want any
money."

She turned to see him running his fingers through his hair
in obvious frustration. "I just want you to tell me why you're
so afraid. So I can help you. I want to fix it."

A tear trickled down her cheek. "You can't fix it. No one
can."

Kincaid came toward her where she stood at the hearth. He
brushed away her single tear with his thumb. This time she
made no protest when he took her into his arms. It felt so
good to feel his heart beat against her chest.

Meg lowered her head to his shoulder.

"Meg, Meg," he whispered, his breath warm in her ear. "I
don't care what you did. How many times must I tell you? I
swear by all that's holy, I don't. Just let me help you." He
stroked her hair, not as a lover would, but as a mother would
stroke his child.

After a moment, Meg looked up into his eyes. She would
never forget this man, no matter how far she went or how
many years passed. "I . . . I think I was spotted this morning," she said softly. "I need to get out of here before they
come for me."

"Who?"

When Meg didn't answer, Kincaid gave another one of his
exasperated sighs. Then, taking her hand, he led her to the

tiny table where they shared their meals and whiled away the hours playing cards and dice. "Tea?" he asked her.

She pushed a heavy sheet of hair off her shoulder. "Wine."

"Excellent choice." He came back with two battered tankards and a dusty bottle. He poured them each a dose of the superior Italian wine. "According to Monti we've but a few more palms to grease and the plan should be set. Arrangements should be complete by the end of the week."

She took a drink of the wine. It calmed her stomach and her nerves. "Tonight."

He laughed. "You know, these iron bars, the guards,"—he gestured with an open palm—"they're here for a reason. Even infamous Captain Scarlet can't scale these walls without a plan."

She took another drink of the wine, avoiding eye contact. "Kincaid, I can't explain it to you except to say that I have to get out of here before he finds me."

"He who?"

She didn't answer.

"Your husband?

"Not my husband. I told you he's dead. Another man."

"Sweetheart, it can't be that bad. Whatever you've done, there would be a trial. You have a right to prove your innocence."

"You don't understand, Kincaid. There'll be no trial. He'll just kill me."

Kincaid stared at her for a long moment. Then, "You're serious, aren't you?"

She studied his dark brown eyes with their dancing specks of green. "Yes"

Kincaid drained his cup and poured himself another. She could see his mind was turning. "Well, I'll just have to send word to Monti to quicken the pace. I'll tell him we have to be out of here by tomorrow night, the next at the latest."

"He'll torture me," she said softly, staring at the glowing

embers in the hearth. "Then he'll kill me." Her words came from her mouth as no exaggeration.

"The escape won't go as smoothly as it would if we had more time," Kincaid warned.

She didn't know if he had heard her or not, but suspected he had. She looked back at him, knowing this man and his friend were her only chance. "I don't care," she insisted. "Just get me beyond these walls and I'll never trouble you again."

He frowned, looking hurt and she realized how serious he was about wanting a relationship once they were gone from this place.

"Beyond these walls, and then where will you go? You don't seem to have any family, or anywhere safe to hide until your name is cleared. No. You'll go with me. Monti's already found a place we can stay until the pardon is secured."

Meg chose not to argue. What was the point? How could she make Kincaid understand why she couldn't stay with him, when she didn't understand herself? All she knew was that she couldn't. So once they made their escape, she would simply slip out of his reach and into the darkness. She would be forever thankful to him, not just for helping her escape, but for making her feel alive again. Suddenly she was filled with a tenderness for this rough highwayman.

As Kincaid watched her, she rose from her chair and walked around the table to his. He just sat there, seemingly entranced.

"I know you'll do what you can to get us out of here," she said.

He put out his hand to her and she took it. How familiar she had become with his hand, so broad and warm. It was as if she had known his hand . . . known Kincaid, a lifetime.

Meg pressed her lips to his palm. There was a lump in her throat. She wanted to escape. She was ready, but now she realized that escape meant parting, and parting meant living without the security Kincaid had provided her these last weeks. "I don't know how to thank you," she murmured.

He looked at her with that lazy grin of his. "To see you

smile is enough." His gaze never strayed from her face as she sat down on his lap.

He smiled. It was obvious he was pleasantly surprised. In the month they had spent together he had never attempted to be intimate with her in any way. He had sensed her need to be left alone, despite their mutual attraction. He had respected her. Yet, at this moment his display of affection seemed right.

Meg settled on his knee, looping her arms around his neck. She felt giddy inside. It gave her a sense of power to know that she was in control here; she was sitting on his lap because she wanted to, not because she was forced.

"Ah, Meg, Meg . . ." He kissed her earlobe. "Ye don't have to do this out of gratitude."

She smiled, staring at his full lips, wanting to kiss them. For days she had wondered what he would taste like. For days she had wondered what it would be like to kiss for the fun of it rather than to be kissed for punishment or out of pure lust.

"I'm not," she said, her voice breathy. "I'm doing it because I want to. Because you want me to." Meg touched the corner of his mouth with her fingertip. He sat perfectly still, his arm around her waist. He made no advancement, just continued to watch her.

Slowly Meg lowered her mouth to his, enjoying the anticipation. As her lips touched his lips, she stroked his jaw with her fingertips. She smiled as their mouths met. He tasted of sweet wine and raw masculinity. A trill of pleasure leapt in her breast as he parted his lips slightly, still letting her take the initiative.

Meg sighed, settling deeper into his lap, tightening her embrace. When his tongue touched her lower lip, she stiffened for an instant. She thought of Philip and his sardine breath as he had thrust his tongue into her mouth so many times, trying to hurt her, to shame her. But the memory faded in a flash. All Meg could think of was Kincaid and how intoxicating his taste had suddenly become.

"Kincaid," she whispered against his lips.

"Meg," he echoed, stroking her back. "My sweet Meg."

She dared to meet the tip of his tongue with her own. He pulled her closer, rocking her back in one muscular arm. She clung to him, reveling in the new sensation. A strange feeling of want crept up from her tingling toes, a feeling she had never known before but could immediately identify.

It was Kincaid who broke the kiss and pulled away as breathless as she.

Meg smiled down at him, still cradled in his arms.

He smiled back, a grin as broad as his hand. "You know, Meg," he gave her a playful peck on the lips, "if I didn't know better I would think that was your first kiss."

Her smiled faded. "Why?" She touched her fingertips to her lips. "Did I do something wrong?"

He laughed, hugging her tightly. "Wrong? Sweet heaven no! It's just that," he grasped for words, "you seem in such awe. Like a child discovering a patch of sunlight for the first time." He laughed again and she realized his voice was shaky. She had affected him as greatly as he had affected her.

"Come to think of it, I feel like it was my first one too, and I have to admit it was not."

She just kept smiling at Kincaid, pleased with him, pleased with herself. "Spare me." She held up her hand. "I want to hear nothing of your conquests." She drew her breath in slowly. "Though I am curious, why hasn't a man like you married?" she crossed her arms over her breasts. "I assume you're not married."

He shook his head. "Not married."

"Why?"

He shrugged. "Never met a woman I wanted to marry before you."

She frowned at his mention of wedding her, but said nothing.

Kincaid went on. "Even if I had found a woman to call

my own, my life has been such that there would have been no place for her, for children."

"You want children?"

"What man or woman doesn't?" He brushed a stray lock of hair from her cheek. "But a man with a wife and babes needs a home, an income."

"No, I don't suppose a highwayman can keep a permanent residence can he?" She kept her tone light, but she was definitely probing. She had been so careful to guard her own past that she'd not asked him of his, but suddenly curiosity was getting the best of her.

He laughed. "I wasn't always Captain Scarlet of the highway, you know."

"No?" She stroked his chin with her finger.

"No. Before our king returned I was a soldier."

"Where?"

"France. Spain. Wherever I was needed. Wherever I could find a musket and crock of ale. There were thousands like me, men without a country, like our own sovereign."

"Then you came from a family of Royalists? Your father supported the Stuarts."

His face hardened. "My father?" His voice was suddenly thick with sarcasm. "My father supported the coin, whichever side it landed upon." He gave her a gentle push and she slid off his lap. He rose. This was obviously difficult for him to speak of. She admired him for trying.

"While Cromwell bled our countrymen dry, my father and his family profited. They bought seized lands at a fraction of their worth. They robbed royal coffers. They paid and accepted bribes." He spat the words that were bitter in his mouth. "So you see, my love, I took after the father I ran from after all. We are both thieves."

Meg stood watching Kincaid as he paced on the far side of the room. The shadows behind him danced jaggedly. It was obvious to her that there was more to this story. She longed to reach out and comfort him. Not only could she hear the anger in his voice, but also the pain.

"Kincaid." She took a step toward him, but he shook his head, lifting a hand to stop her. It seemed he had secrets, too.

It was Meg's turn to respect his privacy.

After a moment he spoke, changing the subject entirely. "If we're to have a chance at escape, Meg, I need to prepare you. You'll have to memorize the layout of the gaol." He picked up a scrap of paper and a bottle of ink and quill from the rough hewn mantle piece. "I'll go over the details that Monti has already secured." He crossed the small room and pushed the stool out for her at the table. He took the seat opposite her.

Meg sat down. As he began a crude sketch, she watched him by the light of the flickering tallow candle in the center of the table. The longer she knew Kincaid, the more complex he became. The fact that he was a common thief seemed of less importance to her each day. In him, she saw more than a thief.

Meg sighed, looking away from him, focusing on the light at the hearth. It was just as well that they would be leaving Newgate and parting this week, she decided. She feared that if she didn't depart from the thieving scoundrel soon, she just might fall in love with him.

The Earl of Rutledge held fast to the strap on the wall of his coach as he was jarred from side to side on the heated leather bench. It was sleeting in London this dreary night. A mixture of snow and rain fell from the dark sky, making Holborn Street slick with ice and freezing mud.

The earl tightened his wool cloak at the neckline. "How much farther?" he demanded between clenched teeth.

His secretary, Higgins, stared at his master with limpid, gray eyes that reminded the earl much of a shark trapped in a net. "Not far, my lord," he eeked out as he tried to wedge himself between the earl's shifting traveling bags and the coach wall.

Percival didn't care much for Higgins. He was a nasty, dwarfted man with a hawk nose and a liking for little girls. But he was devoted to the Rutledge name, which was all that mattered to the earl. Higgins would lie, steal, cheat, murder for his master without so much as a blink of an eye. He had no conscience, as far as Percival could detect. For that, he paid Higgins well, and ignored his disgusting perversion.

The earl lifted the brocade window shade and peered out. Visibility was poor. Sleet came in sheets from the sky. He could see only the blur of buildings and the occasional burst of lamplight as they careened down the center of the narrow, rutted street.

It was near midnight and the keeper of Newgate was not expecting him, but the earl knew that as soon as he sent Higgins in with his name, the keeper would make haste to receive such an important man. No one in London dared not show Rutledge every courtesy, for fear of retribution. Theirs had been one of the few families that had gotten away with switching allegiances to whomever was in power. The earl was in favor with the king, just as he had been in favor with Cromwell only a few years ago. It was said the Rutledge hand reached as far as Paris and as deep as a man's soul. It had been that way for more than a hundred years . . . since the curse began.

The earl sighed heavily. The inside of the coach was cold and dank. It smelled of wet leather and the garlic Higgins wore around his neck to ward off the threat of plague.

The carriage lurched sideways and the flickering lamp nearly went out, drowning in its own stinking oil.

Higgins grabbed the edge of the seat, his already pale face going whiter.

Rutledge chuckled. He enjoyed seeing men in distress, especially eels like Higgins. He glanced out the window again as the carriage righted itself. "Relax, Higgins," he offered, bored. "Once I find my dear sister-in-law, we'll settle in my town house for the night. Think of a warm bed and a tiny white ass snuggled against you."

Higgins made no reply but to look up at his master.

The earl smiled to himself, glancing away, staring out into the darkness through the window.

The vicar had come immediately to him. It seemed the old man thought he had spotted the Lady Surrey in the visiting room of the gaol no less. The interesting aspect of his observation was that he swore she was on the prisoners' side.

Imagine that! His sweet Margaret, a prisoner. What crime could the little mouse have committed? The idea was absurd, but the vicar seemed so sure of himself that the earl chose to investigate the matter personally. He had business with Buckingham anyway, so even if his sister-in-law did not surface, the trip would not be a wasted one.

The carriage turned sharply, then rolled to a halt. Outside, the earl could hear his driver speaking to a guard. After a moment the iron gates swung open and the coach was permitted to pass through. They had arrived at Newgate.

Higgins immediately alighted from the carriage, raising his hood to shield himself from the elements. A good five minutes passed before he returned, soaked, his face twisted in an agitated frown. He hoisted himself back into the coach and slumped onto the seat opposite Rutledge, slamming the door behind him.

"Well?" the earl demanded.

Higgins gave a loose bag a shove, making room for himself on the seat. He pushed back his hood so that the earl could see his ugly face. "The keeper, it seems, my lord, is presently occupied."

"Then tell him to leave his warm bed and his whore or there will be hell to pay!"

Higgins wiped the rain from his pox-scarred face. "I told the turnkey that you must see the keeper at once, but he insists he's preoccupied. We've been invited into the keeper's private apartments for warm refreshment and he will meet with you just as soon as he can."

The earl picked up the gold-tipped cane left leaning against his seat and tossed it angrily. Higgins covered his head with his arms, lest he be struck. "Does he realize who I am? Does he know his position could be in danger, should he not attend to me immediately?"

Higgins winced with each word the earl sputtered. "He . . . he says his position will be in jeopardy if he does not deal with the present matter at hand."

"And what matter is that that's more important than mine?" The earl showered Higgins with spittle.

Higgins's eyelids fluttered. "A jail break, my lord. It seems one of the inmates is attempting to escape . . ."

Seven

Meg ran down the unlit corridor beside Kincaid. He said they couldn't risk carrying a candle, so the moment they stepped out of their Press Yard room, they were launched into darkness. Fearful of tripping, she had pulled the hem of her gown up on both sides and looped it through a leather belt she'd borrowed from Kincaid. Tucked in the belt, as heavy on her mind as on her waist, she wore a primed pistol.

After a few moments of following Kincaid by the mere sound of his footfall, Meg's eyes began to adjust to the darkness.

"Steps," Kincaid instructed so softly that she wasn't certain if he spoke or she had heard his thoughts.

Meg brushed her hand against the cold, wet wall. Her footsteps echoed on the stone risers so loudly that she feared everyone in the prison could hear her. A rat scurried past and she gasped, flattening herself against the wall, but she made no sound. One sound, one step in the wrong direction, Kincaid had warned stoically, might betray them. And if they were caught, he said, she'd be hanged, he'd be drawn and quartered. No questions asked.

At the bottom of the staircase, at the entrance to the Press Yard and Castle where she and Kincaid had been held, they turned toward the common felons' side. She knew which way they went, not because she recognized the narrow passageway, but because she had memorized Kincaid's sketch of the prison's layout.

Kincaid stopped suddenly and pressed his back to the wall. Meg did the same. Ahead, footsteps echoed. Someone was approaching.

Meg stared at her highwayman by the dull light that escaped through a crack in a closed door. He was armed with two blunderbuss pistols and a blade tucked into the waistband of his breeches. Dressed in tight sailcloth breeches and a dark brown shirt open to the middle of his chest, he had discarded his coat, and cloak. He had tied his hair back with a red sash wrapped around his forehead so that he appeared more like a Caribbean pirate than a footpad.

But what was even more startling to Meg than the odd costume or the fortitude of his weapons, was the look in his eyes. This was not the man she had spent the last month with. This was some stranger, focused and intent upon escape. Behind in their cell he had left his gentleness. This man standing beside her, waiting, watching, was the epitome of strength and brawn. All six foot three of his stature was muscle and power. He appeared to Meg to be a man looking for a fight.

She brushed her lips with her fingertips, remembering the kiss they had shared just before they slipped out the door of the cell. In the last three days there had been many shared kisses, each one building on the last until Meg feared she would explode. But thankfully, Kincaid had made no attempt to touch her intimately. She was thankful, because if he had, she knew she would have been powerless to stop him, to stop herself. To touch and be touched was what they both wanted . . . needed.

That was why Meg had to run. She couldn't become intimately involved with Kincaid. The man was a highwayman, a common thief. And she was a murderess. She had to run, to hide from the Earl of Rutledge. She couldn't become involved with a man right now, perhaps she never could.

Meg peered into the darkness, listening as the footsteps came closer.

Kincaid held up two fingers. *Two men.*

She nodded.

Slowly Kincaid inched his way toward an impression in the wall of the corridor. It was only a slight indentation, perhaps eight to ten inches deep. It looked to be a doorway that had been walled up years ago.

Kincaid slid over, making room for her, and she imitated his action, pressing herself into the tiny alcove. She willed herself to become invisible.

The footsteps grew closer. Meg could hear the men's voices now. She tried to breathe steadily like Kincaid, staring straight ahead.

"So I says to Tadpole, you either pay yer debt or yer feedin' the fish on the black bottom of the Thames."

The other man cackled. "And what'd he say then, Artie?"

Artie was one of the guards. Meg remembered him from church services on the third floor where all the prisoners were herded every Sunday. Artie was missing one eye and wore a leather patch over it.

"He started sweatin' hard and makin' excuses." Artie snorted. "Hog crap! I love to see a man sweatin'!"

The other guard laughed with him. The men passed by the alcove where Meg and Kincaid stood, so close she could smell on their clothing the bacon the men had eaten for supper.

Meg held her breath as the two guards passed, exhaling only after they turned the corner in the corridor.

Kincaid slipped from the alcove, on his way again, and Meg followed. All around her she could hear the night sounds of the prison. Even though it was midnight, it could have been noon for the sounds that reverberated off the miserable walls. The air was filled with the cries of men and women. For the inmates there seemed to be no day or night, only the endless hours of dim light and hopelessness. Meg could hear laughter; she could hear screams. Chains clanged. Doors slammed shut. From somewhere above she heard the groans of a man being satisfied, perhaps by a woman, perhaps by his own hand. All of the sounds mingled until they were one, sounds she knew would haunt her forever.

The odd thing was that as they walked through the prison no one of authority seemed to be about. The turnkeys and guards who were normally stationed in different sections of the prison were oddly absent. Was that how bribes for break-outs worked? A man simply paid the authorities to look the other way?

Kincaid stopped and Meg was so intent upon trying to ig-nore the cries of a woman that she bumped into him. He turned to her, the look on his face chastising. *No mistakes,* his expression said.

Meg watched as he tapped lightly on a wood and iron door. After a moment it swung open. She stepped directly behind Kincaid as he put out his hand to pay their passage. In return, the man at the door turned his back and allowed them to pass through. Behind her, she heard the door bang shut and the iron lock turn.

Please get me out of here safely, Meg prayed in silence. Though so far their escape had gone smoothly, the closer she got to the outer walls, the more frightened she became. She had never seen a man drawn and quartered, but her imagina-tion was sufficient to know that she didn't want that for Kin-caid. No man should have to die such a gruesome death.

Kincaid led Meg down another stone corridor. On the floor above, she suddenly heard commotion. Men were shouting. There were footsteps hard and fast on the floorboards above.

Kincaid looked over his shoulder, their gazes meeting. Without words he conveyed the same thought that ran through her mind. *Had their escape been detected?*

Meg had wanted to ask what their chances of escaping would be if they were detected, but she didn't dare speak. Her nerves were stretched so taut that she was shaking from head to foot, but she kept up with Kincaid, her lifeline.

How much farther could freedom be?

Something banged into Meg's leg and she gave an invol-untary cry. She stumbled, going down on one knee, and Kin-caid grabbed her hand, yanking her to her feet.

She clutched her breast, her heart pounding. A mop and bucket! She had tripped over a mop and bucket left in the hallway. She almost laughed at herself and her own foolishness. She was just being skittish. Kincaid said the bribes had been paid. The wheels of the gates had been greased. They would slip out of Newgate and into the London streets without anyone ever knowing they were gone.

They started up another staircase and Meg hurried behind Kincaid, resting her hand on the small of his back for guidance. Halfway up the staircase, he turned unexpectedly and started down again.

"What?" The words were barely out of her mouth when she heard the pounding footsteps coming directly toward them, down the staircase.

"Halt!" a gravelly voice commanded.

Kincaid grabbed her arm, and broke into a run, leaving Meg no choice but to keep up. Lantern light came from behind them, filling the corridor with shadows. A shot was fired and the lead bullet whizzed past them to strike a wall and ricochet back.

They kept running.

Now Meg could smell the stench of the black powder. Acrid smoke lingered in the dank air.

"Run! Faster!" He was half pushing her, half dragging her.

Meg could hear the footsteps pounding in back of her. The guards were not more than twenty paces behind them. Her lungs ached. Her heart was racing.

Down another corridor, left, through a doorway, right, down another corridor. Kincaid seemed to know where he was going. Meg was completely lost.

"Halt," the voice called again. "You cannot escape! Give yourselves up, Scarlet, and we'll be lenient on the woman!"

"Faster," Kincaid hissed in her ear.

"I'm trying," she moaned, her slippered feet pounding on the damp flagstones.

"Plead *belly.*"

"What?" She shook her head in confusion. "Plead belly? I don't understand."

"If we're caught, plead belly. Tell them you're going to have a child. It will keep you from the noose. Give Monti time to get you out."

He meant if they were caught. If he was killed. Meg ran faster.

They made two more turns, putting more distance between themselves and the angry guards pursuing them.

"This way," Kincaid whispered. He turned down a narrow hallway that appeared in the darkness to be a dead end. Ahead loomed a stone wall.

Meg was trembling from head to foot as they came to a halt. She could hear the guards behind them. She leaned over gripping her stomach, panting from the exertion. Kincaid had made a wrong turn, an error. An error that would cost them their lives.

But to Meg's surprise, rather than turning to prepare to defend himself, Kincaid dropped down on all fours and began to slam his fist against the wall. "It's here somewhere," he muttered. "But, damn you to hell, Monti, where?"

"They're coming," Meg whispered, more afraid for Kincaid than for herself. "What are we going to do?"

Then she heard the sweet sound of scraping wood and stone. Out of the flat stone wall, a small door miraculously appeared. Kincaid swung it open and gestured for her to pass. It was pitch dark beyond the secret door, but what choice did Meg have? Without another thought, she dove through the hole. Kincaid followed behind her, swinging the door shut.

Meg laid on her hands and knees for a moment, trying to collect her wits. Behind the door she could hear the guards shouting and cursing. Something about 'disappearing into thin air.'

Finally she picked her head up, only to strike it on the ceiling. They were in some kind of tunnel. "Kincaid?" she whispered.

"Here." He reached to touch her, his hand accidentally caressing her bottom. "I'm here; let me pass and lead the way."

She squeezed herself against the cold, sweating stone of the wall. "The pleasure is mine, sir."

With a dry chuckle, he passed her on his hands and knees. Meg followed. She hated enclosed places. She felt like she was inside a coffin, but she'd come too far now to turn back. If Kincaid said this was the way to safety, then this was the way Meg was going.

She didn't know how far they traveled on their hands and knees, but it seemed like miles. Thankfully, there were no rodents or insects inside the stone tunnel, but it was pitch black and cold and wet. As she crawled, she felt completely disoriented. Her pounding heart was in her throat. Could Kincaid really get them out of Newgate alive?

The air inside the tunnel was stale and cloistering, but slowly Meg began to feel moving air. At first it was just a wave of fresh air, barely a breath. Then another. Meg breathed deeply taking in great gulps of the air that had to be coming from outside the prison walls.

When Kincaid halted, Meg stopped. "Are we there?" she whispered. "Does this lead outside the gates?"

"Almost."

Her heart sank a little. Freedom meant fresh air and a chance at that new life, but freedom also meant parting. She wasn't going to tell Kincaid goodbye. He would only argue with her, perhaps even try to physically restrain her. Once they were outside the prison, on the street, she would just run.

"This leads to a small courtyard, where the vehicles come and go. We've but to pass through the courtyard. A gatekeeper with coin in his palm will open the gate on the far side." She heard Kincaid take a deep breath. "So are you ready, sweet?"

"Ready," she whispered.

They crawled another length before Kincaid stopped and pushed another door. A rush of fresh air poured into the tunnel and Meg closed her eyes in pleasure. It was raining. She could smell it. And the air was cold, but she didn't care. The rain and the cold were freedom; they were a new life.

Kincaid disappeared ahead, then she felt his hand reach back into the tunnel for her. She gripped it and allowed him to pull her out.

Rain immediately struck her bare face and she put out her tongue to catch a drop.

Kincaid still held her hand. "This way," he whispered, pointing.

Meg stared through the darkness. They had to pass a waiting coach to reach the gate which was barely visible in the driving rain.

"Ready?"

She turned to him, "I'm ready, but thank you." She threw her arms around his neck. The hood of her cloak fell back on her shoulders. The cold rain hit her hard in the face, but it felt good.

"Whoa. We're not out yet, sweet. But there'll be plenty of time for you to express your appreciation once we're on the other side of that wall."

"Thank you anyway," she whispered. Then she lifted up on her toes and kissed him hard on the mouth, hugging him. "Thank you so much."

When she looked into his eyes, he was looking at her strangely. "Women," he muttered. Then he took her by the hand. "Let's go."

They were halfway across the dark courtyard, just passing the coach and four when light appeared behind them. "There they go!" a man shouted. "I found them!"

"Through the gate," Kincaid hissed under his breath as he turned to draw his knife. "It's unlocked. Monti'll pick you up on Holborn."

Meg backed up through the mud puddles. Guards were pouring from the prison entryway. She heard a dog growl ferociously. "What about you?" She grabbed Kincaid's sleeve, afraid for him.

"I'll be coming directly." He dashed at the rain in his eyes. "Now get the hell out of here whilst I hold them off."

Meg took one look at the guards, then another at Kincaid.

"Go!" he ordered.

Meg made a run for the gate. Sure enough, it was unlocked. Just as she slipped through, she saw the first guard attack Kincaid. She knew she should run, but she couldn't make her legs move. From outside the gate, she peered inside.

The guard that advanced on Kincaid had a club. He swung it over his head to crack Kincaid, but Kincaid was too fast for him. He moved so quickly that Meg didn't see the knife. Suddenly the guard howled and pulled back. By the light of the lanterns she saw blood gushing from the guard's forearm.

Slowly Kincaid was backing toward the gate. Another guard advanced, this one with a wooden staff. He swung it viciously at Kincaid's head. Kincaid ducked. He bobbed, he wove. Then with one leap forward, he managed to grasp the opposite end of the man's staff and rap him on the head with it. Now Kincaid had his knife and the guard's staff.

Then someone sicced the dogs on him. A yellow and a black hound charged, barking and snarling. Meg cringed. If the dogs attacked Kincaid, their powerful jaws would tear him apart. The dogs circled him, drawing closer. Kincaid moved slowly, still backing toward the gate. Both dogs lunged at the same instant. Kincaid raised the staff and struck the yellow one in the head. With one booted foot, he caught the other hound in its belly. The dogs yiped in unison. The yellow one was knocked unconscious. The black one just lay on the ground rolling and yelping.

"Hey! He hurt my hounds! The bastard tried to kill my hounds!"

Kincaid was nearly to the gate now. Meg knew she should run. This was her chance. She could be gone before Kincaid escaped from the prison courtyard. But what if he didn't escape? There were so many guards now. She stood in frightened silence, watching, in awe of how lithely her highwayman moved.

Kincaid swung his knife again and again, slicing the air with the steel blade. He struck another guard and when a fourth advanced on him, he caught him clean in the thigh. Meg wondered why Kincaid didn't just shoot them with the pistols on his belt, but she sensed it had something to do with his strange ethics. Apparently he could rob, he could shoot and wound English soldiers attempting to stop him, but he didn't want to kill prison guards.

The courtyard was filled with confusion. The skies had opened up in a downpour. Men were shouting. There was more light. Someone of authority in a black cloak, the jailkeeper no doubt, stood near the crested coach barking orders, calling for more guards. Another man was dragging the injured dogs across the courtyard.

Kincaid had nearly reached the gate now. It would be safe for Meg to run. But still, she hesitated. She turned to look up and down the dark, deserted street of Old Bailey. She could see the hired hackney coach waiting in the shadows. A man stood at the door, cloaked in black. It had to be Monti.

Kincaid burst through the gate, slamming it shut. "Let's go, Meg," he snapped, throwing out his hand for her. She had already turned right onto Old Bailey instead of following Holborn Street. There were perhaps twenty paces between her and Kincaid.

Meg took one look at Kincaid and the hackney beyond him, and ran.

"No, Meg!" She heard him swear foully. "This way."

She ran along the prison wall, down the street. "Go," she called over her shoulder. "Get the hackney and go."

"Not without you!"

The guards burst through the prison gate. "There they go!" came one shout after another.

"Stop them! Stop the bastard or it'll be your hides!"

Meg ducked down an alley, running as hard as she had ever run in her life.

"Meg!"

"Just let me go," she cried over her shoulder.

"No!" She ran through the maze of fetid alleys between the main streets. It was raining so hard that it was difficult to see. She needed a place to hide. She couldn't outrun Kincaid. But everywhere the shops were locked up. Doors closed. She raced around a dog cart, climbed over a barrel of stinking fish.

She turned a corner, out of Kincaid's sight. God help her if he caught her, because he was enraged.

She turned another corner, out of breath. Her clothes were so water-soaked that they were becoming heavy. She was tripping over her skirts that had come undone from Kincaid's belt. She couldn't run much farther. Then she heard the guards and their dogs again. They were on another street, perhaps in another alley, but they were still chasing her Kincaid.

She wondered why Kincaid didn't just give up his pursuit of her and make a run for it. For sweet God's sake, Monti was waiting with a coach. The guards were on foot.

Meg tripped over something in the street and fell headlong, striking her hand on a wooden gate. A gate in the alley? On her hands and knees, she fumbled for the latch in the blinding rain. The alleyway off the alley was so small, it was barely visible, the gate so narrow, she had to turn sideways to get through.

Meg slammed the gate behind her and set the latch. She was in a tiny courtyard with only the gate and a door that led into a building. A private home, perhaps. She checked the door, but it was locked. She was trapped if anyone found the gate, but if they missed it, she was safe.

Exhausted, Meg found an old crate to sit on and drew it under the eaves to get out of the rain.

"Meg?"

When she heard Kincaid's threatening voice, she froze. What would he do with her if he caught her? Would she react like Philip? Philip's anger was always accompanied by a cuff to the chin. Or would Kincaid be able to control his temper as she had seen him do in the past. She shivered in the rain. A part of her wanted to answer him when he called.

She heard his footsteps pounding, water splashing as he went by. "Meg? Damn it! Where the holy hell are you?"

She held her breath.

He passed by.

Not three minutes later, two or three men and a barking dog ran by. Guards. She prayed Kincaid got away.

Once the men passed, the little alcove was quiet again. Minutes passed. Then an hour. The rain still fell and Meg huddled under her wet cloak, trying to stay warm. Suddenly she felt so alone. Kincaid was gone. Surely by now Monti had picked him up and they had disappeared into the London night.

So now where did she go? She had no money. No possessions. Only the clothes Kincaid had given her and the loaded pistol on her waist. She supposed she could sell the blunderbuss for money, to eat and for a room to stay in. But she would have to find employment eventually, else she'd starve or freeze to death.

Time dragged on. Kincaid and the prison guards were long gone, but Meg hesitated to leave her alley. Still, it would be dawn soon. She had to go somewhere. Maybe she'd find a tavern and get a hot meal. There she could dry out and collect her thoughts. A hot toddy would do wonders for her outlook on her situation right now.

Slowly, Meg rose from her crate, her bones stiff from sitting so long in the cold and rain. Cautiously, she opened the gate and peered out into the alley. She could see nothing, but the black night had turned to gray. The rain had stopped.

Meg stepped into the alley, listening for any sound of the men who had pursued them. She heard a cat meow. Somewhere overhead in the two-story building a woman shrieked for her husband to get his lazy arse out of bed.

Meg walked down the alley to its exit onto the street.

"There you are, you ungrateful jade!"

Kincaid.

Meg swung around in astonishment. Where did he come from?

Before she could speak, he grabbed her roughly by the shoulders. "Let me go!"

"Shut up."

She struggled. "Let me go, Kincaid. I don't want to go with you!"

"Shut up before someone hears you!" He dragged her along the dark street. There were a few men and women about now, shopkeepers, those employed in stables and wealthy households.

"Let me go!" she insisted under her breath, angry at him for thinking he could force her to do what she didn't want to do. So, he was no different than any man, than Philip and his brother.

He turned the corner and stopped at a hired, closed coach. "Get inside." She could hear the edge to his voice that came just before he lost his temper.

"Kin—"

He grabbed her around the waist, opened the coach door, and shoved her inside. "Go!"

Even before he climbed inside, the coach lurched forward and he made a jump for it. The door slammed shut and he fell onto the seat.

Meg looked up from where she lay in a heap on the floor. The coach was rolling fast down the street, swaying so that she could barely balance herself as she climbed onto the seat. "Bastard! This is kidnapping."

He grabbed the handle that came out of the wall, steadying himself as she was thrown against him when the coach careened around a corner. "Kidnapping? After that stunt you pulled, you're lucky I didn't wring your pretty little neck . . ."

Eight

"I cannot believe she escaped in a futtering jail break! And with a highwayman, no less!" The Earl of Rutledge stood in the center of the bedchamber of his London townhouse. He was clothed in an East Indian dressing gown, his wig removed, with a silk turban around his nearly bald head.

Percival had arrived from Newgate at almost three in the morning and roused his caretaker from his bed. The man had not been expecting his master, as Percival had not sent word he was coming. Since then, the fire on the marble hearth in his lordship's bedchamber had been lit and tallow candles illuminated the room in the hour before dawn. Most of the furniture was still covered with its dust drapes.

"Y . . . yes, my lord. A jailbreak." Higgins stood inside the bedchamber door, but out of striking distance of his master.

"And was she my brother's wife?" Percival had never had an opportunity to speak to the keeper, but Higgins had talked to one of the guards at the gaol.

"Well, could be. The woman who escaped went by the name of Meg Drummond, but she resembled the Lady Surrey."

The Earl of Rutledge sipped sherry from a fluted glass. In his anger, some of the red spirit trickled down his chin. "And what, out of curiosity, was this woman incarcered for, Higgins?"

"Highway robbery, my lord. She was a rum-pad's wench."

"What did you say?" Rutledge boomed.

"This . . . this Meg Drummond, she was arrested for being an accomplice to attempted robbery. Along with a well-celebrated highwayman, Captain Scarlet." Higgins cringed with his own last words.

"Highway robbery!" Rutledge spat, sending sherry sputtering into the air. "And you think this jade could have been my sister-in-law? A highwayman's whore indeed. S'death, Higgins, have you lost what little sense you ever possessed?"

"No. Yes. I . . . I don't know, sir. I mean I don't know if it was her. I'm trying to get information on the arrest."

"Margaret, an accomplice to robbery?" The notion was so preposterous that now he thought it was funny. "Chaste little Margaret would be less likely to play a part in such a crime than I would be to sprout wings and fly over the London Bridge!"

"Yes, my lord."

"So why are you wasting my time, Higgins? The wench who escaped couldn't have been my little Margaret."

"It is a coincidence, sir, that the woman's name was Meg and that she was arrested on the road from Kent to London the same night your brother, Lord Surrey, was murdered. I just thought that I would—"

"Do I pay you to think, Higgins?"

The servant held himself erect in the doorway. "N . . . no, sir. Not usually."

The earl wiped his mouth with the back of his hand. "Then restrain yourself from doing so." He set his glass on a draped table. "I want her found."

"Yes, my lord."

"She's here. I can smell her. I want her."

"Yes, my lord."

Rutledge glanced about his bedchamber. "I've decided I'll stay in London for a time. I want the house opened. I want my clothing and personal items brought from Rutledge."

"Right away, my lord."

"And I want her found. Not tomorrow, not next week." He was spitting again. "Today, preferably this morning. Surely the woman could not have gone far. Christ's blood, she barely had enough sense to find her own way back from the shithouse!"

"Well, it has been more than a month, sir. She's obviously—"

"Higgins!"

The man dropped his cold-eyed gaze to the hardwood floor. "My lord?"

"I want no excuses. I simply want her found."

"If you don't mind my asking, sir." Higgins looked at him with his gray, shark eyes "How do you propose I find a particular woman in Londontown? It . . . it has grown rather large since the king returned."

"I do mind your asking!" Rutledge snapped. "Must I do everything myself? Check with any relatives we have here in town, no matter how far from the castle wall the lineage might be. Then check the markets. The woman must eat! Check every tavern and house that rents to women without escorts. Look in the Royal Exchange for bloody Christ's sake. Where else would a woman go, but to buy trinkets?" He was now counting off on his fingers. "The parks. The theater. Listen to the gossip. A lady of her ilk just doesn't disappear. Someone has seen her and someone has aided her!"

"As you wish, my lord."

"Now, go." He fluttered his hand in a dismissal. "I must have some sleep. Hire what servants are needed to run the household."

"I'll take care of the matter, my lord."

Rutledge sat down on the edge of his bed, made with fresh linens he brought in his own travel bags. "And Higgins . . ."

The man stopped in the doorway, but did not turn to-face the earl. It was a game Higgins played, to act subservient one moment, discourteous the next. The earl only tolerated it because the dog couldn't be easily replaced.

"Get me an invitation to the king's next supper. I've been away from court too long."

"Yes, my lord."

He closed the door behind him and Percival laid back on a heap of pillows. His Margaret a highwayman's whore, indeed! He leaned over to blow out a candle, laughing aloud.

Kincaid dragged Meg by her arm along a narrow street. In the early morning hours there were few people about. Doors were closed, shutters drawn. They must have been very near to the Thames because she could smell it. "Where are you taking me?" she demanded angrily. Monti trailed behind them.

"You deserve to go straight to hell after that trick." Kincaid gave her arm a jerk, forcing her to keep up. "I spent four hundred pounds and risked my life to get you out of *crapings!*"

She jerked her arm out of his hand. "I didn't ask for your help! I never asked for anything! I certainly didn't ask for you to pick me up and drag me into your criminal behavior."

"You'd rather I'd left you on that road to freeze to death?"

"I'd rather not have ended up with lice in Newgate!" she snapped.

"Just like a woman." Kincaid looked at Monti, pointedly ignoring Meg. "Never happy. No matter what you give a wench, what you do, it's never enough."

Meg glanced up at the boarded windows that loomed on both sides of the narrow street. A vender walked by hawking breakfast breads. It was a strange place, somehow different than the London street she had studied from the Press Yard window. "You still haven't told me where we are."

Monti hurried to catch up, flanking her side. "Ram Alley, in Whitefriars, Mrs. Drummond."

Meg glanced at Monti. She noticed he addressed her as Mrs. rather than Miss and she was thankful for his tact. Miss was a term reserved only for very young girls and whores.

She politely turned her attention to Monti. If Kincaid could ignore her, she could certainly ignore him. "And where, or what might I ask is Whitefriars?"

Despite the chill of the morning air, Monti's forehead was damp with perspiration. He wiped it with the sleeve of his coat, seemingly nervous in her presence. "A place in the district where the less fortunate can take haven."

"Thieves, criminals, debtors," Kincaid offered gruffly.

A scowl puckered Meg's eyebrows. "And this is the sanctuary you bring me to?"

Kincaid eyed her dangerously. "You were expecting Whitehall, madame?"

"It's really not so bad," Monti went on. "Some here are good men and women that bad times have simply befallen. Here's a place they can be accepted . . . and hide from the constable."

Kincaid stopped at a closed door and Monti stepped forward to unlock it with a key. Kincaid stepped into a dimly lit entranceway and when Meg hesitated, he grabbed her hand and pulled her inside. The hall was dark and quiet. She heard the door close behind her and Monti turn the lock. She was trapped.

"Where are we now?" she whispered.

"This is where we'll be staying for a short time. Until our pardons can be arranged."

Meg followed Kincaid down the hallway which opened into a large eating room. She wondered if they were in a tavern. Rich drapes hung from the ceiling to partially cover the windows, blocking out the morning sunshine. The walls were painted in some kind of murals, though in the dim light she couldn't make them out. There were tables everywhere still littered with bottles, nuts and oyster shells, and dirty plates. Chairs were overturned. The room smelled of stale liqueur and heavy perfume.

Monti lit several candles illuminating the public room. To Meg's shock she could now see the painting on the walls clearly. They were nudes. Naked women embraced naked men on two of the four walls, their bodies tangled in various lewd sexual positions.

She heard Kincaid chuckle and she looked at him to find him smiling at her. Meg knew her cheeks burned red with embarrassment. "What kind of place is this you've brought me to?" she demanded.

He laughed, dropping his hand onto her shoulder. But Meg was in no mood. She pushed his hand aside.

Kincaid shrugged and walked away. "Monti has rented a room here for us. It's the best he could do on short notice." He went to a sidetable along the wall where bottles of liquor stood half-empty. He grabbed a dirty glass from a table and poured himself a draught of cherry brandy. "Remember, you were the one who insisted we escape immediately."

Meg grabbed a chair that lay on its side and righted it. She was so tired she could barely think. "I want you to let me go." She sat down.

"Go where?" Kincaid downed the brandy in a single swallow and poured himself another. Monti poured his own.

"I don't know. Anywhere but here. I . . . I'll seek employment . . . as a lady's maid."

"And you think someone will hire you with no references? Would you, if you were a lady of quality, hire a woman without references? How would you know she wasn't a swindler?" He shrugged his broad shoulders. "An accomplice to highway robbery even?"

She hadn't thought of that, but Kincaid had, the bastard. He was obviously set on keeping her with him, though why, she didn't know. Meg dropped her head into her hands. So now what did she do? This man who had been so kind to her was now holding her prisoner. Would her luck with men always run badly?

Meg heard a chair scrape as it was pulled up beside her. She glanced up. It was Monti.

"Mrs. Drummond—"

"Call me Meg. Considering the circumstances, I should think we could be on a first name basis, wouldn't you Monti?"

He smiled. "Thank you, madame. Meg." He wiped his mouth with a lace handkerchief. "What . . . what I wanted to say is that you really will be safe here. I . . . I'm working on the pardons for you and the captain, but these things take time. Here . . . here at Mother Godwin's, you'll not be discovered."

"Mother Godwin's?"

"Mother Godwin's Home for Girls," Kincaid offered from where he stood at the window, sipping his brandy, staring out.

"You'll be safe here," Monti assured her. "I . . . I checked with my astrologer just last night. The stars are with us."

Meg glanced at Kincaid. She had heard that some men and women paid close attention to astrology and governed their lives by it, but she'd never known anyone like that. She'd been well isolated from the rest of the world at Rutledge Castle. Of course that was how Philip had wanted it.

"Captain Scarlet!" An unusually tall woman in a black silk dressing gown appeared in the room. She was a comely woman somewhere in her mid-forties with tousled ebony hair piled on her head, as if she'd just risen. Her face was handsome for a woman her age, though strangely she lacked eyebrows.

"Mother Godwin." Kincaid turned from the window, smiling in greeting.

Mother Godwin went to him and threw her arms around his shoulders, kissing him on the lips. Meg straightened up in interest. She couldn't help being just a little jealous. Why was this woman kissing Kincaid?

"How are you, sweet?" she cooed. "Oddsfish, I feared I'd never see you again but at Tyburn. I thought I'd have to fight the crowd for your remains."

Kincaid grinned boyishly as she took his empty glass from him and went to refill it. "Come now, Angel, you know me better than that. A few king's soldiers, a wall, a bar or two, could certainly not keep me from your side."

She laughed, her voice light and airy. "Ah, Scarlet, I've missed you." She returned his glass to him, her fingertips brushing his as the brandy changed hands. Then she turned to Meg. "And this must be the dear Mrs. Drummond Monti spoke of."

Meg didn't rise from her chair. She was too tired and too confused to know what role she was expected to play here at Mother Godwin's. She nodded cordially. "At your service, Mother Godwin."

The black-haired woman turned to Kincaid. "Pretty."

"Unavailable."

Mother Godwin sighed, apparently disappointed by something. She turned back to Meg. "I know you must be tired and hungry. Could I have a bath drawn for you, Mrs. Drummond?"

A bath? Meg couldn't resist a smile. Kincaid had managed to have clean water and soap brought into the Press Yard, but there had been no way to bathe in Newgate. "A bath would be heavenly."

"Let me take you to your room and have my son bring up the heated water." She offered her hand to Meg and Meg rose from her chair. "I'll have him bring a nice raisin porridge and hot chocolate, as well. Something to eat, a bath, and a soft bed and you'll be your beautiful self by evening."

As Mother Godwin led Meg away, she glanced over her shoulder at Kincaid. As angry as she was with him, she was still uncertain enough with Mother Godwin that she looked to him for reassurance.

He smiled as if no disagreement had taken place between them. "Go have your bath and I'll join you shortly."

Feeling a little more self-assured, Meg allowed Mother Godwin to lead her down the hall and up a wide staircase to the second floor. They passed several closed doors as they went down the hall. All was quiet.

"The girls are still sleeping, but I'm sure you'll have an opportunity to meet them later." Mother Godwin walked along in a pair of expensive black silk mules.

Meg wondered who *the girls* were, but she didn't ask.

Mother Godwin halted and pushed open the last paneled door on the left. "This is the room our captain uses when he stays with us. I hope it's suitable."

Meg stepped inside. A fire had already been lit in the chamber. Heavy crimson drapes hung on the windows, old, but graceful. The furniture in the room was mismatched and aged, but of excellent quality, good enough to have once rested in the king's chambers. Dominating the room was a massive bed with crimson curtains to match the velvet drapes on the windows. A big brass bathing tub had already been placed at the hearth and towels rested on a warming rack before the crackling fire.

"I've left a dressing gown on the bed for you. If you give my son Noah your clothing, I'll have it cleaned and returned by the evening's festivities." She stood at the door. "A morning tray will be up directly. Is there anything else I can get you, Mrs. Drummond?"

Meg stood near the bed, running her fingers over the lace counterpane. She couldn't help wondering if Mother Godwin was expecting her to share this bedchamber with Kincaid. What had Monti told her? Did she think Meg was Kincaid's woman?

"No." Meg smiled graciously. "It's perfect. Thank you for thinking of a bath. I've desperately wanted one for weeks."

"Well, enjoy it, and if there's anything you need, just tell Noah. He runs the house around here."

Mother Godwin made her exit and Meg walked to the window to pull back the crimson drapes to look down at the street below. A moment later the door opened with a bang, startling her.

A man her own age came through the door carrying a

bucket of steaming water in each hand. He had the same blue-black hair as Mother Godwin. It had to be her son Noah.

"Got yer bath water," the man said, loping toward the tub with an odd gait. "Mother said, hot Noah, so I got it hot." He grinned at her like a child waiting for approval.

Meg smiled hesitantly. By the way the man spoke, she could tell he was mentally deficient in some way. She watched him pour first one bucket of hot water into the brass tub, and then another. Then he set down the buckets and pulled a square of brown paper from inside his coat. Carefully, he unwrapped it, producing a bar of soap. Even from across the room, Meg could smell the scent of lilacs.

Gingerly, Noah set the bar of perfumed soap down on the wooden stool beside the tub. " 'Nother two buckets and that'll make," he counted on his fingers, "eight. Eight's what it takes to fill the tub. Always eight."

Meg walked toward the tub, drawn by the thought of soap and water. "It looks like enough to me." She dragged her fingers through the water. "Warm enough, too. Thank you." She waited for him to pick up the buckets and go, but he just stood there staring at her.

"You goin' to live here with us now?" he asked after a moment.

Meg shook her head. Noah had a handsome face, innocent. "No. I . . . I'm just staying a few days and then I'll be going."

He nodded. "I like you. You got nice hair."

Self-consciously Meg reached up to smooth her tangled hair. How long had it been since it had been washed? Just thinking about it made her want to scratch. "Thank you."

"Red. Mother dyed her hair red once, but she said it made her look like a Fleet Street whore." He grinned.

Meg gave a laugh, taking no offense at his words. She glanced at the tub. She wanted desperately to get in before the water cooled. "Well," she said.

"Well," he mimicked.

So he wasn't going to budge on his own. "I think I'll take

my bath now." She lifted one of the buckets and handed it to him.

"You want me to leave?"

"So I can bathe while the water's still hot."

He picked up the other bucket. "You don't want me to be scrubbin' yer back?"

Meg's eyes widened. "No. No, that won't be necessary."

"Mary Theresa always lets me scrub her back. Sometimes her front. Her and Miss Maria." Noah was grinning bashfully from ear to ear now. "I like to scrub their fronts."

Meg walked to the door. "No, thank you," she said firmly, giving the knob a tug. "But I do appreciate the offer." She ushered him out the door and closed it behind him.

The moment she heard him clomp away down the hall, she began to strip off her clothing, leaving it in a trail behind her. By the time she reached the tub, she was down to her shift. Dropping it to the floor, she climbed naked into the tub, sighing as she sank into the soft, warm water.

"Ah," she breathed. The water was heavenly. First she washed her hair with the lilac soap, scrubbing away the weeks of oil and dirt. Then she scoured her whole body head to toe, ooing and ahing with pleasure. Meg was just finishing with her toes when she heard the door open behind her. "Yes?" she sank into the tub, covering her bare breasts.

Noah came loping in, as if he'd been invited, a bucket of water in each hand.

"What are you doing here?" She crossed her hands over her breasts, protectively.

Noah poured the first bucket of water into the tub, making no attempt to avert his eyes. "Eight buckets. 'At's what the tub takes. 'At's how Miss Maria and Mary Theresa likes it. That's how Mrs. Drummond likes it."

Meg could see there was no reasoning with Noah, so she let him pour the second bucket of hot water in. "Thank you. Now go," she said, pointing toward the door as she awkwardly attempted to keep her breasts covered.

But instead of retreating to the door, he set down the bucket and reached into his coat. "Wait, I gotta show you somethin'. He held up a drawstring money purse. "I been savin' two weeks. I was s'posed to marry Miss Maria come Friday night, but I decided I want to marry you 'stead. Mother says it's up to you."

Meg's brow furrowed. "I . . . I don't understand."

He clinked the coins inside the purse. "Marry ye. I save my coin every month and Mother let's me marry one of the girls." He scratched his head. "I like Miss Maria. She's a good marryer. But I like Mary Theresa, too. Sometimes it's hard to choose."

"Noah. I don't know what you're talking about. Now you'll have to leave. Captain Scarlet will be very angry if he finds you here."

Noah slid his purse back into his coat looking thoroughly chastised. "You mean you won't marry me, even if I'm quick about it? Miss Maria says I'm quick. Don't give 'er no bother with my little piddle." He broke into a smile again. "Sometimes if business is good, Mary Theresa gives me a free one, but don't tell Mother, because she'll get very angry. No free futters here. No, sir. No, madame."

Suddenly Meg realized what the young man was talking about. He wanted to buy sex from her, for heaven's sake!

So was that was what *the girls* of Mother Godwin's School for Girls did? They were all whores? Was this a whorehouse Kincaid had brought her to?

Meg tried to remain calm. After all, none of this was this addlepated boy's fault. She just couldn't believe it had taken her this long to figure it all out. Her life at Rutledge truly had been sheltered, hadn't it?

"Noah, I'm sorry, but I can't marry you," she said firmly.

He looked so disappointed. "Why not?"

She stared up at the ceiling in exasperation. "Because . . . because Captain Scarlet wouldn't like it, that's why."

"You only marry him?" Noah was trying so hard to understand.

Meg exhaled. A few months ago she would never have been able to deal with this. Now all she wanted to do was get Noah out of there so she could finish her bath. "Yes. Exactly. Now, please go."

He picked up his buckets. "Well, you let me know if you need anything else."

"I will."

Finally she heard the door open and close behind her. She sighed, relaxing into the water.

A moment later the door opened again.

"Noah! Get out!"

"Excuse me? You were expecting another gentleman?"

It was Kincaid's voice. She relaxed again. She and Kincaid had lived in such close quarters in Newgate that she was no longer shy with her body, or his for that matter.

She chased the bar of soap along the bottom of the tub. "Noah. He was here wanting to *marry* me."

Kincaid laughed, setting something down on the table near the bed. It smelled like breakfast. "Marry you?"

"That was his word, not mine. He meant . . . you know."

"Ah, and did you take him up on his offer?"

Meg turned in the tub. "That isn't funny. Is this the kind of place I think it is? I have a right to know!"

"I told you, Mother Godwin's—"

"I know. I know. A School for Girls." She eyed him as he took a seat on the low stool beside the tub. "This is a whorehouse, isn't it?"

He was smiling at her, that smile of his that made her forget what she was saying. That smile that made it so difficult for her to be angry with him.

"Sort of."

She splashed water at him. "Knave! How could you?"

"I told you, the queen's chambers were full. This was the best Monti could do on short notice."

"I will not stay in a whorehouse." She lathered her hands and scrubbed her arm viciously. "I will not be propositioned."

"Not even by me?" He ran his finger along her bare arm. It wasn't so intimate a gesture, yet his mere touch sent sparks of excitement through her.

"Kincaid."

He sighed, sitting back to rest his hands on his knees. "I'll get us an apartment of our own as soon as it's safe. New topic of conversation. Why did you run from me?" His voice was gentle, but persuasive. The anger was gone.

Meg couldn't stand to look at him. She studied the bar of lilac soap in her hands. "I told you I couldn't stay with you. I thought it would be better if I just disappeared."

"Why can't you stay with me?"

She let go of the soap and sank back in the tub, closing her eyes, resting her neck on a towel that had been draped for that purpose. "Because I can't."

"That's not a reason. I love you. That's the reason I want you to stay."

She didn't know how to respond. No one had used those words with her since she was a child. Her grandmother was the only person who had loved her, and she was gone. "Kincaid." When she opened her eyes, he was staring intently at her.

"Yes. I'm waiting. Tell me why you can't stay with me. Tell me why you won't let me take care of you."

"You're a criminal."

"I'll quit. Soon. I never intended to do this for a lifetime anyway. Next problem."

She studied his dark eyes, not knowing what else to say. All she could think of right then was kissing him. She rose in the tub. He jumped up to hand her a warm Turkish towel and would have wrapped it around her if she'd let him.

"We've gone over this time and time again, Kincaid." Securing the towel above her breasts, she reached for another to dry her hair as she stepped out of the tub. "We just go around in circles."

"We go around in circles, because you won't tell me why you won't stay with me. I don't think it's because you don't care for me. That you're not attracted to me."

She walked to the bed and presented her back to him. Letting the towel fall, she slipped into the dressing gown Mother Godwin had left for her. When she turned back to face him, tying the sash, he was right there.

"Meg?"

She shook her head. "I don't want to talk about this. I just can't stay with you. That's all."

"God help me, you're beautiful." He reached out with one broad hand to caress her cheek. "You know I could protect you from whomever you're running from. Your husband—"

"Not my husband," she said firmly. "I already told you more than once, he's dead."

"Whomever." He massaged her shoulder.

Not the Earl of Rutledge, she thought. *No one can protect me from a man so brutal. So powerful.*

Meg stood there, trembling inside. It was like this every time Kincaid grew near her. Every time he touched her.

He took her into his arms and she made no protest. He ran his hand down her arm, over the silk sleeve. "Meg, love, I could make you happy if you'd let me try."

Meg closed her eyes as he brushed his mouth against hers. His offer was so tempting. She wanted so desperately for someone to care for her, love her. "I have to go away from here," she whispered. "If the one who's looking for me finds me, he'll kill me."

"Then I'll go, too. I'll finish my business here and I'll go. We'll go together, anywhere you want."

His offer was tempting. Why couldn't they just disappear, the highwayman and the murderess? When his lips brushed hers, she kissed him back. But she didn't want to think about this right now. She didn't want to think of the earl or her husband, or even of her dead son, all she wanted to think about was Kincaid and how he made her feel. He said he loved her and she believed him.

"Let's not talk about this anymore," she murmured in his ear. She wrapped her arms around his waist. "Let's do this, instead." She lifted up on her toes to press her lips to his.

"Ah, Meg, you do this to me time and time again." He kissed her full on the mouth with a groan. "And this is how the argument always ends. This is always how you win."

"Hush and kiss me," she answered. "Kiss me while I'm still here to be kissed."

Nine

When Meg kissed Kincaid, she had no intentions of making love with him. All she wanted was to feel him close, to brush her lips against his. But suddenly, now that she was in his arms, she craved more. His dark-eyed gaze swept over her, slowly, languorously, with a heat stronger than his touch. Without words, her thoughts passed from her mind to his. *I want you,* she whispered silently.

And I you, he answered.

Meg knew it made no sense. Kincaid had forced her to come here to Mother Godwin's. He was holding her prisoner. What woman in her right mind would want to make love to her captor?

What woman in her right mind wouldn't want to make love to a man who had been so kind, so loving? Logically, it made no sense for Meg to become physically involved with Kincaid. But she quickly realized that love had nothing to do with logic.

"Meg, my sweet Meg," Kincaid whispered in her ear, brushing his fingers against the nape of her neck, beneath her loose, damp hair. Then he closed his open mouth over hers, and she clung to him with an urgency that for days had been lurking just beneath the surface of rational thought.

When he slipped his hand into her robe, she made no protest. His warm hand cupped one full, aching breast and she sighed. Philip had never touched her like this; he had never made her feel this way.

Kincaid kissed her again and again, not just one kiss, but a dozen. He brushed his lips in tiny butterfly kisses over her eyelids, her cheekbones, the tip of her nose, the cleft of her chin, until she was melting into his arms, eager and trembling.

Kincaid rubbed the rough pad of his finger against her nipple and Meg heard herself moan as surely no lady would dare. But then she was not a lady any longer, was she?

"Do you like this?" he whispered in her ear. His breath was warm and labored in her ear. "I only want you to feel good, Meg."

"Yes," she whispered. She let her eyes drift shut. "So good."

"And what of this?" He went down on one knee, parting her robe as he lowered himself.

When his lips touched the bud of her breast, she could feel his mouth, wet from her own. She ran her fingers through his thick, dark hair, arching her back as he took the nub of her nipple between his teeth and tugged ever so gently.

"Yes," she murmured.

Meg let her head fall back as she reveled in the shivers of pleasure Kincaid was creating with his mouth. All at once she was unsteady on her feet. She rested her hands on his broad shoulders for support.

Kincaid held Meg's breast in the cup of his hand, teasing, taunting her nipple with the tip of his tongue until she thought she would go mad for want of more.

"Kincaid . . ." Cautiously she lowered herself to her knees on the faded red Turkish carpet. Now she was practically eye to eye with him again.

"Is this what you want?" he whispered. "I don't want to hurry you. I don't want to hurt you, to make you regret later—"

She pressed her finger to his lips, silencing him. "It's what I want," she breathed. "What I've wanted for days. To be touched." She ran her hand over his broad chest, feeling the beat of his heart through his linen shirt. "To touch you."

Meg put her hands up, palms out, and he raised his hands

to meet hers, their fingers interlocking. "Please," she whispered. "I cannot promise how long I can stay. I cannot promise how long I can love you, but for today, perhaps tomorrow, could you—" She closed her eyes, not knowing how to say what she felt in her heart. Her blood raced. A strange, unaccustomed ache filled her. How could she tell Kincaid she wanted to share his love if only for a few hours?

But when she opened her eyes again, she realized no words were necessary. Kincaid understood what she was trying to say. So for a moment, on their knees, facing each other, they stared into each other's eyes. Then, without breaking eye contact, Kincaid took her by the hand, raised her to her feet, and led her to the bed.

He eased her onto the feather tick and, fully clothed, he lay down, rolling onto his side beside her. He brushed his fingertips against her skin where the black silk dressing gown had fallen open. He took his time, tracing an invisible pattern between her breasts with his hand, over her rib cage, over the flat of her belly.

He whispered in her ear, calling her name, telling her he thought she was beautiful.

Meg closed her eyes, guiding his head until he rested his cheek on her breast, his breath warm and tantalizing on her nipple.

Kincaid brushed her breast with soft, fleeting kisses as his hand drew lower, teasing her, tempting her. His hand circumnavigated the bed of curls to touch her thighs, heat against hot flesh. With his hand, he slowly parted her legs. His fingertips moved from the inside to the outside of her legs, close to the source of her heat, but not close enough.

Meg heard herself moan, still amazed and just a little shocked that such wanton sounds could come from her lips. 'A cold fish,' Philip had called her. 'Frigid.' And she had believed him. Only now she knew he was wrong and she smiled at the thought of her own vengeance. She *could* feel. And from the sound of Kincaid's breathing, she knew she could make a man feel, as well.

Kincaid drew his hand in a circle around her woman's place, now damp, its scent heavy in her nostrils. She lifted her hips, straining to meet his fingertips, praying they would accidentally brush the quivering folds.

"Meg, Meg . . ."

His mouth brushed hers and she pressed her lips to his with a fever of desire she hadn't known could exist. Her entire life, men had meant nothing but fear, pain, and entrapment, and now without warning, here was Kincaid, here for nothing but her pleasure.

Meg explored the inside of his mouth with her tongue, tasting the brandy that had passed his lips. She shifted against him, turning on her side, pressing her hips against his.

"Aren't you going to take off your clothes?" she whispered, feeling only a little shy.

"Hadn't made up my mind yet." He grinned boyishly, pushing a damp lock of hair off her cheek, "I had thought this might be a morning for my lady's pleasure."

Meg looked at him, perplexed. Did he mean that a man and woman could make love only for the woman's pleasure? She nearly laughed aloud at the thought of this wonder. In her marriage bed, all that had mattered to Philip was his own satisfaction.

Meg slipped her hand inside the open neck of his linen shirt, wanting to feel his bare skin under her palm. The idea of making love only for her pleasure was enticing, but right now, she needed Kincaid. She needed, for the first time in her life, to feel a man inside her.

Meg leaned to whisper in his ear, too shy to speak the words aloud. "Please," she begged breathlessly. "I want . . ."

"Yes?" He kissed the corner of her mouth. "What do you want, Meg?" he teased.

She closed her eyes, trembling all over. "I want . . . I need . . . you. I . . . I'm no virgin, obviously." She gave a nervous laugh. "But no one . . . *my husband,* he never made me feel like this." Meg realized her cheeks were damp with her own tears and embarrassed, she made a motion to brush them away.

But Kincaid tenderly pushed her hand aside and brought his lips to her wet cheeks. "Please don't cry, Meg," he whispered, his voice filled with husky emotion. "I'll do whatever you want, just don't cry." His fingers caressed the nape of her neck and he kissed her lips. "If only I could take away the pain the bastard has caused you—"

"Shhh, not now." Her eyelashes fluttered as she opened her eyes to look into his. "Let's not talk about that now." She caught his hand and brought it to her bare hip. "Just love me. Let me love you. No one has let me love them in such a very long time."

With a groan Kincaid brought his mouth down hard on hers. In the drop of a grain of sand in an hourglass, all regard for Philip was gone from her mind. Kincaid was all she could think of, Kincaid and his magical touch.

He rolled her onto her back, pressing his mouth to the valley between her breasts. He grabbed the back of his shirt and pulled it over his head, tossing it carelessly over the side of the bed.

In the early morning sunlight, Meg marveled at the sight of his broad bare chest, rippling with muscle and brawn. Never before this moment had it occurred to her that a man's body could be beautiful.

As he unlaced his breeches and kicked them off, Meg grazed her hands over his chest, feeling the springy, dark hair beneath her fingertips. When her thumb brushed over his nipple she was astonished to see that his response was much like her own. Kincaid's male nipple grew hard beneath her thumb, a sound of pleasure escaping his lips.

"Witch," he accused.

She laughed, bringing her mouth to his again, pressing her hips against him. She could feel his member hard and hot on her bare leg. He was running his hands over her, caressing the curve of her hip, the length of her leg. He kissed her again and again as he slipped his fingers between her thighs to the spot that burned hot and wet for him.

Meg moaned aloud at the feel of his hand in that place from which she had never known such pleasure could come. His slid his fingers up and down, and she ground her hips against him.

"Please, Kincaid," she begged. "Inside.

His gaze locked with hers as he removed his hand and swung over her, kneeling between her parted legs. "Are you certain?" he whispered, leaning to brush his lips against hers.

She raised her hips, squeezing her eyes shut. "Yes," she heard herself moan.

Kincaid braced himself above her and slid inside with one smooth, deep thrust.

Meg heard herself moan and was shocked that she could feel such pleasure. She grasped his shoulders for support, opening her legs wider, lifting her hips to meet his next thrust.

The new and gratifying sensations seized Meg and tossed her high into the heavens. She panted, she moaned, allowing Kincaid to lift her higher and higher. When the explosion hit her she cried out with such force that he covered her mouth with his to muffle her sounds. It was so unexpected, so glorious. She clung to him as he drove deeper, spilling into her, giving instead of taking as Philip had.

For a long moment Meg just lay still beneath Kincaid, reveling in the tiny tremors that still ran the length of her hot, perspiration-covered body. Kincaid covered her face with kisses as he slowly slipped out of her. Then he rolled onto his side and drew her into his arms, still kissing her, touching her, making her feel loved.

When she opened her eyes to look at him he was smiling. "Was I loud?" she asked, still feeling too good to truly be mortified. "No one else heard me, did they?"

"I heard not more than a peep," he teased, kissing the tip of her nose.

She snuggled against him and he threw the rumpled counterpane over both of them. Then, in comfortable silence, they drifted off to sleep.

Much later, Meg woke to find herself still wrapped in Kincaid's arms. He slept completely relaxed, his hands flung out, his breathing deep and slow. For a while she just lay there, still in wonder of what had happened in this bed, in wonder of him.

Meg had not known it was even possible for a woman to get pleasure from a man's bed. She had always assumed it was duty, as she had been told. Her duty to give her husband pleasure. But Kincaid had not been concerned with his own desires, only hers. She smiled at the thought, remembering the intense pleasure she had experienced for the very first time in her life.

Growing warm just thinking about it, she slipped out of the bed, careful not to wake him. Rewrapping the silk dressing gown around her body, she retrieved the tie from the floor where she'd left it and covered herself. Curling up on a chair beside the table, she uncovered the breakfast meal Kincaid had brought hours ago and delved into it. The bread was cold, the coffee only lukewarm in its pot, but Meg was certain it was the best meal she had ever eaten.

Meg was drinking her second mug of coffee when she heard Kincaid stir. Sleepily, he put his hand out to where she had laid beside him in the bed. Not finding her there, he sat straight up. "Meg?"

"I'm here." She picked up her coffee and went to sit on the edge of the bed beside him.

He took the coffee from her hand and rubbed his eyes, taking a great gulp. "I was afraid you'd run again."

She looked down guiltily at her folded hands. "I'm sorry. I shouldn't have done that. I just thought it would be simpler if I disappeared."

"It would be if I wanted you to go." He finished the coffee and set the cup on the table beside the bed. "The thing is, Meg, I don't want you to go." He sat back against the pillows, crossing his arms over his bare chest. "I've spent my entire life waiting for you, looking for you in every face of every woman I've ever kissed. Now that I've found you, I have no intention of letting you get away."

Meg didn't look at him. His words made her uncomfortable. How was it that she had come to sit on this pedestal of his? If he knew what she'd done, the sin she'd committed, she'd not shine so brightly in his mind.

"Kincaid . . ." She made herself look at him.

He took her hand, turning it in his. "All right, love, we'll not speak of the matter . . . now." He kissed her palm. "But you have to promise me you'll not try to flee again."

She sighed.

"If you leave me, I have to know. That's fair enough. I have to see you go."

Meg's gaze met his. Suddenly everything was more complicated. What had happened here in this bed made it more complicated for her. She didn't know what she would do now. His offer to stay with him was enticing. Of course, she wanted no marriage. She had already had a sour taste of that. But the idea of being Kincaid's woman was attractive. The thought of them living together in some far off land was a dream worth dreaming. "I'll not go without saying goodbye," she conceded in a whisper.

Kincaid lifted the counterpane. "Good answer. Now I won't have to keep such a tight watch on you." He patted the sheet. "Come here."

Without a moment's hesitation, Meg slid out of her dressing gown and under the sheets, resting against a pillow.

He brushed his lips against hers. "I have to go out for a short while this afternoon. Do you mind?"

Meg felt a strange sense of panic inside. "Could . . . could I go with you?"

" 'Fraid not, sweet. Robber's business."

She pushed the heel of her hand against his chest. "Please tell me you're not going out to steal. If the soldiers catch you again—"

"No work for me this afternoon. Just men's business." He kissed her temple. "I want you to stay here with Mother Godwin where you'll be safe, but I'll bring you something back."

"A cake if I'm good?" she teased, pressing a kiss to his muscular biceps.

"If you're as good as you were this morning," he growled playfully, "I'll bring you a dozen." Then he lifted the counterpane to cover both their heads, and Meg dissolved into laughter.

She had never fathomed such happiness could come from a man.

The Earl of Rutledge stood impatiently in the center of his bedchamber, his arms widespread as his tailor knelt on the floor, his mouth filled with brass pins. "Just one moment more, monsieur and I will be completed," Monsieur DeMoir begged, in heavily accented English.

Percival rolled his eyes. He had stood so long in this position in his new coat that he was growing faint. "Don't you think I have more pressing business than this fitting, DeMoir?"

"Oui. But my lord, you will be so handsome this night at Whitehall,"—he plucked a pin from his mouth and stuffed it into the hem of the burgundy silk coat—"zat dare I say, zee king will be envious of your costume."

Percival dared a glance into the long gilded mirror the tailor toted with him. Rutledge avoided mirrors most often and did not usually allow them in his presence because he had no desire to see his own hideous face. But for Monsieur DeMoir, he made an exception. The man was talented with a needle

and highly in demand at court. It had cost him twice the price
of the coat just to get him here on such short notice.

Percival studied his new outfit with his eye for color and
form and was impressed by the elegant simplicity. For Percival, there would be no silly starched bows, so popular at court
these days, no billows of lace vomiting from his throat.

He turned slightly to get a better look at his own profile,
ignoring Monsieur DeMoir's protests. Percival's new burgundy
breeches were cut conservatively, to present a fine leg beneath
his clocked stockings. His coat was indeed magnificent with
its brocaded burgundy silk and gold garnitures. The subtle
lace of his new cravat was exquisitely spun by some wretched
Irish cottar.

It was only when Percival looked into his own eyes that
his face soured. How he hated his twisted lip and the gaping
hole that ran toward his cheekbone. If only Monsieur DeMoir
could do the same wonders with his harelip as with his ward-
robe, but of course, he could not.

There was a tap at the door and Percival looked up, thankful
for the reprieve from his own reflection. "Enter."

Higgins stepped inside the bedchamber, moving as he always did, as if under suspicion. "You called, my lord?"

The tailor bid Percival make a quarter turn and he complied.
He didn't need to see Higgins face to face to give him orders.
"It's come to my attention that we've not notified the brat,"
Rutledge said with peevish coldness.

"My lord?"

"Philip's brat." He lowered his arms, not caring if it mussed
the straight line of the hem in his new coat or not. He was
bored standing there and his arms were fatigued. "James.
Surely you remember him? Who could forget the only perfect
Rutledge spawned in more than a hundred years?"

For a moment Higgins was actually taken off guard and it
amused Percival.

"James, sir? I . . . I assumed he was long gone. Dead."

"We can hope," Percival answered tartly. Monsieur DeMoir

was carefully removing from his lordship's shoulders the burgundy coat with the pins protruding from its many seams. "But if he is dead, I've never received word." Set free from the tailor, the Earl of Rutledge strode to the mantel and took up his glass of claret. "I suppose it's necessary that I notify him of his father's death. After all, he is the only heir to my deceased brother's title and moneys." He sipped the red claret. "Should I not notify him, I fear the courts would eventually become suspicious. Why would I not inform my sole living relative of the vast fortune he's acquired? Why would I not apprise him of his father's tragic death?"

"I suppose you're right, my lord."

"Of course I'm right!" He waved his hand, the lace of his sleeve fluttering at his wrist. "So see to it. Find the turd and bring him to me."

"You want me to inform James of his father's death?"

"No, save that treat for me." He shrugged. "Of course, perhaps he's already heard. News of death, the pox, and inheritance travels quickly in Londontown. But I would predict not, else he'd have already been at my doorstep, greedy for his lot."

"Have you an idea of where he lodges?" Higgins crept closer to the door. "Where I might try finding him, my lord?"

Rutledge sighed irritably. He often forgot how greatly he hated the perfect James until mention of him. Then suddenly all of the loathing was there on the tip of his tongue, a bitter, vindictive drink.

"No!" Percival exploded, turning on Higgins, as his manservant probably anticipated. Claret spewed from Rutledge's mouth as he shouted, lunging at him. "No! I have no clue as to where my brother's son resides. I haven't seen him in a decade!"

Higgins ducked out the door just before the glass struck the doorjamb and shattered in a rain of blood-red claret and splintering shards.

With Higgins gone into retreat down the corridor, Percival

turned around, feeling better. Then he realized Monsieur De-Moir was still there, staring at him, his eyes wide with terror.

"Oh, what are you gaping at?" the Earl of Rutledge demanded. "Get out! Get out, and have the coat prepared by the week's end."

Monsieur DeMoir raced for the doorway, the burgundy coat clutched in his hands.

"I've an engagement with the king come Saturday eve and I wish to wear it then."

The tailor made no sound as he took his leave, but for the sound of crushing glass beneath his slippers as he ran.

Ten

"Do you have to go out again?" Meg knelt on the bed, clutching the bed post, watching Kincaid as he dressed.

"I have to go." He adjusted his lace cravat in the looking glass on the wall.

"More gambling?"

He chuckled. His sweet Meg sounded more like a wife every day. To some men, that thought might have been a burden, but to Kincaid, it made him smile. "A man has to make a living, sweetheart. How do you expect me to keep you in this finery," he indicated the tawdry bedchamber with a sweep of his hand, "without the financial means?"

The truth was, he was not just going gambling tonight, although gambling was how he made his living. First he intended to go to the apartments he kept at Charing Cross. Actually, they were the apartments of his *nom de guerre*. Captain Scarlet took up residence in a variety of rooms for rent or in the bedchambers of ladies.

Kincaid felt guilty about hiding his other life from Meg, and in time he would make his confession, but the time hadn't yet come. He had to be certain he could trust her before he revealed his dual existence.

Tonight he wanted to go by the apartments, pick up some clothing, and then make an appearance at the local ordinary. The Pork Belly, and similar establishments, were ideal for gleaning information from drunken patrons. In such public places he discovered who was in town and who was on his way out. Eavesdropping provided him with access to the men on his list.

When Kincaid turned from the mirror, Meg was holding his coat for him. He allowed her to help him into it and stood still while she smoothed the brocade of his cuffs.

He watched her as she fussed with the lace cravat. His Meg Drummond was truly a wonder. She had been angry with him for forcing her into Mother Godwin's, but once she was here, she had adapted quite easily. She didn't approve of the profession of the women of Mother Godwin's, but she didn't hold their poor luck against them. Instead, in only a week's time she'd made herself available to the women to serve them in any way she could, gently urging them to find a better life. She wrote letters for the trollops, for none of them could read or write. She counseled them on illness and female ailments. She listened to their tales of woe with a gentle heart.

"Will you be late?" she asked wistfully.

He grasped her around the waist. She was dressed this evening in a pretty green cotton gown he'd purchased for her from a secondhand dealer in Houndstitch. She wore her rich, dark brown hair with its blond highlights loose down her back like a schoolgirl. One look at her heart-shaped face, her mouth made for kissing, and he wanted to forget about his evening's intentions and tumble into bed with her.

Unfortunately, duty called. He had been too long in neglecting matters of business. The weeks he had spent in Newgate, though made nearly enjoyable by Meg's presence, had put him behind schedule.

He kissed Meg's forehead. "What will you do with yourself tonight?" he asked. "Monti will go with me, so he'll not be available to play knap and slur."

She let go of him and moved toward the fireplace to warm her hands. "I don't know. Stitch a little, perhaps. I'm making myself a shift with that linen you brought me. Or perhaps I'll read."

Kincaid was glad he had thought to go to the bookseller

in Cheapside and purchase several volumes for her. They had not come inexpensively, but she had been so pleased with his gift, that it wouldn't have mattered to him if they had cost a hundred pounds apiece.

In talking with his Meg, late in the evening after he returned from his business in the taverns, he had discovered she was very well educated for a woman, even a woman of noble birth. She knew much of ancient history, art relics, music, astronomy. Wherever she had come from, someone had taken a good deal of time and money to see her well tutored. Her education piqued his interest in whom his mysterious Meg was, but he had held his tongue and did not question her as he would have liked. In time he hoped she would come to trust him enough to tell him her secrets. Besides, deceiving her as he was, what right did he have to demand to know anything of her true identity?

"Well, give us a kiss and I'll be on my way," Kincaid called, putting his hand out to her.

Meg came to him, pressing a kiss of promise to his lips. "I'll wait up for you."

He squeezed her hand as he let her go. "Don't. I prefer waking you up when I return."

She smiled at his sexual intimation, walking him to the door. "Take care and watch for the constable," she whispered.

The concern in her voice made Kincaid hate to go and leave her. But he had to. If he was going to attempt to strike up a new life with his mystery woman, he first had to put an end to the old life.

Another kiss from her lips and he was out the door.

Meg leaned against the paneled door, listening to the sound of Kincaid's footsteps as they died away. The first few nights he'd left her, she'd been so frightened that she'd barely been able to breathe the entire time he was gone. But, as in Newgate, that passed. Now, after a fortnight, she almost looked forward to spending a few hours alone.

Meg wandered to the chair next to the fire, trying to decide what she would do with herself. She did have stitching to do, but sewing had never been one of her favorite pastimes. She could read, but she wasn't in the mood for that, either.

Her gaze strayed to the quill and paper Kincaid had left on the table near the fireplace. Perhaps she would write. Kincaid knew nothing of her scribblings. She never told him for fear he would laugh and make light of it. But to her, they had become important.

It had all started in the lonely hours Meg had spent alone in the Press Yard cell when Kincaid went to the taproom. Meg's heart had ached so for her dead son that the quill and paper had been a means to ease that suffering. At first all she had written were jagged thoughts scrawled across parchment that she immediately burned. But later, when the pain had eased, she began to write poetry. Some were about the pain of the death of her son, but others were simply about the sunshine that sprinkled fairy dust onto the pine floor.

Now she was working on a satire. She had come up with the idea last week when Kincaid had brought her the most recent lampoonery being passed at Whitehall. It was about the king, his mistress, Castlemaine, and her cuckolded husband—and quite amusing. Meg's satire was about a deformed earl and the twisted heart beneath his breast.

She crossed the room to her clothes press. Inside she kept very little, simply because she possessed so few belongings. Beneath her cloak, tucked inside a book of Chaucer's poems, she found her own parody.

Rereading what she had written, she walked to the hearth and sat down, pulling her skirts up to her knees to allow the heat of the fire to warm her. Nodding to herself with approval, she reached for Kincaid's quill and ink. She already knew what the first line to the next stanza would be.

Meg became so lost in her thoughts and the words she put down on paper that time passed quickly. Before she knew it, the case clock beside the bed was chiming midnight. Sprinkling sand on the ink to dry it, she rose with a yawn. Kincaid usually didn't return until three in the morning, so maybe she would lay down for a few hours.

Carefully removing the dress Kincaid had bought her, she stripped off her underthings and pulled a sleeping gown over her head. It was another of Kincaid's gifts, delicately embroidered with green leaves and pink rosebuds across the bodice.

Padding barefoot across the cold floor, she returned her satire to Chaucer's pages and tucked the book back into the clothes press. She stoked the fire and then climbed into bed, snuggling into the soft tester. She was just reaching to blow out the candle at her bedside when she heard a soft rapping at the door.

Meg sat up, pulling the counterpane to her chin. "Kincaid?" He had added a lock to the door more than a week ago, but he had his own key. "Is that you?"

The knock came again.

"Who is it?" Meg called.

"Mrs. Drummond?" came a quivering voice. "Mrs. Drummond, it's Saity."

"Saity?" Meg climbed out of bed. Through the door, she could hear the young woman crying. "Saity, what's wrong?" But the moment she swung the door open, she could see what was wrong.

Saity, a blonde who once must have been pretty, no more than seventeen, stood barefoot in her smock and stays, her tiny breasts thrust above the bone undergarment so that her pink nipples were bared. Tears ran down the girl's cheeks. She had been beaten. Severely. Her eye was blackened and already turning a sickening color of purple and green. Her cheekbone was already so swollen that it protruded, making her face lopsided. Across her immature breasts were bite marks where some bastard had drawn blood with his teeth.

Meg put out her arms to Saity, her heart going out to the woman still barely more than a child. Philip had never broken any of Meg's bones, or brought more than a trickle of blood from her lip, but she knew the shame of being struck. She understood the frustration of being physically incapable of fighting back against a man's brute strength.

"Oh, Saity," Meg breathed, hugging the girl. "What happened?"

Saity sniffed back her tears, resting her head on Meg's shoulder. "Sorry son of a cur, that Jack. He don't get feisty often. And he always pays me extra. I just don't know what gets into him." She wiped her running nose with the back of her hand. "Only this time it was worse. His wife run off with a haberdasher, and he was sorely nettled."

Meg led Saity into the room by her arm to get a better look at her injuries. "You mean he's done this before?" Meg helped her into the chair before the hearth and went to the wash basin for a cool rag.

Saity lifted one thin shoulder in a shrug. "Don't they all?"

Meg went down on one knee on the cold floor in front of Saity and pressed the wet cloth to her bruised cheekbone. Already the eye was swelling shut. "No," she said firmly, thinking of the kindness Kincaid had shown her since they'd been together. "Not all men strike women. Some are of a better ilk. That's one thing I've learned as of late." She smoothed the girl's wispy hair. "Isn't there anywhere you can go, any relatives, to get away from here?"

"I got no one since my ma got drowned. A girl's got to make a living." Saity took the cloth from Meg. "At least here I got a nice bed to sleep in and food fer my belly. Afore Mother found me, I was sleepin' on the docks and tradin' tail fer bread."

Meg stood, so angry she wanted to break something, hit someone herself. "I cannot believe Mother Godwin allows this to happen!"

"She says it ain't allowed in her 'stablishment. But she asks us what we expect, us bein' whores."

Meg glanced at the door, her indecision lasting only a second. "Come with me, Saity," she said, striding toward the bed to grab her dressing gown. Kincaid had replaced the black silk gown Mother Godwin loaned her with one of creamy flannel with lace cuffs and a ruffle at the high neck. She stuffed her arms into it, not even taking the time to button up the buttons.

"What'd you say, Mrs. Drummond?"

Meg was already headed toward the door. "I said come with me." She stopped and waited for Saity.

"Where . . . where we goin', Mrs. Drummond? I . . . I didn't mean to make no trouble for you. Only I was scared and hurtin' and you said if I ever needed ye—"

"It's all right," Meg soothed, putting her arm around the slender girl and leading her out the door and down the hall. "I just want to get to the bottom of this. There's no excuse for this happening. It's bad enough you have to sell what shouldn't be sold, you ought to at least be safe while you do it!"

Saity stared at Meg with frightened, round eyes. "Yes, Mrs. Drummond."

Meg walked up the hall toward the staircase, stopping at the last door before the steps. Still keeping one arm draped over Saity's shoulder, she beat on the door with her fist. "Mother Godwin?"

"Go away. I've got company."

Meg turned the knob and pushed her way in, not caring that she'd not been invited. To her surprise, Mother Godwin was bare-breasted and seated in the lap of a man in a chair before the fireplace.

Meg was too angry to be embarrassed. "I have to speak with you." Saity ducked from under Meg's arm and took a step back behind her.

"Can't you see I'm busy?" Mother Godwin indicated the big man beneath her. He had a face like a steer and he smelled of hay.

Meg nodded to the man who was obviously well into his cups. "Pardon, sir, but I must have a word with Mother Godwin."

Mother Godwin leapt up from the steer's lap and reached for her black silk dressing gown. Meg noticed that in the place where she normally lacked eyebrows, thick, black ones had been carefully painted in. She covered her large, sagging breasts. "How dare you burst into my chambers when I'm entertaining!"

Meg pointed to Saity. "Look at her. Look what some man has done." She pushed the girl's hand down from where she held the rag so that Mother Godwin could see the damage.

Mother Godwin barely glanced at Saity. "It happens. Mary come up! These girls aren't milk maids."

"Well, it shouldn't happen. You're in charge here." She pointed an accusing finger. "You have a responsibility to see these women are not hurt."

Mother Godwin tied the sash on her dressing robe and reached for a glass of wine left on a sidetable. "Who was it, Saity?" she asked with a sigh.

Saity hugged herself "Jack. Jack Creel, the ink man."

Mother Godwin let out another one of her impatient sighs. She glared at Meg. "I'll talk to him about it again. He knows we don't allow this kind of thing in my place. He knows he has to go to the Red Roost for that foolery."

Meg tapped her bare foot. She'd still not taken the time to fasten her dressing gown and was covered hardly better than the two whores. "You'll talk to him *when?*"

Mother Godwin swallowed the last drop of her wine and started for the man again. "When I'm done here, Mrs. Drummond." She put out her hand to the steer with a smile. "Now why don't you go back to bed and let Saity get back to work. I'm certain you-know-who would not approve of your wandering about this time of night."

Meg stared at Mother Godwin, who was already climbing back into her customer's lap. She couldn't believe that was all she was going to say. She couldn't believe she didn't care.

Meg turned to Saity, grabbing her hand and pulling her out of Mother Godwin's room. "Where is he now?"

"What?" Saity still held the wet rag to her cheek. "Who?"

Meg stepped into the hall with Saity at her side and slammed Mother Godwin's door behind her. "Where is the man who did this to you? Jack whomever?"

"D . . . downstairs I s'pose. Havin' another drink. He likes a drink after his pecker's spent."

Meg grabbed Saity's hand and went down the staircase. If Mother Godwin wasn't going to do anything about this, damned if she wasn't. At the bottom of the stairs Meg pushed through heavy red crimson drapes and into the public room where Kincaid had brought her that first morning.

Light blazed in every corner of the room, showing off the lewd murals that covered the walls. There were too many men and women for the size of the room. Some played cards. Others were eating and drinking while a fiddler played a lively tune. Most of the women were in some state of undress. One young girl Meg knew, Maria, lay stark naked on her back on a table, two men playing a hand of cards on her flat belly.

The room was so full of smoke that Meg could barely breathe. "Where is he?" She stood in a wet puddle, of ale no doubt.

Saity hung behind Meg, peeking over her shoulder. "There." She pointed. "The back table. With Mary Theresa."

Meg scanned the room until she spotted Mary Theresa perched on a table beneath a parrot cage. She was wearing nothing but a pair of men's fashionable wide-legged breeches and a cocked hat with a lime-green cockade. Across her breasts she'd written her name and her price with red lip pomade.

A man sat in a chair beside her. They were feeding bits of bread dipped in ale to the green parrot in the cage that swung overhead.

"There?" Meg asked, pointing. The man with Mary Theresa was no taller than Meg, with a pox-scarred face and sparse, peppered hair.

Saity nodded her head, grabbing Meg's arm. "But you don't

have to do this, Mrs. Drummond. I'm all right. Really, I am. I was just scared. That's why I bothered ye. I was just scared!"

Meg started across the sticky, wet floor, her hands planted on her hips. "Jack Creel," she shouted.

The man looked up, popping a bit of ale-bread meant for the parrot into his own mouth. His eyes were glazed over from drink and poverty. "Yea?"

"Jack Creel," Meg sidestepped a drover's hand as he reached into her open gown. She was too angry for modesty. "I've need of a word with you."

Some of the patrons chuckled. Someone shouted that Meg must have been sent by Jack's wife.

Meg headed straight for Jack Creel, dragging Saity with her when the girl wouldn't come of her own accord. "Did you do this?" she demanded, even before she'd reached his table.

Mary Theresa climbed off her stool, but stood beside the table, a captive audience.

Meg held Salty firmly by her frail shoulders. "Did you?" she demanded.

Jack Creel stared bleary-eyed at Saity. "M . . . might 'ave."

Meg let go of Saity's arm, stepping up to the accused. "You ought to be ashamed of yourself! You should be riding a cart to the gallows for this."

He stumbled to his feet as Meg shoved her face into his. He stank of ale and mutton but she didn't care. She was so damned mad, she wanted to rip those last few sparse hairs out of his bald pate. "What is wrong with men that they think they have to beat up women?" she appealed. "Look at her! Look at her!" She pointed at Saity. "God's bones, man! She's young enough to be your daughter. Why would you hit her? Why would you break a pretty face like this?"

Jack stared at his feet, mumbling. "Didn't really mean . . . said sorry . . . won't happen 'gain."

"You're damned straight it won't happen again." Meg

stepped back so that he could see Saity straight on. "Now, I want you to apologize to this girl."

Suddenly the laughter died down. The fiddle music ceased in mid bow-string. Everyone was staring at Meg, listening.

"I want you to apologize," she went on, "and then I want to see compensation!"

"I already done said—"

"I want you to say you're sorry in front of everyone," Meg raged. "And I want you to say you'll never do it again."

"You ought to be ashamed of yourself, Jack," one of the men hollered from near the window. "Hittin' a nice girl like Saity."

"Yea," called another and then another in agreement.

"What kinda man thinks he's got to hit his whore?" cried one of the women.

"No man at all," answered another.

Jack stared uneasily at the crowd that was suddenly turning hostile against him. Then he looked at Meg, then his gaze wandered to Saity.

"I'm waiting." Meg tapped her bare foot, her arms crossed over her chest.

Jack ground the ball of his foot on the floor, crushing a bit of bread crust. "I . . . I'm sorry, Saity, girl. I . . . I didn't mean to whack ye."

"Tell her you won't ever hit her again." Meg prodded him with a finger. "And mean it."

Tears were coming to the man's eyes now. He brushed them away. "I . . . I won't never do it again. I swear I won't. I was just mad at my wife . . ."

Saity lowered the wash rag, giving Jack a shy smile. "It's all right, Jack. Yer one of my best customers. But I don't want to be gettin' hurt every time you come around. It just ain't right you or any man hittin' a woman, and I ain't gonna stand for it anymore."

Meg looked back at Jack. "Excellent. You've both had your say, now empty your change purse."

He staggered a little. "What?"

"I said, empty your blessed change purse. Your pocket, wherever you keep your damned money!"

He blinked slowly. "You want my coin?"

"I don't want it. I want you to give it to Saity. Compensation."

"Comp—"

"Compensation," Meg repeated. "For your ill behavior." She tapped the rickety wooden table impatiently with her knuckles. "Now cough it up before I really lose my temper."

Jack stared at Meg, and for a moment she feared he wouldn't give up his coin. She had no idea what she would do then. It had been her anger that had gotten her this far. She had nothing to threaten the man with, except perhaps Kincaid's wrath.

But after a strained moment, Jack backed down and reached into his breeches to pull out a ragged leather purse. Slowly he opened the drawstring and turned the pouch upsidedown. Dirty coins clinked onto the table.

"Now give it to her," Meg instructed.

Jack only hesitated a second before he scooped the coins up one by one and made his peace offering to Saity.

For a long moment the public room of Mother Godwin's Home for Girls was quiet. Then, from the rear of the room came a clap. Then another. At first it was one loud, steady beat, but then others began to join, and before Meg knew what was happening, the entire room of whores and men were clapping in approval.

Meg wasn't certain why they were clapping, but fearing it was because of what she'd done, she started a hasty retreat across the congested floor. It wasn't until she reached the crimson curtains at the stairs that she spotted Kincaid.

He was clapping. Even when the others died down, he was still clapping . . . for her. Then she realized it was he who had started the clapping to begin with, which meant he'd seen what she did.

Flustered, she parted the red curtains and headed up the staircase.

"Meg!" Kincaid called after her. "Wait up, sweetheart."

She stopped on the staircase and waited, but she didn't turn to look at him. He had told her to stay in their chamber. Would he be angry that she'd ventured out? Would they have to come to words over the matter?

"That was a hell of a brave thing you did down there," he said before he reached her.

"You're not mad I left the room without you?"

"I'd rather you stayed where I think you'll be safe, but I'm not your turnkey, Meg. I don't want to keep you here by force."

"I just couldn't let it go. I tried to talk to Mother Godwin, but she wouldn't do anything." She rested her hand on the stairrail. "A man has no right to beat a woman. Not even a whore deserves to be beaten."

Catching up to her, he rested his hand on her shoulder, staring at her, demanding she look back. "You're right, Meg. No man should hit a woman, nor a child, nor an old man."

They exchanged a look that made Meg's throat constrict. Suddenly this wasn't about Saity. It was about Meg and Kincaid and how she felt about him.

How had this happened? How had she fallen so madly in love with this great brute of a man?

She linked her arm through his and they started up the staircase, just as a man and wife would start up the stairs to their own bed in their own home. "How was your evening? Profitable, I hope."

"Profitable. But I missed you."

"Then you should take me along—for good luck. Monti says I was born under a lucky star."

"Actually, I was thinking . . . I was thinking maybe it was time you went out with me." He watched her for her reaction.

Meg broke into a smile. She had felt so cooped up these last few days. From her window she watched the dirty, bustling streets of London and she wanted desperately to be a part of it, a part of the world she'd been sheltered from all these years. "Could I?" She tugged on his arm. "Could I go out with you? I wouldn't be any trouble. I swear I wouldn't, Kincaid."

"Oh, I wager you'll be a handful of trouble." He kissed the top of her head. "But I think I'll take you just the same."

At the top of the stairs Meg halted and threw her arms around his neck, jumping up to kiss him. "Oh, I can't wait. Where shall we go? What shall we see? Am I to be the gambler's lady?"

He lifted a dark eyebrow, ushering her down the hallway to their bedchamber. "We shall see about that." He opened their door. "But I brought something home for you tonight. Something you'll need if you're to venture out with me."

Meg ducked under Kincaid's arm and raced for the bed where she spotted a brightly wrapped package. With the excitement of a child on Christmas Eve, she ripped open the colored paper. Inside was a handsome green wool cloak and a matching green vizard. With a cry of delight, she swung the cloak over her shoulders to cover her nightclothes. Then she picked up the vizard, which served as a mask to shield a lady's identity, and lifted it to her face to hold it with its button between her teeth.

Kincaid slid the bolt on the door and came to take her hand, spinning her around him. "You're a beauty, my mysterious Meg. And this only adds to the mystery."

Then he pulled her hard against him and Meg dropped the mask. The cloak fell from her shoulders halfway to the bed. And when she dropped onto the feather tester with his weight upon her, all she could do was laugh.

"I love you, Meg," he whispered, lowering his head over hers.

Meg stared up into his dark eyes, threading her fingers through his magical hair. "And I you," she dared softly. "God above, save me from my sin, I love you, too."

Eleven

The Earl of Rutledge stood in the shadow of a headless Venetian statue, watching the crowd of ladies and gentlemen who gathered at the Mummford House next to the old Mulberry Gardens to the west of the palace. The cause for celebration was the Earl of Mummford's fiftieth birthday. The invitation had come only the day before, which meant Percival was a last-minute guest, but he'd accepted just the same.

In a week's time his name would appear on everyone at Court's guest list, from the lowliest country earl's to the Duke of Buckingham's. No one would dare slight him. He would be invited because they feared him, not because they actually wanted him to attend their suppers and parties. Percival would like to have been invited just once because he was wanted. But since he and his hideous face were not desired, he would bully his way into their homes and drink their French wine, eat their stuffed partridge, and win their coin at the gaming tables.

The earl sipped champagne from his fluted glass, his gaze moving from one clump of gallants and their ladies to the next. He had forgotten how much he detested these affairs, perhaps because he had always been an outsider, even when he was on the inside.

The house was overrun with earls and dukes and knights, countesses, duchesses, and ladies. A thousand candles burned, illuminating the dance floor, the rooms of gambling tables, the lavish trays of food and drink. It was a most exquisite party, so exquisite that Rutledge considered throwing one himself just so that he could outdo Mummford.

Percival had taken care in dressing this evening, knowing the king would most likely make an appearance in the earl's honor. It was always a good idea to look prosperous to one's liege, especially if one was interested in procuring a portion of the royal coffers for one's latest business venture.

Rutledge had had a new periwig made for himself, blond, with thick sausage curls. His suit consisted of black velvet breeches, a gold brocade coat, and a long green satin vest that flashed when he walked. On his hip, he wore a plain gilded sword that had been in the Rutledge family for half a millennium.

A servant in black livery walked by and Rutledge gave him his empty glass and took a full one. As he lifted the crystal rim to his lips, he noticed a young woman staring at him from behind the folds of her painted fan. She stood perhaps twenty feet from him, with several young coxcombs. The host, the Earl of Mummford, a great fart of a man with hanging jowls, held her on his arm.

The earl was well used to stares. Everywhere he went in London—the Royal Theater, local ordinaries, the India House—people stared, but most had the good manners to turn away when they were caught looking. This little strumpet was different. She stared openly, flirting with her eyes. He wondered if she might be his lordship's daughter, as the earl had not seen the lady at Court. That or the earl's new mistress.

The earl smiled at her, feeling a stirring in his loins. She was a pretty piece with sleek, black hair and a petite frame. Not beautiful like his Margaret with her long limbs and heart-shaped face, but quite pretty. Quite perfect.

Rutledge nodded his head in acknowledgment, setting the young woman's fan to fluttering. As was proper, she lowered her lashes, but still she watched him from the corner of her slanted eyes as she pretended to listen to the air the earl exhaled.

Rutledge finished his champagne, and leaving the glass at the foot of the statue, he walked directly across the room to where the dark-haired beauty stood.

"Pardon the intrusion," the earl stated, laying on all the charm he knew he was capable of demonstrating. "But I must thank you, Lord Mummford, for the invitation tonight. A happy birthday to you." Rutledge bowed deeply, keeping one eye on the engaging piece of fluff.

The earl nodded, his jowls vibrating as he spoke. "Rutledge. Good to see you." He bowed, the cartilage of his knees popping as he attempted to bend at the waist.

The young men in the circle scattered, tripping over themselves, mumbling awkward farewells as they made a hasty retreat. Most young Court fops didn't have the stomach to speak with Percival.

Mummford shooed away the dandies with a brush of his hand. "Allow me to introduce you to my daughter, the Honorable Mary Mummford."

"Your servant, madame." Again Rutledge bowed, showing an excellent leg.

"Your servant, my lord." She fluttered her fan, as she dipped a curtsy, allowing him a peek at her rice-powdered cheeks and the moleskin patch at the corner of her pink lips. Her eyes were blue, as clear as the blue water of a spring pond.

The earl was instantly infatuated. He could barely take his eyes off her.

"And how do you find London, Rutledge, after your time in the country?"

Rutledge smiled his lopsided smile, dabbing his mouth with a lace handkerchief so that there was no spittle on his chin. "Quite out of control actually. Women strutting upon the stage. Ladies and gentlemen of the Court who make no attempt at fidelity. The state of the royal coffers in ruin."

The earl laughed, making a snorting sound. "I firmly

agree." He raised his beefy shoulders in childlike excitement. "Stimulating, isn't it?"

Stimulating, is this daughter of yours, Percival thought. Just then the musicians struck up another lively tune.

The earl made a graceful gesture. "Would you mind, sir, if I were to dance this corranto with your daughter?"

The rotund man glanced at the child of his loins.

Mary Mummford fluttered her fan and for the first time Percival realized it was painted with pink nudes. So she *was* in London seeking a husband . . .

"Father?"

"Go. Go, daughter. But don't allow his lordship to monopolize your evening. Remember, you promised Acres's and Hanzel's sons dances, as well."

Mary dipped a curtsy to her father and then allowed Percival to lead her away by her gloved fingertips.

They joined other guests on the dance floor for the tune. They barely touched as they danced, often changing partners, but Percival couldn't keep his eyes off the young woman. She smelled heavenly of violet water and each time she passed him, he caught a whiff of the scent. Each time they stood face to face as dance partners, Mary looked directly into his face, almost as if she didn't see his deformity.

By the time the corranto ended, Percival had fallen in love.

"Would you care for a drink?" Percival asked, not wanting the young woman to slip away from him. For the first time he realized just how lonely he was with Philip and Margaret gone.

Mary smiled, fluttering her fan, her pert bosom heaving. "A drink would be excellent, your lordship. I fear I'm so overly warm, I'm near to fainting."

"Let me take you outside, then, where you can catch your breath." Percival took another glass of champagne from a servant and smoothly ushered her across the floor toward the balcony.

Out on the balcony, he led her to the far corner, away from the few others scattered there.

"Are you chilled?" Percival asked. "I can find a wrap for you."

"God's bowels, no." She laughed, taking the glass from his hand. Her voice was like a crystalline bell.

Heavens, how old could this girl be? Percivil conjectured. Seventeen? God help him, his taste was running close to Higgins's!

A man who was rarely unsettled, Percival searched his head for something to say that would interest the child. He didn't want to let her get away. He didn't want to turn her over to the fop, Acres, her father had spoken of. "A fine party, your father puts on," he stumbled.

Mary leaned over the rail of the balcony to look down into the winter garden. Below water ran from a fountain. "Father?" She laughed her bell-laughter. "That lazy turd can kiss my lily-white ass." She laughed again.

Percival blinked. Surely such a young woman of innocent appearance could not be so vulgar. "You . . . you don't care for your father, Lady Mary?"

She turned to face Percival, leaning against the rail, lifting her foot beneath her gown to steady herself in a most unlady-like pose. "That pimple-pocked hypocrite? He kept me locked up in the country for years and now suddenly he's parading me before the Court like a Fleet Street whore, looking for the highest bidder." She drained her glass and tossed it over her head.

Percival heard the glass shatter on the rocky pool below. Surely the young Mary didn't realize the cost of such a glass. He immediately despised her lack of respect for her father and her father's property. But her lovely face, even drawn down in a frown, was irresistible. "Your father has brought you to Court to find a husband?"

She held out her hand, swinging her fan on her wrist. "He has. My mother passed years ago attempting to give birth to another Mummford brat. I was under the tutelage of my aunt until last year when a fishbone lodged in her throat and she expired at the dining table."

"I'm sorry for your loss."

She looked at him, her clear blue eyes illuminated by the rushlights on the ground below. "Don't be. She was a corpulent, prune-faced prig. I hated her."

A smile played on the healthy side of Percival's mouth.

She smiled back. "I amuse you, my lord?"

"You certainly have strong opinions."

"And why shouldn't I? I know what I like and what I don't." She reached out and brushed her hand down the center of his chest, over the green silk vest. "And I like you."

Percival held his breath, hoping she wouldn't take her hand away too quickly. Of course her gesture had been entirely indecorous. The earl could call him to the dueling field for dallying with his daughter thusly. But Percival couldn't help himself. He covered her hand with his. It was tiny, smooth, and cool. "And why do you like me, Mary?"

"Because, *Percival,* when you see someone you are attracted to, you go after her. The minute you saw me, you marched right across the room, up to my father practically demanding an introduction." She fluttered her dark lashes drolly. "Half the dandy fops in London are still trying to get up the nerve to ask to be introduced to me."

"And you don't find my . . . deformity repulsive?"

She looked at his face, studying the hole in his lip carefully. Percival held his breath until she spoke again.

"It's certainly ugly, but not repulsive," she finally said, and Percival was able to exhale. "I once had a kitten with five legs. I kept him under my bed and charged the cottars children a price to see him."

Percival was taken aback at her comparison of him to a freak cat. The girl was ill-mannered, discourteous to her elders, and most likely a slut. But still he was fascinated with her, perhaps only because she would look him in the face.

"I highly doubt your father would allow me to call upon you," Percival offered boldly. "I'm much too old to be a suitable escort."

She let out a bored sigh. "You're probably right. But come by for me in your coach at two and take me to the theater. Cleopatra is playing at His Highness's and I'm dying to show off my new gown."

She pulled her hand away and regretfully, he let go. Suddenly he felt twenty years younger. "Your servant, madame." He nodded, amused by her forwardness. "I shall arrive promptly."

"Well, I'd best go inside before my father realizes I'm missing and begins to bellow. He's trying desperately to protect my virginity until he can get a decent proposal." With a flip of her curls, Mary Mummford sashayed off the balcony and back into the light of her father's ballroom.

Percival did not escort her, but rather stood back in the shadows and watched the sway of her hips as she walked. His instincts told him to back off; the young woman could be nothing but trouble. But it was too late. His heart and his cock already ached for her.

Meg slipped her feet into her slippers and then stood and spun on the balls of her feet. She couldn't remember the last time she'd been this excited. She couldn't remember that she'd *ever* been this excited. Kincaid was taking her out to an ordinary for supper and cards.

"Going like that, love?" Kincaid looked up from where he sat on the edge of a chair, rolling up his stockings.

Meg pranced before him. "You don't care for my attire, sir?" She was dressed in a sheer linen and lace ribboned smock with full sleeves and skirts. Over the smock she wore a short boned busk that lifted her breasts high and cinched in her waist. "Everyone else in this home traipses about in their underclothing. I thought I should like to try the same."

She was laughing as he caught her hand and stood, his stockings in place. "While you're most attractive in this, madame," he kissed the swell between her high breasts, "I fear you might grow cold in the winter chill." He winked. "Take my advice tonight and go with the gown, as well."

Still laughing, Meg spun out of his arms, dancing her way to the bed where she'd laid out the latest gown Kincaid had brought her from the seconds shop in Houndstitch. The gown was probably not as fine as the ones Philip had had made for her in the years they were together. The Randall brothers would have nothing but the best; only the finest china on their dining table, the best horses in their stable, the most exquisite art in their gallery. Meg had fit somewhere in between the horses and the artwork. She was always dressed in the latest fashion, with jewels from the Rutledge coffer.

Even though the pearl-gray satin gown with a mulberry petticoat was not the finest she'd ever worn, it made her feel good each time it fell over her shoulders. It made her feel good because, though it was given used, it was given out of love.

"Need some help there?" Kincaid crossed the room, his high-heeled shoes making a sound on the wooden floor as he walked. "I really think you need your own maid, Meg. I'm not good at this women's business." He held the gown over her head as she wiggled into it.

"No maid," she protested as her head popped through the neckline and she smoothed the satin over her abdomen. "I told you, no maid."

"I can afford one, darling." He turned her in his arms and began to work the buttons up the back. "My winnings have been good at the tables."

She held her breath as he buttoned the gown at her waist. "I need my life simple at the present, Kincaid. Please, just let me make my own choices right now."

He was silent for a moment as he finished with the buttons. Then he kissed the back of her neck and turned her in his arms again so that they were facing each other. His gaze searched hers, for understanding, no doubt.

"All right," he conceded after a moment. "If it's that important to you, though I don't see how a lady's maid—"

"The maid is not the point, Kincaid." She pressed her lips together. "It's the fact that I want to make the choice myself. Not have you make it for me."

He let go of her, raising his hands in surrender. "Fair enough." He walked to the clothes press to retrieve his blonde periwig.

She walked to the full-length mirror she'd borrowed from Saity. "You're not angry with me, are you?"

"No." He dropped the periwig over his pinned hair. "I only wish you would help me understand. I'm trying damned hard, Meg."

She smiled. He *was* trying. "I know you are." She went to him and lifted up on her toes to kiss his mouth. "That's why I love you." She adjusted the periwig, tucking a stray lock of dark hair beneath it.

"That's why you'll stay with me? Marry me and bear my heirs?"

She laughed, refusing to be drawn into this conversation tonight. Nothing was going to spoil her evening out. She'd not allow it. "That's why I won't clunk you over the head while you slumber, take your gold *cheat,* and be gone in the morning."

"My cheat is it? Where have you been picking up our local cant?"

She lifted her shoulders delicately. "A lady must amuse herself when her gentleman is traipsing about town without her."

Kincaid slipped into his mulberry coat and was fully dressed. "Ready?"

She grabbed her cloak and muff and the mask off the bed. "Ready."

He put his arm around her, blowing out the last candle as

he led her out the door. "Ah, Meg, you're such a tearing beauty. I don't know what I did to deserve you."

She stopped in the hallway, allowing him to tie her cloak beneath her chin. "Is that why you're attracted to me, Kincaid?" she asked, suddenly serious. "For my appearance? My face?"

"Oh, sweetheart." He raised the hood of the cloak to cover her tumbling dark curls. "I appreciate your beauty but I love you for what's in here." He tapped her left breast lightly. "And here." He touched her temple.

"Good answer." She was smiling. "The only answer."

He swept his hand across his brow. "Phew. That was close."

She elbowed him, chuckling, then took his arm and allowed him to escort her down the stairs.

Arm in arm, Meg and Kincaid cut through the public room of Mother Godwin's House for Girls. It was already beginning to fill with patrons. In the front hallway Meg spotted Monti waiting for them.

She nearly burst into laughter with one look at the absurd costume he'd chosen tonight.

Monti swept off his cocked hat with the pink feather and bowed deeply from his waist. "Madame, you are most magnificent tonight."

She curtsied playfully. "Why thank you, sir, and you are most handsome."

Together the three stepped outside. While Kincaid signaled for the coach he'd hired for the night, Meg took in great gulps of the night air. It was a clear, cool night, the first week of March. The street smelled of greasy cookshops and lye soap used by the laundresses of Ram Alley, but for Meg it was the smell of freedom. Her fear of the Earl of Rutledge had kept her inside too long.

The coach rolled up and the three climbed inside. "So just where are we going?" Meg asked, taking a seat beside Monti so that she could look at Kincaid as they rolled down the street.

"An ordinary on Drury Lane near his Highness's Theater. It's quite popular with the gallants. A place to stop and sup after the play. I believe Cleopatra is playing currently. I could take you one day if you like."

"Perhaps." She studied Kincaid's face. He looked so different in the blond periwig that she wasn't certain she'd have recognized him herself if she'd met him on the street. "And who might I ask, are we supposed to be?"

"Be?"

She kittenishly kicked him with the toe of her slipper. "You know what I mean. This," she indicated with her gloved hand, "is not Captain Scarlet. And that," she hooked her thumb, still trying not to laugh and offend their mutual friend, "is certainly not the Monti I know."

Monti was dressed in a velvet coat and breeches of a hideous lime green, with a pink vest and hose and a pink feather in his cap. His periwig was dyed an eggplant red, which clashed greatly with the pink and green of his costume.

"Oh, that is Montigue Kern. He's quite well known about Londontown for his taste in clothing."

Monti was chuckling with Kincaid as if it were a joke between them. "But I . . . ," Kincaid went on. "I am known as James Kincaid. Rejected son of a country Viscount. Once a student at Middle Temple. When I could no longer tolerate the political injustice of Old Noll, I left England."

"His father sent him packing," Monti offered in an aside.

Kincaid frowned, but Monti went on with his story. "James sailed with privateers preying on Parliament's shipping. I served in the Spanish Army against France and England and gambled my way through Europe. When my king returned to the throne, so did James, though no longer a boy."

Kincaid made light of his description, but there was an underlying seriousness to his tone. A bitterness she couldn't help but detect. "And is that true, Kincaid?"

He looked away, the laughter gone from his handsome face. "A good bit of it."

"I found him in a whorehouse in France," Monti said, "if you'll pardon my bluntness."

It was Meg's turn to laugh. "Really, Monti. Surely you don't think I'd be offended by your use of the word. I live in a whorehouse."

"Touché." Monti grinned at her as he often did, obviously infatuated. "Anyway, that was where we met, in a bed with Miss Lori Darling."

"You were sharing her?" Meg's eyes widened with a mixture of disgust and fascination. She knew such perversions took place but surely Kincaid hadn't participated in such depravity.

"Have no fear, sweet." Kincaid took her hand, patting it. The shadows she had seen on his face only a moment before were gone and he was his jovial self again. "We didn't share the lady as I was so inebriated I had passed out and quite missed the festivities."

"I dragged him home with me as he had no place to sleep but the tart's bed."

"And we've been together ever since, haven't we, Monti?"

"So let me get this straight." She fiddled with the velvet of her muff. "The two of you are highwaymen part of the time, gambling fops the remainder?"

Kincaid looked at his friend with amusement. "I suppose so."

Meg sighed, glancing out the window, watching the city houses made of flimsy lath and plaster construction pass by, her tone light. "Thieves and impersonators. Why could I have not fallen in with a pair of a better ilk?"

Kincaid leaned forward, catching her chin with his gloved hand and kissing her mouth. "Because we were meant for each other, my love."

She frowned.

"It's quite true," Monti explained. " 'Twas in the stars, I assure you. Were you to consult an astrologer as all sensible ladies and gentlemen do, he could give proof of that which you see merely as a coincidence, my dear."

Kincaid rolled his eyes. He thought little of Monti's beliefs in astrology, although it was all the mode at court these days.

The coach halted and Monti jumped out to help her down. "I'm nervous," Meg said over her shoulder as she put her mask in place.

"Don't be." Kincaid, behind her, squeezed her shoulder reassuringly. "Tonight we'll just sup, play a few hands of cards, and go home. Nothing is expected of you but to enjoy yourself."

On the ground she turned to face him. "There's no chance we can be caught?"

"Monti says the pardons are all but secured. We're old gossip by now, my love." He offered his arm. "Now let's go sample the fare. Mistress Neaman makes a superior tart of marrow bone."

Inside the ordinary of the Fish and Bone, Mistress Neaman, proprietor, escorted Meg and her two gentlemen to a discreet table at the far side of the room, near the kitchen door. After a few minutes of talk and a glass of strong Alicante, Kincaid persuaded Meg to remove her mask and enjoy the outing.

Mistress Neaman's cooking was indeed superior. She served the marrowbone tart she was so well known for, along with roast snipe and carbonados. There was rye bread and sweet butter, mashed turnips with onions, and cups of wine. For dessert she served comfits and marzipan.

After the supper dishes were cleared and more wine was poured, two young fops, half drunk, joined them for a game of ombre. The two young men were quite pleasant, flirting with her, laughing and joking with Monti and Kincaid. Meg sat back, warm from the wine and Kincaid's company, content to watch the men play.

The more time she spent with Kincaid, the more she realized how difficult it would be to leave him when the time came. His offer to marry her and for them to run away to some far-off place was becoming more appealing each day. Why couldn't they both leave their identities behind and start a new life. Meg had always thought she would like to see the American colonies. Why couldn't they go there?

Meg watched Kincaid as he scooped up a handful of coins he'd just won. He was indeed charming, this alter ego of his. Everyone seemed to know James Kincaid and enjoy his company. It seemed hard to believe that one man could be two in the same city, but it seemed that Kincaid had indeed pulled it off.

Kincaid piled his coins before him and waited for the cards to be dealt again. "Enjoying yourself, sweet?" he whispered, slipping his hand beneath the table to take hers.

She smiled. "I am," she answered in the same hushed tones. "But I must admit I'm growing anxious to return home."

"Tired?"

Her gaze met his. "No."

He broke into a grin, scooping up his coins. "Gentlemen, it's been a fine evening, but I fear we must part company."

"Hang it, James," the one called Carter complained. "You've beaten me again and now you give me no time to redeem myself?"

"I apologize, my friends, but the hour is late and Mrs. Drummond is tired and desires the comfort of her chamber." He rose from the bench to help Meg with her cloak. "But I assure you we shall meet again soon."

"Well, do bring the lovely Mrs. Drummond when you come again, as we much prefer her company to yours," Carter replied, standing haltingly to bow.

Meg turned away with laughter, lifting her vizard to cover her face. It was then that she spotted the Earl of Rutledge.

Twelve

Meg's first reaction was one of terror. As she clutched her mask to her face, she could do nothing but stare at the Earl of Rutledge. He was with a young woman with dark hair. She was laughing lightheartedly as he led her to a table at the other end of the room.

Once Meg realized Percival hadn't seen her, that he couldn't recognize her concealed by the mask, her fear slowly dissolved to anger.

As cruel as Philip had been, Percival had always been crueler. It was he who had insisted that there would be nothing but perfection in the Randall ancestral home. It was he who had driven his younger brother Philip to murder his deformed son. In Meg's eyes, Percival was as much a murderer as Philip.

Meg stood where she was, frozen, as Kincaid made his farewells. Seeing Percival brought back a sudden flood of memories that she had been able to staunch for weeks. Suddenly her breasts ached for her dead newborn. Suddenly her heart ached for the child who had grown into a woman in that horrible house surrounded by treasures and opulence. She ached for her own pain.

"Ready, love?"

Meg barely heard Kincaid's warm voice in her ear. She couldn't drag her eyes off Rutledge. He was laughing with the young woman who looked no more than sixteen or seventeen. He was playing the gallant she had seen him play so many times in the high dining room at Rutledge Castle. The poor woman didn't realize what a monster he was.

At some point Meg had assumed she would regret killing Philip. At some point in her life she was certain that she would come to the conclusion that she should have let Philip murder her and be done. But as she stared at Percival's ugly face, watching him in gay conversation with the unsuspecting woman, the only regret she felt was that she had not taken his life, as well, God save her soul.

"Meg?"

Meg blinked. "I . . . I'm ready." Kincaid took her arm and led her through the public room, now bursting at the seams with ladies and gentlemen just come from the playhouse or elsewhere, seeking supper and the company of other noblemen and women.

"Meg, are you all right?"

She glanced at Rutledge one last time. Kincaid didn't seem to notice him. "Fine. I'm fine." She knew she was trembling. Seeing Rutledge. Remembering the son she suckled only once. It made her angry. It made her determined. The Randall brothers had no right to take from her what they took. They robbed her of her childhood. Of her innocence. They robbed her of her confidence and self-esteem. Both the bastards deserved to burn in hell.

Meg tightened her grip on Kincaid's arm. Seeing Percival made her recognize how lucky she was to have Kincaid. Percival Randall, the Earl of Rutledge, wasn't fit to wipe Kincaid's dung-covered boots, highwayman or not.

As Kincaid assisted Meg into the carriage, she realized for the first time that Monti wasn't with them. "Where's Monti?"

"Found a lady friend." He slid onto the seat across from her, closing the carriage door. "Didn't you notice?"

"I . . ." She stared at her gloved hands. "I was distracted." She was silent for a moment as the coach rolled off. Then she looked up at Kincaid. She could barely see his face in the semi-darkness. "Kincaid, were you serious when you said we could go away together. Far away, I mean."

His gaze met hers. "Entirely."

She slid from her seat across the rocking coach to his, taking his hand. All she could think of were her years of unhappiness, of fear, of hopeless desperation. "Then let's do it." She nodded her head decisively. "Tonight. Let's leave England. Let's go to America. I don't care what I have to do. I'll wash dishes in a tavern. I'll sweep someone's floor. Please, let's just go far from this place."

"Meg?" He pushed back her hood so that the yellow light from the oil lamp shone on her face. "What brought this on so suddenly? Did you see someone you knew?"

She glanced down at her lap. It was hard for her to lie. "No. No it's just that . . ." She looked into his eyes again. "Tonight was so wonderful, just being with you. I . . . I think we could have a good life together, you and I."

"I told you I would marry you, Meg." He kissed her gloved hand that smelled of oiled leather. This was the moment he had been waiting weeks for. "And I mean it. I can call a parson tonight if only you'll have—"

Meg covered his lips with her fingers. "No marriage," she said softly. "I've tasted that bitter tea. But love. Happiness? Freedom?" She traced his lips with her fingertips. "We could have that, you and I, couldn't we?" Before he could speak, she covered his mouth with hers.

"Meg, Meg," he protested.

She kissed him again, thrusting her tongue between his lips. This time he made no attempt to protest. Kincaid didn't know what had come over his Meg, but he was learning that all he needed to do at a time like this, when her past seemed to haunt her, was to be there for her. To listen. To tell her he loved her.

"Meg, my love . . ." His dark brown eyes sparkled with life.

Suddenly where they were seemed unimportant. All that

mattered to Kincaid was the desperate need to comfort his Meg in any way he could. At this moment making love to her was what was important.

Their mouths still molded, Kincaid raised her gently from the seat beside him and pulled her onto his lap, straddling his legs. Her fingers brushed the nape of his neck sending a shiver of desire down his spine. Their tongues intertwined, he savored the taste of the wine on her breath.

He reached with one hand beneath her cloak, finding the curve of her breast. She moaned in encouragement.

The coach swayed as they careened around a corner. She had knocked off his hat, his periwig. She yanked off her gloves, his. She unpinned her hair and splayed it over her shoulders.

Kincaid tried to remain calm and keep his breathing steady. But his Meg made it difficult. He could feel himself growing hard, straining against the taut material of his breeches.

She flung off her cloak, pulling down the bodice of her gown so that he could touch his lips to her breasts that thrust above her corset. Kincaid groaned, teasing her nipple to a ripe bud as she settled down deeper into his lap, pressing her groin to his.

Meg's breath was ragged in his ear as she murmured his name again and again.

Taking her other nipple gently between his teeth, Kincaid slipped his hand beneath her abundant petticoats to a place he knew would be warm and wet.

Meg lifted slightly on his lap, parting her thighs. Suddenly the scent of desire, his and hers, was heavy in the dark coach.

Kincaid pressed his lips to Meg's again, smoothing the soft down of curls between her legs. She squirmed against him, aiding his caress. She threw back her head, running her hands through his hair. He kissed the pulse at her throat, the warm spot at the valley between her firm, peaked breasts.

The sound of Meg's soft moans made Kincaid shudder with desire for her. He had been with so many women, women whose names, faces he'd long forgotten, but no woman had ever made him mad like this. No woman had ever made him desire her as he desired his Meg.

So this was love? The desire to give without feeling the need to take? Was this what he had searched for his entire life? As his mouth met Meg's again and again, he came to the conclusion that this *was* love. This ache in his heart.

Lowering Meg in one arm, he continued to stroke her, parting the soft, sweet folds of her femininity.

"No, no, not so fast," she murmured breathless and panting. "I'm not ready. Let me . . ."

Then she slipped to the floor of the coach, down on her knees. Before he could protest or even try to calculate how close they were to Ram Alley, Meg was pulling on the tie of his breeches. The moment his breeches fell open and she slipped her warm hand inside, he was lost to any objection he might have tried to express.

Kincaid exhaled heavily as she wrapped her nimble fingers around his stiff rod. "Meg, you don't have to—"

"Shhh," came her voice out of the darkness. "Let me give to you something of what you've given so many times to me, Kincaid. Let me express my love as you express your love for me."

What else could he say? He slumped back against the leather of the coach bench, running his fingers through her hair that had come tumbling down from the hairpins.

Kincaid heard his own groans of pleasure as the tip of her tongue touched the tip of his engorged shaft. He closed his eyes, riding the waves of pleasure until finally he feared he could not stand her ministrations another second.

"Meg!" His voice was sharp. "Come here, love." Then he lifted her by the waist into his lap.

She lifted her skirts, fighting the yards of billowing satin. Their mouths met hungrily, both Kincaid and Meg desperate for release.

With a little maneuvering Kincaid was able to lift her and

guide her down on his shaft. They both moaned in unison as the union was made.

"Kincaid," she panted in his ear, lifting and lowering.

"Sweet, sweet Meg." He kissed her temple, the rhythm of his breathing reaching a frenzied high.

Again and again she rose and fell in his lap, and he shuddered with each thrust. Realizing by the sound of her voice that she was near to spent, Kincaid lifted himself halfway off the seat, gripping her bare bottom. Meg cried out, shuddering, and he fell back, spilling into her, calling her name.

Meg dropped her hands onto his shoulders, laughing. In the dim light he saw tears rolling down her cheeks.

Then suddenly the coach stopped. Meg's eye widened in such surprise that Kincaid burst into laughter.

Meg leapt off his lap, falling into the seat across from him. Kincaid was just closing his breeches, she pushing down her skirts when the driver opened the door.

Stifling their laughter, the two of them gathered their discarded clothing, the cloaks, gloves, his periwig and hat, and stepped out of the coach into the cold night air.

Kincaid paid the driver, who was now straining to see inside the coach. Then Kincaid grabbed Meg's hand and led her down the street, their cloaks still bundled in their arms.

It was a glorious night. Perfect.

Much later, after they made love again, Kincaid lay sprawled in their bed with Meg cuddled up beside him. It was that quiet before they slept that Kincaid enjoyed so much. When they spoke of their day, their plans for tomorrow. This was the time when Meg made him feel like he finally belonged somewhere . . . to someone.

Since they had arrived back at Mother Godwin's, he'd been thinking about Meg's asking to run away together. He kept thinking about the commitment he had made to himself and he had come to the difficult conclusion that he couldn't leave

London, not yet. The question was, how could he explain it to Meg? How much did he tell her? All of it, he finally decided.

"Meg?" he said softly. "You still awake?"

She stirred, snuggling deeper into the feather tick, her hand brushing over his chest. "Um hmm."

"Listen, sweet. We need to talk. I . . ." He exhaled. "I can't leave London tomorrow."

She opened her dark eyes to stare up at him. "You can't?" Her voice was sleepy.

He ran his hand over her bare shoulder. "No, I can't," he answered equally hushed.

She pushed up on her elbow, pulling up the counterpane to cover her breasts. "Why not Kincaid? We don't have to go to America if that's not what—"

"No. It's not that, Meg." He took her hand in his and traced one of the long lines of her palm with his finger. Monti would know what the line represented, but he didn't. "Meg, I can't go because I have a commitment here."

She wrinkled her nose. "Who made a commitment? Kincaid? James? Or Captain Scarlet? Just so I know which man we speak of."

He liked her droll wit. "All of us. You see . . ." He looked away, still caressing her hand. "I haven't been entirely honest with you."

"Oh?"

He exhaled. Why was this so difficult? He wanted to tell her he wasn't the thief she thought him to be. That he had a purpose to his crimes. That he was avenging injustices. But he knew he was afraid because in explaining Captain Scarlet to her, he would be baring a part of himself.

"No. I'm not really a highwayman."

She chuckled. "Innocent like the rest who went to the gallows are you, Scarlet? Come now, that won't work with me. Remember, I was the one arrested with you that night you tried to rob that coach."

He let go of her hand and laid back on the bolster. A fire crackled in the hearth, giving off the room's only light. He stared at the ceiling, watching the jagged shadows dance. "The robberies are not random, as the High Sheriff believes."

She was watching him closely now, studying his face. "Go on."

"And I do not keep the profits. Never have. Not half a shilling."

"Where do the profits go? For surely there are profits. I read only last week in the papers that the dashing Captain Scarlet had stolen a sapphire necklace the size of a plum from some unsuspecting woman."

He appreciated her making light of the conversation. She made it easier for him to go on. "I donate the profits to those who live in the slums of the city. To the citizens of Whitechapel, Fisbury, Southwark, and the like."

"A Robin Hood of modern day?" Her face lit up and she was laughing, but not at him.

Now he was a little embarrassed. It did sound silly when he spoke the words out loud. "Not exactly, Meg."

She placed both hands on his chest and leaned on him, looking up at his face. "So who are the victims? You said the choices are not random. What did they do to you that you feel you must rob them of their coin and jewels and distribute it to the poor?"

"I have a list."

"I'm not surprised."

"Meg." He frowned. "Can you not see that this is hard for me to explain?"

She kissed his chest. "I'm sorry, sweet. Go on."

He reached for the half-glass of brandy left beside the bed. "Monti and I, we came up with the list just after we arrived in London last year. The men . . . the men whose names are on the list committed crimes against fellow Englishmen. Fellow Englishmen less fortunate than themselves."

"What do you mean *crimes?*"

"These men took advantage of the change in the political climate. They jumped ship. One day they were supporters of the Crown and the next they were loyal Parliamentarians." His voice grew edged with steel. "Men like my father claimed allegiance to that bastard Cromwell and his Puritan ways and profited from their friends who refused to abandon their king, though he was exiled. Sick bastards like my father accepted lands, moneys, even women, confiscated from loyal Royalists." He wiped his mouth with the back of his hand, tasting his own bitter anger. "Then, when Charles returned, the turncoats simply crossed the plank again. Suddenly they were supporters of the Stuarts, claiming they had been supporters all along. And our king, attempting to truly restore our country took them in with open arms. He felt he had no choice." He shrugged, a catch in his voice. He was thankful he saw no laughter in Meg's eyes now. "So you see there was no price for their disloyalty."

"So you are punishing them one by one by robbing them on the highway?"

" 'Tis a small enough gesture. I certainly cannot take the riches from them that they have accumulated, I know that. But once the list is complete, I intend to publish a satire naming the men and explaining why they were chosen. At least they will lose face. Some will lose business with the men who remained loyal to the king despite their hardships."

"You're going to write a satire?" She was smiling.

"Aye. 'Tis one of James's foibles." He lifted a hand lamely. "I didn't tell you because I didn't want you to think me silly."

She laughed lightly, obviously amused.

His forehead creased. "Why do you laugh?"

"I'll show you later. But for now, I want you to tell me, when you've visited each man you intend to visit, will your work be complete? Will your commitment be done?"

"It will, Meg."

"And then will you be free to leave your anger behind?" She looked down at him, her gaze concentrated and serious.

"Not just your anger with these men, but your anger with the father you rarely mention?"

He closed his eyes, unable to withstand her scrutiny. How was it that this woman could always understand him, always know what was closest to his heart? "I believe I can," he answered.

"How many men are left on this list?" She was talking practicalities now.

He opened his eyes, thankful she had not asked him about his father. "Not a dozen."

She sat up, drawing her knees to her chest. "And when this list is done, you would go with me? To America?"

"I would go to the ends of the world with you. And it's not that they are more important than you Meg, it's only that—"

She kissed him lightly on the mouth. "You don't have to explain it to me. I understand." She rested her chin on her bare knee, lost in thought. "A dozen men," she reasoned aloud. "That wouldn't take you long to accomplish if you could track them all down."

"That's James's job. He earns money to support us and gleans information on who is coming and going out of the city."

"I feel like I'm in bed with several men at once." She laughed. "All right. If James gets the information, then Captain Scarlet can see the deeds through."

"Yes."

"And the sooner the remainders on the list have been visited, the sooner you and I can get on with our lives."

"Aye. But I've been careful not to commit the robberies too close in time or physical proximity."

"And you only rob on the highway around London? You've no other method of operation?"

"No. Why do you ask?"

"Well, you're not being creative enough. Sounds like you need some help from a lady."

His gaze narrowed. Did she mean what he thought she meant? "Pardon?"

"You need a woman's help. And I'm your woman." She was grinning, obviously pleased with herself.

"You're no thief."

She rose up on her knees, letting the counterpane fall so that she was naked. She kissed him again. "And neither are you, my love."

Thirteen

"Percival, how good to see you again." Mary Mummford fluttered her fan, glancing away from him so that, to a wandering eye, she didn't appear to be speaking to him.

"Madame." Percival nodded. He stood two feet from her, in the shadows, watching a hand of laterloo at a gaming table. Whitehall's privy gallery was filled with ladies and gentleman tonight, their faces flush with good wine and foul gossip.

"I waited for you to call on me again, sir, yet you did not and I'm sorely vexed with you. I even sent you a note by way of my handmaid. I received no reply." She pouted, her lips pursed seductively.

The Earl of Rutledge allowed himself a sideward glance at the engaging strumpet. She was dressed this evening in a pink and maroon taffeta gown, her busk so tight that it pushed her round little breasts up and over the neckline of her bodice. He was certain it was the ring of her dark areolas he saw at the lace edging. Her face was painted and patched as was the fashion, but overly so. He wondered if the girl realized she looked more like a child who had played in her mother's lip pomade than a woman.

"I apologize for not calling upon you," he murmured so that others couldn't hear him. "But I encountered your father at the East Indian House where we were both seeing to business." He watched her as she lifted a wine glass to her rouged, bee-stung lips. "He asked that I not call on you again as you have several suitors already interested in matrimony."

She drank down the last of the wine with a tip of her wrist. "Screw Father!" She dropped the glass on the edge of the nearest gaming table, ignoring the frown of some matronly baroness. "I'm bored, Percy. Will you walk with me?"

Percival licked his dry upper lip, feeling the curve of his deformity. He glanced up and down the gallery teaming with satin coats and brocade gowns. The Earl of Mummford was nowhere to be seen.

"Percy?"

He knew he shouldn't, but he couldn't resist the girl. He came out of the shadows to offer her his arm. "Mary."

She smiled, linking her arm through his. "It will be our little secret, won't it, Percy?" She patted his arm like she must have patted the deformed kitten.

"Madame?" He led her along the north wall of the gallery, remaining out of the direct light of the thousands of candles that burned in chandeliers and wall sconces.

"Our trysts."

A smile tugged at the corner of his mouth. He liked the vein of the conversation, and yet it disgusted him at the same time. Where had the morals of Mother England gone? "I assure you my intentions are completely honorable."

She glanced at him over the edge of her painted pink fan. "Mine aren't." She giggled. "The lambs must play whilst they have the chance, don't you believe? I'll be wed soon, Percy—to *someone*. Whoever is the highest bidder, I suppose. And I don't like the thought. Not one bit. The idea of a beautiful young woman like myself marrying some old crook-back like Arnold Blithe is as welcome as a looking glass after the pox!"

"The Earl of Acres is a wealthy man of considerable influence at Court. He possesses many holdings, including a fine home in Dover. I've been his guest there."

"Yes, well, he's been through three wives in the last ten years. All of them dead of childbed or the pox in less than three years." She smiled innocently at a lady and gentleman passing, her frown reappearing the moment they were gone.

"I don't like the odds, sir. Not one bit. And what do I want with a home on those godforsaken cliffs? I want a home in London and one in the country nearby so I can escape the plague when it comes in the summer."

Percival couldn't help but laugh at Mary's naivete. Nor could he help but compare her to Margaret. Had Margaret ever been so young and simpleminded? She had certainly been young. She couldn't have been more than nine or ten when she came to Rutledge Castle. But she had never been such a simpleton.

"You laugh at me, sir?" Mary cut across the galley, leading him into the bright light.

Rutledge squinted. How he was beginning to despise the light that revealed his failings. "You know so little of life, my dear."

"I know what I like and what I don't. What I want and what I do not want." She ducked down a dark, vacant passageway, pulling him along.

Again Percival knew he shouldn't be here with her. He had no right to dishonor her father thusly. But the scent of her supple, young skin . . . skin unmarked by pox or time. It was intoxicating.

In the darkness Mary pushed him against the wall. For a woman of small stature, she was strong. "Why don't you kiss me?" she whispered with her wine breath. "Can you kiss with that mouth?" She was pressing her body against his, those pert breasts, straining against him, begging for release.

Percival could hear his own breath, heavy and labored. To this point he had been able to restrain himself.

He grabbed her shoulders and yanked her roughly against him, forcing his mouth to hers. His original intention was only to frighten her.

She squirmed a little, squeaking with surprise.

Percival opened his mouth, thrusting his tongue between her blood-red lips. She tasted of wine and unmarred perfection. The thought that she was so willing, yet forbidden, excited him. It made his blood rush. Freeing one hand he squeezed her breast cruelly, reveling in its softness in his hand.

"Ouch!"

She brought her hand under his coat, caressing his chest with her small hand. "Easy, boy," she whispered huskily. "You don't want to damage the goods."

He pressed his mouth against her neck, sucking until he knew he would leave a bruising mark. He wanted to possess her. He wanted to hurt her for her insolence. To hurt her because she was so pretty and he was so ugly.

Pushing down the taffeta bodice, he found her nipple with the pad of his thumb. She moaned softly in his ear, almost mewing. He kept thinking of the deformed kitten she had owned. *What a sick bitch.*

Percival caught the button of her breast between his thumb and forefinger and pinched hard.

"Ouch." She slapped at him lightly.

He reached around behind her and slapped her ass hard.

She fell forward against him, exhaling in a rush of wine breath. "Easy, Percy." She was giggling. Her voice was husky. She liked it.

Percival smiled in the darkness. A part of him wanted to warn her against a man like himself. A part of him wanted to tell her to run while she still had the chance. She was no match for the Earl of Rutledge. But a larger part of him wanted to possess her—the part of him that was blue-veined and rigid, throbbing in his breeches.

"Do you suck, Mary?" he whispered in her ear. "You like that, too?" He squeezed her breast hard.

She was giggling, panting. "I suck," she whispered, nipping his neck with her pearly teeth.

He unbuckled his breeches, letting them fall to his ankles. In the semi-darkness he watched her lower herself to her knees in a puddle of pink taffeta. He caught a curl of hair at her temple and twisted it until he felt it tighten and pull at the tender flesh.

"So suck me," he whispered. "And suck me well, my little slut, or there'll be hell to pay."

She reached out to catch him expertly in her mouth.

So, sweet Mary Mummford had done this before . . .

"Tomorrow I have to see to a widow who's sent word to Scarlet through Monti." Kincaid sat down on the chair near the hearth as Meg had instructed. "She says she's in desperate need. One of the men on my list, Joseph Auger, is forcing her out of the inn she's been running since her husband's death because she cannot pay his exorbitant rent."

"Good. I'll accompany you. It'll be a good way for me to get started."

He sighed. "It's pointless to go through this again, Meg. You will not become involved. Not in the Elizabeth Small matter. Not in any matter that concerns Captain Scarlet."

"You're being obstinate without just cause." She lathered her hands with a wet bar of soap and applied the suds to his broad, angular face. "If you would think about it logically, you'd admit I'm right."

He wrinkled his nose. "What kind of soap is that you're using? It smells like flowers."

She grinned. "Violet and chamomile. It was all I had left." She picked up his razor. "Now close your mouth before I slice off your lips."

"So this is why you offered to shave me? You knew I'd be a captive audience!"

She slid the long razor down his cheek and he clamped his mouth shut. She chuckled. "That's better. You listen. I'll talk." She wiped a streak of soap and dark hair on a towel resting in his lap.

"I could help you on your missions."

"I have a partner," he mumbled, tight-lipped.

She brought the razor close to the tip of his nose. "This

is the first time I've ever done this. I wouldn't move if I were you."

He groaned.

Meg went on shaving. "I could help you alter your methods of operation. I don't mean to criticize, love, but you're not a terribly creative highwayman."

"I—"

"I'm talking. You're listening." She stroked his chin with the razor, the blade making a scraping sound as she shaved the skin clean. "I already have several ideas. My theory is that the sooner we knock the men off your list, the sooner you and I can get on with our lives. The sooner we can make plans to go to America." She kissed his lips, wiping the shaving soap from her own chin. "I was thinking we could purchase some land with some of that money you're making at cards. What's your feeling on growing tobacco?"

"Meg. It's not that I wouldn't welcome your help, but it's dangerous. We could be caught—"

She dipped the razor blade into a basin of warm water. "I could be thrown into Newgate, for heaven's sake!"

"This is not a matter to joke about. In aiding me, you would become as guilty as I. A criminal. You could be shot and killed. You could be hanged at Tyburn."

He had used that argument over and over again until Meg was sick to death of it. She would be a criminal? She was already a criminal, one of the worst kind. She was a murderess. The fact of the matter was that she didn't care. She wanted a life. She wanted a life with Kincaid and she was willing to fight to get it.

"Meg, this isn't your fray. It's mine. I know it's foolish, the entire notion of punishing these men for what they did, but—"

"It isn't foolish. It's noble. And as for it being *your* cause, it has become *mine*." She squatted in front of him, resting her elbow on his knee so that she could look into his eyes. "I knew men such as those who are on that list. I knew some of them personally. They supped at my husband's dining table." Her voice grew bitter. "My husband and his brother were men that should have been on that list of yours, Kincaid. I don't know how you missed the curs."

"Meg." He tried to take the razor from her hand, but she refused to let it go. "I'm just trying to protect you."

She stood up, turning his cheek roughly to finish the other side of his face. "Would you do it for me?"

He opened his mouth to speak, but she grabbed his chin. "Just nod. I'm the one who's supposed to be talking, remember?"

She could tell by the glimmer in his dark eyes that he was growing angry with her. He jerked his chin in a nod.

"All right, let's reason this one out, Captain Scarlet. You would aid the woman you loved—you do love me, don't you?"

He nodded.

"All right. You would aid the woman you loved in a dangerous task, yet you do not believe that I should aid the man I love? Do I understand you correctly?"

Again he opened his mouth to answer. She shut it by touching the tip of the blade to his chin.

He nodded.

She smiled. "So how, in that man's brain of yours, does that make sense?"

He grabbed the razor out of her hand. "Because you're a woman, damn it, Meg!" He jumped out of the chair and headed for the mirror to finish his own shaving. "And women do not fight for causes. Women do not get involved in politics. Women do not get wounded or killed trying to hold up coaches."

She followed him to the mirror, refusing to give an inch. "No. Women stay at home and care for their husband's lands while men fight each other over honor. Women are sold into marriage, beaten and raped at the hands of brutal men in the name of political righteousness. Women die giving birth to men's sons." She watched his face in the mirror.

"It's not the same thing and you know it, Meg."

"The blessed hell it's not!"

His face shaven, he brushed by her, tossing the razor into the bowl. Water splashed over the sides, dripping onto the towel laid out on the table. "That's the end of the discussion." He yanked his clean muslin shirt over his head. "Tomorrow I go to see Elizabeth Small and you remain here where you'll be safe."

"You can't tell me what to do," She accused, her own temper flaring. "You don't own me. There's no wedding vows between us, *Captain Scarlet.*"

"You're making me angry, Meg." He perched himself on the edge of the chair and shoved his stockinged foot into his boot. "Don't make me lose my temper."

"That won't work with me, because I'm not afraid of you and your temper!" She dropped her hands to rest on her hips. "I don't care if you run and shout, jump up and down. I'm going."

The other boot on, he grabbed his coat, headed for the door. "You're not going." He flung it open and stepped into the hallway, practically slamming the door in her face. "End of discussion!"

Meg lifted the reins of her mare, urging her to move faster as she followed Kincaid down the muddy road just outside of London. Darkness had just fallen. The evening was cool, but not cold, and there was the smell of the budding spring in the air.

Meg adjusted her seating on the side-saddle, having no trouble keeping up. Philip had made certain that from an early age she was well educated in horsemanship, as any lady should be.

"Is it much farther?" Meg urged her spotted mare up beside Kincaid's steed.

He glared without answering.

He was still annoyed by the fact that she had won their argument. But she didn't care. She'd won. Well, a small victory. He'd agreed to allow her to accompany him to the Widow Small's inn on Ratcliff Highway. Once he heard the widow's full story, if he chose to seek out Joseph Auger, Meg would have to remain at the inn until Captain Scarlet's business was complete.

"Monti's not coming?" she asked, trying to make conversation to lighten his black mood. An owl hooted in the maple and elm trees that hung low over their heads.

"Should I need him, he'll come." He nodded in the direction of the lamplight that shone ahead. "There 'tis. The Cock and Crumb."

They rode toward the hanging sign that bore a rooster and a slice of bread with falling crumbs. Outside the door, under lamplight, Kincaid dismounted and helped her off her horse. A young boy who appeared out of the darkness took the horses to the barn in the back.

"Now you let me do the talking, do you understand me?" Kincaid took her by the arm and led her inside, suddenly possessive of her.

Meg nodded, smiling. "Whatever you say, dear."

Kincaid threw her a disapproving glance as a tall, beefy woman approached them, wiping her hands on her apron. She wasn't pretty, but she had an honest face. "Good even', madame, sir. Do you seek sup or a bed or both?" She had a warm voice that exuded hospitality.

"Widow Small?" Kincaid addressed her in a gentlemanly fashion.

She patted the damp hair at her temple, momentarily flustered. "Yes?"

"You sent for me," Kincaid said softly so that the few other patrons in the public room did not hear him. "I came immediately as was requested."

The widow's honey-brown eyes suddenly grew round with surprise. "Captain—"

"Could you show us to a discreet table?" he said loud enough for the others in the room to hear. "The lady is famished, but we prefer privacy."

Flustered, the widow led them to a trestle table in a cubby hole in the corner of the room near the staircase. A cherrywood fire crackled, giving off warmth and the sweet, pungent smell of cherries. Kincaid helped Meg out of her wool cloak and she took the chair Kincaid offered her. Kincaid took the seat directly across the table. "A meal, Mrs. Small. We truly are famished. Something hearty. Have you sack?"

" 'Course, sir." She bobbed a nervous curtsy, obviously uncertain of what she was to do next.

"Then bring us our refreshment." He smiled, then lowered his voice. "And we'll talk."

The widow rushed off, reappearing a few moments later with three dusty green bottles. She set them down with a bang, knocking one over in her apprehension. "I got clary water if your wife would want it . . . sir," she stumbled, righting the bottle.

"That would be fine." Meg smiled, trying to set the widow at ease. The poor woman was so apprehensive that her clean, wrinkled hands were shaking. "And a bit of bread whilst we wait for our meal."

The widow nodded. "Be right back. With fresh butter, too, sir."

This time she returned with a glass of clary water. "Your . . . your meal will be ready soon. My son is dishing the stew."

Meg sipped her drink, speaking softly. To anyone in the room, she knew she appeared only to be making conversation with the innkeeper. "Your message stated you could not pay your rent on this establishment." She ignored Kincaid when he cleared his throat to get her attention. "That suggests business is poor, and yet I see a public room of hungry guests."

Mrs. Small shook her head that was covered with a stiff white cap. "Oh my, business is good ever since His Majesty came back, only . . ."

"Go on," Meg urged. Out of the corner of her eye she saw Kincaid frown. She knew he'd said he would do the talking, but it was obvious he made the widow nervous. And why wouldn't he, as large and imposing as he was in his black cloak and feathered cavalier's hat? It simply made sense that it would be Meg who would speak with the widow.

"He . . . Mr. Auger, has raised the rent three times," she whispered. "It's now more than double the cost when my husband lived." She crossed herself hastily. "God rest his soul."

"And his price is unreasonable?"

"My husband always said he was high to start with, but when our own tavern burnt to the ground some years back, we didn't have no choice but to take Mr. Auger's offer." She leaned over the table, speaking so softly that Meg had to strain to hear her. "My husband was always suspicious of the fire that put us out. It was set by some unknown villain."

Meg glanced up at Kincaid, satisfied with what the widow had to say. "When is this rent due?"

"Last Saturday. I'm two months behind. He says that if I don't have the coin day after next, he'll put my babies and me out on the street." With the corner of her flour-dusted apron she wiped a tear that trickled from her eye. "I got nowhere to go, ma'am. No way to feed my three boys but from this place. No skill but my cooking."

"Where is he now? Will he come himself for the rent or does he send a messenger?"

"Oh, he comes himself, the old skinflint. He wouldn't pay a messenger." She curled her upper lip. "He collects the rent and stays to eat twice a man-sized meal. More bread. More honey. More potatoes." She swept her arm with a flourish. "Then he takes brandy from my larder to comfort him on his ride home without ever leaving a ha'penny to cover the expense."

"He comes from his home?"

"From his home to his daughter's where he stays the night, then here the next day. Like a good clock he is. I could give you the way to his place. The daughter's, too." She paused for a moment, then turned to Kincaid, clasping her hands. "Please, Captain Scarlet. You're my only chance. My only hope. My sister, she lives in Whitechapel, she said that was what you did. You helped folk like us."

This time Meg didn't even bother to look at Kincaid. "We'll see what can be done."

The widow turned to Meg, taking her hand. "Thank you," she whispered, her emotion sincere. "I will never forget your kindness." She glanced at Kincaid. "Nor yours, sir."

Kincaid sighed. "Is our meal ready, Mrs. Small?"

"Oh, yes. Of course." She threw up her hands. "I'll be back directly."

Kincaid waited until she was gone, then turned his eyes on Meg. "Why did you say we would help her? You don't know—"

"The oaf is going to put her and her children out on the road. And he's one of the men still left on your list." She took a sip of her clary water. "How could we not help her?"

"We?" He brought his face closer to Meg's. "When did this become *we?* I only brought you with me for fear of the trouble you'd cause if I left you with Mother Godwin."

"Don't worry, sweet." She rubbed his hand. "I already have a plan that will work perfectly. You're going to love it . . ."

Fourteen

"This is insane, Meg. I cannot allow you to—"

"It's a good idea." Standing beside the road in the late afternoon light, she pulled off her cloak and handed it to him. "Monti, tell him it's a good idea. It will lead the suspicion away from Captain Scarlet." She removed her riding hat and her hair fell loose over her shoulders. "Won't it, Monti?"

"It's a very good idea, actually, Kincaid. Clever."

Kincaid gathered her cloak in his arms, ignoring Monti. "Auger will never fall for a *lady in distress!* He's an addlepate, but not *that* senseless."

"Bet me." She ran her fingers down the tiny buttons of her gown. "Put your coin where your mouth is, *Captain,*" she taunted.

"Meg?" Kincaid stared at her, suddenly realizing what she was doing. "Meg, why are you taking off your gown?" He glanced at Monti who was watching with obvious interest, then back at Meg. "You can't take your clothes off in the middle of Ratcliff Highway!"

She stepped out of her gown and tossed it to Monti. "I'm not going to take it all off, just a few layers." She unlaced her busk. "I do want to appear to be seriously in distress."

"She's not taking it all off," Monti repeated with a grin. He accepted her undergarment, cocking a thick eyebrow. "Just a few layers."

"I will not be a part of this," Kincaid fumed.

"You're not." She stepped out of her first petticoat. "Just

go stand in the woods and let Monti and me take care of business. All you have to do is have our horses ready to make the get away." Her tone was light and teasing. She stepped out of the second petticoat. The air was cool, but she wasn't chilled. Her nervous excitement kept her warm.

Monti took the two petticoats from her arm. She was now standing at the roadside in nothing but a cotton and lace smock, white stockings, and pearl-gray heeled slippers with grosgrain bows. "What o'clock is it?" she asked.

Monti checked his pocketwatch. "Near five."

"Good. If the Widow Small is correct, our Mr. Auger should be passing through on his way to his daughter's home at any moment."

Meg took the dagger from Monti's sheath around his waist and picked up a coil of rope at her feet. She walked off the road, up the bank. Years of coaches, horsemen, and tradesmen on foot and in carts had cut the road in a trench. Once she set foot in the grass roadside, she headed toward a grassy spot beneath an ancient, gnarled sycamore tree.

"Meg!" Kincaid called after her. "Meg!" Angrily, he thrust her cloak and hat into Monti's arms and followed her up the slight incline. "I don't like this whole idea. Not one bit."

"Monti said it will work. You even said last night that the idea was brilliant."

"That doesn't make it safe. That doesn't mean I want you to do it!"

Meg backed up to the tree, Monti's dagger in her hand. "I think I hear a coach. Could you help me?"

"Meg." His balled hands fell to his sides in exasperation.

"Kincaid, my mind is made up. I want to be a part of this. For you. But for personal reasons, too."

"Ah, that wicked past of yours."

"Don't make fun of me." She grabbed a hank of her thick, honey-brown hair and raised it high over her head.

Kincaid exhaled slowly in rankled indecision.

"I could use some help," she repeated softly.

After a moment's hesitation, he took the dagger from her hand. "If you need me, all you have to do is call. I'll be directly behind you in the woods. I'll be aiming for the bastard Auger's gut."

She leaned forward giving him a peck on the lips. "Hurry and do it. Can't you hear the coach?"

Holding the handful of her silky hair, Kincaid sank the dagger into the tree bark above her head, pinning her hair.

"Perfect. Now the rope. Tie my hands behind me 'round the back of the tree." She tucked her hands behind her.

Kincaid walked behind the tree, tying her hands. "I think I'd prefer this in our bed," he mumbled.

She laughed huskily. "So perhaps we'll try it one night. Now *hurry.*"

"Done." He came back around the tree to face her.

"Go." She lifted her chin. "Go with you, and take my clothes into the woods." She looked for Monti in the dying light. "Monti, are you ready?"

"Ready."

Meg blew Kincaid a kiss as he walked around the tree, disappearing behind her.

Meg let her breath out steadily. She could hear the coach approaching. She was hopeful it was the right man. This morning Monti had been able to coax a wench from Auger's daughter's kitchen into admitting they were expecting Auger this evening. Monti was excellent at innocently obtaining information. He even managed to bring back a few freshly baked apple tarts.

Meg took another deep breath. Overhead, the skeletal tree limbs swayed, the scent of their new leaf buds filling her nostrils. She could hear the hum of insect song along the roadside. The dry grass of the previous summer tickled her legs. It was strange, but she wasn't a bit afraid of the events that were about to unfold.

"Approaching," came Monti's voice in a shout.

The moment the coach appeared around the bend in the

road, Meg threw her head back. "Help me! Please help me!" she cried dramatically. *"Pleeease, help me."*

Behind her in the woods she heard Kincaid's dry chuckle. "I'm going to put you on the stage," he said softly.

"Hush!" she whispered. Then she pretended to struggle against her bindings, directing her pleas to the approaching coach. "Sir! Kind sir, won't you help me?"

The driver pulled back hard on the reins, halting the covered coach.

"What is it?" called a grumpy voice from inside. "Why do you stop, Albert? Don't you know there are thieves about these woods. Marauders?"

The white-haired driver, a man who surely had to be older than Moses, tapped on the roof of the coach with a short leather quirt. "Look, see for yourself, sir. It's a woman with 'er 'air pinned to a tree."

"A woman? Hair pinned to a tree? What the blast are you talking about, Albert?"

"Please help me," Meg begged the driver. "I've been robbed and left for dead."

The man inside the coach threw open the door. He matched the Widow Small's description right down to the hairy wart on his clipped chin. "What is this?" he demanded, stepping onto the road. "What is this about?"

Setting the brake, the driver slowly eased his ancient bones over the bench and down onto the ground. "A . . . a woman, Mr. Auger," the driver stammered. "See." He pointed.

Mr. Auger jerked his head back as if he didn't believe his own eyes. He was a short, portly man dressed in sober clothing, but even at a distance Meg could see the glimmer of gold rings on his pudgy fingers. "God's bowels, madame! What has happened to you?"

"I've been robbed, sir," she moaned. "My horse stolen, my servants run off."

"Thieves?" Auger glanced nervously into the dark woods.

The sun was just setting in a blaze of orange light in the western sky. "Are they still about?"

"Oh, no," she tried to reassure him without him becoming suspicious. "Long gone. I've been here for hours." She even managed to squeeze out a tear. "Could you help me, kind sir?"

Auger started up the slight embankment, aiding himself with his silver-tipped rosewood cane. "They stole your clothing, too, madame?"

Meg quickly feigned modesty, hanging her head. "I fear so, sir. I'm so ashamed." She looked up at him, lowering her bottom lip in a slight pout. "Couldn't you help me? I'm so cold. So afraid."

The moment Auger stepped into the grass, Monti appeared at the coach door, a blunderbuss in each hand. "Stand where you are, sir, else you'll have a bit of lead in your gullet."

Auger whirled around, throwing his arms high in the air in surprise. His cane fell into the grass.

"Heavens, they're back!"

"Old man." Monti pointed one pistol at the driver. "Go to your master and take his purse."

"Don't shoot," the driver begged, moving rather quickly for a man his age. "Just don't shoot." In a moment's time, he had Auger's fat purse and was coming down the bank to the road again.

"Thank you." Tucking one of the pistols beneath his arm, Monti checked inside. "Excellent." He looked up, smiling. "And now, if you would be so kind as to step inside the coach." He waved his pistol at Auger. "You too, sir, and do hurry. I've a schedule to keep like everyone else."

A smile twitched on Meg's face as she watched Auger climb into the coach behind his driver. The old crony hadn't even attempted to free her. All he cared about was saving his own leathery skin!

"Now," Monti instructed, looking into the coach. "I want you to cover the windows. Good, good. Next I'm going to close the door. It must remain closed for the following ten minutes. Have you a clock?"

"Y . . . yes," came Auger's frightened voice.

"Excellent. Now, if you should open the door in the next ten minutes, I fear I shall have to blow your nuts off. Do we understand each other?"

"Perfectly."

"Excellent. Now of course I shall have to let your horses go. But I don't believe it's a long walk to the next home. Enjoy your evening, sir."

Monti bowed gracefully and then slammed the coach door shut with his knee.

The moment the door was closed, Meg heard Kincaid come out of the woods behind her. "I cannot believe this flimsy scheme worked," he muttered, untying her hands.

"I told you it would," she gloated. With her hands free, she reached above her head and pulled the knife from the tree trunk, releasing her hair.

Kincaid came around the tree, pushing her cloak into her arms. "I'll get the horses. Monti?"

On the road, Monti was just slapping the backside of the second of Auger's horses. It bolted down the road after the first.

In a minute's time all three were astride their mounts, barreling down the road toward London.

"Good job, Monti." Meg grinned, pleased the robbery had gone so smoothly. "Now, haven't we a poor widow to visit?"

"I don't see him yet." Meg peeked from behind a curtain, watching the road below. She and Kincaid had taken a second-story room in the Widow Small's inn. Here they would stay until the matter of Mr. Auger was settled and his name could be struck from Kincaid's list.

"Come away from the window, Meg. You want him to see you?"

She let the curtain fall. "I don't understand why you're so grumpy."

"I am not grumpy. I'm concerned." He kept his eyes on the pages of the book in his lap, though she knew full well he wasn't really reading. "This is dangerous business and you treat it as a lark."

She walked slowly toward him. She was dressed only in her shift and petticoats with a flannel dressing robe thrown over her shoulders and matching mules on her feet. Tonight they would sup here in their cozy room, avoiding the public room where they assumed Auger would dine if he was truly the creature of habit the widow said he was.

"Kincaid, I understand that it's not a game," she said softly, coming to stand before him. "But you must also understand that I have led a very sheltered life. In a way, everything is a lark to me. Just being alive is a lark."

He set his book down and pulled her into his lap. "Tell me about the child," he said softly. "I can't stop thinking about it."

Meg looked away, tears immediately welling in her eyes. She tried not to think about her baby. She tried not to worry whether or not the midwife had found a place for him in the churchyard.

She smiled bittersweetly. "A boy. A male child, what every man should want." A tear ran down her cheek.

"His father did not?"

Meg bit down on her lower lip. She considered telling Kincaid the truth, or part of it, but she stopped herself. What was the point? There was no reason to drag him into her shame. Besides, she still feared he might hate her for it, even turn her in. Men were like that, the way they always took up for each other. "Let me say he was not as pleased as I would have hoped."

"The child died immediately?"

"Yes."

"And the father?"

Meg wiped at her tears with the back of her hand. "I told you, he died. Shortly thereafter."

Kincaid pulled her against him and she snuggled in his arms, laying her head on his shoulder.

"There can be other children, Meg," he said softly. "Ours. Would you like that?"

She sniffed. "I don't know that that's possible. It took me many years to conceive the one son, and even then he was . . ."

"He was what, Meg?"

She closed her eyes. "I would like another child, Kincaid, if God chooses to bless me. I'd like to have your son."

He kissed her forehead. "Or daughter?"

She laughed. Unlike the men she had known, her highwayman put the same merit in female children and male children. Yet another reason to love him. "Or daughter."

"And then she would have your silky hair." He brushed her hair with his hand. "Your soft skin." He kissed her cheek. "Your intelligent mind." He tapped her head with his knuckle. "I mean any woman who could come up with a scheme like this and make it work has got to be brilliant."

She laughed, her sadness gone. "It is going to work, isn't it? The widow is going to pay the miser with his own coin." She giggled. "And then—"

"Hush, and kiss me, Meg. I tire of talking business."

Meg slipped her hand to the nape of his neck and leaned to press her mouth to his. Just as their lips met, she heard the sound of carriage wheels on the gravel below.

"He's here!" She jumped off Kincaid's lap to run to the window to take a peek. "Wouldn't you love to be a fly on his window tomorrow night?"

Kincaid sat astride his horse, impatiently watching the road from where he hid in a copse of trees very near to the place that Meg and Monti had robbed Mr. Auger only two nights before. The coach would have to slow to make the hill. It was the perfect place for a holdup.

It was late afternoon, not yet twilight. A gentle breeze blew out of the north, ruffling the mane of the gelding he rode. The horse nickered softly and Kincaid patted its arched neck. The beast seemed to be as anxious to get on with this as Kincaid was. "Easy boy, easy," he murmured. It won't be long now. The old widow was right, the man runs like a clock." He chuckled. "Even in adversity."

He glanced overhead, checking the time by the position of the sun. Sunlight still filtered through the trees that were beginning to blossom with new life. Birds sang and the grass swayed in the breeze.

Kincaid grinned despite himself. That was how he felt these days, like a new leaf, blossoming after a long winter. And he had his Meg to thank for it. The idea of a life with her in America was becoming more appealing each day. Just as soon as this life could be put aside, as soon as he could close the book on the list of men he bore his grudge against, he could open a new book. A book of hope and happiness. And Meg would be the source of his contentment.

A slight rumbling noise signaled the approach of the vehicle Kincaid waited for and his body tensed. Each time he stepped onto the highway as Captain Scarlet, he prayed there would be no violence. That wasn't his purpose. Humiliation alone was. Kincaid had seen enough death to last him a lifetime.

The coach came into view, slowing for the grade. Kincaid took a deep breath, checking to be sure that his face was covered by the red swath of his highwayman's costume. Then, lifting his primed pistol, he sank his heels into his mount and wheeled out onto the road.

"Stand and Deliver!" Kincaid boomed, riding up along the side of the coach to peer into the window. It was Auger, all right. He recognized him from the widow's excellent description. "Your coin or your life!"

"Merciful father!" Auger swayed against the seat as if he were going to faint.

"Oh, my God! Oh, my God," came a feminine voice. "Father, it's thieves!"

"Driver," Kincaid commanded, lifting his pistol to take aim. "Halt."

The driver was already sawing on the reins, and the coach slid sideways to an abrupt stop.

"Step outside," Kincaid instructed. "Both of you. Driver, climb down."

Auger tumbled out of the coach, shaking from head to foot. The woman inside followed, hanging onto his coat tails, still shrieking.

Kincaid swept off his hat, nodding in greeting. The young woman, Auger's daughter, had a face like a heifer, but that was what was appealing about the highwayman Captain Scarlet. He loved all women.

Suddenly she was silent.

"So sorry to detain you, madame," Kincaid said smoothly. "I hope your trip has gone smoothly to this point."

She pressed her hand to her heaving bosom. "Please don't hurt us. Please. Father." She prodded him. "Give the nice thief your money. Your rings, too."

"I cannot believe it. I cannot believe it," Auger groaned, fumbling in his coat. "Twice in one week! I've been robbed twice in one week, daughter. Am I cursed? What have I done to deserve this?"

When he didn't move quickly enough, the daughter reached into her father's coat and snatched the coin bag herself. "Here, here you are, sir."

"The rings, too. She's right." Kincaid smiled. "A very clever girl, your daughter."

But when the woman started to pull a ring off her own plump finger, Kincaid shook his head. "No, no. I couldn't, madame, just the gentleman's will be enough. You're a woman too pretty not to be lavished in jewels."

The girl blushed with a giggle. "Thank you, sir."

Pulling off his gold rings, Auger thrust them into Kincaid's glove.

"Excellent," Kincaid said with a satisfied nod. "Now the next matter."

"Next matter?" Auger was visibly trembling. "Are you going to kill us?"

"This is Captain Scarlet," the daughter whispered, her cheeks still pink. "He doesn't kill his victims. Do you, Captain?" She giggled, openly flirting with Kincaid. "Sometimes he even kisses them."

It was hard for Kincaid not to laugh. "The matter, sir, concerns a widow by the name of Elizabeth Small. Do you know her?" His horse shifted its weight back and forth, Kincaid knew making him an imposing figure astride.

"Small . . . Small. Let me think, let me think." He pressed his finger to his sweaty forehead. "Yes . . . yes, I recall now. I believe I do know her."

"She pays you rent for an inn you own?"

"I believe so."

"I want you to give her the inn."

"Wh . . . what?" Auger choked.

"Did I stutter?" There was a sudden edge to Kincaid's voice. "I said I want you to give the inn to the widow. Legally."

"I . . . I can't. It . . . It's very profitable."

"It will not be profitable if you are robbed on this road each and every time you pass on it. You will not profit if I begin visiting some of your other establishments. I understand you own an excellent tavern on the Strand, also one near Bridewell. Need I go on?"

Auger's face turned a bright red. "You . . . you can't do that. I . . . I'll call the High Sheriff. The king's soldiers will—"

"Have soldiers been able to stop me in the past?"

The daughter shook her head. "He's very good, Father. He

never gets caught. There was a rumor he was in Newgate, but then later I heard it was false."

Kincaid lifted his shoulder. "So there you have it." The smile fell from his face. His tone hardened. "Now take care of the widow, or I will take care of you. I have not found it necessary to take any lives as of yet, but the possibility is always there. Do you understand?"

"I . . . I understand. But . . . but why are you doing this to me? Why do you mock me?"

"A time will come when you will know." Kincaid looked to the driver. "Sir, could you be so kind as to pull the linchpin on the coach? That way it won't be necessary that I dismount."

The driver hurried to follow Kincaid's bidding.

"Excellent." Kincaid smiled again beneath the swath of red. "And now I must go. Remember, Auger, I will check on the widow. Do as I instruct or there will be hell to pay."

Kincaid pulled his horse closer to the daughter and leaned over, pressing his mouth to hers. "Have a nice evening, madame," he said as his gaze met hers.

"Oh, oh, thank you, Captain," she hyperventilated.

Then with a wink, Kincaid was gone. Down Ratcliff Highway, headed toward London and his Meg.

Fifteen

"Marry me, Meg."

"Could you hand me the mallet?" Her voice was garbled by several nails she held in her mouth to keep her hands free. "I think I'd like the mirror here." Standing on a chair, she pointed to the bare spot on their bedchamber wall.

"Meg, you're not taking me seriously." He passed her the mallet. "I truly want to marry you. What if there was a child? I don't want my son or daughter born under a veil of illegitimacy."

She took a nail from between her lips and tapped it into the wall. Monti had finally secured their pardons after another exchange of money, so, yesterday, on the first of April, Meg, Kincaid, and Monti moved from Mother Godwin's to the apartments James and Monti kept at Charing Cross.

At first Meg had been annoyed that Kincaid had kept her in a whorehouse when he had a perfectly good five-room apartment at a fashionable crossroads in London, but she understood his reasoning. She understood his need to slowly reveal to her his life as it truly was.

She banged a second nail into the wall. "I . . . don't . . . understand . . . why . . . we . . . can't leave things as they are." She peered down at him from her perch on the chair. "The idea of being *kept* is deliciously wicked. I rather like being the highwayman's woman."

"Hush. The walls are thin, sweet. I'm James Kincaid to

this part of town and it's important that you remember that—unless you want to end up in Newgate again."

She pointed toward the bed. "Could you bring the mirror, there?"

He went to retrieve it, obviously exasperated. "I can do this for you, Meg."

She took the heavy gilded oval mirror from his hands. "I can do it myself." She had bought the mirror at the Royal Exchange, an inside market where anything from bolts of cloth to rare birds in cages could be purchased. At Rutledge everything was brought in, she'd never had a chance to make any choices on her own. It had been an exciting outing for Meg, one of her first as James Kincaid's woman.

She hung the mirror on the nails. "Straight?"

"I don't know." He stepped back a couple of feet. "Meg, you've managed to change the subject again. To the left a tad."

"Here?"

He nodded. "Perfect." He grabbed her hand. "Now get off the damned chair before you trip on your petticoats and break your neck."

She allowed him to help her off the chair, then buzzed away, busying herself tidying the very disorderly apartment he'd brought her to. "Why change our relationship when there's nothing wrong with it? I think we'd just be asking for trouble neither of us would welcome."

He leaned against the doorjamb, watching her as she picked up dirty clothing and soiled boots from the needlework carpet. "This isn't about me, it's about you. So don't turn it around. Now look, from what little you've said, I can gather your husband was a bastard, may he rot in hell. But that doesn't make me a bastard."

She dropped his soiled clothing into a pile on the end of the bed. It was one of her favorite pieces of furniture in the apartment with its curtains in bronze silk, trimmed with lace and lined with taffeta. "These need to be cleaned. I want to be one of Saity's first customers. If she's going to make it as a laundress we have to help her." She deposited his boots on the hearth to be cleaned and polished later. "And these need to go to the shoeshine."

"Meg. Damn it. Will you stop a minute? Stop and listen to me?"

"I want the apartments to look nice for your friends when they come to sup tonight. It's bad enough having everyone know I'm your whore." She turned to him, her arm filled with two of Kincaid's discarded coats and a pair of breeches that needed mending. Her face was practically concealed by the mountain of clothing. "I don't want them to think I'm untidy, as well."

"You're not my whore. You could be my wife if you'd have me."

She spun around, holding up one of his heeled shoes. "Do you know where the match to this is? I've looked everywhere and I can't find it. I don't understand how a man can lose a shoe in this room."

Kincaid strode across the room and took the clothing and the shoe from her arms. He dropped them onto the floor beside them. "Could I have your attention for just one moment, Miss House Maid?"

Meg sighed, blowing air through the wispy hair that had escaped her bone hair pins to fall over her forehead. She forced herself to look at him. "I'm avoiding the conversation," she said softly, "because I don't want to talk about it. I want to leave our relationship as it is. A good one."

He took her hand. "I'm offering to marry you. To care for you. To give our children a name. Marriage would only make our relationship better. Why must you be so obstinate?"

Unexpected tears welled in her eyes and she was unable to meet his gaze. "Because I'm afraid, Kincaid."

He was silent for a moment, then brought her hand to his lips. "And you think I'm not?"

She smiled, turning her head to look into his dark brown

eyes that at this moment were speckled with green. "I can't say yes right now. Give me some time. I want to marry you, I'm just scared. Scared my past will catch up with me and ruin everything. Let's wait a few weeks, a few months, and then we'll talk of it again."

Kincaid drew her into his arms, easing her head onto his shoulder. "I'm just petrified I'm going to lose you. I have to finish the list Meg, but when that matter is closed I'll be ready for a new life. I want to be certain you'll still be here when that time comes."

"I told you I wouldn't leave you without you knowing it, should I decide to go." She lifted up on her toes to kiss him. "And I can honestly tell you that with each passing day I'm more inclined to stay." She rubbed the tip of his nose with hers.

"And more inclined to marry me?"

There was a hasty knock on the open bedchamber door and Monti sauntered in, carrying a sheet of print in his hand.

"Thanks for the warning," Kincaid called sarcastically.

Monti ignored his remark. "Who's getting married? Ah, Meg, so you told our friend here our little secret? Can I have the banns cried for you and me today, my love?"

Meg wrinkled her nose, stepping out of Kincaid's embrace. "I couldn't bear to tell him he's been cuckolded. You'll have to break the sorrowful news to him yourself, my love." She blew Monti a kiss off her hand. Then she picked up the clothing Kincaid had dropped on the floor and went back to her task of straightening the room.

"She's turned me down again, Monti." Kincaid raised his hands lamely, only half joking.

"Tsk, tsk." Monti perched himself on the arm of a damask-covered chair near the cold hearth. "I apologize, my friend, we just didn't know how to tell you." Then he waved the piece of parchment he carried. "Look what I picked up at the 'Change this morning when I was buying myself a pair of new stockings."

"Did you find the stockings you were looking for?" Meg was making a separate pile for mending. The new laundry shop Saity opened would also repair clothing.

"Oh, a lovely magenta pair, to go with my salmon coat." Monti bent his wrist like one of the court dandies he imitated so well. "You know, the one with the silver garnitures."

Meg could only laugh at the thought of the horrific ensemble Monti was fashioning. "Will you wear it tonight to our supper?"

"Just for you, my love."

Kincaid groaned. "Enough prattle, you two." He took a seat in the chair beside Monti's. A small writing table separated them. "You barged into my private sleeping chamber for a reason, my friend?"

"Oh, yes." Monti handed the sheet of paper over.

"What is it? Another letter from the widow?" Meg stacked several dirty dishes that had come from a local cook shop. From the look of the green mold on them, she surmised they had to have been here for months. "I thought Augers had turned the tavern over to her, wine cellar and all."

Kincaid scanned the page. She heard him chuckle.

With a smile of curiosity, she came to him. "What is it?"

Kincaid glanced up. "James's latest satire. I had heard it was already circulating through the withdrawing rooms of the best households in Londontown."

She raised an eyebrow with interest. "Can I see it?"

"It's not very good, really."

"Not good? Bloody hell, you've a droll wit." Monti directed his next comment to Meg. "Buckingham's are nothing compared to the writings of Sir James. Everyone at Court says so. The duke is insanely jealous."

"Sir James?"

"That's how he signs his satires. Of course everyone knows it's James Kincaid."

Now Meg was truly intrigued. "Oh, let me see it." When Kincaid didn't offer the paper, she tried to grab it.

Kincaid held the satire just out of her reach. "If you don't care for it, my manhood will be crushed."

She laughed "Don't be silly. Monti's already crushed your manhood this morning by telling you we're secretly lovers." She grabbed for the paper again. "Now pass it here or I shall have to go to the 'Change and ask Buckingham for a copy myself."

Kincaid sighed, lowering the paper to his lap. "If I show it to you, will you show me one of yours? You told me you write, but I've not seen a splatter of ink yet."

Meg nibbled on her lower lip in indecision. She wanted to read what Kincaid had written. Her curiosity was overwhelming. But she wasn't sure how much of herself she was willing to give to him yet. And her writing was surely a part of her. "Oh, all right," she finally conceded. "But there'll be no jokes at the dining table tonight should you find my words shallow and poorly written."

He offered the satire and Meg snatched it from his hands, backing up for fear he would recapture it.

The moment she scanned the first few lines, her face lit up in a smile of pride. It was good, truly good.

She went to sit on the edge of the bed to read the rest of it. It was a short poem, only six stanzas, that spoke of the treatment of the poor by the rich. It made the ladies and gentlemen of the Court seem trite and without honor.

When she was done, she looked up at Kincaid. "This will certainly set some tongues wagging. You're practically naming some of the men from that list of yours."

"He always does," Monti commented, buffing his nails on his coat hem.

Kincaid shrugged. "Again, it can do no real harm. More foolishness."

Meg folded the sheet of parchment carefully. "It can make people think long and hard about their own lives." She got off the bed to come up behind Kincaid's chair and lower her hands to his shoulders. "And the writing is excellent. I mean that sincerely." She smiled down at him. "I'm impressed by your talent."

"All right. I shared mine." He shook a finger at her. "Now you have to share yours."

"Is that similar to the 'I'll show you mine if you show me yours' game? I was playing that game with a lady just the other night." Monti grinned.

Meg started to laugh. "I cannot believe how you two have corrupted me. Such bawdy talk never went on in my household, I'll warrant you that."

"Not even between you and your husband?" Kincaid's tone was light, but Meg could tell he was searching for understanding of her past. He was sly like that, gaining insight day by day, though not really knowing any particulars.

She gave a derisive snort. "Certainly not between my husband and me. I was his ward first, then his wife. He always treated me like his child. Now his brother," she went back to picking up Kincaid's discarded clothing, "he was a different sort." She shuddered at the thought of Percival. "He was always saying crude things under his breath to me, touching me under the dining table with my husband sitting beside me."

"And your husband allowed it?" Monti scoffed. "I'd have killed the bastard, brother or not."

Meg sighed. "My husband said it was my fault. That I encouraged it with my feminine wiles and I got what I deserved."

"Cur," Kincaid muttered, getting up from his chair, suddenly in a foul mood. "Every time I think about you living with that man," he flexed his fingers as if choking some invisible apparition, "I want to—"

"Kincaid, please don't start. What's done is done. Now let's talk about something cheerful. What shall I order from the cookshop for supper tonight? I want your friends to have a good time."

"Plenty of sack is all that's necessary with that bunch." Monti rose from his chair. "Well, I've business to attend to.

I'll see you tonight." He bowed formally to Meg. "Your servant, madame."

Meg blew him another kiss and Monti sauntered out of the room.

"You two have gotten to be very good friends," Kincaid observed when Monti was gone. He busied himself shuffling through some papers on the writing desk.

Meg placed a folded stocking in Kincaid's clothes press. "Does that disturb you? There's never been any impropriety. We just tease each other."

Kincaid turned from what he was doing. "No, sweetheart, it doesn't bother me. I'm glad to see you learn to trust someone else. Friendship is good for a man's soul . . . and a woman's."

She smiled. "I love you, Kincaid," she said, the stockings still in her hands.

"And I you, sweet. Now finish making your piles and we'll take them to Saity. Then we'll stop at an ordinary for a bit of bread and be back in time to meet the dressmaker with your new gown."

"Dressmaker?" She placed his stockings inside and closed the mahogany doors. "I called for no dressmaker."

"No. I did. I thought a woman needed a new gown for her first party."

She came across the room to wrap her arms around his neck and stare into his sparkling eyes. "And how did you get this gown fitted without my knowing? Did the dressmaker come in the night when I was stark naked and asleep in our bed?"

"No. I took the brown taffeta of yours to him. You'd remarked it fit well."

"So that's where that gown went. I thought Saity had taken it to mend the hem."

"Saity was in on it." He smirked, obviously pleased with himself.

Meg tipped back her head, her laughter light. "You are very clever, not only on paper, but in deed."

"Whatever makes you happy." He kissed her lips. "I mean that. I want what you want."

Meg kissed him again and laid her head on his shoulder. *How could my life have become so perfect?* she wondered. *Too perfect. My luck has to run out.*

Then she smiled at her own morose thoughts. *Heavens,* she mused, *now I sound like Monti.*

"What do you mean he's disappeared without a trace?" The Earl of Rutledge was seated at a small table, tackling an evening meal of blood sausage and pickled eel. "The boy has got to be here somewhere!"

Higgins stood inside the doorway of the earl's bedchamber out of striking distance of his master. "I mean I cannot find him, my lord. I've only been able to glean a few morsels of information."

Rutledge stabbed a succulent piece of eel and popped it into his mouth. "Go on."

The manservant cleared his throat of phlegm. "Your nephew was a mercenary like so many of the dullwits before the king returned. He was wounded when he was serving in the French army. He also did a stint on a privateer's vessel, raiding Parliament's shipping."

The earl tipped his wine glass. "The little pustule!"

Higgins folded his pale white hands patiently. "Then he simply disappeared. I can find no one who actually knows the Honorable James Randall, only of him. I don't know that he ever returned to London. Perhaps he was seized with pleurisy and died, my lord."

"More likely the clap." Rutledge poured himself another glass of Alicantes. "No. He's here. I can smell him. He's here in the city and so is she." He held out the empty wine bottle. "So find him. I'll find her, too."

"I've exhausted my sources, my—"

"Oh, shut up, Higgins, will you? Just stop your whining and follow my charge! Now take this bottle and bring me another."

Higgins snatched the empty wine bottle from his master's hand and backed out of the room. "Yes, my lord."

Rutledge gave an agitated sigh as the door shut. "Damned servants," he muttered.

The door opened again.

"Higgins!"

"A lady to see you, my lord . . ."

Rutledge looked up to see Higgins step aside and Mary Mummford come sailing into his bedchamber in a sea of pink and yellow rustling organza.

He rose from his chair, smiling. "Mary, my dear."

"Percy." She smacked her lips near his cheek.

"I apologize, but you've missed supper."

"Not dessert, I hope," she purred. Then she glanced over her shoulder. "Higgins, that will be all for tonight." She turned her back to Percival to allow him to remove her ermine-edged cloak.

"My lord?" Higgins questioned from the doorway.

"Do as you're told. And close the door. I don't wish to be disturbed again until morning."

"Then you do not want more wine, my lord?"

"Out!" the earl shouted, spraying the air and Higgins with spittle.

The bedchamber door closed and Percival tossed Mary's cloak onto a chair. He wiped his lips with a damask napkin from the table. "I wasn't expecting you tonight."

She toyed with the silk sash of his dressing robe. "I know, my love." She pouted. "But it's so difficult for me to get away. I come when I can."

"And no one saw you? Not from my household nor yours?"

She tossed her head of glossy black curls. "Of course not. Only that snake of yours, Higgins." She shuddered delicately.

"I don't know where you found him, Percy. The man's so repulsive, I vow he gives me the vapors."

"I'm glad you were not seen." Percival retrieved his wine glass from the table. He had intended to turn in early, thinking he had no real appetite for bedsport tonight, but now that Mary was here, perhaps he could rouse himself after all. He reached out and tweaked her breast. "How long can you stay?"

"Long enough to wear you out, old man." She batted her eyelashes, flitting away, leaving a trail of clothing behind her.

The earl stood back for a moment watching Mary disrobe, watching the way the firelight played off the pale skin of her naked buttocks, marred only by a few fading red lines.

He licked his dry lips, grasping the tie of his dressing gown to release it. "So what have you in mind, tonight, my pet?"

She dropped naked onto his bed, spreading her legs, caressing her mound of dark curls playfully. "Oh, I don't know. Something fun. Something different. I'm rather bored with last week's game."

Percival let his robe fall to the floor and immediately his member sprang up, already pulsing in anticipation of what he would do to her.

"Bored are we? Well, let's look in our little chest of toys and see what we can find, shall we?"

Mary rolled over in the silky sheets, laughing that laugh that had amused him at first, but now only annoyed him. "Surprise me, Percy."

Percival reached into the black metal trunk beneath his bed and extracted a pair of leather gloves and a coil of rope. "Oh, I shall, my little strumpet. I shall."

Sixteen

Meg hung onto Kincaid's arm as they wound their way through the street, down toward the river. It was a warm evening in April and it seemed that every man, woman, and child in London from lady or gentleman to beggar had come out to see the water pageant on the Thames. Again and again Meg was jostled by the crowd that seemed to move as one body and smelled of unwashed flesh, heavy perfume, and ale. The air hummed with voices and laughter.

Because weeks had passed since Meg had seen the Earl of Rutledge, she had grown less fearful of him and more willing to go out in public. By now he had certainly returned to Rutledge Castle. All the years she had known him, he had never spent more than a few days a year in London. By the time he came again next year, she and Kincaid would be long gone from the city and far from her brother-in-law's reach.

"So many people," she murmured from behind her vizard. "They make me nervous"

"First water pageant of the season," Kincaid replied, making his way down the center of the street. Because of his size, he was able to move easily through the jovial crowd. "Just hang on. I'll not let you be trampled."

She glanced up at him. Garbed as he was, in a black cloak and black felt hat pulled down low over his brow, he would be difficult to identify from any distance. "You sure it's safe to be out? I thought you wanted to lie low a few days." She lowered her voice. "You came so close to being caught on St. Alban's road."

"I'm safe enough. My face was covered, but for my eyes. I couldn't be identified."

"You were shot at, Kincaid," she whispered harshly. She touched the arm she had bandaged. It was naught but a powder burn, but the thought that it could have been far more serious frightened her. If he was caught again, there would be no second pardon. If he was caught, tried, and found guilty, he would be hanged at Tyburn as a thief.

"A spot of bad luck." He shrugged his broad shoulders. "I ran into a constable."

Meg kept a steady hand on her skirts to prevent them from being dragged in the animal dung and rotting refuse that typically littered the streets. "Bad luck? Not in the stars, you say?" She rolled her eyes. "That's Monti's nonsense. Perhaps he's right, perhaps you should begin checking with his astrologer before you step onto the highway."

He laughed. "Perhaps. And maybe I should find a unicorn horn to wear around my neck, as well."

She peered into his eyes, unsure of what he was really thinking. "Be honest, was it coincidence or had the constable been tipped off?"

"I'd like to think it was coincidence."

"But you're not sure?" When he made no reply, she tightened her grip on his arm. "Forget the rest of the list, or leave it behind for Monti. Let's just go, Kincaid. To America. You'll be safe in the colonies."

He shook his head. "I can't do that, Meg, not yet. I'm sorry." He glanced down at her. "But it won't be much longer, sweet, I swear. Look, there's the barge Monti rented. See it?" Kincaid pointed and waved, dropping the subject of his safety. "Everyone else is already aboard."

The Thames was ablaze with light as skiffs and barges floated down the river, illuminated by lanterns and torches.

The vessels were decorated with flower garlands and multitudes of brightly colored banners.

In the distance, behind her, Meg could hear the shouts of men and women who watched the pageant from balconies up and down the river.

"Thought we were going to have to shove off without you." Monti grinned, his nose bright red from the great quantity of liquor he'd already consumed. From behind him came the sound of a lute and the sweet voice of a young girl who sang a lively folk song.

"Good even', Monti." Meg smiled, offering her cheek to be kissed. She waved to one of his friends on the boat who was waving at her. "The street was so crowded."

He took her arm, helping her aboard. Kincaid climbed onto the barge behind her and the hired sailors pulled in the mooring lines.

"Happens every spring. The city simply goes mad." Monti pushed a jack of wine into Kincaid's hand. "Going to take off the disguise, Captain?" He grinned. "You're among friends now. It's truly not necessary."

After greeting several men and women on the barge, Meg and Kincaid settled on a settee beneath a curtained pavilion in the bow of the boat. Kincaid laid back on the chair and Meg nestled between his legs, resting her back against his chest. The barge floated out into the center of the river, joining the other vessels in the pageant.

For hours Meg and Kincaid laughed and talked with their friends. They sang songs, they played cards, they made bets on trivial matters. The wine flowed and there were platters of meats and breads to sup on.

As the evening grew later, Meg found herself withdrawing from the group, content to lay in Kincaid's arms and soak up his love. Each time he touched her hand, or gave her a sip of wine from his cup, she found herself growing more aroused. Though they were among two dozen others, she felt as if there was no one on the barge but the two of them.

Gooseflesh rose on the back of her neck as Kincaid casually laid his hand on the nape of her neck. "Want to go for a little walk, Meg?" he whispered in her ear. She recognized the husky sound of desire in his voice.

"I would." She pressed her mouth to his in a kiss meant to tempt him.

"Minx."

Meg climbed off the settee, and Kincaid rose behind her. "You make it rather difficult for a man to walk," he teased, shifting his legs.

"Where you going?" someone called to them as they left the covered pavilion through the swaying, transparent curtains.

"Just a little fresh air, Edward." Kincaid gave a wink and the others burst into bawdy laughter.

Meg elbowed Kincaid playfully as they walked away from the others, out of the lantern light. "Is it really necessary that you make it that obvious why we're coming out here?"

"Why are we coming out here?" he teased, slipping his arm around her waist. They walked toward the relative privacy of the stern of the barge. "For no reason but to draw a breath of fresh air and gaze at the stars."

Meg was just about to make a retort when a skyrocket shot from the far side of the river screamed into the sky. It exploded in a thousand twinkling lights, falling like stars from the heavens.

"Oh, did you see that?" Meg ran to the rail just as another rocket burst in the dark sky and fell hissing into the muddy water. "Aren't they beautiful?"

Soon streaks of yellow light criss-crossed the sky up and down the river. Men and women on the skiffs and barges clapped and shouted their approval. Lanterns dotted the dark shoreline as others gathered to watch from the edge of the city.

"It is beautiful." Kincaid came up behind Meg, wrapping his arms around her waist and resting his chin on her shoulder. "And so are you."

She turned her head, lifting her chin until their lips met.

"Mmmm, you taste good," she whispered. She turned in his arms, molding her body to his, stroking his buttocks with her hand as she pressed her mouth to his again. "I just can't get enough of you. What a miserable hussy I am."

He chuckled, his voice husky and warm in her ear. "Ah, sweetheart, you don't know what most men would give to have a woman like you love them."

Meg's gaze met Kincaid's in the darkness. "And I do love you," she whispered passionately.

"Then why not—"

"Hush." Meg silenced him with a searing kiss that left them both trembling with desire.

"Want to sit?" Kincaid asked when she finally broke the kiss. He indicated a lounge chair nestled against the curtained wall of the lighted pavilion.

Meg's heart was pounding. All evening as she had sat in Kincaid's lap she'd thought about what she would do with her man when she got him alone. "Can they see us?" she murmured, watching the silhouette of a couple dancing.

"No." He stroked the small of her back. "They're in the light, we're in the dark. We can see them, but they can't see us." His lips touched hers in a kiss of promise. "Come on, sweet, just sit with me a moment."

Meg listened to the others' laughter. They were singing and clapping now to a gay tune the lute sang. "I don't suppose anyone will come out."

Kincaid led her to the lounge chair where someone had piled some of the same transparent fabric that had been used to drape the walls of the pavilion. "Of course not." He kissed the pulse at her throat, settling on the chair, pulling her down with him.

Though Meg was hesitant, she put up no protest. It seemed that any sense of decorum she had once possessed was gone. She wanted to lie with Kincaid under the stars in the searing light of the skyrockets. She wanted to touch him and be touched. She could feel her loins burning for want of him. Her breasts ached for the weight of his hand.

Meg lay on her side in Kincaid's arms, half reclining. "All right, but I'm not going to take off my clothes," she warned softly.

"What kind of gentleman do you think I am?" His eyes twinkled merrily as he dangled one hand over her shoulder, his fingertips brushing the swell of her breasts.

"I know what kind of man you are—that's what concerns me."

"Ah, you are so beautiful, my Meg," he whispered as they lay on their sides facing each other. "Your smell." He nuzzled her neck and inhaled deeply. "The taste of you." He leaned forward and licked the pale flesh of her breast.

Meg moaned softly, threading her fingers through his silky hair that fell over his shoulder.

Kincaid slid his hand inside the bodice of her watered silk gown that was the color of violets. Meg held her breath in tingling anticipation. His mouth touched hers, their breath mingled. He took his delicious time in stroking her, his tongue darting out to tease her upper lip.

Meg could feel herself trembling all over as he began to knead her breasts. She moaned, her mouth twisting hungrily against his.

"Kincaid . . ." His name passed her lips, breathy. She tugged at the hem of his shirt beneath his coat, pulling it out from his breeches. Finally she was able to slip her hand beneath the linen and graze his bare, broad chest.

Kincaid kissed her again and again until she was breathless, until her head spun. All the while he was touching her . . .

Kincaid brushed the pad of his thumb against her nipple and she laughed softly, still in awe of the pleasure he could bring her. He knew her body so well.

When Kincaid unhooked the first few buttons of her gown, she watched him by the faint glowing light that came from the pavilion. Then, when he lowered his head to her breasts, her fingers wrapped around his neck, encouraging him, guiding him.

Shivers of pleasure rippled through her as he suckled first one taut nipple and then the other.

When Kincaid reached down to pull up the layers of her gown and petticoat skirts, she pulled at the silk with him. His fingertips brushed the creamy flesh of her inner thighs. Instinctively, she parted her legs slightly.

"Meg, Meg . . ." he whispered. "I'll love you forever . . ."

Hot, pulsing desire leapt in her veins as he brushed the dark curls at the apex of her thighs. She could already feel herself wet; she could smell the perfume of her own desire.

She took a shuddering breath as he delved deeper with his fingers. All conscious thought slipped from her mind. He was kissing her face now, her cheeks, her chin, the tip of her nose.

He rolled her onto her back and lowered his body over hers, straddling her with his knees. His hair fell in a curtain over her face and she lifted her head to kiss him on the mouth.

She knew she must have looked a sight with her bodice unbuttoned, her breasts bared, and her skirts hiked to her naked thighs, but she didn't care. All she cared about was the sound of Kincaid's voice, the touch of his hand.

Kincaid sat up, straddling her on his knees, his face looming over her. He stroked her calves, running his hand over her silk stockings. He touched her inner thighs, tracing invisible patterns with his index finger. She could feel the silky material that covered the chair under her buttocks, sensuous against her skin.

Meg kept her eyes open, watching him, reveling in the desire for her she saw plain on his face.

"Can I kiss you here?" he whispered, brushing his fingers over her woman's mound. His gaze never left hers. "Can I taste you?"

She reached up to stroke his cheek with her hand. "Touch me," she whispered, a hint of a smile on her lips "You know how . . ." Then her eyes drifted shut as he lowered his mouth over her.

With the first stroke of his tongue, Meg raised her hips off the chair. Her head reeled with the pleasure of his lovemaking. Kincaid gave of himself completely and freely and it was that thought that excited her as much as his touch.

Throbbing, incandescent heat radiated from her stomach. She could hear her own breath, ragged, as she called Kincaid's name. The excruciatingly sweet pleasure of his tongue was almost more than she could stand. Time slipped through her fingers like the silky sheets she lay upon.

"Kincaid," she finally panted, stopping him. "Make love to me."

He lifted his head from between her thighs. "I am, my dearest."

"No." She tugged on his shoulders, pulling him toward her and he rose until his body was parallel over hers again. "You know what I mean." She knew color suffused her cheeks. "I want you. I want to feel you . . . inside me."

Kincaid's lips brushed hers as he fumbled with the buttons of his breeches. He tasted of her . . . of her passion, of his own.

Meg felt the burning heat of Kincaid's rod against her bare thigh and instinctively she lifted her hips. She was so close to release . . . she could feel her muscles strung tight with pent up desire, demanding release.

Kincaid knelt between her legs and with one movement he took her. Meg cried out with pleasure, lifting in response to his hearty thrust.

Kincaid buried his face in her hair, his own ragged breath matching hers. Their movements were quick and hard. Suddenly this was no gentle lovemaking, it was sheer passion. It was hard, and hot, and sweaty.

Half sobbing, Meg clung to Kincaid, arching, crying out. The pinnacle of her pleasure hit her with such force that it made her dizzy. Somewhere in the back of her mind she heard

Kincaid groan, felt him thrust one last time to spill his seed into her.

Then he collapsed over her and she sighed, enjoying the feel of his body pressed fully against hers. Aftershocks of pleasure rippled through her body and she panted.

After a moment, Kincaid rolled off her onto his side. He pulled her against him to cradle her in his arms. He reached down and lifted some of the silky material of the chair over her exposed body. The sheer sheeting felt cool on her hot, prickly skin.

"I'm sorry, sweet. I didn't mean to get in such a hurry there at the end." He kissed her temple.

She looked up at him, her smile wide. "It was me as much as you. I swear I'll go straight to hell for my lust."

"Not for a man you love," he whispered, kissing her again.

She snuggled against his chest. "Not for a man who was my husband?" She didn't know where the thought came from, it just popped up out of nowhere.

Kincaid's gaze met and held hers. "Don't trifle with me, Meg. You'll break my heart."

She brushed her lips against his, intoxicated by the scent of him, of their lovemaking. "I've decided," she whispered, as surprised by the words coming out of her mouth as she knew he was. "I'll marry you, Kincaid. I'll be your wife."

There was a knock on the door to their apartment. Kincaid looked up from the table where he was studying a map of the American colonies. It was early afternoon and they were enjoying a quiet afternoon alone. "Meg? Door."

When she made no reply from the bedroom, he rose from the table still set up in the drawing room from a party two nights before.

The knock came again, this time impatiently.

"I'm coming!" he called. As he turned the corner, he stumbled on a new carpet Meg had recently laid in the entranceway.

He was certainly trying to appreciate her feminine touch in their home, but change was always hard for a man to get used to.

The banging came a third time.

"I'm coming, blast it!" At the door, he hesitated, his hand on the knob. Suddenly he had a bad feeling. "Who is it?"

"Message for the Honorable James Randall."

Seventeen

Kincaid knew he must have paled. He looked behind to be certain Meg wasn't there. He'd not heard that name in more than a decade. Suddenly spirits of the past rose out of the ground to wrap their wispy arms around his ankles. His hand trembled as he opened the door, feeling if he opened the gates to the underworld. "What the hell is it?" he demanded.

A short, ugly fellow with cold eyes stared up at Kincaid. He reminded Kincaid of an eel on a dinner plate with its cold, lifeless gaze. "James Randall?"

"What do you want with him?" Kincaid snarled. "Out with it, I'm a busy man."

The man fluttered his eyelashes. "I've been sent by the Earl of Rutledge to retrieve his nephew, the Honorable James Randall." The eel fingered the garlic amulet he wore around his neck. "Are you James?"

Kincaid rested his hand on the doorjamb for support, his mind numb. Suddenly he was short of breath. His uncle had sent for him after all these years? It could only be for one reason. His father . . .

Kincaid hung his head, the guilt, the shame, the pain of the past falling on his shoulders like a shroud. "I'm James," he said softly.

The eel smiled smugly. Then he bowed, sweeping his hat off his head. "Abner Higgins, your uncle's personal secretary. It is a pleasure to meet you after all these years, young James.

I have heard much about you." He dropped his cocked hat onto his head. "I shall wait in the coach."

Kincaid stepped back inside the apartment.

"Something wrong?"

He looked up to see Meg. His dear Meg. She was going to be his wife. He was going to start a new life with her. Children, a home. Why the hell did this have to happen now?

"I have to go somewhere," he snapped, not meaning to be harsh with her, but knowing it came out that way.

"Do you want me to come along?" She held her graceful hands together at her waist.

"No." He jerked his coat off the chair where he'd left it. She met him at the door to hand him his black cavalier's hat with the plum feather "I don't know how long I'll be. Don't wait up for me." He kissed her hastily, then was out the door.

Kincaid didn't know what news his uncle had that he would seek him out after all these years, but knowing his uncle, it couldn't be good.

Kincaid stood on the steps of his uncle's townhouse, fighting the constriction in his chest. He took a deep, cleansing breath, trying to slow his pounding heart. He felt like a boy again, summoned by his father. He was bitterly angry and at the same time, somewhere deep inside, frightened. He detested feeling like this. He detested his father and uncle for making him feel this way.

Taking another deep breath, Kincaid hit the door with his fist. He remembered this house from when he was a child. He had hated it as much as he hated Rutledge Castle.

The door swung open and there was Higgins. Kincaid thought it absurd that the man would drop him off at the front door, then run around to the back door so that he could let him in. But his actions were no odder than anyone else's in his uncle's household.

Higgins's thin lips tugged back in a patronizing smile.

"Come in, sir. Your uncle awaits you in the withdrawing room."

Kincaid handed over his hat, striding down the hall directly toward the room. The sooner he got in there, the sooner he could get out.

He entered the room without knocking. His uncle was standing near one of the windows gazing out into the garden, his back to the door.

"James."

That eerie voice. It would follow Kincaid to his grave. "My lord." He did not bow as was proper. He was no boy to be rapped across the palms with a rod for disrespect.

Rutledge turned slowly to face him. "Good to see you, dear nephew." He lifted a demi-glass to his lips, sipping an amber-colored liquor. "I have often wondered through the years how you were faring."

Kincaid reached behind him, closing the recessed, paneled door to give them some privacy. He wondered, though, why he bothered. No doubt the eel, Higgins, would be listening through the door, a glass cupped to his ear.

Kincaid cleared his throat. "That must be why you've contacted me so often, uh, *Lord Rutledge*." He stared into his uncle's ugly face, his distaste plain in his voice.

The earl sighed with agitated boredom. "Dear boy, after all these years, I cannot believe you are still so tight-fisted with your grudges. I thought you would have matured."

Kincaid stood stiffly, his hand aching to reach out and strike the man who had caused such terror in a young boy's life. "You and my father put me out of your house with good riddance and not a shilling to my name. You did not expect me to be angry?"

"I didn't expect you to still be so stubborn after so much time has passed," the earl snapped. "I expected you to return with at least some semblance of respect."

Kincaid tightened his hands at his sides into fists. "You sent word for me for a reason, I assume?"

"I've been looking for you for months." Rutledge set down his glass, pacing behind an overstuffed chair. "I couldn't find you. My manservant tells me it's because you have dropped your family name. And I must tell you, I was both hurt and shocked."

"Where is Father? Is he ill? Have his evil ways finally caught up with him?"

"Will you never learn to hold your tongue?" Rutledge drew back his disfigured lip in a half smile. "My brother, your father, is dead."

Kincaid knew he blanched. He had assumed his father was ill, perhaps even dying. He assumed that he had called him to reconcile their relationship before he passed. Naive as it might have been, it had not occurred to Kincaid that his father might be dead. Dead . . .

It took Kincaid a moment to recover. He looked up at his uncle, wishing he could wipe the delight off his face. He had always been a man who took pleasure in another person's pain. "How . . . how did he die? What illness?"

"Oh, there was no illness." Rutledge gave a laugh that lacked amusement. "Philip was quite healthy." His brown-eyed gaze met Kincaid's.

Kincaid recognized those eyes as the same ones he looked into each morning as he shaved. "Not ill? An accident, then?"

"Not an accident at all," the earl responded acidly. "It was quite cold and calculated."

"Sweet heaven, will you just come out with it and let me be gone from here?" Kincaid burst in anger. "How did my father die, damn you!"

"Oh, that temper of yours, nephew. Never could control it, could you?" Rutledge toyed with the keyboard of a spinet in the corner of the room, striking idle keys. "Murdered. Your dear father was murdered."

"Murdered?" Kincaid felt the breath rush out of him. Still he kept his place at the door. "By whom? Someone he cheated out of their property? Or perhaps one of the cottars? One of those that he charged such an exorbitant rent that their children had starved?"

Rutledge's head snapped up. "How dare you speak of your deceased father in that manner!"

Kincaid's gaze met his uncle's, cold and unyielding. *"How* did he die?"

"Stabbed." The earl went back to striking the keys on the spinet, the single notes as disturbing as his voice. "Bled to death," *ting,* "on his own bedchamber floor," *ting.* "Murdered," *ting,* "by his beloved bride." *Ting.*

Kincaid looked away, his stomach ill. "His wife murdered him? Anne?" He shook his head in disbelief, remembering his father's second wife. Anne had been painfully shy. She had been frightened of the Rutledge men, even of him.

"Not Anne," the earl spat, sending droplets of spittle falling onto the ivory keys. "That simpering bitch's been dead for years. *Margaret.* The little strumpet, Margaret."

Kincaid's brow furrowed. The name sounded familiar, but he'd tried so damned hard to wipe the past from his memory that the recollection was hazy. "Father remarried again?"

"Of course he did. After Anne died . . . in childbirth." Rutledge struck two keys at once, "he married Margaret Hannibal."

Suddenly the image of a thin blond-haired girl with a sad face came to mind. "Little Margaret? The orphaned child Father took in?"

"Not a child any longer." Bored with the spinet, the earl wandered away, dropping into a chair. He crossed his legs. "I can tell you from firsthand experience, she had rounded out nicely."

Kincaid looked away in disgust. His uncle had always lusted after his father's wives. One would have to have been blind not to notice it. Eventually Kincaid had come to the conclusion that his father simply hadn't cared.

Kincaid stared at the polished hardwood floor at his feet.

He couldn't believe it. His father was dead . . . "How long ago? When did he die?"

"January."

January? All these months Kincaid had thought he was alive, alive to still hate, and here the bastard had been dead. It was just like his father to rob him of that little pleasure. "Why, why did she do it?" He stared at his uncle's face not really seeing the deformity.

"Gone mad, I suppose. She gave birth to a dead, deformed child and she simply snapped. It was a bloody, brutal mess," he finished, seeming to take pleasure in the gruesome description. "Philip was hacked to death."

Kincaid turned on his heels. "Thank you for bothering to find me." Suddenly he couldn't breathe. The withdrawing room smelled of dust and old furniture and faintly of peppermint. It was making him physically ill. He had to get out before he embarrassed himself by vomiting. He reached for the door.

"James, there will business to attend to. Papers to sign."

Kincaid glanced over his shoulder at his uncle, his hand on the open door. "Papers?"

"Your inheritance."

Again Kincaid was jarred. He turned back around. *"Inheritance?"*

"Of course. You are his only living heir. There's money. The title. You are now quite wealthy, nephew, no thanks to your own doing."

"But I thought . . . I thought that when he put me out, he disinherited me. He said he was going to disinherit me."

The earl rose and came toward Kincaid, putting out an arm to comfort him. "He was angry, yes, but he didn't disinherit you. You were his son."

Kincaid stepped back out of his uncle's reach, the brush of his fingertips burning like acid on his shoulder. His uncle's awkward attempt at being kind was as distasteful as his outright hostility, perhaps more so.

"So he never disinherited me?"

"You are his legal heir, the new Viscount of Surrey." Rutledge let his hand fall, staring into Kincaid's face. "Of course it was one of our father's lesser titles, but—"

"He left me as his heir?"

"There was no one else. And now you're mine, as well I'm afraid, nephew."

Kincaid began to back out of the room. This was all too much to think about. Too much to consider. The bastard, he had gone and died on him! He'd left his money and futtering title to him and then got himself murdered?

Kincaid stumbled backwards, then whirled around, heading for the door. His anger was choking him, sucking him into some black void. If he didn't get some air . . .

"James, come back," the earl called after him. "We've matters to discuss."

Kincaid barreled down the hallway, concentrating on the front door. "Go to hell," he shouted, throwing open the door.

"Sir, your hat," came Higgin's voice from behind.

Kincaid stepped out into the late afternoon sunshine, slamming the door behind him. Though his uncle's coach still waited to return him to his apartment, he passed the vehicle, crossed the street, and headed for the nearest ordinary.

He needed a drink.

Percival reclined on the bolster, tucking his arm behind his head. Mary lay panting beside him, her lips still wet from his seed. "You were late again, tonight." He reached for a glass of rich burgundy on the table beside the bed. "I don't like it when you're late, Mary."

She rolled onto her side, propping herself up on one elbow. She was still deliciously naked, the sheet draped over the curve of her hips. She stroked her own breast casually. "I told you, I come when I can. I made no promises, Percy."

He reached out and pinched one nipple just the way she

liked. "You come when I say you come. To this house . . . to my bed."

She rolled her kohl-lined eyes, slapping his hand away. "You can't tell me what to do. I started this. I come when I please." She stroked her dainty fingers between her damp thighs. "Without need of your permission."

Percival sipped his burgundy. He was not in the mood for Mary's impertinence. Not tonight. Not after his visit with that turd of a nephew of his. Christ, he'd forgotten how handsome his brother's child was. How tall and muscular. How well he carried himself.

He'd forgotten how much he hated him.

"Don't push me tonight, Mary." Percival finished the glass and reached for the bottle to pour himself another. "I'm not in the mood to be gracious."

"Well, screw you." She got up from the bed, licking her fingers that had just rested between her thighs. "I don't have to put up with this!"

"Get back in bed." He pointed. "I'm not finished with you. You know the punishment for disrespect."

She dropped her shift over her head, covering her pert breasts with their dark nipples still long and hard. "I'm not afraid of you! This was my game. Not yours."

He smiled, wondering if she realized how dangerous her words were. But then his smile drew back into a threatening frown. "Get into bed, Mary. I'll not tell you again."

She yanked her busk off a chair and slipped it on, lacing the ribbons with jerky movements. "I'm tired of this and I'm tired of you!"

Percival sighed. "You're treading in dangerous waters, my love. Get back into bed and hush that pretty mouth of yours before I lose my temper."

She stepped into her petticoat and fastened it at the waistband behind her. "You want to know why I was late?" She dropped her pink and yellow organza gown over her head. "I was late because I took another lover. Couldn't you smell him on me?"

Percival felt his heart flutter. He wouldn't give her up. It was too good, having a partner who volunteered her services. One that wasn't forced or paid. And their likes were so similar. They were perfect together. He wouldn't let her go. It was out of the question. His anger flared. "Shut up, shut up, you stupid little bitch." He got up, slipping into his silk robe.

"Bitch, am I?" She slipped her tiny feet into her yellow silk slippers, foregoing the stockings. Her gown was still unbuttoned down the back. "Bitch? Maybe so," she spat, her dark curls bouncing as she spoke. "But at least I'm not ugly. Not a freak! Freak!"

Percival reached out and slapped her hard across the face, so hard that she stumbled, catching herself on a chair before she went down. "Get back into my bed, now," he ordered.

"You disgust me, do you know that?" She was backing up toward the bedchamber door, her stockings in her hand. "You've always disgusted me. I just did this," she indicated the bed, "because I wanted to defy my father. Because I was bored." Her hand rested on the doorknob. "Well, now I'm bored with you, you sick bastard!"

"Don't leave!" Percival shouted, sending his spittle flying in the air. "Don't you leave me or you'll be sorry, you little cunt!"

Mary made an obscene gesture and walked out the door.

Kincaid tipped back the leather jack of ale and downed half of it in one long drink. Dropping the jack onto the table, he wiped the foam from his mouth with the back of his hand. His fingers were numb. He was drunk. But not drunk enough to forget.

"Another," he shouted to anyone who would listen.

He was in a seedy tavern down by the river. He wasn't quite clear on how he'd gotten there. He could smell the

Thames's stench through the window where the glass had been broken and never replaced. The floor of the tavern was dirt, the crude tables rough-hewn slabs of wood thrown over barrels. The food was maggot-ridden, the ale watered down. He didn't know why the hell he'd come here except to escape.

"Ye called for another?" The barmaid, with her bleached hair and smeared lip pomade, sauntered toward him. Her smock was streaked with dirt and stained yellow at the armpits. Her face and the full breasts that hung over her bodice were marred with deep smallpox scars. She might have been pretty once, but a hard life and the disease had taken its toll.

He eyed her impatiently. "That's what I said, didn't I?"

She grabbed a pewter pitcher off the tray she balanced in one hand and poured a portion of ale into his jack, running it over the side. As she poured, she drew close enough for him to smell the perspiration of another man's body on hers.

"Anything else, sweet lips?" She lifted a thick eyebrow suggestively. "We've a room for sportin' above, if ye be wantin' my services."

"Just the ale." He flipped her a coin. "Keep your clap to yourself."

"Well, ain't you Mr. High and Mighty." She dropped the coin between her breasts and moved on to the next table.

Kincaid lifted the jack to his lips. They were numb, too. He knew he should go home. Home to Meg. But he didn't want her to see him like this. Maybe he wouldn't ever go home.

"Bastard," he muttered under his breath. "How could you die on me?" He ran his hands through his disheveled hair. He'd lost his hat somewhere.

How could his father have up and died without him knowing it? Murdered no less. Kincaid had never gotten a chance to say good-bye. To say he was sorry . . . Hell, who was he kidding? Sorry for nothing.

His father had always been a rotten bastard. Never once in his life had he had a kind word or gesture for his only son.

All Kincaid recalled of his childhood was fear . . . fear and an intense desire to please his father. As a child he had always thought it was his fault his father didn't care about him. *Bad boy. Stupid child. Clumsy oaf.*

His mother had told him it wasn't his fault. He remembered her cuddling him, kissing his bruises, results of his father's heavy hand. He closed his eyes, vaguely remembering her face. His mother had smelled so good.

Then she had died. Died giving birth to another one of his father's freaks. It was the Rutledge curse.

Kincaid took another drink of the ale, welcoming the spinning sensation that was settling in his head. He didn't want to think about this. Not any of it. Seeing his uncle and his deformity dredged up questions he'd long ago suppressed. What if he carried the curse? What if his father had passed that along in his blood? Would he sire no children but those with deformities? Not that he feared he couldn't love a child who was in some way imperfect. The question was, could he do that to Meg?

Sweet God in heaven, had his father given him nothing good?

Kincaid rested his forehead on the heel of his hand. His uncle said Kincaid's father had left him his portion of the Rutledge fortune. So he *had* cared for him, in his own way . . . hadn't he?

"So why didn't you find me while you were still alive?" he questioned aloud, taking another drink. *"Futtering bastard."*

"You talkin' to me, boy?"

Kincaid looked up to see a burly seaman with a tarred pigtail staring into his face. He was a big man, no taller than Kincaid, but he had to outweigh him by two stones.

"I said, you talkin' to me?" The sailor struck his fist on the table, tipping it slightly.

Kincaid's eyes narrowed dangerously. He could feel his blood rushing. "Could be, *sister.*"

The sailor suddenly swung his fist at Kincaid, but Kincaid saw it coming. With one swift movement, Kincaid knocked the tabletop upward, sending the jack of ale and the whole board sliding onto the refuse-covered dirt floor.

Kincaid's first swing caught the sailor square in the jaw, sending him reeling backward. Before the man had picked himself up off the floor, Kincaid was on top of him, pummeling his face.

The sailor caught Kincaid by the back of his coat, tearing the dove-gray damask as he lifted him up with one beefy arm, his biceps bulging.

Kincaid fell backwards onto the dirt floor, striking his head on the edge of a table as he went down.

"Son of a whoring bitch!" the sailor accused, hurling himself through the air, landing on Kincaid's chest. "You talk to me thata way? I'll crush you, pretty boy! I'll crush you, grind your bones, and serve you in meat pudding!"

The sailor's fist hit Kincaid's nose so hard that his head snapped back. Blood spewed down his white linen shirt and on the sailor's striped red and white shirt, as well.

"Shit-eating cur," Kincaid shouted, grabbing the sailor's sticky, tarred pigtail. "You got my shirt dirty. My fiancé's gonna kill me, so I'm gonna kill you first!"

"Fiancé, hah!" The sailor threw back his head in laughter. "Whore, you mean. Prick-sucking whore!"

"Don't you call my woman a whore!" Kincaid flew into a rage, charging him. "Now I *am* going to kill you!"

They fell to the dirt-packed floor of the dimly lit tavern, locked arm in arm. Over and over they rolled. Swing after swing, fist meeting flesh. Kincaid was now blind with fury. No one would call his Meg a whore and live to tell the tale!

Somehow both men managed to separate and stumble to their feet again. A crowd of tavern patrons had gathered around them, sloshing back ale and making bets on the outcome of the fight. One enterprising barmaid took a place at the door, allowing men to come in off the street to see the fight for half a shilling each.

The sailor charged Kincaid with a chair and Kincaid barely sidestepped being skewered against the wall. He tore his coat off, pushing back his bloody sleeves. "Come on, come on!" he encouraged. "Take me if you can, *sister,* cause you're going down!"

The sailor bellowed like a bull and charged with the chair again. This time Kincaid caught one of the rungs and swung him full around, sending him crashing into a table set with playing cards. The cards went flying into the air and the four men who had been seated at the table made a hasty retreat over several overturned chairs.

The sailor caught Kincaid by one arm and swung him around, ramming him into the wall and butting him with his head. Kincaid grabbed him by his tarred tail, practically jerking his head off his shoulders, and sank his fist into his soft gut.

The sailor went reeling backward and the crowd cheered. More coins were changing hands and Kincaid ran his hand over his face, wiping away the sweat and blood that blinded him. "Come on *sister!* Go another round?" he baited.

Someone caught the sailor by his shoulders and shoved him forward, straight for Kincaid. Kincaid was just drawing his fist back when the sound of a shot from a blunderbuss exploded in the air. The sound of a lead ball from the pistol whizzing past his head shocked him back into reality.

What the hell was he doing here down by the waterfront in a tavern full of crooks and thieves? What was he doing drunk, fighting a man that could easily kill him?

"Enough," called an ugly, squat man from where he stood on a table near the back of the room. "Enough fightin', men. Ye want to fight, ye take it into the street where you won't be wreckin' my fine establishment."

Before Kincaid knew what was happening, two burly men appeared at his side and half-carried him, half-dragged him across the tavern floor and shoved him out the door. Right behind him came the sailor and the two landed in a heap in the stinking gutter.

Kincaid's head swam. There wasn't enough ale or fists to take away the pain he felt in his heart.

"Hey, you all right?" The sailor sat up, giving Kincaid a boot in the hip. "Souse, you still livin'?"

Kincaid just lay there in the gutter that smelled of shit, panting, wishing he could just forget about his father. Wishing desperately that a part of him didn't still want the bastard to love him.

Eighteen

"Where do you think he could be?" At the sound of a coach halting below, Meg raced to the window to draw back the curtain and stare down into the dark London street. Each time she did it, she hoped Kincaid would materialize. The door of the hired hackney swung open and a middle-aged man and woman appeared. Meg let the chintz curtain slip from her fingers with disappointment.

"You don't think he went out without telling us? As Captain Scarlet, I mean."

Monti stood in the shadows of the doorway watching her. "I know it's not like him not to tell one of us where he's going." He glanced up. "But I'm sure he's all right, Meg."

She sat down in a chair, wrapping her flannel nightrobe tighter around herself, hugging herself for comfort as much as for warmth. "He was very agitated when he left. A coach took him away, a private coach, but I didn't see the shield on the door. I don't know who it was."

"You didn't ask where he was going?"

"He was in one of those black moods of his. I didn't dare."

Monti came to lean on the back of the chair behind her. "Oh, you know our captain. He probably just lost track of time. He's playing cards somewhere, tipping an ale."

"He said he wouldn't go out on a mission without telling me. He promised."

Monti rested his hand on her shoulder. "Meg, he's all right."

She stood, pushing a lock of hair off her shoulder. "It's after midnight." She began to pace. "Something's got to be wrong. He's been picked up by the soldiers. Caught."

Just then Meg heard the turn of a key in the front door. She had heard no carriage on the street, so whoever it was had to have come on foot.

She hurried out of the withdrawing room with Monti directly behind her. Before she reached the front hall, she heard the door swing open and a crash, followed by the sounds of shattering glass.

"Kincaid?" She ran down the hallway in the darkness of the unlit entryway. "Kincaid, is that you?"

She immediately recognized his silhouette laid out on the hall carpet. She went down on her knees beside his crumpled body. The table next to the door had been overturned and a Chinese vase he'd purchased for her was shattered on the hardwood floor.

Panic rose in Meg's chest. Had he been shot? Run through with a sword?

"Kincaid!" She tried to sound calm. "Kincaid are you all right?"

But the moment she raised his head off the floor, she detected the heavy odor of liquor on his breath and clothing, among a myriad of other ill smells. "Kincaid, damn you Are you dead or just drunk?"

Monti squatted on the floor beside her and helped her roll him over onto his back. He ran to get a lamp and returned to the front hallway. Meg was just pushing the front door shut when he appeared with the light.

"You can check him over, but I don't see any injuries," she spit with an irritated wave of her hand. "I think he just passed out."

Monti righted the small table and set the oil lamp on it. He quickly scanned Kincaid's body while Meg stood over him, her arms folded against her chest.

"Nope." Monti ran his hands the length of Kincaid's prostrate body. "He's not hurt. No broken bones. No wounds." He pulled a handkerchief from his sleeve and waved it over Kincaid. "But God's bowels, he stinks."

Meg set her jaw. "Wake him up."

Monti chuckled. "Don't know that I can. Don't believe I've seen him this drunk since Paris."

Meg pushed Kincaid's ribs with the toe of her wool slipper. "Kincaid!" she snapped. "Wake up!"

Kincaid groaned and tried to roll onto his side, but Monti stopped him with the heel of his lavender slipper.

"C'mon old boy. Wake up. The mistress isn't terribly pleased with you, so I suggest you come to." He slapped his cheeks lightly, rolling his head back and forth.

Kincaid muttered something under his breath about tripping on the damned carpet. His eyelids fluttered.

"There we go, friend."

Kincaid opened his eyes staring up at Monti. "God's s . . . steeth," he slurred. "You're an ugly . . . sight to see."

Monti glanced at Meg. "See, he's not hurt."

She walked around so that she faced Kincaid as Monti helped him to sit up. "Where the blast have you been?" she demanded. "I thought you were dead. I thought you were run through on some highway outside of London."

Kincaid blinked slowly. "M . . . Meg, l . . . love."

"Don't you Meg Love me," she spat, so angry she could have slapped him. "Where did you go? Why didn't you send a message that you were all right? You've been gone nearly ten hours!"

Kincaid lurched to his feet with Monti's aid. "L . . . lost track of . . . t . . . time."

He swayed toward her and she took a step back. "You stink like a chamber pot!"

He glanced at the floor covered with broken shards of colored glass. "B . . . broke your vase, M . . . Meg."

"Oh, shut up." She glanced at Monti. "I guess you can lead him to our bedchamber. There'll be no getting anything out of him tonight." She shooed them both. "But I want those clothes off him! He won't sleep in my bed stinking of a sewer."

Monti chuckled his way down the hallway, leading Kincaid. "My friend, you're in deep refuse this time," he murmured. "I warrant you I won't be here come morning and you wake."

Meg passed them on the hallway headed for the bedroom. "Leave his clothes in the hall."

She went into the chamber, fully lit with candles, and began to put away her quill and ink and the paper she had splattered with ink smudges attempting to write while she waited on Kincaid.

Her heart was pounding. He had scared her, scared her to death. She felt like their time together was running out. She felt like he wasn't going to live long enough to see that last name crossed off his list.

Outside the door in the hallway she could hear Monti as he attempted to help Kincaid disrobe. Kincaid was putting up a mighty protest, but Monti seemed to be getting the better of him.

Meg was furious that Kincaid could have frightened her like this. Yet, she was immensely relieved. He was all right. He hadn't been shot, or arrested. He'd just had too much to drink.

But what had set him off? What had the man in the carriage said? Where had he taken him? In the time Meg had known Kincaid she had never seen him drunk. What had happened that made him go out and consume so much ale that he couldn't walk.

Meg looked up to see Monti, a full head shorter than Kincaid, stumble through the door, half carrying Kincaid, stark naked. She strode across the room, tossing back the counterpane. Helping Monti get him to the bedside, she gave Kincaid one hard shove and he fell into the bed with a groan.

Meg jerked the counterpane over him. He lay on his stomach on the tester just as he fell with his arms thrown out and his legs askew.

"Sleep well, my love," she muttered, covering his shoulders. "Because you've got a hell of a lot of explaining to do come morning."

Meg looked up from her chair where she sat reading a book. Kincaid was just beginning to stir. It was nearly noon.

He groaned, covering his face with his hands.

Meg closed her book and set it down beside her. She took her time walking to a table to retrieve a pot of coffee she'd kept warm for him since her breakfast at seven.

"Still among the living, my love?" Her sarcasm was thick.

He closed his eyes. "Hell, what stinks?"

She poured him a mug of thick, strong-smelling brew. "You."

Slowly he sat up to lean against the headboard, accepting her offering. He squinted in the sunlight that poured through the open windows. "I feel like my head is going to crack open."

She sat down on the edge of the bed. "I feel like I could crack it open myself."

He took a sip of the coffee, looking at her, then back at the coffee. "You were worried about me. I guess I should have sent a message I was all right."

"Kincaid, I thought you'd gone out on a mission. I thought you'd been arrested. Shot. I—"

He tried to take her hand, but she pulled it back. He took another drink of the coffee, focusing on her face. "I apologize. It was just—"

"Just what? I heard you speaking to someone in the hallway. Then suddenly you have to leave. You go without telling me where or how long you'll be and then you just don't come back. I thought maybe you were being interrogated, tortured."

He exhaled, running his fingers through his hair. "I need a bath."

"I'll call for one." She continued to look at him, waiting for an explanation.

He exhaled. "Oh, hell, Meg. I don't have an excuse but to say I was a little out of my head last night. I wasn't thinking clearly." He rubbed his temples with his thumb and forefinger. "You won't believe what's happened."

The distress in his voice made her realize something really was wrong. Suddenly she forgot about herself and her own worries. Her anger fell away. "Tell me."

He handed her the cup. "More coffee."

She poured another cup and pushed it into his hands. "Who was that man I heard you speaking with?"

"My uncle's manservant."

She blinked. "You have a living uncle?"

He looked away from her toward the window. "I didn't tell you because I was ashamed of him. Ashamed to be related to him."

"You're not responsible for the actions of others." She folded her arms over her chest. "You've told me that more than once." She waited for him to go on and when he didn't, she prodded him a little. "So it was your uncle who sent for you?"

He nodded, still staring out the window, obviously avoiding eye contact with her. "He wanted to tell me my father's dead."

Meg's response would have been to say that she didn't know his father had still been alive. But that had been part of their agreement from the beginning, hadn't it? It had all been her idea. He was supposed to keep his secrets, she was to keep hers.

"I'm so sorry," she said softly.

"Don't be." He wiped his mouth with the back of his hand. "He was a bastard. Same as my uncle."

Meg kept her voice soft, realizing that his words, the thoughts that were in his head, were painful to him. And she didn't want to hurt him. No matter how angry she was with him, it distressed her to see him in pain. "To you?"

"To anyone. Everyone. He was a futtering non-discriminatory bastard!"

She stared at the counterpane, surprised that the man she loved could have such hate for another. "How did he die?"

"Murdered. Some bitch murdered him."

Meg felt her chest tighten. Most of the time she was able to suppress any memories of her past, of her life before she woke up in Newgate with Kincaid at her side. But suddenly she saw Philip on the floor. She felt the knife in her hand. She swallowed against the emotions that bubbled up inside her. "W . . . why? Why did she kill him?" She hoped he didn't hear the strangeness in her voice.

"I don't know. My uncle didn't really know. Something about a dead baby."

Meg knew she must have paled three shades. Her instinct told her something was terribly wrong here. Something she could feel, but couldn't touch. Something she could sense, but couldn't see. Her heart beat erratically. "A . . . a *baby?*"

"His wife killed him, Meg." He turned his gaze toward her, reaching for her hand. She could have sworn she saw tears in his eyes. "Murdered my father! And then she ran."

Meg could barely breathe. Suddenly she knew who Kincaid was. It was some horrible, unbelievable coincidence, but she knew it even before she asked the question. "Tell me the truth. Your name isn't James Kincaid, is it?"

"No." He didn't seem to noticed how frightened she suddenly was. "When I came back to London after the king's crown was restored, I dropped my last name because I didn't wanted to be associated with my father or his family."

Meg heard his words as he went on with his confession, but they sounded as if they came from far away. She didn't need to ask him what his name really was. She already knew. James K. Randall. The Honorable James Randall. Her husband's long lost son . . .

Nineteen

Meg knew she was trembling; she only prayed that Kincaid, wrapped up in his own emotions, wouldn't notice. Her heart was pounding in her ears. She felt like she was falling . . . falling into a black hole, blacker than hell.

She stood up, trying to act casual, and moved away from the bed. Kincaid was still talking.

". . . I know that. I know I should just be able to walk away, Meg. Take his inheritance and say good riddance to the bastard." His tormented gaze followed her. "But he was my father. *My father.* I have to find her. I have to find the woman who did this and see that she pays for her crime." He ran his fingers through his hair, pushing it over the crown of his head. "Am I making any sense at all, sweetheart?"

Meg rested her hand on the back of a chair to steady herself. "You. . you said he was a bastard. That . . . that he was cruel to you."

"He was." Kincaid stared at his hands in his lap.

She wished she could catch her breath. "So . . . what if he deserved to die?"

"No man deserves to be brutally murdered!"

And what of a babe? her heart cried. *Did my son deserve to die because he was less than perfect?* Her stomach twisted in agonizing knots. "Could it have been self-defense?" she asked softly.

"Of course not," Kincaid scoffed. "My father was a bastard,

but he certainly wouldn't have tried to kill Margaret. She grew up in our house! He loved her."

Hearing Kincaid speak her name, the name of the woman she had once been, sent a chill down her spine. It was almost more than Meg could bear. How had everything that had been so right between her and Kincaid turned out so wrong so quickly. "So you'll avenge your father's death, even though you hated him. Why?"

He groaned. She knew it was difficult for him to express his true feelings. To reveal his emotions to her. But she had to know. Why was he doing this? Why was he doing this to her?

After a long moment of silence, he spoke, his voice stark in the sunny room that suddenly seemed chilled. "I guess a part of me still wants him to love me," he said softly, shrugging.

Meg picked up one of Kincaid's discarded shirts and began to busy herself folding it. She had to do something with her hands to stop their shaking. "You can't make a dead man love you, Kincaid."

"I know this is difficult for you to understand." He threw his bare feet over the side of the bed, holding his hand to his forehead again. "But it's something I have to do. I'd never feel right taking his money and title, money you and I can use to buy that land, without at least attempting to find the cold bitch who did this to him. Do you understand?"

She dropped the shirt into a small basket she'd been collecting soiled clothing in to take to Saity. It wasn't even dirty. "I understand," she said softly, feeling numb from head to foot.

She took a deep breath, trying to sound matter-of-fact. She had to get out of the room before she suffocated. "I . . . I'll have Amanda bring in the bathing tub and hot water so you can bathe." She picked up a pair of his discarded stockings and dropped those into the laundry basket as well. "Then . . . then I have to go out for a while."

He slipped into his dressing robe. "You're leaving?"

She started toward the door with the laundry basket, fearing that if he drew too close, if he touched her, she would shatter. "I . . . I'll be back later."

He caught her at the doorway, wrapping his fingers around her arm. "Meg, I said I was sorry about last night. I know I scared you and I didn't mean to. I also know this is a lot to foist on you. I should have told you about my father, about the whole futtering family of freaks, but I . . ." He sighed, looking away.

Meg's heart was breaking . . . for Kincaid, for herself. For their love that she knew now could never last.

"I . . . I guess I was afraid you wouldn't love me if you knew," he went on, caressing her back. "He always said no one would ever love me. He said I wasn't worthy."

Meg didn't say anything. She couldn't. She just turned on her toes and kissed him. Then she left.

Meg rested her head in her arms on the battered table piled with folded laundry. After fleeing their apartment, she had taken the new, painted green carriage Kincaid had just bought her, to seek Saity's advice. The whore-turned-laundress was the only female friend Meg had.

"Holy bones, Meg." Saity shook her head, glancing out the window of the tiny shop she'd rented on the fringes of White-friars slums. "A sadder tale, I ain't never heard." She dipped a man's linen shirt in a pot of hot water and reached for a bar of laundry soap.

"I'm so sorry to burden you with my terrible secret." Tears ran down Meg's flushed cheeks. "But I didn't know where else to turn."

"There, there, now." Saity patted her shoulder with a wet, soapy hand. "A burden like that'en can be a terrible one for a woman to carry. I'm glad ye told me." She winked. "And I'm glad ye killed the bastard, too."

Meg lifted her head from her arms. "Why did this have to happen?" she cried miserably. "We were in love. Kincaid was going to marry me, Saity. He said we would have children. He wanted my sons and daughters." She closed her eyes. "I miss my baby so much. And I know I can't replace him, but I wanted another so badly."

Saity pushed back a lock of her blonde hair. She went on scrubbing the shirt. "He says he loves ye and you believe him?"

Meg nodded. "I honestly think he loves me."

Saity began to wring out the shirt, moving it to the rinsing tub. "So tell 'im you killed his father. Then go off and have your happy life with the old bastard's coin."

Meg hugged herself for comfort. "I can't do it." She shook her head. "I just can't, Saity."

"Why not?" She lifted the shirt from the tub, watching the water run off it in rivulets.

"Because he'd hate me, and I couldn't stand that."

"If he loves you and he hated his father, how could he blame ye?"

"He won't believe me. His uncle said I did it in cold blood. He said my baby was already dead. Kincaid will believe his uncle. The earl is a very powerful man, Saity."

"You don't know yer man won't believe you. Ye got to trust that love ye have between you."

Meg pushed away from the table, getting up off the stool. "He's had this thing with his father all these years. His father kicked him out of the house and said he was going to disinherit him, only he didn't. Kincaid feels like he owes Philip. Even if he is dead."

Saity wrung out the shirt and laid it over a line strung across the room. "You're right about one thing for certain. Men are funny about their fathers. Their fathers kick 'em around for twenty years, callin' 'em no good bastards, and a man loves his father anyway. It don't make no sense to me. But you're right, you definitely got a problem, Meg."

Meg paced the uneven floorboards of the tiny shop that smelled of lye soap and wet wood. "Besides, I couldn't hurt Kincaid by telling him I was the one who murdered his father. It would break his heart."

"Self-defense ain't murder."

"I couldn't tell him I was responsible." She balled a fist. "I won't hurt him like that after all he's done for me." She looked up at her friend. "He saved my life. He made me realize I wanted to live. I just can't do this to him," she finished softly.

Saity reached for a pair of soiled stockings. "Well, the only other thing you can do is run," she finally said sadly. "You ran from the earl, so run from Kincaid."

"That's all I can think of, too," Meg conceded.

"You know where you can go?"

Meg looked out the large window, watching a boy and his father go by, pushing a two-wheeled cart filled with sheaths of wheat. "I was thinking of going to the colonies."

Saity wrinkled her pretty face. "Where?"

"The American colonies."

Saity's eyes grew wide. "With all them redskins?"

"I always wanted to go there. They say it's a land of rebirth. A place where a man or a woman can start all over again."

"You'd do that? You'd get on one of them little ships and go across the world?"

Meg watched the wheat cart roll down the muddy street. "I would."

"Braver soul than me." Saity wrung out one of the pink men's stockings.

"Oh, nonsense, Saity, you're brave. It was brave of you to leave Mother Godwin's and strike out on your own."

"Ah, I'd never 'ave done it without you and Kincaid."

"Nonsense. You're a bright, strong woman. You knew there was a better life for you out here."

Saity waved a hand, obviously embarrassed by Meg's words. "We ain't talkin' about me right now. We're talkin' about you." She tossed the stockings over the clothesline. "I still think you ought to risk it and tell your man." She took a deep, thoughtful breath. "But if you won't do that, you're gonna have to have a plan. Ye just can't stand here and declare you're goin' to America."

"You're right." Meg paced. "I do need a plan."

"Ye got to have money. Ye got to find a ship and book yer passage. They don't just leave from London to America every day of the week."

Meg twisted her hands. "I don't have any money."

"So take some of Kincaid's."

Meg looked up. "I couldn't do that. That would be wrong."

Saity batted her eyelashes. "They ain't gonna take you for free, girl. Though I can't figure why they'd charge ye to starve ye on a ship and leave ye with a bunch of red savages."

"I'll have to find out when the next ship is going. And the cost. Maybe I can make a few coins gambling. I'm not bad with the dice."

"Good idea. Then you could just give your man back his money, and he'd never be the wiser."

Meg leaned on the back of a rickety chair. "Oh, Saity. This wasn't what I thought was going to happen. After Kincaid rescued me, after we fell in love, I thought everything was going to be all right." She hung her head. "I was such a fool."

"You weren't no fool." Saity pinched Meg's arm. "Ye took what the good Lord handed you. And you'll take what 'e gives you now." She reached for another soiled shirt. "You'll be all right, Meg. You come too far not to."

Meg looked up at Saity, dressed in her ragged clothes, damp with soap and water, and smiled. "You're a good friend, Saity. Thank you."

"Thank you, for all you done to put me here. Now, you leave it to me to find out about a ship."

"And what should I do in the meantime?"

"Ye go home to your man and ye love 'im until the last hour ye got with him, that's what you do. 'Cause a man like Kincaid don't come often to a woman." Saity sank the shirt into the water bucket. "They just ain't out there, I'll vow to that."

Meg glanced out the window again. She ached for what she and Kincaid would have now, and she had to smile. Their time had been short together, but what Saity had said was right. Most women never knew the love Meg had shared with Kincaid. And for that she had to be thankful.

Meg stepped out of the coach onto Drury Lane with Kincaid and Monti on either side of her, taking her arms.

"Blast it, the play has already started," Monti complained. "My astrologer warned me it would be a day of delays."

Meg laughed. "Oh, it's all right if we're a little late. You don't go the playhouse to see the performance anyway." She tapped her fan on his shoulder. "You go to flirt and you well know it."

Kincaid laughed, ushering her across the street toward the entrance to the king's playhouse. There were dirty-faced beggars everywhere, putting out their hands, pleading for food or money. Kincaid pitched a few coins to them, parting the crowd to make way for Meg. "She's got you, Monti. She knows you better than you know yourself."

Monti only sighed, smoothing the ribbon of his purple and yellow coat with the matching high heels. His cocked hat was yellow with a ridiculously large purple feather protruding from the back. His purple clocked stocking, sewn with the initials C R for Charles Rex, were tied with yellow bows.

Once inside the playhouse, Kincaid led Meg upstairs to the balcony where he had rented a box. Meg had been to a play several times before, but was still fascinated by the bawdy excitement. The return of King Charles had not only opened the playhouse doors once again, but women were actually playing parts. It was the scandal of the city.

The moment Meg was in her chair, she leaned over the rail to look down into the pit where the benches were filled with handsomely dressed men and women. She had been shocked the first time Kincaid had explained that the overly painted women were whores, openly selling their wares. But now that she had gotten used to the fact, it was just one more element of the playhouse that fascinated her.

The play was already in progress, though the audience seemed to be more interested in themselves and those around them than in the performance. It was a light comedy where men and women danced in bright costumes singing merry songs. Pretty young Orange Girls down in the pit walked about with their tin boxes, selling fresh fruit and sweet cakes, getting nearly as much attention as the players on stage.

In the balconies above and below her, Meg could hear men and women laughing and calling to each other. They came not to see the play but to talk and flirt. To gossip. Overall, the playhouse was loud and ill-smelling, but Meg delighted in the excitement.

Kincaid sat beside her holding her hand, and though he had seemed preoccupied since his visit with his uncle a few days ago, he was obviously pleased that she was enjoying herself.

Meg's heart twisted in her chest each time she thought of all the things she and Kincaid would never do again. And each moment she shared with him, she couldn't help wondering, *is this the last time?* The last time to tickle his feet, the last time to share wine from the same glass, the last time they would make love on the floor before a blazing fire? But she made herself enjoy each moment to the fullest. Now she was aware of every word that he spoke, every caresses of his hand. If they were not going to live out their lives together as Meg had hoped, at least she would have these memories.

Meg was chatting with Monti about one of the women in the next box over when Kincaid leaned to speak. "Did you see who that was that just entered Lady Sutter's box, Monti?" He indicated with a nod.

Monti scanned the seats three boxes over. "Gads, is that Horatio?"

Kincaid was already getting out of his upholstered chair. "Indeed it is and I'll bet he can give me information on old Crocket." He squeezed Meg's hand. "I'll be right back. Horatio had been helpful in the past. Then he ran into a bit of trouble with a man's daughter and had to lie low in the country for a few months. Will you be all right here with Monti?"

"Of course." She gave him her best smile. "Go and see to your business. But remember, you promised me supper at the Red Crow. Don't go anywhere without me or you'll risk my wrath."

Kincaid leaned over her shoulder to brush his lips against hers. "You know I only live for you, my sweet," he whispered.

Meg exhaled softly, enjoying the feel of his lips against hers.

"Be right back." Then Kincaid was gone.

Meg settled in her seat to try and see if she could follow what was happening in the play. Monti was now busy talking to two young women, blonde twins in the box directly to his right. From where Meg sat, it appeared he had a good chance at escorting one, or perhaps both of them, from the playhouse to supper.

Meg listened to a song sang by one of the lead actresses, amused by her little dance. As Meg watched, her gaze strayed to a box to the far left of theirs, nearly across the playhouse. She was admiring a woman's floral, forest-green gown, when she suddenly realized she recognized the man entering the box just behind her.

Meg's breath caught in her throat. "Sweet heavens," she whispered. It was him. *Rutledge.*

Before she could look away, he made eye contact with her. Unlike that night in the tavern, he recognized her this time. She saw it in his eyes. Eyes she realized now were the same color as Kincaid's. The difference was, in Kincaid's eyes she had only ever seen kindness. Rutledge's were pure evil.

For a moment Meg was stunned that she couldn't move. She couldn't lower her lashes. She couldn't look away. She didn't know what had come over her. It was as if she was daring him.

The earl stood there at the rail of the box for what seemed an eternity, openly staring, openly accusing. Once he glanced at Monti, then back at her.

At least he had not seen Kincaid. He didn't know she was there with him.

Rutledge held her gaze a moment longer, then bolted for the door of his box.

Meg jumped up at the same instant. "Monti, help me," she ordered, snatching his hand from one of the twins'. "I'm ill. I have to get to the coach."

Monti rose from his chair, apologizing to the young woman. But Meg didn't wait for him. She was already at the door, the skirts of her grass-green sarcenet gown bunched in her fists.

It would be a race to the playhouse doors.

Twenty

"You're ill? *You don't run like an ill woman!*" Monti hurried to catch up with Meg in the narrow hallway that now thronged with gaily clad men and women. The playhouse exploded with applause as the final curtain dropped. The sound was deafening. He grabbed for her elbow. "Slow down, Meg."

Meg took Monti's arm, still rushing. They had reached the staircase and she was pushing her way through the crowd, down the stairs. "I have to get out of here, Monti," she murmured desperately. "You have to help me."

"What, someone's looking for you?" Monti glanced over his shoulder. "Who is it? Not that husband of yours? Because if it is, I shall just have to run him through with my—"

"He's dead," she hissed between her teeth. "My husband is dead and buried, God rot his bloody soul. I've told you that, I've told you both a hundred times. Why won't you believe me?"

"We just thought maybe that was why you didn't want to wed our highwayman," he answered under his breath. "Not that Kincaid cares if you're married or not at this point."

At the bottom of the steps, Meg elbowed a woman in an orange taffeta dress. "So sorry." She pushed through the crowd, pressing toward the door where she knew outside the coach and driver would be waiting. "Excuse us. Pardon."

Monti held tightly to Meg's elbow, remaining at her side. When a tall woman with an elaborate coiffure turned to make a rude comment, Monti stuck his tongue out at her. "Christ's bones," he muttered. "That woman should have checked her charts before she left her bed this morning."

Reaching the double doors that were held open by men dressed in royal livery, Meg stepped out into the twilight. "Where's the blasted coach?" She hurried along the street lined with coaches, both hired and private.

"Meg."

"It's got to be here somewhere. Kincaid told the driver to wait."

"Meg."

"That's why we pay him the two pound six a year for, right? To be at our beck?"

"Meg," Monti whispered in her ear. "Are we running from the ugly fellow with the misshapen mouth?"

Meg was too scared to turn around to see. She knew it was the earl of Rutledge. Who else could he have been referring to?

"What if we are?" she snapped. "Oh, thank the sweet lord. There it is!" She ran across the filthy street toward their newly painted green coach on the far side.

"Oh, it matters not to me," Monti panted from the exertion of the run in his high heels. "It's only that I like to be able to spot the enemy from across a room." He took a quick look over his shoulder again. "And that cuttlefish certainly isn't hard to spot, is he?"

When their driver saw Meg running for the coach, he started down off the bench to assist her, but she beat him to the door. "Drive on!" she ordered.

"But, Mistress, Mr. Kincaid—"

"I said, drive on, Axle! You can return for Mr. Kincaid later!"

Meg leaped into the coach without assistance, with Monti right behind her.

"Drive on!" he shouted as he slammed the door.

As the coach rolled away, Meg glanced out the window to

see the earl running beside the carriage. He reached with his fist to hit the door.

"Faster," Meg shouted, banging the paneled ceiling with her fan. "Faster, Axle!"

The two horses increased their speed and the coach went careening around the corner, leaving the earl behind in a spattering of mud and dung from the street.

The Earl of Rutledge halted on the street, clutching his chest as he attempted to catch his breath. There was an odd aching that trickled from his breast down his left arm. "Bitch," he muttered, wiping the spittle from his mouth. "I knew I'd find you, Margaret. I just knew it."

"Sir, are you all right?"

Percival heard a familiar voice behind him. It sounded like his dear brother Philip, but of course Philip was dead. That perfect little slut had murdered him. Percival turned, the ache in his arm easing. "James."

"Sir, are you all right?" His nephew hesitated to offer his hand as if he found the thought of touching his own uncle repulsive.

"I'm all right. There's my coach." Percival pointed to the vehicle with the Randall coat of arms painted on its door.

"Let me escort you." James walked beside Percival.

"You'll not believe this, nephew." Percival straightened his back, the pain gone. "I saw her! She's here. Right here in the city just as I suspected all along, the clever tart."

Her? My father's wife?"

The earl's footman opened the coach door for him. "Your father's *widow.*"

James stood on the street putting his head through the doorway. "Where did she go?" He looked down the street now congested with theatergoers and their vehicles.

"I don't know." Percival sat down on the leather bench,

still puffing. "Will you join me? Friends and I are going to the Plump Partridge to dine."

His nephew hesitated, glancing over his shoulder. "I came with someone, though where she is right now, I'm unsure."

"A woman?" The earl smiled. "Don't tell me you've finally found a woman to settle with? Are you married, nephew? I didn't get a chance to ask when last we met."

"Not yet. Soon." He turned back to Percival. "It looks as if my coach is gone. I don't know what could have become of her."

"You know women. Fickle." The earl patted the seat beside him. "Come, James, dine with me and we'll discuss the little witch, Margaret. Now that I know she's here, we must make our plans to find her."

"Rutledge!" a strong voice called from the street. "Gads, why did you run off? Chasing another whore?" Lord Roberts nodded to James as he climbed into the coach, followed by Albert Marlin.

The two men had come to the play with the earl. Percival didn't particularly like the men. They were both loud and obnoxious, but they owned ships he was interested in purchasing.

"Gentlemen, my nephew I've told you so much about," Percival introduced. "James Randall, Viscount of Surrey, since he has inherited."

"Lord Surrey."

"Lord Surrey."

Both men paid their respects as they seated themselves inside the coach.

James stared at the crowd of men and women still pouring from the theater doors. "I just don't know what became of her. A friend said he saw her and another leaving our box." He stroked his handsome chin. Percival had always envied his nephew's fine-lined jaw. "Now she and the coach and the friend are gone."

"Cuckolded, perhaps, James?"

He laughed. "I think not."

"So dine with us, or at least let me carry you somewhere." The earl tapped the leather seat again. It was odd how he hated this man, the perfect son that Percival knew he would never have. He hated James for his handsome looks and goodness of his heart, but he also loved him. That same part of him that hated perfection, also desperately loved it.

With a sigh James stepped up into the carriage. The footman shut the door and in a moment they were bouncing down Drury Lane.

"I appreciate your giving me a ride, sir, but I can't sup with you. Could you possibly take me home to Charing Cross? I fear my Meg might be ill."

Rutledge sighed. He'd much rather have spent the evening conversing with his nephew than the simpletons sitting across from him. "Very well." He pushed open a small window to his left. "Charing Cross," he shouted to the driver.

"Yes, my lord."

The earl settled himself back on the seat, smoothing his coat. The pain in his chest frightened him. This was the second time he had experienced it in the last week. Was this yet another curse of the Randall blood, a weak heart? His father had died of a heart ailment.

"Hang it." The earl sighed. "I utterly forgot Lady Ashford. Wasn't she with you, gentlemen?" He directed his question to the two fops seated across from him.

Marlin fiddled with the ruffles of his silk sleeve. "She went with Carlos and Abney. Good riddance, I say. I've had a taste of that piece and I must admit she's as dry as a French Merlot."

Rutledge chuckled.

"Say, heard the latest gossip?" Roberts asked. He opened a woman's fan he must have confiscated at the theater. It was all the mode among the fops these days to carry a lady's fan.

"I seriously doubt my nephew is interested in filthy Court gossip," the earl commented.

"Oh, this is too good." Roberts fluttered the fan with his hands that were as delicate as any woman's.

"Do tell," Marlin insisted, patting Roberts on the knee.

Percival watched his nephew glance out the window smiling politely.

"I swear if men spent less time gossiping and more time taking action," James said, "I doubt this country would be in the state of disrepair that it is."

"Well." Sir Robert fluttered his fan, making the golden yellow curls of his periwig bounce. "Do any of you know the Baron Mummford?"

"Oh, I know him," Marlin chimed in. "Wonderful parties."

"A rotund man?" The earl nodded with disinterest. "I'm acquainted with him."

"Well," Roberts drawled, "the baron is quite disturbed, for it seems that his darling virgin daughter is missing."

"Virgin, indeed." Marlin gave an indignant snort. "Had a piece of that, as well."

"Do you know her, sir?" Lord Roberts directed his question to the earl. "Pretty little strumpet with inky-black hair and a pert mouth made to be crushed by a man's lips."

Percival removed his hat, tossing it onto the seat. He hadn't expected the conversation to turn to Mary Mummford. "Met her at the baron's last supper, I think. You remember that one, don't you? The one where Lord Cassidy caught his wife upstairs with his friend Acres?"

Lord Robert grinned. "I remember it well."

Percival lifted one shoulder, having no desire to discuss Mary Mummford with these men or anyone else for that matter. " 'Twas my only acquaintance with her." Then he looked out the window, relieved to recognize the street. "Ah, here we are James, Charing Cross."

The coach rolled to a halt and Percival felt the coach shift as the footman leaped off the back and ran around to let James out.

"Thank you so for the hospitality, your lordship." James backed out of the carriage, bowing stiffly.

Percival stared at his manicured hands. "James . . . James let's not be so formal, you and I." He glanced up hesitantly.

James hung on the coach door. "It was the way you said you wanted it."

The coolness in his voice stung Percival. Would no one ever care for him, just a little? "That was a long time ago, James." He fiddled with his thumbnail, surprised by his own emotions. "I'd like it if you called me Uncle."

James looked away. "Could we talk about this another time? More privately?"

Percival wished his nephew would look him in the eyes. He wished he would show just a little compassion for a man who was growing older, a man that perhaps had made some mistakes in his lifetime.

Percival patted his lips with his handkerchief. "Of course, James. Why not call on me this week and we'll discuss the matter of Margaret."

"Thank you again for the ride." James nodded to the two fops. "Gentlemen."

"Good even' to you, Surrey."

"Evening, Lord Surrey. Hope you find your woman," Marlin finished with a hint of a snicker.

James closed the door with a slam and then settled down in his seat again, wishing he had a drink. He could see it was going to be a long evening, entertaining these two simpletons.

"Feeling better, darling?" Kincaid stretched out on their bed and stroked Meg's temple.

Meg let her eyes drift shut, savoring the feel of his loving touch. It was so unfair, all of this. When her grandmother had left Meg in Philip's care, when she was dying, it had been the understanding that when she came of age she would marry Lord Surrey's eldest son. His son James. Grandmother had arranged the match made in heaven. But then James was sent away when she was still a child, secluded in another part of the castle, and Philip had taken her for his own wife.

Meg rolled onto her side, throwing one arm over Kincaid's hips. She still couldn't believe that she had once lived in the same home with Kincaid and not recognized him. Of course she had just been a child then, and he a young man not yet fully developed. And Meg had not been permitted to dine with the family, but rather ate in the kitchen with her nursemaid. Kincaid . . . *James* . . . had mostly been at school. Meg had only admired him from afar. From the top of the castle wall, she remembered watching him ride away that last time, off into the mists of the morning, an outcast. Philip had been in a rage for weeks after that even though he had been the one who had ordered his son from his house never to return.

"You certain you don't want me to call a physician?"

Meg looked into Kincaid's eyes, her memories fading away. "I'm fine, really." She smiled. Sweet heavens, she loved this man. "It was just hot at the theater."

"I'm sorry you missed the supper I'd promised you."

She snuggled up against him. "That's all right. It could be nice to stay home this evening. Monti's gone out and we have the house to ourselves."

He lifted her unpinned hair, brushing the nape of her neck with his fingertips. "I already gave the servants the night off. We could chase each other naked through the house."

She giggled. She really did feel better. Since Kincaid had arrived home and Rutledge hadn't shown up on their doorstep, she was much better. Still, time pressed her from all sides now. Seeing the earl, having him see her, made her realize she and Kincaid had very little time left together.

"We could take a bath together," she suggested wickedly. When he lowered his mouth to hers, she brushed his lower lip with the tip of her tongue.

"A bath, indeed." He flattened his tongue and licked her cheek.

Meg giggled, trying to roll away from him. She was dressed only in her shift. When he had arrived home, just after she and Monti, and realized something was wrong, he had immediately assumed she was sick. She allowed the assumption. Kincaid had ordered her straight to bed, bringing her tea himself. Then Monti had gone out for the night, whispering to Meg that she had some explaining to do later. Now Meg and Kincaid were just lounging in their bed, enjoying being together.

Kincaid tickled her and she burst into another fit of giggles. "Stop!"

"You said yourself you're not sick any longer." He tickled her again.

"I'm not." She pushed him away with her bare feet. "But you know I hate to be tickled." She grabbed one of the pillows by its linen cover and whacked him playfully in the head.

Kincaid fell back, feigning he'd been hit much harder than he had.

Meg burst into laughter as she rolled onto her knees and hit him again.

Kincaid grabbed another pillow and hit her back.

Squealing with laughter, she hit once and, before he lifted his head, she hit him again.

Now both of them were laughing wildly as they crawled across the bed hitting each other again and again, Meg trying to stay an arm's length away from him. Somehow in the tussle she lost the case of her pillow. She kept hitting him, sometimes ducking his swings, other times catching a pillow in the head or across her shoulder

Winding up, Meg hit Kincaid hard across the back and the seam of the pillow burst. Suddenly the air beneath the bed's canopy was filled with small, white goose feathers. Meg cried out with delight as she watched the feathers fall like a first snow.

"Now look what you've done!" Kincaid declared, tossing his own pillow aside.

"Look what I've done," she echoed, delighted by the soft feathers that floated down around her. "Can you believe there would be so many?"

As the feathers floated down they brushed her arms, her cheeks, her legs left bare by her shift now tangled around her waist. Each feather that touched her felt like the caress of a butterfly's wings. Meg caught the feathers with her hands and tossed them into the air in handfuls, oohing and ahing with the delight of a child.

Kincaid caught a feather between his thumb and forefinger and rolled it between them in fascination. Then he reached out to brush the feather across her chin.

Meg giggled. "That tickles."

He brushed the feather at the valley between her breasts. "And that?"

She still giggled, but her voice was huskier this time. "It tickles, but it feels good."

He picked up another feather so that now he had two. With each hand he brushed her bare thighs.

Meg sighed with pleasure.

"Hmmmm," he whispered. "We may have stumbled upon something interesting, my love."

Meg closed her eyes as he brushed her collarbone, the pulse of her throat, with the feathers. Suddenly her skin was tingling with delight, with anticipation of his next move.

Meg sat on her knees, perfectly still, facing Kincaid as he continued his delightful assault.

Kincaid brushed her earlobes, her lips, her eyelids. The first time he kissed her, her eyes flew open in surprise. She brought her fingers to her lips where he had just touched them.

He smiled. "No, no, close your eyes, my love. You have to guess. The feather . . ." he brushed her bare shoulder with a feather, "or me." He then brought his mouth close to the same spot so that she could sense, more than feel, the heat of his breath, the graze of his lips.

Meg closed her eyes with a sigh that resembled a moan of

pleasure. He was surrounded by feathers still. They were in her lap, piled in the bed around her bare legs, caught in her hair, stuck to her shift. With her eyes closed it was like floating on a cloud with her lover.

"You are so clever," she whispered.

"Shhhhhh."

He brushed a feather . . . or was it his lips across her cheek?

Meg sighed again and again as Kincaid teased her flesh with the feathers, his mouth, his tongue until her senses soared. He didn't touch her breast or the private place between her thighs except through the linen of her shift, and yet she felt as if her flesh was on fire. Every nerve ending tingled. She was lightheaded, her mind as light as the feathers that still brushed against her.

When Kincaid finally took her in his arms and laid her gently on the bed of feathers, Meg wrapped her arms around his neck, craving the taste of his mouth. Their breath mingled. She kissed him again and again, caressing the muscular plane of his back and bare shoulders, not knowing when his shirt had come off. Had she removed it or he?

"Meg, Meg," Kincaid whispered. With a broad palm, he stroked the length of her body, following the curves of her breasts, her hips, her thighs. As they moved on the bed the feathers rose and fell in their fluffy cloud.

Meg rolled Kincaid over, pressing her body against his, his back into the soft bedding. She laughed, watching him through heavy-lidded eyes, drunk with her passion for him.

She pulled off his breeches, his stockings, and then straddled him. She watched him watch her remove her shift. Feathers stuck to her here and there where her body was damp with want of him.

Then Meg flattened her body over his, pressing her hips to his hips, her breasts to the flat plane of his broad chest. She felt his manhood hard and pulsing against her damp thigh and marveled at the thought that no matter how many times they made love, he still desired her.

It would be so hard to leave. A tear slipped from Meg's eyes, down her cheek, and fell on his chest.

"What is it, love?" Kincaid asked. The light of the flickering candle beside the bed cast eerie shadows across his face. She could see the brown of his eyes, speckled with green.

"Nothing," she whispered, wiping the place on his chest where her tear had fallen. "Only that I'm so happy."

"Women are strange creatures," he answered after a thoughtful moment. "But I'd not have you any other way, my sweet Meg."

Meg leaned over him and kissed his mouth, her tumbling hair falling in a curtain around his face. "Make love to me," she whispered desperately, her gaze locked with his. "As if it were the last time."

"There will never be the last time," he answered, rolling over, taking her with him until it was she who laid in the bed of feathers with him on top.

Meg reached up with both hands, her gaze never straying from his face. How handsome he was with his angled cheekbones and wisps of hair just beginning to gray. Their hands met and their fingers interlocked.

Meg was still staring into his dark eyes when he raised his hips and sank his shaft deep inside her. She closed her eyes, moaning, reveling in the feel of him and the brush of the goose down feathers that still rose and fell with every breath, every movement.

Soon Meg was lost to the ancient rhythm that joined two lovers as one. Again and again she raised her hips to meet his thrusts, crying out with ecstasy, sinking her blunt nails into the flesh of his shoulders.

She twisted beneath him in the agony of her pleasure. The rapid rise and fall of her breath matched his as he lifted her higher and higher on the bed of feather clouds.

Meg heard herself cry out. She felt her muscles contract

and then release. She felt that burst of ultimate joy. But Kincaid continued to move, to thrust.

His fingers tangled in her hair as he dug his knees deeper into the mattress. Meg gasped for breath, her body still trembling from the last orgasm, struggling to reach the next. Seconds later she cried out again, this time her entire body convulsing with the pleasure of his thrust.

Kincaid groaned, rising and falling one last time before his body was still.

For a moment Meg could do nothing but fight to catch her breath. She was lightheaded, her body still trembling with the aftershocks of their lovemaking.

With a moan Kincaid slipped off her damp body, falling onto his back. Feathers fluttered upwards, floating down to rest across his bare body, the crisp hair of his groin now spent. "Sweet mother of God, I believe you've done it this time, Meg. I'll be the butt of every satire come next week. Man dies from making love . . ."

Meg heard her own laughter in her ears as she rolled onto her side to rest her head on Kincaid's shoulder. "I like the feathers," she whispered in his ear. "Could we try it again?"

He lifted his head only a hand's length and then let it fall as if too exhausted to hold it up. "Now?"

She dissolved into a fit of husky laughter. "All right. I'll get you some wine and a bit of bread to fortify you. But I won't be cheated. The evening is yet young." She pressed her lips to his in the kiss of a lover that was also a wife.

If only this night could last forever.

Twenty-one

Meg walked along the street, her arm linked through Kincaid's, her vizard carefully in place to shield her identity. She certainly didn't expect to see the Earl of Rutledge in Whitefriars, one of the slums of the city, but there was no room for error. She knew her life was at stake. If Rutledge caught her, she was dead. No one would be able to save her, not even her beloved.

"This really isn't necessary," Meg said, looking up at Kincaid. "I can get to Saity's on my own."

He shrugged, nodding causally to someone who passed them on the congested street. "I feel better escorting you, so let me do it. The close calls are coming too close for my comfort these days. I think we all need to be cautious."

Of course Meg knew what he was talking about. The robberies. The closer Kincaid came to finishing off the list of offenders, the more dangerous the hold-ups were becoming. Meg smiled, enjoying the feel of the sun on her face. "No one could recognize me in this." She touched the black vizard that concealed her features. Then she leaned to whisper, "And who would recognize you without your swath of red tied around your face, Captain Scarlet?"

He grinned. "Go ahead, tease the captain. Soon he'll be gone from your life, never to be seen again."

"Not even in my bed?" she teased, her eyes sparkling with mischief. Of course she knew her time with Kincaid was nearly done. She knew the evenings of fun and games were over, too, but it was nice to think about them, to dream, to pretend they were going to last forever.

"Well, he may call upon a certain lady in her bedchamber on occasion." He winked.

Meg giggled behind the mask. *Sweet heavens, how she loved the man. How would she live without him?*

They had just turned the corner onto the street where Saity ran her laundry, when Meg spotted a woman with a baby. The woman, lost in conversation with another woman, was standing in front of a cook shop, the baby attached to one brown teat.

A lump suddenly rose in Meg's throat. The baby looked just like her little John. True, the infant's mouth was not misshapen, but it was the same dark head of hair, the same roundness of his cheeks.

Meg stopped in the middle of the street to stare at the baby. He was so perfect. Her John had been so perfect . . . well, nearly so.

A tear trickled down Meg's cheek. Most of the time she could keep herself from thinking of her baby, gone to heaven. She just didn't think about him. Usually she could look at an infant and not feel the ache in her arms for the child she would never hold again. The aches felt so strongly now. For some reason this baby brought all the memories tumbling back. It brought the pain . . .

"Meg," came Kincaid's gentle voice. "You all right?"

She couldn't answer him. All she could do was stare at the baby. She knew it was wrong to covet what belonged to another, but she wanted that little baby. She wanted him for her own.

At that moment she realized how desperately she wanted another child—Kincaid's. Secretly she wanted to be pregnant. She wanted to take a part of him with her when she went. So what if there was a stigma attached to giving birth unwed? She'd lie. She'd tell the settlers in the colonies that her husband the carpenter, the jeweler, the pickle man, had died. What would they know living so far from England?

"Meg . . ." Then Kincaid looked in the same direction she was looking and saw the baby. He wrapped his arms around her trembling shoulders and gave her a hug. "We'll have children," he whispered against her cheek. Then he kissed her temple. "I promise."

Meg took a deep, shuddering breath. What a miracle that would be, she thought. Mentally she counted the days since her last flux. It was too early to be sure, but the possibility was there. If only God would give her Kincaid's child.

She started down the street again, forcing herself to look away from the baby, to return him in her mind back to the bosom of his mother. That wasn't her baby. It never would be. Her son was buried, in the churchyard, she hoped.

"I'm all right," she told Kincaid, breathing evenly, making herself think of other things. "It just makes me sad sometimes."

He took her hand, squeezing it. "I know this has been hard for you. Newgate and Mother Godwin's. The list. The matter of my father's death. His property and title. But when it's settled, we'll go away from it all."

Kincaid's father. Now here was something she needed to be worrying about. Philip, the bastard. He had ruined her life once, and now he was ruining it again. She couldn't protect herself from the pain, but she could protect Kincaid. She would, no matter what the cost.

"There's Saity now!" Meg forced herself to smile, lifting a hand to wave.

Saity was standing on the edge of the street pouring a wooden tub of dirty water into the open sewer that ran the length of the street she lived on. Saity spotted them and waved, dragging the tub back up her front stoop. "Meg."

"Saity!" Meg let go of Kincaid's hand and left him behind. "I was hoping you would be here."

Saity stood on the top step, wiping her forehead with the

corner of her damp, soapy apron. She was looking good these days, not so haggard. Though she obviously worked long, hard hours, she appeared happy to Meg.

"And where else would I be but here wringin' out stockins?" Saity asked, lightly.

"I don't know. Having tea with the king?"

Saity threw her head back in laughter. "Maybe you, but not me." She lifted her skirt and bobbed a curtsy. She was always a little shy around Kincaid. "Afternoon, sir."

He swept off his hat, presenting his leg as if she were the Queen Mother, Henrietta Maria. "Madame . . ."

Saity fluttered her apron, blushing. "You rogue, you!"

Kincaid returned his hat to his head. "I'll return shortly," he told Meg. He was already starting back down the street. "Stay put until I come back for you, and don't talk to masked strangers." Then he blew her a kiss.

Meg could only smile as she returned the kiss and stood there on the step watching his back until he disappeared into the crowded street.

"A woman couldn't ask for a better man," Meg sighed.

Saity stood on the step beside her, watching Kincaid go. "Indeed, a woman couldn't." She eyed Meg. "That mean you're reconsiderin'?"

"No." Meg stepped into the shop with Saity behind her. She dropped her vizard on the table her friend used to fold clean, dry clothing. "I won't reconsider. I can't hurt him any more than that bastard Philip has already hurt him."

Saity dropped the washtub on the floor and began to fill it with buckets of water she'd already brought in through the rear of the shop. "Well, if your mind is made up, I won't stand in your way." She watched the water pour from her bucket into the tub. "I'll even help ye. But I want you to know it's 'cause you're my friend, not 'cause I agree with it."

Meg removed her cloak made of a pale blue, lightweight damask. Kincaid had brought it home for her only this week. It bothered her to take such expensive gifts from him, especially now that she would have to leave him, but she didn't know how to refuse them without hurting his feelings or making him suspicious.

"So, have you found any information on passage to the colonies?" Meg sat down on a three-legged stool and began to fold a pair of yellow clocked stockings that must have belonged to a man with calves like a tree trunk.

"Very little." Saity took a pot of water from where it boiled on the hearth and lugged it toward the wash tub. "But I got a friend working on it."

Meg noticed a hint of color in Saity's cheeks. "A friend, you say?" She lifted an eyebrow inquisitively. She wanted desperately for Saity to be happy. "And might that friend be a man?"

Saity poured the steaming kettle of water into the tub. "A man who's got no wife." She looked at Meg slyly. "But he's lookin'."

Meg laughed, reaching for the other yellow stocking. "What does he do?"

"He's just a fishseller." She shrugged her thin shoulders. "But he's real nice to me. He brings me fresh fish." She nibbled on her lower lip. "And he don't smell like a fish, either. He smells . . . clean," she finished with a grin.

"He sounds wonderful." Meg looked up from the table. "Is he courting you?"

"I think he is. I just think he don't realize it yet." She set the kettle back on the hearth and picked up an armful of soiled white table linens. "I guess I ought to tell 'im what I did before I come here, but I'm afraid I'll run him off."

"You wouldn't have to tell him."

"Yea." Saity dropped the linens into the steamy water. "But I wouldn't feel right, me stalkin' him, thinkin' wedding, and he not knowin' I been a whore."

"So wait a little while. See what comes of the relationship and tell him if he brings up marriage. If your fish man loves you, he won't care about your past."

"I guess you're right. If my Clancy ever comes to love me, he shouldn't care what I was. Or at least he should forgive me." Saity stirred the clothes soup with a big wooden paddle. "But you could make the same argument talkin' of Kincaid." She looked up at Meg.

Meg sighed, keeping her hands busy folding laundry. "It's not the same thing. I killed a man. I killed Kincaid's father." Her hands fell still as she thought about her dead baby again. "Saity, what would you say if I said I might be with child?"

Saity spun around, her paddle coming completely out of the tub. "I'd say I'm glad it's you and not me, sister."

Meg laughed. Leave it to Saity to lighten her burden. "I'm serious. I'm only a little late. A few days. It took me years to quicken with my John, but . . ."

Saity's brow creased. "But a part of you is hopin'?"

"I know it's wrong, a sin to bring a bastard into this world. But a part of me wants desperately to take a part of Kincaid with me when I go."

"Phew-eee!" Saity pushed the paddle back into the water, throwing in a lump of her soap for good measure. "Now that really would set a hardship on your shoulders. An unmarried woman carrying a child. In the village I came from, they put girls like that in the stocks. That's why I come to the city in the first place."

"You were pregnant?"

She frowned. "The boy said he'd marry me. His papa owned the town tavern. It woulda been a good life." She glanced out the window. "Only he married the blacksmithy's girl instead of me, and there I was in my father's house, fifteen years old with a babe growin' inside me. If my father had known, he'd've beaten it outta me."

"So you came to London?" Meg asked sadly.

"Yea. Lost the baby. It was best anyway. I couldn't feed myself," she gave a little laugh, "how'd I have fed a squalin' babe? You know the rest of my sad tale."

"I'm sorry," Meg said softly, genuinely feeling Saity's pain.

"I know someone who could rid you of it," Saity said hesitantly, "if that's what you want."

"No." Meg looked up at her friend. "I don't even know if it's true or not yet, but if it is . . ." She looked at the child's linen shirt she held in her hands. "If it is, I'll care for him or her. I'll sell myself into servitude if I have to, but our son or daughter will have food on the table and know that he or she is loved. By me, and by the father who couldn't accompany us to the colonies."

Saity gave a long sigh, leaning on her stick. "You got dreams, I'll give you that, Meg."

Meg smiled, feeling better now that she'd confessed her fears, her hope. "So you'll have your friend Clancy find out about a ship? It has to be soon, Saity. The Earl of Rutledge saw me at the theater."

Saity's eyes widened. "No!"

"Yes. And now that Kincaid has contact with him, it's only a matter of time before one of them realizes—"

Saity held up her palm, raw from the lye soap. "You don't have to say any more. If you want to go to them Indian colonies, babe in your belly or not, I'll help you find a way, even if I got to swim across that ocean with ye on my back."

"Someone say something about swimming?" Kincaid stepped inside the shop door that had been left open to let a breeze blow through the hot room.

Startled, Meg popped up off the stool. "Heavens, you gave me a fright." She laid her hand on her breast, feeling her heart patter.

"Sorry. Ready to go? I promised Monti we'd meet him for sup and cards at the Roost tonight."

Meg picked up her vizard and cloak. "Sorry I couldn't stay very long, Saity." She allowed Kincaid to drop the cloak over her shoulders.

"Always good to see your sweet face." Saity brushed her palm across Meg's flushed cheek. "You come back when you can, dirty sheets or no."

Meg laughed, leaving the shop with a wave. "Back in two or three days."

"Bye, Saity." Kincaid waved farewell.

Out on the street Meg and Kincaid walked side by side. "Have a good visit?"

"Yes."

Kincaid glanced down at her. "I'll never understand what you two women talk about. Me?"

Meg laughed, breaking the tension she felt in her chest. "Now isn't that just like a man to think every conversation must revolve around him."

"I just asked." He acted innocent.

"We talk about women things, if you must know." She raised the mask, putting it in place.

"Well, I like to talk about woman things," he answered with a chuckle. He lowered his voice until it was husky and sensual. "Especially your woman's things."

Meg broke into laughter at his lewd remark and smacked him playfully on the arm with her folded fan. "Honestly, Kincaid, I don't know how I live with you!"

He grinned roguishly, slipping her arm over his. "But you couldn't live without me, either. Could you?"

She laughed, hoping the gaiety in her voice covered the pain.

Rutledge took the steps one at a time, allowing the aura from the single tallow candle he carried to light his way. He took his time on the stairs, entering the bowels of Rutledge Castle. More than one Randall family member in the last centuries had met his or her death on the treacherous steps.

At the bottom, he veered right. The labyrinth of halls and rooms below the main floor of the castle stank of wet earth and rock, and years of darkness. The air was damp and cool and hung over his shoulders like a shroud.

He wanted a particular bottle of wine from the wine cellar,

a superior brandy. When he returned to London tomorrow, he was to take it as a gift to a business acquaintance. He could have sent a servant, but it was one of those matters he preferred to handle himself. A man who did not freely roam his own palace, his father always said, was a man who would never quite be in control of it. And of course Percival would not give up control. It empowered him.

He whistled to himself as he walked deeper into the dungeons. A large rodent squeaked and scuttled past him on the dirt floor. He made a mental note to have one of the servants throw a few cats down the steps. That would take care of the rats.

"So, how are we are today?" he called, his voice echoing off the dank, filmy walls.

From somewhere ahead came a scrape of wood against stone. "Quiet today, eh?"

He listened to the sound of his own footfall as he continued down the corridor. "Tom and Sam said as much. Pity. I thought we could chat. Would you like that?"

Still, there was no sound but his own footsteps and the rise and fall of his breath.

"You'll be happy to hear I'll be staying tonight and not returning to London until tomorrow. Doesn't that please you, my dearest?"

Percival chuckled, feeling warm despite the chill of the dungeon. He liked it down here. Perhaps when he found Margaret—*not if, but when*—he would bring her here. They could spend some time together, time Percival had always wanted when she was Philips's wife.

Down here in the dungeon, perfect little Margaret would have no place to flee. It wouldn't be like it had been before. She'd not have Philip to hide behind. She'd not be able to escape to her apartments, pleading a headache. Her attention would be utterly his.

Percival smiled at that thought, a smile he knew was

crooked. A smile that if he held too long, would cause spittle to drool from the corner of his mouth.

He wiped his lips with the back of his hand, brushing them with the Brussels lace of his cuff. Then he reached to his groin, shifting the bulge in his breeches to a more comfortable position. Just the thought of bringing Margaret down here, having her all to himself, made him hard.

He passed a closed plank door in the narrow corridor that led to the wine cellar. "Do you hear me, darling?" He banged on the door with his closed fist as he passed it.

Again came the sound of wood scraping against stone. Then nothing. He couldn't help wondering why he hadn't thought of any of this before. How much he had missed for his lack of creativity all these years!

Percival smiled a thin smile. "I'll go for the wine and then come back," he called over his shoulder. "Perhaps I'll even bring two bottles and we shall share one. Would you like that, my love?"

He didn't wait for a reply. He knew there would be none. Instead, he tipped back his head and roared with laughter. Down here his disfigurement meant nothing. Down here in the bowels of the earth he was in charge. *He* decided between life and tortured death. *That* was power. And he liked the taste of it.

Twenty-two

Meg held so tightly to the reins that the leather bit through her calfskin gloves into the soft flesh of her palms. Her horse danced impatiently beneath her, snorting and pawing at the ground.

"You all right?"

Kincaid's voice was brusque, but not unkind. Meg had participated in enough robberies by now to know he meant no harm in his sharp words. He was now Captain Scarlet, not her Kincaid, not James Kincaid, not even James Randall. He was cautious, with a single intent in mind.

She patted her mount's neck with a gloved hand. "Fine."

The half-moon hung low in the dark, cloudless sky over Maidenhead Thicket. They were awaiting the Bath coach on which a Lord Hardgrove was said to be traveling with his whore.

"I don't know what's become of Monti. He said he had a friend to visit in Bath, but he would meet us in time." Kincaid looked up into the sky, guessing the approximate time, no doubt. "I hope he's not run into trouble."

"You know Monti." She urged her roan gelding forward until she was beside Kincaid on the rutted road. "He's probably soused in a tavern with a woman on his knee." She chuckled, but Kincaid didn't join her.

"Did you hear something?"

Meg was still for a moment, listening. At first she heard

nothing, but then a rustle in the trees across the road. "That?" she whispered.

Kincaid nodded.

She listened another moment. Now she heard nothing. "Just a deer foraging for food, I suspect," she said after a moment.

Kincaid nodded, glancing up the road in the direction of Bath. "I'm sure. I'd just feel better if Monti were here."

She lifted an eyebrow. *"I'm* here."

"Exactly."

She frowned. "I've done a superior job to this point. Monti said so. So did you, if I recall correctly."

He sighed. "I don't know how I let you talk me into this. Each time, I tell myself you'll stay home this time, home where I know you'll be safe. Then here you are, dressed like a highwayman in a black cape and mask.

"Highway *woman,"* she corrected, refusing to take insult from his words. She understood his reluctance. "And it will be over soon. You've only another three on your list after our dear Lord Hardgrove, who travels with his whore while his wife is still in childbed in London."

"I see, so you want to punish him not just for his crimes against all English citizens, but also for his poor husband-ship?"

She smiled. "We all have our agendas, Captain. The longer I have to contemplate the characters of the men on your list, the more I realize that those who do not treat their fellow countrymen well, do not treat their family and friends much better. The betrayal is only more subtle."

A smile twitched on Kincaid's face, yet he said nothing.

"What?" Meg asked after a moment. "What did I say that you find so amusing?"

He reached out and took her black gloved hand in his own to caress it. "I smile, not because you amuse me, but because I realize how lucky I am to have found a woman so innately good, and so intelligent, too." He exhaled. "I cannot help thinking my father could have chosen a bride more carefully. He'd not have died as he did then, would he?"

A lump rose in Meg's throat and she pulled her hand from his. "Is . . . is that coach wheels I hear?"

Kincaid lifted his head, listening. "It is." He reached down and brought up the scarf he wore around his neck, winding it about his face.

Meg raised the hood of her cloak so that it shadowed her feminine features. Beneath her cloak she wore a pair of men's breeches, a linen shirt, and German leather riding boots. From the saddlebag she extracted a primed pistol. Her nerves were on edge. She could hear the coach drawing closer now, the sound of the hoofbeats and the roll of the wheels obvious.

"I can do this alone," Kincaid whispered. They had backed off the road so that the coachman wouldn't immediately see them in the shadows of the forest. "Just go into the woods and wait for me. I'll make short work of Hardgrove and meet up with you."

"Yes, you can do it alone, but it's far more dangerous. I want to keep you in one piece, my love."

Just then the coach and four appeared on the dark road, rumbling toward them.

"If there's any trouble," Kincaid warned, "get the hell out of here. We'll meet at the tavern we agreed upon."

"Just be sure the whore gets her kiss," Meg teased, making light of what they were about to do. "You know Monti heard the woman at Gerard's Cross was quite disappointed you didn't kiss her."

Kincaid rested his pistol across his lap. "I'm practically a married man. I cannot continue to kiss these women forever."

Meg smiled. The coach had nearly reached the designated point. "Ready?"

"Ready."

Meg sank her heels into the gelding's flanks and shot onto the road before the stagecoach. The driver pulled back on the reins and the coach horses rolled their eyes and shied right in fear of the horse and rider that had appeared out of nowhere like a ghostly apparition.

As the stagecoach rolled to a halt, Kincaid appeared out of the darkness beside the door. "Stand and Deliver," he shouted in the voice of Captain Scarlet. "Comply and no one will be harmed."

Then Meg heard the first gunshot.

She wheeled around in fright, realizing the fire came not from the coach, but from a rider behind it. Where in sweet heaven's name had he come from?

"Kincaid!" Meg shouted, knowing she mustn't panic.

Another shot blasted in the darkness, filling the air with streaks of light and black powder smoke. As she wheeled around the side of the coach, she saw Kincaid return fire.

There were two horses and riders that had been following the coach! An escort?

"Go," Kincaid shouted into the darkness. "I'm right behind you!"

Meg's horse reared as another shot rang in the air and she fought to remain in her saddle. She had sworn she would be no burden to Kincaid. She had promised she could take care of herself if they got into trouble. She'd not disappoint him.

Meg jerked hard on the reins, veering around the coach, her horse rearing again. Inside the coach she could see the shadows of a man and woman huddled together. The woman was screaming. There was a great din between her shrieking and the men shouting, the horses neighing.

"Kill them!" the man, Lord Hardgrove no doubt, shouted. "Kill the thieving bastards."

Kincaid fired again, this time hitting one of the men's horses. Horse and rider went tumbling down.

Now there was only one man who could pursue them.

Meg leaned over her mount's neck, urging him into a gallop. Behind her she could hear Kincaid shouting. He was still astride and hot on her heels.

She dared a glance over her shoulder as she rode into the

forest. The other rider was pursuing them. She had one shot left. . . . Could she really shoot a man? After all, she and Kincaid were considered the criminals. In the eyes of the court, this man was only defending his employer.

Meg fought her conscience as she rode deeper into the thicket. Surely by now Kincaid had reloaded. She knew he could do it astride as quickly as standing.

Then Meg heard a man's voice from the roadside. "Come back, you stupid bastard! Don't leave me here alone in the dark!"

Meg couldn't believe her own ears as she heard the rider behind Kincaid fall back. Still, she rode hell-bent through the woods. What if he went back to check on his lordship and then pursued them again?

Branches tore at the hood of Meg's cloak, knocking it back, dragging the leaves through her hair. Briars scratched her legs through the breeches; insects flew into her face, but she kept riding. Occasionally she looked over her shoulder to be certain Kincaid was still there.

They must have rode twenty minutes hell-bent through the dense forest, in the darkness, following a narrow game path. Finally Kincaid called for her to slow down.

She halted beneath an ancient oak tree to wait for him. Moonlight peeked through the branches nearly filled out with leaves. "Something to be said for Monti's stars, eh?" She smiled. "He said the luck would be with us tonight."

Kincaid rode up behind her, scowling. "I don't understand this, damn it!" He shook his fist. "They always went off without a hitch until that night I found you on the road."

"So maybe I'm the bad luck." She reached to take his hand as he rode closer. A thin shred of moonlight crossed his face. Suddenly Meg realized he was pale. Deathly pale.

"Kincaid?" Panic rose in her chest. "Kincaid, are you all right?"

"I'm all right."

Then she saw the bloodstain on his breeches. "Sweet,

heaven," she whispered, covering her mouth for fear she'd cry out. "You've been shot."

"How's the leg?" Meg rolled onto her side. They had just woken to the morning sunshine pouring through the window-panes onto the bed quilt.

Kincaid flexed his bare leg, bandaged at the thigh with strips of linen Meg had gotten from the innkeeper. Because they had already reserved a cottage at the quiet inn down by the Thames outside of the city, and because Kincaid had paid the innkeeper a healthy fee, there had been no questions asked. The innkeeper's wife had supplied bandages, healing balm, hot tea, bread, and cheese at nearly four in the morning.

Meg herself had extracted the lead ball that was just be-neath the surface of the skin on Kincaid's thigh and then ban-daged it. After a dose of tea laced with brandy-wine she had tucked Kincaid beneath the colored quilt that smelled of fresh lilacs. Then she watched over him as he slept, monitoring him for any signs of fever or infection.

Kincaid flexed his leg again. "It's a little stiff, but I'll be fine." He kissed her forehead. "You'd make an excellent phy-sician, my love. Better than those cuttlefishes in the masks."

Meg smiled, but then it faded. "It's time to end this, Kin-caid. I don't know what's happening, but I think you need to give up on the list."

He tucked one hand beneath his head, still reclining in the bed. "I can't, Meg. I set out to do a task and I'll complete it."

"Kincaid! Do you hear yourself? Are a few coins, a couple of emerald necklaces, a gold watch or two, worth your life?"

"It's not the things I take, and you well know it. It's the principle of the matter. The embarrassment of the robbery. And I must admit I enjoy going into the slums to take the coin, the food, the medicine the thievery provides." He reached out to tug on a lock of hair that fell forward on her cheek.

"You know, Monti said he heard last week that those that have been robbed by Captain Scarlet have formed an association. They realize that they all have something in common. And when my satire begins to circulate with all their names, they will lose business. There will be those who will no longer wish to associate with them. Perhaps the king himself will even look into the matter once a finger is pointed in their direction."

Meg sat up, hugging her knees. "I understand your reasoning, but we're talking about your life here!"

"I'm almost done. The list is almost complete."

"Kincaid! Surely you don't believe that it's by accident that you've nearly been caught half a dozen times!"

He shrugged. "Poor luck. Nothing more. Only a few of my contacts even suspect who I might be, and even to them, I have given no confirmation."

She looked away, angry that he could be so stubborn. Out the window, through the part in the chintz curtains, she could see a goose girl herding her charges over a hill. "Someone is giving up information. Someone knows."

"If someone were betraying me, I'd have been caught and hanged by now. It's just the luck, like Monti says."

"Monti." Meg looked back at him. "And where is he? What if those men who fired at us came upon Monti last night? What if he's lying in some ditch, dead or bleeding to death?"

"If there's one thing I've learned in all these years with Monti, it's that the man can take care of—"

A knock at the door cut Kincaid's sentence short. He jumped up from the bed, lifting his loaded pistol from the night table.

Meg drew the bedcovers up to her chin. The cottage they had rented was small, only one room. There was nowhere to hide if they had been caught. No place to run. They had assumed that this was such a small, obscure village that no one could find them here.

Kincaid walked to the door, limping just a little. At the door, he pressed his back to the wall. "Who is it?" he called.

Meg held her breath, reaching for her own pistol. Perhaps she couldn't shoot a man pursuing them to save herself, but she thought she could shoot a man to save Kincaid.

"Who the hell do you think it is?"

At the sound of Monti's voice, Meg exhaled with relief.

Kincaid unbolted the door and jerked it open.

Monti stepped inside, dressed neatly, every curl in his red periwig in place, a plumed hat in lime green in his hand. "Good morning to you. Or should I say afternoon. I never thought the two of you would wake. I've been waiting outside for hours."

Kincaid kicked the door shut with his heel and limped back toward the bed.

"Where have you been?" Meg demanded: "I thought you were dead."

"Me?" Monti indicated himself with a flip of his manicured hand. "I'm like a cat, my love. I always land on my feet."

Kincaid sat down on the edge of the bed and pulled on a pair of wrinkled breeches. Meg had not yet unpacked the clothing they'd brought along.

Monti's gaze settled on Kincaid's bandaged leg. "Gads, wounded, friend?"

"Where the hell were you, Monti?"

Monti walked to the small table painted blue with its quaint matching chairs. From a wooden bowl, he plucked an apple. "Got caught in the tavern with a group of the king's soldiers. I couldn't well excuse myself, telling them I had a robbery to commit, could I? Especially since the bottleheads were losing their purses."

"You were gambling?" Meg jerked the counterpane up higher. She was dressed in only a thin shift. "I was afraid you'd be killed or caught and you were drinking and throwing the die?"

"I'm sorry, Meg." He bit into the apple. "But a man has

to assess every situation. Don't you think the soldiers would have been suspicious, had I excused myself suddenly in Bath and then a robbery had taken place shortly thereafter?"

His breeches tied, Kincaid sat back down on the edge of bed, laying his pistol on the bedtable. "He's right, Meg. I'd probably have done the same thing."

Meg let her hands fall to her lap as she sat in silence for a minute. "So now what do we do?"

"I take it you were shot at?" Monti took another bite of the apple. "So old Hard Ass Hardgrove was lugging a pistol?"

"No." Kincaid got up and walked stiffly to the table where he retrieved a half-empty glass of last night's brandy. "He had escorts, Monti. Futtering escorts going from Bath to London!" He sloshed back a gulp of ale.

Monti chewed, thinking. "Someone on the inside giving us away?"

Kincaid slammed the glass back on the table. "Who? No one knows the exact particulars. Some of the regulars, Roberts, Parker, Candle, they might suspect who we are, but they couldn't know for sure."

Monti sighed, tossing his apple core into the cold fireplace across the room. "It wouldn't be a crime to give up here. Write your scathing satire, distribute it, and get the hell out of London."

Kincaid ran his fingers through his loose hair that fell to his shoulders. Since he had gotten word of his father's death he looked haggard to Meg. The character lines of his face were more pronounced, his worries etched in his smile. He looked like he needed a good night's sleep.

"I can't do that, Monti." He flipped his inky hair over the crown of his head. "You know I can't."

Monti opened his arms. "Could have just been a fluke. Maybe Hardgrove is paranoid and travels regularly with an escort."

Kincaid shook his head. "Parker would have told us."

"Well, my suggestion, friend," Monti said, "is that I go

back to London and pay a visit to our friendly cobbler, Mr. Parker. You and Meg stay here a few days, rest, let the gossip simmer down. By the time you return to London, I might have an answer for us."

Kincaid picked Meg's dressing robe off the back of one of the blue chairs and carried it around to her side of the bed. He held it up to shield her from Monti as she slipped into it.

"I suppose Monti's right," she said, looking up at Kincaid as she knotted the tie of the robe around her waist. She reached up to stroke his beard stubble. "You look like you could use a day or two of rest."

Kincaid walked away, agitated. "I suppose it makes sense, though I'm anxious to be done with this matter." He looked over his shoulder at Meg. "I'm anxious to get on with our life. To marry. Suddenly America seems like home to me even if I've never set foot on its ground."

"That means you're going to take your inheritance and run?" Monti questioned. "I thought you were going to find your father's killer. I imagine your dear uncle will be hurt if you go."

"The earl," Kincaid said with distaste, "is tracking the witch as we speak. He's spotted her in London and seems confident he'll have her in a matter of days."

Monti nodded. "Then once the list is complete, you'll be a free man."

Meg stood at the window watching the goose girl in her blue tick dress and scarf tied around her head. The conversation made her shaky inside. Suddenly, for the first time, she realized how hard it was to live so many lies. Only now did she recognize what a toll the whole farce was taking on her. The sooner she was gone from London, the better. It would break her heart to leave Kincaid, but she had no choice.

"Meg . . ."

She turned around, realizing Kincaid was speaking to her. "I'm sorry, I fear I wasn't listening."

"I asked," Kincaid repeated, "if you'd be content to stay

here a few days while Monti questions our contacts in London."

Meg smiled. The thought of spending a few days alone with Kincaid before she made her escape was heavenly. She knew she was taking chances each day she put off her departure, but she was still waiting for definite word on a ship from Saity. And what would a few more days matter? She was here in the country and Rutledge was in the city. She would be safe enough.

"I think it's an excellent idea. It will give your leg time to heal."

Monti started for the door. "Good enough, then. I'll send a message in a few days." He stopped, his hand on the doorknob. "Now, who are you two again?"

Kincaid followed Monti to the door. "Mr. And Mrs. Albert, come to rest a few days before returning to our estate in some shire, can't remember which one right now."

"Good enough." Monti dropped his ridiculous lime-colored hat onto his head and nodded to Meg. "See you in a few days, dear."

"Be careful," Meg called after him.

Kincaid closed the door behind him and set the bolt. "Now," he said turning to her, a smile on his face. "What shall we do to amuse ourselves in this little cottage for several days?"

Meg laughed, coming to him to put her arms around his waist. "I have a suggestion, if you're so inclined, my lord . . ."

"And that is?" He looked at her in a way that made her heart melt.

How could she leave him? Though leave him, she must . . .

Meg lifted on her bare tiptoes and whispered in his ear.

Kincaid lifted an eyebrow roguishly. "Precisely what I was thinking."

Arm in arm they returned to the cozy bed.

* * *

James heard his own footfall in the darkness. He could smell the dank walls of the stone corridor. "Father?" his little boy voice called. "Father, where are you?"

James ran, his bare feet cold on the stone floor, his nightgown twisted at his ankles. Cold terror ribboned through his veins. "Father!"

His father's voice echoed in his head. "No one could ever love you, boy. That's why your mother died . . . it was the only way to get away from your sorry ass. Idiot. Incompetent. Fool."

"Father?" James called out, still running as if the devil himself was on his tail. "Father, I can't find you . . ."

Up the stairs the boy ran, stumbling on the hard, cold stone, cutting his knees, scraping his shins. But he picked himself up and started up the stairs in the darkness again.

He had to help his father. He had to save him . . .

"Father, I'm coming," he called.

Just as he reached the top step he heard his father's first blood-curdling scream.

"Father!" James cried. He ran from door to door along the corridor, hearing the screams, not able to tell where they were coming from.

"Don't kill my father!" the little boy cried, racing from closed door to closed door only to fling them open to find the rooms empty. "Don't kill him!"

The screams seemed to be coming from the four walls around young James. It made no sense. This was his home and yet it wasn't. Where were the servants? Why weren't the candles in the wall sconces lit? Where was Mother?

Of course Mother was dead. Gone to hell, his father told him.

"Father!" James reached the last door and pulled it open, heavy for a boy of only six or seven.

The screams were coming from inside.

James tripped over the hem of his nightgown and fell inside the bedchamber door. As his hands hit the floor they slipped in something warm and wet . . .

James looked up slowly, his hair over his face, obscuring his view. Then he saw the body.

His father was sprawled on the bedchamber floor, his club foot twisted unnaturally, his arms spread. And the blood . . . It was everywhere. His father's clothes were covered in the dark, slimy blood, but so was the floor, the bedcurtains, even the walls. Blood was seeping through the walls.

"No!" James screamed. "No!" He struggled to rise, but he kept slipping in the blood that now puddled in the room, rising high as he fought to get to his feet.

Slowly the blood surged over his father's dead body, covering the open, unseeing eyes.

James was drowning, drowning in his father's blood . . .

"Noooooooo!" the boy cried.

"Nooooo," Kincaid screamed.

"Kincaid." Meg grasped his shoulders, shaking him. "Kincaid, wake up!" She patted his cheek. He was bathed in sweat, his entire body trembling. "Kincaid, it's just a bad dream, wake up!"

Kincaid came awake with a start, still tasting the metallic fear on his tongue.

"It's just a dream," he heard Meg's soft voice in his ear. She was holding his trembling hand, stroking it.

He sat up, brushing the hair out of his face. He felt like an ass. What grown man still had nightmares?

"Kincaid," came Meg's voice through the fog of his fear, still lingering in the corners of his mind. "You all right?"

He wrapped his arm around her shoulders, hugging her. "I'm all right, sweet." He took a deep breath. "I . . . I was dreaming about my father. I have to go to Rutledge Castle."

"Why?" She clung to him, looking into his eyes.

"I don't know. I just do. It's been years and years since I've been there." He kissed her temple. "Just a feeling I have. A need." He looked into her green eyes that had mesmerized him since that first night he had gazed into them on the highway to London. "Will you go?"

She looked away. "I can't."

"Why not? I could use you at my side. Your strength."

In the darkness, he could see her fiddling with the hem of the counterpane. Waning moonlight shown through the window. "I just can't. Your family, they were so mean to you. I . . . couldn't bear to look into your uncle's eyes."

"Meg—"

"I can't," she repeated sharply. "I just can't."

Kincaid still looked into her face, tenderly brushing her cheek with his knuckles. "All right. You don't have to. I can go alone. Or Monti can keep me company. I'll go after we return to London."

She nodded and then, after looking into his eyes a moment longer, she pressed her mouth to his. "Let me chase away your nightmares," she whispered. As she rose on her knees to kiss him, the coverlet fell away, the moonlight dancing off the curves of her breasts, her hips . . .

And as their lips met, the memory of the dream faded from Kincaid's mind. As long as he had Meg, he knew he would never be alone again. And as long as he had his Meg, he would know his father, the bastard, had been wrong.

Someone could love him . . .

Twenty-three

"You certain you won't go with me?" Kincaid stood on the street, his mount's reins tucked in his hand. It was early morning and there were only a few people on the street at Charing Cross. Only a handful of venders could be seen rolling their carts, bound for one market or another.

Meg tried to smile. It was so early that she'd not yet dressed, but instead come down to say farewell with a cloak thrown over her dressing gown. She woke at dawn with Kincaid, made love with him, and then cooked a farewell morning meal in the kitchen in her bare feet, just like a wife would have done. "No. I won't go with you. And I wish you wouldn't go, either." Meg twisted her hands in the folds of her cloak. "I don't know why you want to dredge up more bad memories. You ought to let them lie."

And she truly felt that way. Of course she was also afraid Kincaid would find some clue to lead him to her, though what that might be, she didn't know. A portrait was never painted of her. Philip had always talked of commissioning one, but never done so. And who could tell Kincaid about her if he asked the staff? No one in the household had ever befriended her for fear of Philip's wrath. Meg knew there was very little evidence in the castle that she'd ever existed at all, but still she was afraid.

Kincaid stared at the ground made muddy by the late spring rains. "I can't explain this to you, except to say that I need to go at least once before you and I set sail. I'd like to look through my father's possessions. There's a portrait of my mother, if the bastard didn't burn it."

Meg nodded because she did understand. "I'll miss you," she said, fearing she would break down and cry. She didn't just mean she would miss him while he was in Rutledge, she meant she would miss him the rest of her life. When he returned, she decided she'd no longer be here. If she had to, she would find a place to hide until she could manage passage on a ship.

Kincaid took her hand in his gloved one and brought it to his lips. "I'll be gone two or three days at most. I promise."

Tears stung Meg's eyes. She'd been so emotional this last week since they'd returned from the inn on the river. She was so emotional that she knew she had to be pregnant. Nothing else could cause such a strange mixture of feelings in a woman's body but pregnancy. Which was yet another reason why it was time she went.

"Take care of yourself."

"I will." This time he kissed her lips. "Meg, are you all right?" He tilted her chin with his index finger, forcing her to look him in the eyes.

A lump rose in her throat. "I'm all right," she whispered.

"Do you want me to put this off another week?"

"No." She bit down on her lower lip. She had to go, and it would be easier if he was gone when she took leave. "I'm just tired, that's all." She gave him a quick kiss. "Now be careful with that leg and remember to change your dressing."

"I will." He swung up into the saddle and raised the reins to go. "Don't worry about me. I'll be fine. I'll go to the castle and chase the demons from my mind for good."

She smiled a bittersweet smile. "I'll try not to worry."

He turned the horse to go and then looked back. "Meg, I was thinking. Why don't you see what can be done about making a wedding gown while I'm gone? It will take a seamstress a few weeks, and by then we'll be packing for America. I want to wed on English soil before we go."

Not trusting herself to speak, she nodded. Then, with a lame wave of her hand, Kincaid was gone. Gone down the street, gone from her life.

"Just a few things and I'll be ready to go." Meg walked at Monti's side. He was carrying a box of trinkets she'd purchased from various booths at the Royal Exchange. She was cloaked in dark green with a vizard covering her face.

Here was the place where wealthy men and women came to purchase items, but also to hear the latest gossip, to meet with lovers, to ruin reputations. Meg had come to buy the things she thought she would need to take with her on her journey to the colonies. She needed a few more things purchased with the coin she'd won at cards in the various taverns and ladies' and gentlemen's hall.

"Goodness," Monti stopped at a stall crowded with chattering women. "Did you see this fine lace, Meg? 'Twould look excellent on a wedding gown." He lifted a piece to the cuff of his coat. "Or on a new shirt for me."

Meg smiled. "I don't need the lace. You buy it for yourself."

"Meg, *look* at this. See the fine detailing? It would be a steal at twice the cost."

She glanced over his shoulder, lowering her mask to get a better look at the exquisite cloth. "It is fine, Monti, but I truly don't—" As she glanced away she made eye contact with a man on the far side of the room at a Chinese import stall.

Rutledge.

"Sweet God, save me," she prayed under her breath, jerking the mask over her face. "Monti, let's go."

Rutledge was already coming toward her. He wasn't running. It wasn't his style now that he had her trapped as she was. His gaze never left hers as he pushed his way through the crowded hall.

Monti set down the lace. "What is it, sweet?"

Meg was already pushing away from the table. "Him."

"Him?" Monti swore under his breath. "All right, I'll get you out of this one," he grabbed her hand, leaving her purchases behind, "but I swear by all that's holy, when you're safe, you owe me an explanation."

"Anything." Meg lowered her head, following him, trusting him because she had no one else to trust.

"Lotie," Monti pushed his way around the stall to whisper in the lace girl's ear.

The bright-eyed teenager nodded her head excitedly and parted a curtain at the side of the stall that kept customers out.

"This way," Monti whispered in Meg's ear. "A shortcut."

"Margaret!" came the Earl of Rutledge's voice as they darted through the opening in the curtain. "Margaret, come back here. You won't get away this time!"

Monti and Meg bolted through the back of the booth, following the lace girl. "This way." She motioned.

Through another part in the multicolored curtains, they found themselves in a corridor, obviously used for the vendors to cart their wares in and out of the 'Change. The girl pointed to the right. "The door is there."

Monti, ever the gallant, pressed a quick kiss to Lotie's cheek as he brushed past her. "If an ugly fellow passes here looking for us, send him the other way, will you?"

Meg lifted up her skirts with both hands, running down the hall with Monti. "Please God," she prayed with each step. "Don't let him catch me. Don't let him win."

They burst through the door, which sure enough, led them to an alley behind the 'Change.

"This way," Monti shouted without hesitation. Rather than taking the twisting flight of steps, he leaped over the railing onto the ground and raised his arms to catch Meg.

She didn't have time to argue. Raising her skirts, Meg threw herself over the wooden rail and Monti broke her fall. She landed on her feet, her knees bent.

"Come on!" Monti grabbed her hand.

They ran along the building, its alley piled high with discarded crates and wooden boxes. At the edge of the alley they met with a busy street. The first hell-cart Monti spotted, he waved down.

Meg heard the earl's voice echoing in the alley behind her as she and Monti leapt into the hired coach. Monti gave him directions as they rolled off, the horse in a canter.

Meg fell back into the seat of the open carriage, barely believing that she'd escaped again, knowing her luck had to be running out.

Monti collapsed on the narrow seat at her side clutching his chest, breathless. "Blast it! I've lost the heel of my slipper." He raised his foot to show her where part of the shoe had broken off. With a frown he lowered his foot to the carriage floor. "We'll go to the Crook and Crown and take a private room. We can hide a few hours and then, as long as it's safe, we'll return to the apartment after dark." He took a breath, his gaze narrowing. For once there was no gaiety in his tone of voice. "Now start explaining, Meg."

Monti sat at the tavern table in the private room above the public room, cracking a walnut. Meg paced the floor.

"Sweet blood of the virgin," Monti muttered, shaking his head as he popped a bit of the nut's meat between his teeth. "No one would believe such a coincidence. It was fate, Meg, pure and unpretentious."

Meg exhaled, dropping her hands to her sides. "I don't have time for your *house of the rising moon* nonsense right now, Monti. I need your help. I need you to tell me what to do."

"The Earl of Rutledge." He made a clicking sound between his teeth. "He really is an ugly bastard. Kincaid never mentioned the harelip."

She stared into the flames of the small fire. A servant had lit it in the hearth to chase away the early evening chill. The sweet smell of applewood filled the room. "All the Randall men had a deformity. Philip's was a club foot."

"All the men but our Captain Scarlet, it seems."

She turned to him, her eyes begging. "Monti, please. Help me. Am I doing the right thing in leaving Kincaid before he discovers the truth? Saity thought I should just tell him. She thought I should take the chance that he would love me enough not to care."

He reached for a tankard of ale and tipped it back. "You never should have let it get this far."

She fought the emotions that immobilized her. *"I didn't know."*

"You didn't recognize him, even though you knew him as a child? Not on the road to London that night? Not in Newgate? Not when he slept in your bed? You didn't suspect?"

"I didn't recognize him because I was a child when he was living at Rutledge Castle. I was kept so far from the rest of the household that I probably caught only a glimpse of him half a dozen times in those years. And after we met here, we were both so secretive about our pasts that neither of us ever had a clue."

"It seems so implausible."

She laughed without mirth. "What is truly hard to believe is that when my grandmother passed my care onto Philip, she thought I was to marry Philip's son when I was of age." She ran her finger along the worn rail of a chair, made smooth by the years. "I should have wed Kincaid . . . hell, James. Not his father."

Monti tossed an empty shell to the floor and took another black walnut. Meg watched him crack the nut and extract the meat, waiting to hear what he had to say.

He took another nut before he spoke. "You're doing the right thing," he said softly. "You're right. The truth of what you did, who you are, would break his heart. I've known Kincaid a long time; we've been to the gates of Hades and back together." He looked at her. "I doubt he'd show you any mercy once the truth was told."

Meg's lower lip trembled. It's what she had feared all along, but hearing someone else say it still hurt. "So I should go away now? Before he returns?"

Monti stood, brushing the crumbs from his lace and linen shirt. He had removed his coat to get more comfortable. They had been here for hours. "You should go now, sweetheart," he said quietly walking toward her, his arms outstretched. "And let me take you where you want to go."

Meg allowed him to take her in his arms because she ached so badly to be comforted. Monti had hugged her before. They were friends. "What did you say?" She lifted her head from his shoulder. Monti was a full head shorter than Kincaid.

He stroked the back of her head, smoothing her hair. "I said you should let me get you out of this mess. I'll take you to the American colonies if that's where you want to go."

Meg took a step back. Something in Monti's tone didn't seem right. "You'd escort me, you mean?" Her gaze searched his ruddy face for understanding. "You would betray Kincaid and his friendship by helping me?"

"I'd do it because I love you," he cried passionately.

Meg stared at him, shocked by his declaration. "What?"

"I said I love you. I've always loved you." He put out his arms to her again, but this time she stepped away. "I'll marry you," he went on, faster than before. "If you *are* with child, I'll give the child my own name. No one ever need be the wiser."

Meg could do nothing but gaze in disbelief. What was he babbling about? *Marry Monti?*

"I have money saved," he continued. "We could buy land in the Virginia or Maryland Colony. We could grow tobacco, you and I." He put out his hand to her. "Oh, lovely Meg. My heart of hearts. I'd love you. I'd love you as much as Kincaid ever did. More."

Meg was close to tears again. She didn't want to hurt

Monti's feelings. She did love him. She loved him for his friendship. She loved him because he and Kincaid helped her when no one else would have. But she couldn't marry Monti. She didn't love him in that way. Perhaps once she could have done it. He certainly would make a better husband than Philip had. But now that Meg had experienced veritable love, she knew she would never settle for less again.

Monti looked at her with the wild eyes of a desperate man, a man who feared his life was slipping away in whore houses and at the gaming tables, and Meg felt his pain.

"If you would just give me a chance," he pleaded, "I can be as gallant as the captain. I know I'm not much to look at, a fat, short man with a red, bulbous nose, but—"

"Monti, Monti," Meg interrupted. She could let it go no further than this. "Monti, listen to me." She took his hand, gazing into his dark eyes. She spoke slowly, gently. "I will forever be grateful for all you've done for me but I—"

He sighed, his face crestfallen. "You don't love me. Not like you love *him*."

"No." Her voice was barely a whisper. "I'm sorry, Monti. I've hurt you. I've hurt you both." She looked away. "I've made such a mess of everything. I should have let Philip kill me that night."

Monti grabbed her shoulders. There were tears in his eyes. "Don't say that." He shook her, forcing her to look at him. "Even if you don't love me, if you never could, I'd still not give up a day of the time we've spent together. I'd not give up a single smile of yours for all the riches of the world or life external."

She smiled, covering his hand with hers. "Thank you."

"Now tell me you don't believe you should have died that night."

This time she gave him a little smile. "I don't believe it. Not even now that I've made such a muck of things. Sinful woman that I am, I still think Philip deserved to die, God save my soul. He deserved to die for what he did to my baby.

He deserved to die for what he did to his son John—and to Kincaid."

"That's my girl." He let go of her, brushing his eyes with the back of hand. "Now." He walked back to the table. "We have to see what we can do about getting you out of this city and on your way. If you won't let me go with you, at least I can ease your way. I have money."

She shook her head. "I can't take your money, Monti. It wouldn't be right. I have some saved. My money, not Kincaid's. I won it gambling."

"Let me pay your passage." He took a sip of his ale. "Please? It will make me feel better."

She turned back to the hearth, massaging her temples. She felt as if she'd been wrung out on Saity's washboard. "We'll talk about it later. I can't think. Nothing makes any sense in my head right now."

"Well, the best thing for us to do this moment is to get you home to bed." Once again, he was the confident, cheerful Monti she knew.

She turned back. "You think it's safe?"

"Rutledge didn't follow us. By the luck of the stars he's only seen you with me, so he'll not be able to make the connection between you and his dear nephew." He reached for his coat and her cloak hanging near the door. "It'll be safe enough. Tomorrow we'll go to Saity's, and if she's not yet gotten information on your passage to the colonies, I'll see what I can do. I have a friend or two down at the wharves."

Meg turned to let him slip her cloak over her shoulders. She was dead tired and her breasts were achy. She knew she was pregnant for certain. "I'll never be able to thank you for your help, your understanding." She stopped in the doorway. "And you won't tell Kincaid, not ever?"

He caught a lock of her dark hair and let it go to watch the curl spring back. "I wouldn't hurt him like that. I wouldn't hurt you." He gestured with a sweep of his hand. "Now, shall we go?"

Meg stepped into the upper hallway of the tavern, a sense of relief washing over her. *Everything is going to be all right,* she told herself. *It will all work out. At least as well as it can at this point . . .*

Twenty-four

Kincaid stood in the front hallway that, despite the sunshine of the afternoon, seemed dark and sorrowful. Just stepping over the threshold made his stomach queasy.

Rutledge Castle. Home.

He smirked. *Home?* Not hardly. The word *home* conjured thoughts of warmth, kindness, a haven in one's mind. Home made Kincaid think of Meg, of the sweet smell of her skin just after she's bathed, the taste of her mouth on his, the sight of her barefoot, in her shift, pouring coffee for him in the morning. This place, this vault, brought no such feelings of warmth to him. This place made his skin crawl.

"The . . . the master ain't in, my lord." The servant called Sam stood in the shadows near a full set of armor said to be worn by one of the Randall men in the middle ages. "He . . . he's gone to London. Sh . . . should I send word y . . . you've returned home, my lord?"

Kincaid squinted in the darkness. "Come closer man." He waved his hand impatiently when he balked. "By the king's cod, I'm not going to strike you! I just want to see your face."

Slowly, Sam came out of the corner, followed by his shadow Tom.

"Now, listen up, men. There's no need to send word to my uncle that I've arrived. We've already met up in Londontown. I simply want to wander around my childhood home. I want supper with a decent English ale and a bed free of bugs. I'll be gone in a day or two."

"I . . . we'll make up your old room, my lord," Sam said, seeming a little more at ease. At least now he wasn't cringing with each word Kincaid spoke.

Kincaid frowned. Just the thought of that dreary room he'd spent so many lonely hours in made him uneasy. "Good enough. Now see that my horse is cared for. You're dismissed."

Kincaid watched as the two men hurried, single-file down the back hallway toward the bowels of the castle. For a moment he just stood there, staring up at the weapons that lined the wainscot-paneled walls and ceiling in typical English fashion. *So many years of Randall history, so many years of unhappiness,* he mused.

At least he had managed to break the chain. Thanks to Meg he would never be unhappy. Not as long as he could hold her in his arms. And now that he had her, he intended to hold her for an eternity.

Kincaid wandered down the hall. The wall decor changed from swords and knives to huge portraits of ancestors dead and gone. They were a prim lot, mostly sour-faced, with their stiff collars and haughty brows. As Kincaid walked through the gallery, he watched the eyes watch him. When the deformities had appeared in the family tree some two hundred years ago, the portraits were painted less frequently. There were many women on the wall in their dull gowns, but fewer men. Occasionally an uncle or a grandfather had his portrait painted from a different angle to disguise the facial deformity that often occurred.

Kincaid stopped to stare up at a portrait of his father's father. Albert Randall had his picture painted from one side, his disfigured mouth shadowed with the oils of the paintbrush. Kincaid touched his own perfectly shaped mouth gingerly. He had often wondered how he had escaped the Randall curse. His mother had whispered to him when he was a small boy it was because his heart was pure that he had not been vexed.

"Poor, ugly bastard," Kincaid murmured, passing his grandfather's portrait. By all accounts by Kincaid's father, Albert had been a raving lunatic. An evil, cruel man. Kincaid couldn't help wondering just how bad the man had been if his own father thought so.

At the front staircase Kincaid halted to stare up the winding banister. He remembered sliding down that banister on his mother's lap. He smiled. When he closed his eyes he could still hear her laughter echoing in the empty hall. He had so few good memories of this house. She had died shortly after that in childbed and then there had been no more laughter for many years.

He started up the staircase. Not until the girl came . . . Margaret. She had laughed. He remembered hearing her when he passed the nursery wing on his way to meet his own tutors. He had only caught a glimpse of his father's charge a few times. She had been a slight, pretty blonde with the saddest green eyes.

Kincaid took the steps two at a time. What had happened to turn that innocent young girl into a murderer? His father had taken her in as an orphan, fed her, clothed her, educated her, and then married her. She should have been nothing but grateful.

"Grateful?" he muttered under his breath.

Was that how he felt about his father? Had Philip ever once given anything without expecting something in return. Had he ever given anything, even the basic necessities, without rubbing it in Kincaid's face? Hell, he could hear him ranting and raving. Even after all these years Philip's degrading voice still haunted his memory.

At the top of the steps Kincaid turned left down the dark corridor that was cold even for early May. Entering the west wing, he stopped at a closed door. His father's bedchamber.

So pretty little Margaret had lost her head, his uncle said. No one would ever truly know what took place behind this door that set her off. Kincaid was a fool if he thought he could believe anything Percival said. Perhaps in the daze of childbirth, in the pain in producing yet another stillborn heir to the Randall name, she had lost her mind. Perhaps Philip had baited and badgered her as he so often had Kincaid.

There were times when Kincaid could have killed him . . .

He pushed open the door.

The heavy crimson drapes were drawn. The bed had been stripped of its feather tick and linens. The room smelled of mildew . . . and ugliness.

Kincaid went to the window and threw open the drapes, dust billowing up. He rubbed his nose and then pushed open the lead window frame to let in a breath of the fresh countryside air.

With a sigh he turned around. That was better.

For a moment he just stood there staring at the room—the walls, the dusty furniture, the floor. Near the end of the bed he noticed a dark stain on the floorboards. Blood?

Anger made him tense again. What was wrong with him that he could possibly think the woman had been justified in her evil deed? It didn't matter what kind of bastard his father had been. She shouldn't have murdered him . . . she shouldn't have.

Kincaid walked to the mantel where there were two tiny portraits in gold frames. One of Philip's first wife, Mary, Kincaid's mother, the other of his second wife, Anne. What a sick bastard to openly display the faces of previous wives before Margaret.

So where was the third portrait he had hoped he would find? What kind of woman had Margaret grown up to be? Was she ugly and pinch-faced, or had she blossomed into a beautiful woman? He guessed she was beautiful. His father liked his women young and beautiful.

Kincaid picked up the small oil painting of his mother. This was what he had come for, really. He walked out of the bedchamber, leaving the door open, not looking back at the bloodstained floor.

Kincaid continued down the hallway, meaning to go to his

own bedchamber, but something made him pass it. He followed the corridor and its twists and turns until he found
himself in the east wing. Here had been the nursery. Here was
where Margaret had lived in the time he had occupied the
castle.

Kincaid didn't know why he wanted to see the apartments
she shared with her nurse. What clue to the person she was
now would he find after all these years? Still, curiosity got
the best of him and he entered the nursery. The first room he
passed through was the same room he had been tutored in as
a small boy. That was back when his mother had been alive,
long before Margaret had come. To the left was a room for
babies with a cradle and a cot for a wet nurse. How many
times had his father attempted to fill that infant's cradle only
to be disappointed? The next room was where Kincaid's nurse
had slept. The last two rooms were for Randall children.

Kincaid pushed open the first door, but it was obvious no
one had occupied it for fifty years. Inside the second doorway
he halted, an eerie feeling coming over him.

This was where Margaret had slept. He was certain of it.
He shivered, despite the warmth of the garden sunshine that
poured through the lead and glass windows. There was something so familiar to him about this room, and yet it was decorated entirely differently from when he had slept here as a
little boy.

The bed hung with wispy chintz bedcurtains, now moth-
eaten and tattered with age. They were a pale green, green
like the spring grass. The same material hung from the windows, ragged and still without a breeze to flutter them.

On a table near the bed rested an old doll, its china face
cracked. He picked it up, watching its head list to one side.
Why had she left the doll here when she'd moved to his father's chamber, he wondered.

*Because she would have been a woman then, and women
didn't carry dolls to their husband's bed.*

Kincaid returned the toy to its place, having the strangest

feeling that here in Margaret's room he could hear her voice, or at least read her thoughts.

He went to the linen press and opened the doors. It smelled thickly of rotting cloth. With one finger he lifted a stack of disintegrating cloth, old bedsheets, a torn shift. He was just about to close the door when his hand brushed something hard beneath a moth-eaten wool cloak folded neatly on the second shelf.

Kincaid's brow furrowed. What was it?

He slid his hand inside the envelope of the gray wool and, to his surprise, extracted a small, cloth-bound book. Leaving the door to the clothes press open, he walked to the window, blowing the wool threads off the cover.

The moment he opened the book, he knew what he'd found. A journal. On the first page was the name Margaret Hannibal. It was dated December 21, the year of our Lord, sixteen forty something. The last number was too faded to read.

Papa grows weaker each day, he read the childish scrawl. *He no longer calls for my mother, dead all these years. Grandmama says our Lord will come for him soon . . .*

Kincaid flipped several disintegrating pages. He felt uneasy reading the girl's words that were obviously never meant to be shared.

Still, he couldn't resist reading a passage here and there. *Gone to the funeral today. Raining. Does God always send the rain for a man's funeral . . .* Further on, . . . *cannot believe Grandmama must go to heavens, too. And then where will I be? Alone without a protector.*

Kincaid carefully turned the pages, feeling more like a thief than he had ever felt on the highway. He was stealing this poor sorrowful girl's thoughts, her innermost fears . . .

His eye caught the name *Rutledge* and he glanced at the words. *"Arrived at Rutledge Castle today . . . Grandmama too ill to care for me . . . A great dreary fortress. No one is very kind and I am afraid . . ."*

He flipped to the last page with writing. *To be wed today*

and wonder if it would not have been better to have gone to the sweet Lord with my Grandmama.

Kincaid closed the book, bits of crumbled paper drifting to the floor. He would take it home to London with him and study it. Perhaps he could even get Meg to look at it with him. She was a woman. Maybe she could make out something of the girl's words. It wasn't that he expected the diary would help him find his father's murderess. The last entry was obviously on her wedding day, though there was no date. The murder had taken place some seven or eight years later. But perhaps somewhere in the scribbles would be some indication of Margaret's mental well-being. Had she been crazy as his uncle indicated?

With a bad taste in his mouth, Kincaid left the nursery, closing the doors quietly behind him. He needed to get outside. He needed the sunshine. Meg was right. He never should have come.

Kincaid followed the servants' hall out of the east wing and through the pantry, into the afternoon sunlight of the kitchen yard. Standing beneath a blossoming apple tree he took great gulps of the fresh country air. He'd seen enough. There was nothing here that would give him any clue as to where he could find the murdering Margaret. Now that he was here, all he wanted was to go home to Meg and rest his head on her breast.

Kincaid picked up a twig and hurled it into the air. That's what he would do. He would go home to London this afternoon.

A sound at the cellar stairs made him turn. The door of hewn wood and forged iron appeared out of a mound of earth near the entry to the kitchen. He remembered being forced as a child to go down into the stone caverns to bring up bottles of wine. Years after he left Rutledge for good, he still had nightmares about that cellar.

But what was that sound? A voice?

Kincaid walked to the oak and iron door that was latched

from the outside. Now he heard nothing but the rustle of the leaves over his head and the trill call of a mockingbird.

Just as he turned away, he heard the noise again. But he couldn't make out what it was. Could someone possibly be down in the cellar?

Kincaid lifted the rusty latch, an ominous feeling coming over him. "Holy mother of God," he muttered, feeling like a fool. He was no longer a child that had to fear the darkness or the demons that hid below the earth in his father's cellar.

Kincaid swung open the door and something leapt out. Startled, he took a step back, focusing on the black pit of the stairwell. "What the hell?"

Meowww.

An orange tabby shot between Kincaid's boots, making a beeline for the orchard.

Kincaid had to laugh at himself as he closed the cellar door and dropped the latch. He'd been at Rutledge no more than an hour and he already had himself spooked. Was that what this place did to people? Spooked them? Made them say things they would never say, do things they would never do? Could that have been what happened to Margaret? Or was she the cold-blooded killer his uncle made her out to be?

Kincaid turned away, presenting his back to the gray stone castle that loomed three stories overhead. He had only one stop left to make.

"M . . . my lord?"

Kincaid looked back to see Sam and Tom. They appeared out of thin air, just like the cat.

"Sam?"

"W . . . what you doing, s . . . sir?" He eyed the cellar door.

Kincaid hooked his thumb. "Heard something in the dungeon," he said, making light of his own scare. "Thought it might be Old Knoll come back from the dead." Old Knoll was the name used for Cromwell when parents wanted to frightened their misbehaving children.

"H . . . heard something?" Sam and Tom both stared at the door as if it would leap to life at any moment. "P . . . probably nothing. P . . . probably just . . . just a rat."

"Actually, it was a cat."

"Y . . . you went down t . . . there?"

"Didn't have to. Cat came up." Kincaid plucked an apple blossom from the tree overhead, thinking he would take it to Meg. If it didn't rain, he'd be home before she went to sleep. "I changed my mind about staying, Have my horse brought to me immediately."

"Y . . . you're not spending the night, my lord?"

Kincaid tried to remain patient. He couldn't figure out if the man was slow-witted or just scared of him. "Yes, Sam. I return to London today. You and the staff are taking fine care of my uncle's estate. I need see nothing more."

Looking rather relieved, Sam and Tom hustled themselves across the garden in the direction of the barn. Kincaid had just crossed the grassy orchard when a stable boy appeared with his horse.

Kincaid tucked Margaret's journal and his mother's miniature into his saddlebag. He kept out the apple blossom for fear it would be crushed. He mounted and waved a farewell to the two servants, who stood side by side like Siamese twins.

Kincaid rode away from Rutledge Castle without looking back. *Good riddance,* he thought. *If I don't set foot here again in this lifetime, it'll be too soon.*

He rode down the hill, away from the estate, toward the little village of Rutledge. Halfway between the castle and the cottages below, he veered right off the rutted road. Nestled in the trees was a small church and churchyard where he had attended private services as a boy. Here was where his mother was buried.

Kincaid dismounted and tied his reins to the iron fence. He walked past the front door of the church that now barely hung on its hinges, around to the cemetery.

"Not much of a man for God, eh, Uncle?"

"What ye say, James?"

Kincaid turned, startled for a second time in the last twenty minutes. Surely the ghosts of the graves weren't calling him.

Upon closer examination he spotted an old woman hunched behind some mulberry bushes, tending to a grave marked by a crude wooden cross.

The old woman cackled as she straightened her crooked back, bringing herself up to her full height of no more than four and a half feet. Even from where Kincaid stood, he could smell the cloves she wore around her neck.

"Mavis?" He squinted in disbelief. "Tell me that isn't you."

She cackled, her gray eyes, nearly hidden with wrinkles, danced with delight. "Hehehehe. Never thought I'd see you again, James, boy."

He grinned. Mavis was the midwife at Rutledge. She'd delivered him and his father, and all his father's dead babies after him. She had cared for his mother on her deathbed after birthing a deformed child. She'd been here forever. As far as Kincaid knew, the old woman had been built centuries ago of the same stone as the castle.

Kincaid walked toward the woman, who was hunched with age, and wrapped his arms around her. Hell, you're still alive, Mavis? I thought you must be long gone to your reward."

She patted his back before releasing him. "Shows what a boy like you don't know, don't it?"

Kincaid crossed his arms over his chest staring at her. I just can't believe you're still here."

"Work's not over," she told him, taking up her digging stick again. "Not over till it's done."

He walked along the fence following her. "What are you doing?"

"Carin' for the graves." She dug at a thorned weed with her stick.

"Surely there must be others who can do that? I could send someone up from the village." He tried to take the stick from her hands but she moved just out of his reach, as stubborn as she had ever been.

"Always taken care of the Rutledge babies. Will till they drop these old bones into the ground."

Kincaid's gaze went to the tiny cross. It was a relatively fresh grave. At once he knew who this had to be. Another half-brother, stillborn. "My father's last?" he asked quietly. *Margaret's son.*

She nodded her pointed chin. "Aye."

He glanced at the fence, perplexed. "Outside the gate?"

"The earl wouldn't let the wee thing in the churchyard proper. Said he didn't deserve a Christian burial. Was only 'cause I dug the hole myself the little'n got a burial at all. That uncle of yours said to toss 'im in the woods and let the wolves eat 'im. Had to call the vicar up in the middle of the night in the rain to say 'is blessing." She spoke matter-of-factly without any malice toward the earl.

Kincaid looked away. A part of him wondered if he belonged here where he could make a difference to these people. But he only considered it for a moment. He could never live here. He doubted he could ever sleep a night within those walls. The past was already etched in the stone, as unalterable as the jutting towers.

He looked back at the grave. Done weeding, Mavis was planting a spring flower in front of the unmarked cross. "Did he have a name?"

"Don't know if his mama named him."

Kincaid nodded. He thought about asking Mavis about Margaret, but decided not to. What was the point? There was no need to drag her into the ugly business.

"Well, I'm going to see my mother's grave and then return to London."

She smiled. "I'm glad I saw your face 'afore I died, James." She didn't look up.

Kincaid turned to go, then on impulse he walked back to

the grave and added the apple blossom twig. He said nothing to Mavis as he walked away, lost in his own thoughts.

He would pay his mother's grave homage and then go. He was anxious to be on his horse headed east toward London. The sooner he escaped the pall of the Randall estate, the better off he figured he'd be.

Meg stood on the steps of Saity's laundry shop in the failing evening light. Monti waited in their coach, but only because she had insisted.

"A week?" Meg twisted her perfumed handkerchief between her fingers. Since receiving his inheritance, Kincaid had been shameful in his gift-giving. "Saity, I can't wait that long. Kincaid will only be gone two or three days."

Saity stood in the doorway in a clean sprigged cotton gown, minus her laundry apron. Her hair had been brushed and pulled back in a sleek coiffure. In the twilight she was rather pretty. "It's the best I could do, Meg. I'm sorry. I told you, my friend said ships don't just take off for the American colonies every day of the week."

Meg glanced over her shoulder at the coach. Monti had climbed down and was now pacing impatiently.

She looked back at Saity, peering at her through the close-cropped hood of her cloak. Since that last close call with the earl, she was hesitant to even step onto the street by the light of day. "Monti said he would see what he could do for me."

She grabbed Meg's arm. "You told him?"

"I had to. I had another run-in with the earl. Next time he'll catch me, Saity. I just know it."

"Don't say that! It's bad luck!" She took Meg's hand in hers and rubbed it. "Now if Monti wants to help you, you let him."

"He wants to give me money to pay my passage, but I don't know that I can take it. I don't like putting him in the middle of all of this. It's not fair to Kincaid; it's not fair to Monti."

"Listen, if there's one thing I learned on the street, sweety, it's that if a man wants to give ye money fer nothin', ye take it."

Meg had to smile at her version of wisdom. "So even if I do take the money later, what do I do now?" She tried to look around Saity, thinking she had seen someone move behind her in the shop.

"Ye pack yourself and get over here where you'll be safe in my neighbor's attic. We already fixed up a nice bed fer ye. Got an invisible door in my wall and everything, just like the king's privy closet."

Meg moved to one side of the step, realizing that Saity was purposefully blocking the door "Who've you got in there?" she whispered, smiling. "Your fish man?"

Saity brought her finger to her lips, blushing. "Shhh. He's just come to sup with me. Brought cod."

Meg tried to get a glimpse of the man, as much to tease Saity as to satisfy her own curiosity. "Oh, I can't come tonight and ruin your intimate supper."

Saity shrugged her thin shoulders. " 'e probably won't stay long. At least not after he gets a taste of those flat biscuits I made."

Meg chuckled. "I'll come tomorrow."

"You'll be safer here," Saity argued.

"No. It's all right. Really. Kincaid's not due for another day or two. Even if he left by the first light of the morning, he'd not be here till nearly noon. I'll be here before noon tomorrow." She held up her right hand. "Honestly." She backed down the splintered steps. "Now you have a nice supper with your man and I'll see you tomorrow."

"He's not my man," Saity corrected, giggling as she leaned over the rail.

Meg just waved a gloved hand in response and stepped up into the coach. She'd spend one last night in the bed that still smelled faintly of Kincaid, and then in the morning she'd leave.

By the time Kincaid arrive home to Charing Cross, she'd have disappeared into the city with her terrible secret, gone from him forever.

Twenty-five

Meg rolled over in bed, her head swimming. She was so tired, she couldn't think. It had been days since she'd slept more than a few hours and it was taking a toll on her.

Kincaid . . . I love him so much and now he's gone. I'll never see his smile again, never feel his lips on mine, never hear him call my name again.

Meg drifted off to sleep in exhaustion, still thinking of Kincaid, remembering every kind word, every touch of his hand, every broad grin.

She could still smell him on her pillow. It was that deep masculine scent that reminded her of the forests of Kent and of her sexual attraction to him that had been strong, even from their days in Newgate gaol.

She snuggled deeper into the feather tick. She could almost smell him here in her bed. In her dream she could feel his weight beside her. She smiled in her sleep.

"*Meg . . .*"

She heard his voice, so real . . .

He brushed his lips against hers, his hand snaking over her bare belly.

He had always known how to touch her.

She sighed as he took his pleasure, brushing his broad palm over her ribcage, lingering at her breasts.

Instinctively Meg curled against him in her dream, savoring his warmth. She caressed his shoulder, all of it seeming so real.

"Meg, I missed you," he whispered in her ear.

And I you, she said in her head. *I miss you now. I'll miss you forever.*

She felt his lips brush hers and she moaned, an excitement quickening in her veins. It was *so* real.

Her hand fell to his hip, stroking the taut, sinewy muscles of his thighs.

In her mind she heard him chuckle.

How she loved the sound of desire in his voice. Desire for her. She would never get over her amazement that a man like Kincaid could want her and want her with such fervor.

"Meg, my love. Meg, my lover."

She felt his weight upon her, pressing her deeper into the feather tick. Hot in her dream, she pushed back the counterpane impatiently. She wanted to feel nothing on her skin but his skin.

When his tongue teased the tip of her swollen breast she groaned. Threading her fingers through his silky hair, she squeezed her eyes tighter, wanting the dream, the sensations, to last forever.

He took her nipple between his teeth and tugged gently, her hands guiding his mouth.

"Like this, my sweet?" he asked.

"Yes," she breathed. "Yes, my love . . ."

She moved beneath him, wanting to feel the hardness of his manhood pressed hot and throbbing against her. She wanted to linger in this dream state of sensations forever . . . and yet she wanted more.

Meg heard herself moan, still amazed at how real this dream seemed. If she could always dream like this, she thought, perhaps she could bear to be without him. Perhaps her life would not end.

Meg parted her thighs, feeling his stiff rod scorching her bare thigh. She could feel the wetness there between her legs. She could feel her urgent need for him.

"Meg, Meg . . ." He cradled her in his arms. She could

feel his hair brush her cheeks, his warm breath on her lips. Then he slipped inside her with a sturdy thrust.

Meg's eyes flew. *Sweet heaven, this wasn't a dream!* "Kincaid?"

"Expecting someone else?"

Meg blinked. "W . . . what?"

Kincaid laughed, propping himself up on one elbow, still deep inside her. "I said, were you expecting someone else? You looked so surprised when you opened your eyes."

She closed her eyes again, panting. Where did he come from? Why was he here? He was supposed to be at Rutledge Castle. Had she wanted him so badly in her bed this one last time that she'd actually conjured him up?

"I'm sorry I woke you," he whispered in her ear. Then he tickled her earlobe with his tongue.

Meg sighed. Her desire for him was so strong that she couldn't think. Not now. Not until she was spent.

"A wonderful way to be woken," she purred, curling her arms around his neck, pulling him closer, deeper.

He kissed the pulse of her throat. "I thought you would think so."

Her eyes closed, Meg let go of all thought of the future or of how she would get away. All that mattered at this moment, was this moment. This last time together, the last time they would make love.

Slowly Kincaid began to move rhythmically, taking his time, teasing her, taunting her, making her ache for each thrust.

Meg's hands fell back on her pillow as she writhed beneath him, lost in the ecstasy of the moment. Again and again he drove her to the brink of fulfillment, only to cheat her, to make her moan.

"Kincaid . . ."

"Yes, my love?"

"Please . . ." She wrapped her arms around his waist, drawing him into her, trying to urge him to move faster.

"What is it? What do you want?" His voice was warm and breathy in her ear. She could tell by his tone that he, too, was close to orgasm.

"Tell me," he encouraged. "Tell me what you want."

"You." She turned her head this way and that, her entire body trembling with arousal. "I want you. Only you. Always you, Kincaid."

He lowered his body over his, his descent deliciously slow. Finally his mouth touched hers and Meg lifted her hips at the same time that she thrust her tongue into his mouth.

And each time Meg thrust her tongue, he thrust. Again and again until she was frantic.

Then finally, when it was he who could stand the sweet torture no longer, Kincaid brought her to the brink and over the side of the cliff. Together they were falling, falling in the moondust of the magic of the night.

Later, when Meg's breath came more evenly, when she was cuddled in his arms, her head resting on his shoulder, she finally found her voice. "Why . . . why did you come back so soon? Change your mind about going to Rutledge?"

"No. I went, but once I arrived, I realized I wanted nothing more than to come home to you."

The maternal instinct in Meg made her reach out and stroke his hair, smooth and silky between her fingers. "Was it terrible?"

He pulled away from her to lean back on the bolster, his arm tucked behind his head. "Yes. Worse than I remembered."

For a moment Meg was silent. She of all people understood the pain of one's past. "Are . . . are you all right?" she asked finally.

He drew her into his arms again. "Now that I'm home again, I am." He kissed her temple. "I'm fine. I stopped at the Green Duck Tavern on the way back into London and lucked upon one of my consorts. He was drinking with Monti, if you can believe that. It seems Mr. Geoffrey Gilbert will be leaving the city tomorrow morning. I believe he and I have a date on the highway."

"The last name on your list," Meg whispered as much to herself as to Kincaid.

"The last name." He hugged her. "And you know what that means. I'll take a few days to write my last satire." He yawned, closing his eyes, his voice already sleepy. "And then you and I will begin preparations for that wedding I was promised." He kissed her again. "Good night, my Meg, my light in the darkness."

Meg snuggled against him, vowing she would stay awake all night just so she wouldn't lose a moment of these last precious hours with him. But finally she, too, drifted off to sleep.

"Are you certain you should go without us?" Meg stood in their bedchamber, still in her dressing gown. She'd woken at dawn in a fit of morning sickness and had only finally just gotten out of bed half an hour ago.

He eased her into the chair and went back to tying his cravat. "I can go it alone. A simple task. I'll rob the man of his coin and jewels, bowl with the king, and be home by supper."

Meg took a sip of the tea Kincaid had brought her, unamused by his joking. She was too concerned for his safety. "Why not wait for Monti's return? If you saw him last night, surely he knows you planned on leaving first thing this morning. I'm certain he'll be home soon."

"It can't wait, Meg. If I don't catch Gilbert on his way out of the city, I'll not get him this trip. How could I possibly know when he'll be returning from his wife's family estate? If I don't go now, this could set us back weeks."

Meg toyed with the Brussels lace tie of her wrapper. She didn't want him to go. She'd said goodbye once. How could she do it again?

"I'll be home by late afternoon . . . in one piece. I swear it." He reached for his plumed cavalier's hat, left on the end of the mantelpiece. Now why don't you get into bed and go back to sleep? If you're not feeling better by this afternoon, I think we should call the physician."

She smiled weakly, rising. "I'm fine. Really." She rubbed his arm, feeling the strength of his muscles beneath the rich woolen coat. "Will you promise me you'll be careful?" She looked into his green eyes, swearing to herself that she wouldn't cry. She'd not have him remember her that way.

"I promise." He kissed the tip of her nose. Then he walked to the bed and lifted the counterpane. "Now lay down and let me tuck you in."

Not having the energy to argue, Meg climbed into bed and let him cover her to her chin. The bed linens still smelled of their lovemaking from last night.

"Go to sleep. I'll be back in no time." He gave her a husbandly peck on the cheek and then sauntered out of the room, his best highwayman's grin on his face.

"Goodbye," Meg whispered to the empty room. "I love you."

Then she slept, too spent for tears.

Sometime mid-morning, closer to noon, Meg woke to hear the front door open. "Kincaid?" She blinked away the sleepy cobwebs from her mind. It couldn't be him again, could it? How would she ever get away if he'd not leave the apartment?

"Kincaid?" She got out of the bed and padded barefoot down the hallway. She found Monti in the front withdrawing room pouring himself a brandy. "Oh, it's you."

He glanced up, a strange look on his face. He looked surprised to find her still here. "You didn't go yet?"

"No. Kincaid returned home early." She leaned against the doorjamb. "But now he's gone again. Gilbert." She frowned. "But you knew he was going. He said he met up with you last night."

"He said that?"

"Yes." She stared at him, uncomfortable, not knowing why. "So why weren't you here this morning? You were supposed to go with him. He waited for you but you didn't come."

He looked at her in her dressing gown. "I'm so glad you didn't go." He squinted. "Why didn't you go? Are you planning to go to Saity's this morning?"

"I was sick, but yes, I am leaving this morning. I want to be gone before Kincaid returns."

Suddenly he appeared concerned. "You all right? The baby?"

Without thinking, she brushed her hand over her flat belly. "Fine. Just morning greenness. But, Monti, you didn't answer my question. Why didn't you meet Kincaid this morning?"

Monti tipped back his head and drank the brandy in a single swallow. He reached for the bottle to pour himself another. "I . . . was detained."

Meg didn't like the sound in Monti's voice. Something was wrong. "Monti?" She stepped into the withdrawing room. She saw his hands shake as he poured himself another drink. "I said, what's wrong?"

He only shook his head as if he didn't want to say.

Meg's heart skipped a beat. "Kincaid? Is he in danger?" She didn't know what made her say it. Gut instinct.

When he didn't answer, she grabbed the sleeve of his coat. "Monti! Tell me Kincaid isn't in danger."

When he looked at her, his usual ruddy face was as pale as a dead man's. His lower lip trembled as if he were going to burst into tears.

"Monti, tell me, damn you! Is Kincaid in trouble?"

"I . . . I had no choice." Tears brimmed in his eyes. "I couldn't stall any longer. Nothing was working out as I planned. They . . . they were onto me."

"Monti! What are you talking about?"

The glass fell as he lifted his beefy hands to cover his face. "What have I done?" he cried. "Merciful Father, what have I done?"

Meg pulled his hands away angrily. Suddenly it was all clear. Too clear. The information leak. The close calls. Kincaid had insisted it was coincidence, a hazard of the trade. Bad luck even. But it had been Monti! Monti all along.

"Please tell me he's safe," she whispered on the verge of hysteria. "Make me believe you."

"I . . . never meant for him to be harmed." Monti started to cry. "I thought I could stay ahead of them."

"Ahead of whom?"

"The Lord Justice's men." He stumbled to a straight-backed chair and crumpled into it, his head hung, his arms lifeless at his sides.

Meg followed him. "You sent the Lord Justice's men after Kincaid?"

"No. Yes." He shook his head, seeming confused himself. "I did, but I never meant for him to get caught. I only meant for the Lord Justice to *almost* catch him. It was just a game, a cat and mouse game."

Meg grabbed Monti by the shoulders and shook him. "You betrayed Kincaid, one of the only friends you have? You were like brothers! Why? Why, damn you?"

When she let go of his shoulders, he slumped forward again. "Why does any man betray another?" he muttered. "Coin."

"Money!" Meg raged. "You betrayed the best man that walks this earth for futtering money!"

He began to blubber. "Kincaid . . . he . . . he had it all. A handsome face, a title coming to him, then he had you. I wanted something for myself. Something he didn't have to give me. I never thought they would actually catch him. I got him the pardon that first time. There was no trouble after that. I never thought he'd get hurt."

Meg crossed her arms over her chest. "You sorry son of a bitch! You never thought he'd get hurt sending the Lord Justice's henchmen after him?"

"I always checked the charts . . ." He looked up at her, his nose running, his cheeks wet from his own tears. "I went to the astrologer each time. I made sure they were lucky days for you both. I knew you were safe, then."

"You relied on the stars to keep us safe?" Meg couldn't believe Monti's words. How could he be so stupid?

Then Meg thought of Kincaid, out on some road about to be ambushed. Maybe it wasn't too late. Maybe there was still time. She looked over at the case clock on the mantel. "Is there still time?"

"I don't know."

She grabbed Monti by the scruff of his shirt and dragged him down the hallway toward her bedchamber. She had to get dressed and get a horse. There still might be time to save him!

"Tell me where he his," she demanded, yanking clothing out of her clothes press. She began to dress immediately, not caring how Monti saw her. Modesty seemed unimportant with Kincaid's life at stake.

"Tell me where he is and why this time will be different."

"Whitechapel Road, toward Mile end."

"You think he'll be caught. Why?"

Monti leaned against the doorjamb. "The Lord Justice lost his patience with me. Said he'd throw me in Newgate for obstructing the king's law if I didn't provide accurate information this time."

She stepped into a riding skirt and hooked the buttons. "And Kincaid's luck?" Her tone was sarcastic.

Monti shook his pathetic head. "Run out. The stars are bad and the Lord Justice has ordered that Captain Scarlet be killed on sight. He's gotten too much pressure from the men we robbed. There's to be no trial. The men just want him dead to spare themselves any further embarrassment."

Meg shrugged into her riding coat, grabbing up her stockings and boots. "Go downstairs and have the coachman saddle me a horse. Are you listening to me, Monti?"

"Listening."

"I want a horse out front in five minutes and then I want you gone from this place. I want you gone forever," she shouted in his face. "Do you understand me?"

"I . . . I can go with you. I can help."

"And what?" She stared him in the eyes. "Betray us again? I think not."

His head lulled. "I'm sorry. I'm sorry. It got out of hand. I wanted to be like him. Rich. I wanted a woman like you to love me. I wanted you to love me."

Meg turned her back to Monti, so angry she feared she might strike him. "Go," she ordered. At the bedside, she pulled a loaded pistol from the table drawer.

Meg rode down The Strand, east on Fleet Street, through the city as fast as she could. But the London streets were crowded and it seemed to take forever to weave through the throngs of pedestrians and the caravans of assorted vehicles.

Please, she prayed as she held tightly to the pommel, riding as fast as she dared. *Please, God, let me get there in time.*

Meg urged her horse faster as she reached the open road of Whitechapel. "Not much farther," she told the horse, trying to remember which was the bend in the road where Monti thought the ambush would take place.

What if it was too late? What if Kincaid was already dead?

Up and over a hill, Meg spotted more than a dozen soldiers on horseback following a coach and four. She pulled back hard on the reins, hoping they hadn't heard her approach. *Please let that be Gilbert,* she prayed.

But it had to be. The soldiers were following far enough behind that Kincaid might not see or hear them until it was too late.

Meg swung into the woods line to pass the soldiers unseen. Luckily they were moving slow enough to stay well behind the coach, so she could outride them. Once within the cover of the forest, far enough off the road not to be detected, she road hell-bent for the next turn in the road.

When Meg entered a thicket, she realized it had to be the one Monti had indicated Kincaid would be waiting in. What if Monti had lied?

Meg lowered her head to ride under a low-hanging branch, pulling her piebald to a halt. She stared in the forest. She could see the road. This had to be the place. But where was Kincaid?

Then she heard the click of the musket trigger behind her.

"Kincaid?"

"Meg?"

She looked over her shoulder, sawing on the reins to turn her horse around. There he was, Captain Scarlet, the highwayman, looking much the same way he had that night when he'd found her on the road from Kent.

"Oh, thank God I found you," she breathed as he lowered the pistol.

"What are you doing here?" Kincaid's voice was gruff and inpatient.

"It's a trap!" Behind her, down the road, she could hear the pounding of the horses' hooves and the roll of the carriage wheels. "You have to get out of here. They're coming for you. Soldiers. You've been betrayed!"

Kincaid yanked down the red swath of material that was his trademark. She could see his face fully.

"Betrayed how? By whom, Meg?"

She thought about her answer for a long second. "I don't know who's responsible," she insisted. "The tip was anonymous." She swung out of the saddle, grabbing his reins. "Now trade horses with me and get the hell out of here. Disappear into the forest while we still have a chance."

"Trade horses?"

"So if they follow you, they'll be following me." She grabbed his arm, practically hauling him out of the saddle.

She took his hat from his head, trading it for her own. "Give me your cloak, too."

"Meg—"

"Blast it!" she said through gritted teeth, pushing his hands aside to untie his black cloak herself. "Don't you see this might save your life? I can hear them coming!"

"And what if they catch you? If they stop you." He lifted her into his saddle. They could both hear the approaching vehicle now.

"If they stop me, what am I but a crazy woman taking a wild ride! Go now. Take a separate path. Go to one of the taverns and lose yourself for the day. I'll meet you at home tonight."

Kincaid mounted, her green cloak, too small for him, thrown over his shoulders, her plumed green wool riding cap perched on his head. She would have laughed at how ridiculous he looked if the situation hadn't been so dire.

The coach was nearly parallel with them on the road. Through the cover of the trees Meg saw the soldiers riding in behind it. Kincaid would have been caught. Once he'd ridden out onto the highway to rob Gilbert, it would have been too late by the time he'd spotted the horsemen.

Suddenly there was the sound of musketfire.

Meg whirled her horse around to see a figure cloaked in black, swathed in red, riding straight up behind the soldiers. From a distance it looked like Kincaid, but of course it wasn't.

Kincaid stared in disbelief. "Who the hell—"

"Ride," Meg insisted. "This is it. Your last chance. Your luck's run out, my love."

Just as the words came from her mouth, the soldiers fired on the man in black and he flew backward off his horse.

Meg squeezed her eyes shut as they fired again and again. "No," she whispered, hearing the body hit the dirt and gravel road.

"It's Monti! It's got to be. We've got to help him!"

Meg reached out to grab Kincaid's reins. "No. It's too late. You know it's too late."

"Meg? What the hell's going on? Why would Monti—"

Her eyes flew open. "This is our chance," she said, knowing it was a chance Monti had given them. "Ride!" She slapped the horse he rode hard on the rump with her quirt and the horse shot between two trees, headed in the direction of London.

"We'll separate farther down the road," she said, catching up with him. "I can meet you at home, later."

"Like hell!" He rode beside her at a gallop. "I'm not letting you out of my sight until you're safe and I've got a futtering explanation!"

Meg cringed at the harshness of his words. Now what was she going to do? How was she going to get away? And worse, what was she going to tell him of Monti?

Twenty-six

"I cannot believe Monti could have done something that reckless," Kincaid repeated. He stood in their bedchamber leaning against the mantel, staring into the flames of the fire he'd built. It had begun to rain on the ride into London and both of them had gotten soaked and chilled. Upon their safe arrival home to Charing Cross they'd bathed and changed into dry clothes. Kincaid wore a plain pair of breeches and a loose shirt. Meg wore her flannel and lace dressing gown.

"I don't know what to say." She chose her words carefully. "I told him not to come. That I would warn you myself."

"He had to have been drunk." He shook his head in obvious grief. "Otherwise he'd not have done something that stupid. What else were the soldiers going to do, but fire on him?"

Meg walked up behind Kincaid and placed her hand on his back, rubbing it. "I guess we'll never know why. The only thing we do know is that he did it to save you. He did it because he loved you. You'd have done the same for him."

Meg had decided on the ride home that there was no reason to tell Kincaid the truth. What would be the point? Monti was dead and there was no bringing him back. Captain Scarlet's days were over. As far as the Lord Justice knew, the thief had been caught. What good would it do anyone to tell Kincaid his friend had betrayed him and then made the ultimate sacrifice to redeem himself?

"Aye, I would have done the same to save him." Kincaid

sighed. "We have to claim his body. I would think the soldiers brought him back to London."

Meg walked to the table where she'd set out a light supper. "Have one of his friends claim his body. Then you can take care of the burial as you see fit. It'll be safer." She rested her hand on the back of a chair at the table. "Now, come. The cook shop delivered lamb stew with leeks and fresh bread. You need to eat."

Kincaid came to the table and sat down across from her. He took her hand and said a blessing over the meal and then began to eat. Meg knew he ate only out of habit, not because he was hungry.

She watched him eat the stew, just pushing her own around her plate. She wasn't hungry, either. Her concern now was how to get away. When they were bathing, she'd asked him to tell her more about his trip to Rutledge Castle, but he'd been strangely evasive and that concerned her. Had he seen or heard something to make him suspect the awful truth?

Meg knew she had to leave. Tonight. Once Kincaid was asleep, she'd just slip away. She knew he'd go to Saity's looking for her, but that wouldn't really matter anyway, because she'd not be at Saity's long. She'd thought long and hard on this today. Before she took that ship to the colonies, she had one more place to go. Somewhere in the back of her mind, she had known all along she couldn't leave England without making the pilgrimage. Like Kincaid, she too had to return to Rutledge Castle.

Later that night, when Kincaid slept on his back, his arms askew, Meg slipped out of their bed. Without making a sound, she dressed and retrieved the small bag she'd hidden in her clothes press. Fearful she would wake him if she touched him, she blew him a kiss from beside the bed, silent tears running down her cheeks. Then, on impulse, she walked to the writing

desk, picked up his quill, and scrawled a simple note across
a piece of parchment.

I love you. I'll love you forever.

I'm sorry I couldn't stay.

No explanation. No lies. It was better this way, she decided.
Then, in the cover of darkness, she took her bag and slipped
out of the bedchamber, out of the apartment and into the dark
city.

"Are you stark raving mad? Should I call a cart from Bed-
lam for ye?" Saity ranted.

It was barely dawn. Meg had slept a few fitful hours in
the attic in the house connected to Saity's shop, and now she
was having a biscuit and tea before she set off on her journey.

"I'm not crazy. I'm a mother."

"It's not safe. What if the ugly earl is there?"

"Kincaid was just at Rutledge. He said nothing of seeing
his uncle. The earl is still here in London."

"And if he ain't?"

"I'll take the risk."

"It ain't worth it. Not a grave. Not even the Virgin Mary's
is worth your life."

Meg paced the tiny kitchen attached to the back of the
laundry shop. A few sputtering tallow candles illuminated the
room. "Don't you understand? It's my child's grave. My son's.
The grave I never saw. I never had a chance to place flowers
on it or pray over it."

"The good Lord's got your baby wrapped in His loving
arms. Same as my dead babe. There ain't nothing in that
churchyard but ashes and dust. That ain't your baby, Meg."

She reached for her mug of tea, her chin set stubbornly.
"A mother should see her child's grave. I don't want him to
think I've abandoned him with my going off to the colonies.
It's already taken me too long to say goodbye properly."

Saity slapped a biscuit and a crock of butter down on the

table. "I think yer pregnancy's gone to your head." She lifted her palm in a solemn oath. "I swear, I do."

Meg buttered her biscuit. Tea and bread seemed to be the only thing that calmed her stomach these days. "You're not going to change my mind, so you might as well give up." She bit into the biscuit, catching crumbs with the tip of her tongue. "All you can do now is help me."

Saity plopped herself down in her chair and reached for the butter crock. She was already dressed for the day with her laundress's apron in place. "Help you how?"

"What are you going to tell Kincaid when he comes? Because he'll surely come."

"Not going to tell him nothing."

"He's not going to accept the fact that you know absolutely nothing of my disappearance."

"I don't care if he holds my head over a flame and singes my ears, I won't say a word. Not if he dips my bare feet in hot wax and—"

Meg had to laugh. "All right. All right. I understand. You won't tell where I've gone." She looked down at her bodice, brushing away the crumbs of the biscuit. "But do tell him I love him." Tears welled in her eyes. "I truly do. You know that, don't you Saity? I'm leaving him because I love him too much not to."

Saity got up from her chair and came around the table to take Meg in her arms. "There, there," she soothed, hugging her tightly. "I don't understand. I'm not smart like you. But I'll tell him what you said just the same."

Sniffing, Meg lifted her head from Saity's shoulder, taking the plain-loomed handkerchief she offered. "Thank you," Meg said. "Thank you for doing this for me. Thank you for being such a good friend."

"Nonsense." Saity opened a small cloth sack on the table and began to stuff biscuits inside. "You got me out of whorin'. I'll never be able to pay you back for that." She thrust out her hand, offering the dusty flour sack.

Meg took the bag of biscuits. "I'll be back in a day or two. You have the coin for my passage." The money Monti had insisted she take would be enough not just to pay her passage, but to keep her a long time in the colonies. Once the baby was born she thought she might set up a business. A store maybe. Surely the English women in the colonies wanted English tea and soap. "Have your fishseller pay and make the final arrangements. I'll be back in time to catch the ship."

"Ye can't get to Rutledge and back in one night in yer condition. Where will ye stay? The castle, mayhap? I'm sure if the earl is there, 'e'll invite you in!"

Meg made a face. "I've got the bed roll your Clancy gave me. I'll just sleep in the woods."

"Sleep in the woods!" Saity threw her arms up in the air. "I got half a mind to go with ye on the crazy journey. That way when yer man comes up my step spittin' and shoutin' like I know he will, I won't be here to hear it!"

Meg took Saity's hand, giving it a squeeze. "It's kind of you to offer, but you stay here. You take care of your business and that fine man of yours. Looks to me like he's getting worked up to ask you to marry him."

Saity blushed. "Think so?" Then she rolled her eyes. "I sure hope so, because I ain't gave 'im a piece. Not one lick and I'm dyin' to tumble with him."

Meg laughed at Saity's bawdiness. She understood what it was like to be in love and want to make love. She was so glad Saity had found that same happiness. "I'd better go now. If Kincaid's up early, he'll be here in no time."

Saity walked Meg to the back door where the horse Clancy had borrowed for her was waiting.

"Take care of yerself," Saity said, lifting the hood of Meg's plain black cloak over her tumble of curls. She tied it beneath her chin. "And be careful. You get scared, or you decide you don't need to go, you come right home to Saity, you hear me?"

Meg used the creaky wooden steps to mount the nag. It

wasn't much of a horse, but she was grateful for Clancy's help. "I'll be back in a day or two. Promise."

Saity stuffed the biscuits into a small leather bag hanging from the back of Meg's saddle. "Good luck to ye, then." Saity kissed her hand and then lifted her palm in farewell. "See you in a few days."

The morning sun was just beginning to rise in the east behind her when Meg rode off, headed for Kent and Rutledge Castle.

Kincaid opened his eyes and squinted in the bright morning sunlight that poured through the draped windows. He'd slept later than usual. Exhausted from the last few days of mental turmoil, he guessed.

Sitting up in bed, he ran his fingers through his hair, pushing it back off the crown of his head. Yesterday had been a hell of a day. Monti was dead. He could barely believe it. And it still made no sense.

But what did make sense in his life these days? He had gone to Rutledge Castle looking for clues concerning his stepmother, Margaret. He had expected to come home hating her even more. Instead, he almost felt a kinship with her. It was eerie. He hated her for killing his father, but he felt sorry for her at the same time. Having grown up in that household, seeing how his mother and stepmother had been treated, he could guess how it had been for young Margaret. Just the thought of his father bedding the pretty, shy young girl with her blond wisps of hair made him sick.

When Kincaid thought about his father's death and his declaration that he would find his killer, he realized now that he was doing it for himself. Not for his father. After all these years he was still trying to make his father love him. Even in death he was still trying to please the man who could never be pleased.

So why not just give it up, he thought, a tremendous weight seeming to lift from his shoulders. *If the earl wants to be vindictive, let him find her. Let him have her thrown into Newgate and convicted. All I really want now is Meg and a new life.*

Kincaid glanced at the empty place beside him in the bed, then around the room. "Meg?" He was quiet for a moment, listening for movement in one of the other rooms. Then he called louder, "Meg, you here?"

When she didn't answer, he climbed out of bed and reached for a crumpled pair of breeches on the floor. "Where are you?" He walked down the hallway, past Monti's room. On the off chance she was there, he looked inside. She wasn't. He closed the door again, unwilling to linger there this morning.

He checked both withdrawing rooms next, and lastly the small kitchen to the rear of the apartments. She was nowhere to be seen.

Gone to get something to eat, I suppose. He poured himself a small bucket of water from a pitcher to carry back to the bedchamber to shave. As he was leaving the kitchen, he heard footsteps on the back stairway.

That was odd. She never used those steps. Maybe she was looking for one of their hired servants that slept in the attic on the top floor. He turned around, smiling. "Meg?"

The door opened and young Amanda, the coachman's wife, looked back at him, startled. "Morning, sir." She turned away, obviously embarrassed by his state of undress.

"Morning." Kincaid frowned. "You haven't seen your mistress, have you?"

Amanda shook her head. "Ain't seen her since I came down this morning and that was just after dawn. Made biscuits to go with the jam I done up yesterday. You want for me to bring you a tray?" She kept her back to him.

"Whatever." He went back down the hall to his bedchamber, now concerned.

Had Meg gone to claim Monti's body on her own? Surely

she'd be smart enough to take her own advice. She'd been right that someone else unconnected with the infamous Captain Scarlet needed to do it.

Pouring the water into his washbowl, he dipped a sliver of shaving soap into the water and began to lather his face, standing at the window, looking down on the street below.

"You shouldn't have done it, Meg," he said to himself.

But he knew how much she had cared for Monti. As much as Kincaid himself. Monti had been a brother to her, a friend. He'd been a good friend to them both.

Kincaid lifted his straight razor to his chin and began to stroke away yesterday's shadow of a beard. He guessed he'd dress and check a couple taverns. Perhaps there would be gossip concerning yesterday's shooting. Maybe one of Monti's friends would know what had happened to his body.

Staring into the small mirror propped on the washstand, Kincaid caught a reflection of his writing desk on the far wall behind him. A piece of parchment on top caught his eye. It wasn't his writing, which was odd because Meg rarely used his desk. She preferred to sit in a comfortable chair with a book and paper on her lap.

Razor still in hand, he padded across the room. His gaze settled on the note. He read it once, his breath catching in his throat. Then a second time.

There was a buzzing in his ears as he came to the realization that she was gone. That she had fled after she swore she wouldn't.

"Son of a bitch!" he shouted throwing the razor at the wall. It hit the chair rail, splattering shaving soap before it fell to the floor and went skittering under her clothes press.

"Son of a bitch, you did it anyway!" He felt as if someone had kicked the wind out of him. He felt utterly betrayed.

Not Meg. Not my Meg . . .

He lifted the note for more careful inspection, noting the blots of ink where something wet had hit the writing. Her tears?

"Why, Meg? Why?" he whispered.

Suddenly a strange feeling came over him. The handwriting. It was familiar. Yes, it was Meg's, but there was something else familiar about the writing. He'd seen it elsewhere before. Recently.

Then it hit him, as hard as a lead musketball to the chest.

Tossing the note back on the table, he spun around. His saddlebags, where the hell were they? He'd just brought them home last night, having never unpacked them from his trip to Rutledge.

He ran to his clothes press and threw it open, tossing clothing over his head as he dug for the leather bags. Stockings, breeches, feathered hats, and lace-cuffed shirts. Nope. The bags weren't here.

He turned back, staring at the room, wracking his brain. "Where the hell are they, Meg?" he said aloud, hearing the tremble in his own voice.

"Amanda! Amanda!" He ran out of the room and down the hall.

She met him at the inside kitchen door, drying her hands on a blue and white towel. "S . . . sir?" She stared at him wide-eyed and frightened.

He grabbed the kitchen towel from her hands and wiped at the shaving soap still on his face. "Where are my saddlebags? I can't find them."

She followed him back down the hall. "I . . . I don't know, my lord. I . . . I haven't seen them."

Kincaid kicked open his bedchamber door. "You clean in here, right? So, where are they?"

She clutched her hands, trembling. "I didn't clean here this . . . this week, my lord. I didn't touch them. I didn't touch anything. I swear I didn't."

"Well," he boomed. "They sure as hell have to be somewhere! They didn't just sprout legs and—"

He halted mid-sentence, his gaze settling on the bed he and Meg had shared. There they were. The saddlebags. Right

where Meg always hung them after he left them on the floor
by the door. Hanging on the bedpost. He almost laughed. The
little jade had straightened up before she fled!

"You're dismissed, Amanda," Kincaid flung over his shoulder, heading straight for the bed. "Shut the door behind you!"

He barely heard the sound of the closing door as he lifted
the worn saddlebags from the bedpost. He stroked the oiled
leather. He'd had these bags for years, since his days in Paris
with Monti.

Monti . . . Meg . . . My life is crumbling before my eyes.

Kincaid thrust his hand into the bag and felt for the journal
he hoped was still there. What if the crafty witch had found
it and taken it with her? At this point he'd have believed anything.

"Ah, ha!" His fingers hit the sharp edges of the book and
he pulled it out of the bags, letting them fall to the floor
without heed.

Kincaid strode to the writing desk to retrieve the note Meg
had left. If he wasn't mistaken, and he didn't believe he was,
he knew the handwriting would closely match. True, one had
been written years earlier by an immature hand, but handwriting didn't change that much over the years.

No wonder the damned writing in the journal had looked
so familiar to him. . . . How could he have been such a fool
not to have realized it two days ago at Rutledge?

He flipped open to a page in the journal. *The earl followed
me in the garden again today* . . . it read. He lifted the note
Meg had left him to compare it to the journal page. What he
saw made his heart skip a beat.

"No," he whispered, staring in disbelief, knowing it was
true, wishing beyond hope that it wasn't.

"How could I have been so stupid? You were a blonde then,
but blondes turn dark with age, don't they Meg?" he said
aloud to himself. "I was stupid and you were smart."

"Meg. Margaret. Dead baby. I never made the connection."

He let the journal and the note drop onto the desk. "You

love me? Right. How could I have been so foolish?" He hit his forehead with the heel of his hand. "How could I have been so blinded by your beauty, your body?"

He hit the closest chair with his hand, knocking it over, enraged. "You set me up, didn't you, Margaret? You set me up right from the beginning?" he shouted at the empty room. "You never loved me. You were just trying to save your own skin."

He grabbed a pair of dirty stocking and his muddy boots. "Well, you may be chuckling now at your clever move. You killed my father, cuckolded me. But we'll see who laughs last, Margaret Randall. We'll just see."

Twenty-seven

Kincaid bounded up the steps to Saity's shop and hit the door with his closed fist, knocking it open. "Where the hell is she?"

Saity turned from the hearth, a dripping wet shirt in her hands. "What?" She looked only a little startled . . . as if she'd been expecting him.

"I said, where the hell is she?" He pointed. "And don't try to pretend you don't know. Who else would she come to?" His tone was bitter. "Who else would have aided in this deception, but another woman?"

Saity lifted an eyebrow. "Excuse me, but you got no right to come into my place of business and start shoutin' at me!" She was a small, comparatively frail woman, but her voice was commanding. "Now you want to talk to me, you talk to me with a civil voice, else"—she let go of one sleeve of the shirt to point—"you get out of my shop!"

Kincaid looked away from her, wiping his mouth with the back of his gloved hand. He was so furious he could barely control himself. Perhaps Saity was right. He shouldn't talk to her that way, but damn it, his life was falling apart!

When he spoke again, he made an effort to keep his voice even. "I want to know where she is. Here?"

Saity played the innocent. "Is who here, sir?"

"You know who the hell I mean! Meg!"

Saity turned her back on him, dropping the shirt into the bucket of water at her feet. "There you go, shoutin' at me again. I'm tellin' you, Kincaid, friend or not, you won't get nowhere tryin' to bully me. The days of Saity Nutter bein' bullied are long gone." Her back to him, she added a bit of soap to the water and began to rub the shirt against the washboard. Apparently she was unintimidated by his physical appearance or gruff voice. Apparently she meant what she said.

Kincaid rested his hands on his hips, taking a deep breath. He knew Saity had something to do with all of this, he just knew it. If Meg wasn't here, Saity knew where she was. He just had to get her to talk. "I need to know where she is, Saity," he finally said quietly.

"Why?"

"To talk to her, damn it!" He kicked at a stool and knocked it over, sending it rolling across the uneven floorboards.

Saity watched the stool roll away with exaggerated disinterest. She glanced up at him. "You don't sound like a man who wants to know where a woman is so you can talk to her." She dropped the shirt into the wash water and faced him, crossing her arms over her chest. When she did so, she left a wet spot on her blue apron. "You sound like a man who's lookin' fer a woman so he can rough her up. I know all about that. Remember? I been there. Had them black eyes."

"I'm not going to rough her up!" He made a strangling motion with his hands. "I'm just going to kill her."

Saity frowned. "Oh, so I should tell you where she is so you can kill her?"

The way she stood there, her arms crossed over her chest, speaking so matter-of-factly, made Kincaid just a little ashamed of himself. He was behaving badly. He knew it. It was just that he was so damned angry. So damned hurt . . .

He stared at his boots for a moment, then looked up. "She can't just leave like this. I know who she is and I want an explanation." He hit his chest with his fist. "Don't you think I have a right to that?"

"You know who she is? So what explanation do you want?" She shrugged. "That she accidentally came upon her stepson after killing his father in self-defense. Only she didn't know it was her stepson until after she'd fallen in love with him?" She lifted a hand. "There. There's your explanation. She killed your father only she didn't know it was the father of the man she'd fall for later. So she left."

"Accidentally my lily white ass! She set me up. She killed my father. Then she hid in the one place she knew my uncle . . . I would never look."

Saity rolled her eyes. "Oh, please! Just like a man to think he's always in the middle of everything. Do you hear what you're saying?" She took a step closer. "You're saying she ran out of that castle, bleedin' down her legs, and tracked you down? You're sayin' she fainted in your path, knowin' you'd pick her up? Knowin' you'd get arrested and have to stay together for weeks in Newgate Prison? You're sayin' she knew you'd fall in love with her and that way save her own skin?" Saity burst into laughter. "That's the best one I heard this week!"

Kincaid picked up the stool and righted it, trying to ignore Saity's laughter. He didn't want to hear this. He didn't want logic. He was too angry for logic. He wanted revenge. Blood.

"So it *does* sound a wee silly to you, eh?" Saity said after a long moment of silence.

Kincaid looked up at her.

"Admit it. It does sound stupid, doesn't it? Only real things can turn out this strange."

He looked Saity straight in the eyes. "Is she here?"

"No." She lifted her hand. "But you're free to look around. You can hang out them shirts on the line whilst yer in the back, if you like."

Kincaid started for the door that led to the attic stair, than spun around. "Ah, the hell with it!" He threw up his hands. "I don't want to talk to her. I don't want to see her. She lied to me. She betrayed me. The little conniving witch never loved me. She just—"

"Now wait there one second." Saity shook her finger angrily. "There's some things you can say. Yea, she told some lies, but she loved you, you jackass. She loved you more than anyone on this blessed earth will ever love you." She set her jaw. "So you tell yourself what you want, but don't be sayin' she didn't love you 'cause it just ain't true. Why the blast do you think she took off?"

"What am I doing here?" He stomped toward the door. "What could have ever made me think you'd be any help?" Before Saity could say another word, he walked out of her shop and slammed the door behind him. To hell with Saity. To hell with Meg. To hell with his uncle. To hell with them all! He was getting drunk.

Meg rode the nag along the path she'd traveled six months before, thinking of how funny it was that a woman's life could change so greatly in such a short time. What was six months? A growing season? The time it took to sew a quilt or embroider a table linen? For heaven's sake, it took more than six months to grow a child in a womb.

She brushed her hand absently over her abdomen that she knew would soon begin to swell with new life. Six months was nothing compared to the time she had spent at Rutledge Castle. And yet look at how differently life was today than it had been six months ago. In that short period of time she had given birth and lost her child. She had murdered a man and lost her husband. She'd spent time in jail and time in the arms of a man who loved her. She'd loved and been made love to. It had been a tragic six months, a glorious six months.

She couldn't help wondering where the next six would lead her. A new world, a new life, as a new person. The thought was overwhelming, and yet it gave her hope. What she carried in her womb gave her hope.

Meg peered up at the sunshine pouring through the ancient pin oak trees overhead. The warmth felt good on her face.

Considering the distance she'd traveled, she guessed Rutledge couldn't be much farther. She was anxious to get there, anxious to see her baby's grave. And anxious to get away.

Kincaid may have felt the need to walk the cold stone corridors of the castle that had been his home for so many years, but Meg didn't. She wished she could burn the damned place to the ground and end its curse.

Less than half an hour later the road began to look familiar. She'd never been permitted to travel far from the castle. Philip always believed her place was at home where he could keep an eye on her, but she'd been this way before, to a county fair. That was in the early days of their marriage, when he was at least occasionally kind to her. She studied the countryside as she rode along at a comfortable pace. She remembered the trees, the turns in the road, the thatched cottage up the hill with the sheep that surrounded it.

Then the sky began to cloud overhead. "Oh, no," Meg muttered, urging her mount a little faster. "Not rain."

The storm moved in quickly. One minute the sky was bright with sunshine and hope, the next minute it was dark and foreboding. "An omen?" she wondered aloud, staring up at the ugly clouds rolling in. Then she laughed at herself and her foolishness. Perhaps more of Monti's superstition had rubbed off on her than she'd thought.

Monti. She'd tried not to think about him all day. She still couldn't believe he'd betrayed Kincaid for money. Greed. Her grandmother had always said greed was the downfall of many a noble man.

Another quarter of a mile and the rain began to fall. It was as if God had lifted a bucket of well water and poured it over the earth. "Oh, no," Meg moaned, huddling beneath her cloak. Despite the fact that it was May, it was still cool. And once the sun was gone, she was chilled.

"It can't be much farther," she told her mount, patting him on the neck. She squinted to see through the blinding rain. *Hadn't it been raining the night she'd fled from Rutledge?* Yes, raining and sleeting. She shivered, remembering that night. She didn't know where she'd gotten the courage to flee. She'd been a different person then, not as strong and confident as she was now. Kincaid had been the one who had given her that confidence.

Kincaid . . . She wouldn't think about him now, nor about the loneliness of the days to come. She needed to concentrate on getting to her baby's grave and getting out of there safely. Then she would make the journey to the colonies. Maybe then, when she was safe with an ocean between them, she'd think about Kincaid.

She passed the place in the road where she thought Kincaid had picked her up the night she fled the castle. She didn't remember much of that night. She was out of her head with grief and the exhaustion of childbirth. But this looked right. And the spot looked like a place Kincaid and Monti would have chosen for a hold-up.

A little farther down the road Meg spotted a cluster of cottages. It had to be the little village of Rutledge. So what did she do now? Go straight to the cemetery? What if someone saw her?

So what if someone did? The earl was in London. Who else would bother her? She was still Lady Surrey to the cottars—a woman of great importance. No one would dare stop her or question her.

Among the huddle of thatched cottages, Meg spotted a young girl standing in the rain. She looked to be eight or nine with long gangly legs and corn-yellow hair. The girl was signaling to her.

Meg didn't recognize the child. Who was she? What did she want?

"Yes?" Meg urged her horse off the muddy road. "Do you need help?"

The little girl pulled her apron over her head to shield herself from the driving rain. She grabbed Meg's horse's reins. "My grandmother says come in out of the rain, traveler."

Meg looked up at the cottage and its lamplight flickering in the tiny sod window.

"She has tea and biscuits," the girl enticed.

Meg glanced up the road toward the castle. She had to go that way to reach the cemetery. She looked back at the child.

"Just a little tea. 'Til you get warm."

What's the harm? Meg thought. She was cold and wet and concerned, not for her own health, but the welfare of Kincaid's baby she carried. "All right. Just a cup of tea and then I must be on my way." She dismounted awkwardly, landing in a mud puddle.

The child led Meg's horse away. "Be right back."

Meg waited under the overhang of the cottage where a vagrant light shone in the window. A moment later the girl returned.

"I put 'im in my uncle's stall and gave 'im a block a hay and water."

"Thanks. I'll pay you for the hay."

"No. Grandmother says that ain't . . . is not necessary. If the good Lord keeps us in hay, we got enough to share." The child opened the door to the cottage and went inside.

Meg followed, having to duck to make it under the low sill. Inside the single sod room it was warm, the light dim. It smelled of clover hay, fresh floor rushes, and ginger. The room was sparse with a battered table, two mismatched chairs, and a hemp-rope bed. Overhead there were rows of baskets and bundles of dried herbs hanging from the rafters. In places, Meg had to duck to keep from striking her forehead on a basket.

"Sit here by the fire and dry yourself." She dragged a chair from the table to the hearth, leading Meg. "I'll get the tea. You make yourself com . . . fortable." She watched Meg as she went to pour the tea that was already brewing in a crock on the table.

Meg removed her cloak and hung it over the chair, rubbing

her hands together in front of the fire to warm herself. "You said your grandmother sent you to get me. Where is she?"

"Gone to deliver a baby. But she'll be back. She saw you when you came into the village. Thought she recognized your face."

Meg took the cup of fragrant tea the child offered. "Who is your grandmother?"

"Mavis, the midwife."

Mavis. Memories of the night she delivered John came tumbling back. Mavis had been a strange woman who smelled of cloves, she remembered. But it was Mavis she had to thank for her escape. If Mavis hadn't given her those old clothes and practically pushed her out the door, Meg would never have had the courage to leave on her own.

"I do know your grandmother!" She sipped the tea that had a strange taste, but was good. "She delivered at my lying-in."

The girl perched herself on the edge of the table, swinging her feet. "Grandmother delivers all the children, bastard brats to the earl's nieces and nephews," she said proudly. Then she looked at the floor. "Well, she did deliver at the castle."

Meg wasn't sure what to say. Did the girl know who she was? Meg decided it would just be better to skirt the whole issue. "So what's your name?"

The girl looked up, beaming. "Annie, Annie Mavis, named after my grandmother. My mother died and my father left me here to find work elsewhere."

Meg nodded. "You speak very well, Annie."

She nodded. "Grandmother teaches me the right words. Someday soon, when I'm bigger, I'm going to work in a big house." She wrinkled her nose. "But not Rutledge Castle. Bad spirits. Grandmother says I'm to stay away from Rutledge and the curse. She says if you got away, I can, too."

Meg stared at the little girl. "Your grandmother knows who I am? Not just that I'm a traveler?"

Annie leaned over to whisper as if someone else could have been in the tiny cottage. "You're the wife who got away. Lady

Surrey. Ye didn't end up in the graveyard same as the others," she whispered. "Grandmother says you're a woman to be *reckoned* with." She crossed her arms, wrapping them around her thin waist. "When I grow up I'm going to be just like you, Lady Surrey."

"Shhh, child. Don't call me that." Meg rose. "I'm Meg now, Meg Drummond. It's just a ghost of the past that passes through here now. Do you understand?"

"The earl said you murdered his brother, but Grandmother called it self . . . self . . ." She struggled to find the right word.

"Self-defense," Meg finished for her. "And your grandmother is a smart woman. I did kill him, but only because he was going to kill me." She saw no need to tell the little girl about the baby. No need to upset her.

"Would you like a ginger biscuit and more tea?"

Meg looked out through the window. If possible, it seemed to be raining even harder. She only hedged for a moment. "Oh, all right. Since the rain hasn't let up. But then I have to go."

"Grandmother said to tell you to spend the night. She won't be back till tomorrow, come a baby born to life or a baby buried. She said you'd need your strength for your trip."

This was all so eerie that Meg considered leaving. How did Mavis know so much about her? "I . . . I don't know if I should stay."

Annie brought her a cake on a clean piece of cheesecloth. "Grandmother said not to be afraid. She's no witch, just a woman who knows about mothers. She said to tell you she knew you'd come back. She knew you'd want to see the grave before you got on with your life."

Meg smiled. "My baby is buried in the churchyard?"

"Sleep in my bed with me tonight and I'll take you in the morning. Grandmother said I could."

Meg sat down in the chair by the fireplace to nibble on the ginger cake. The thought of spending the night and going to the churchyard in the morning was enticing. It was so warm and comfortable and dry in here and so wet out there. And what if she did visit the grave now? Where would she sleep, then? She'd certainly not make it back to London in the storm on the nag she'd ridden here on. And then what would she do when she returned to London? The ship to America wasn't leaving for days. Chances were Kincaid would be looking for her. Rutledge was the place he'd never know to look for her.

Meg took the teacup the girl had refilled for her. "I think I will stay."

Annie jumped up and down, clapping her hands. "Oh, goody. A friend to stay with me. I hate sleepin' here alone when Grandmother's birthing babies."

"So bring your chair." Meg waved her hand. "Come have tea with me and tell me a story. I know a girl as bright as you must have a good story or two in her pretty head."

Annie dragged the chair through the floor rushes. "Oh, I do. Just wait till you hear this one!"

The Earl of Rutledge stood at the window of his library staring at the dreary rain. Even a fire in the fireplace had not been able to take the chill from his bones.

He was in a foul mood. He'd received word from Rutledge Castle that his nephew had arrived. He'd taken his carriage at first light yesterday from London back to Rutledge just to see James, to be here with him in his ancestral home.

But by the time Percival got here, the turd was already gone. Apparently he'd stayed no more than an hour or two, but the messenger had already been sent to London.

Rutledge slapped his hand on the desk, rattling an ink well. His patience was wearing thin with the boy. Here he was to inherit this great estate one day and he barely gave Percival the time of day. He'd expected better of him. Once Percival had released his brother's funds to James, he had expected frequent visits. Perhaps a party thrown by James in Percival's honor. A little ass-kissing. Percival felt he deserved it.

But the boy had a mind of his own. He always had. That was why Philip had kicked him out of the house to begin with. It had all been over politics. The boy hadn't seen the profit that was to come from siding with Cromwell and his Roundheads. He hadn't realized the financial opportunities as Percival and Philip had. The boy's head had been filled with thoughts of loyalty to the Crown, nonsense that could have gotten him killed if it hadn't been for Percival's power. So Philip had sent his son packing and the boy had wandered off to Europe with so many idealist cavaliers.

Percival wandered away from the window and his desk, bored. It was raining too hard to return London tonight. Besides, he had matters to take care of before he returned. He was due for a trip home anyway, so while he was here, he thought he might as well see to them.

Matters to take care of . . . He thought of the dungeon down below, a spark of an idea flickering in his head. Hmmmmm. He was bored. Perhaps that which waited downstairs for him could alleviate some of that boredom. He chuckled at his own cleverness. Of course! Why had he not thought about that before?

"Higgins!" Percival opened his library door and stuck his head into the hallway. "Higgins, where the hell are you?"

He immediately heard timid footsteps in the stone corridor. "My lord?"

"I want my supper."

"N . . . now, my lord?" Higgins kept his head bowed, his eyes averted.

"Yes, now!" Percival reached out and plucked him in the forehead. "You think I meant tomorrow?"

"N . . . no, my lord. It's only that it's early for your supper. You usually insist—"

"You're going to argue with me," Rutledge sputtered, "about when I want my blasted supper? Me, the Earl of Rutledge?" As he spoke spittle flew through the air. He wiped his deformed mouth impatiently with the corner of his handkerchief. "Tell me my household doesn't need disciplining! With that last burst of words, he touched his chest with his hand, feeling a tightening.

Higgins took a step back, just out of Percival's reach. "No, No, my lord, your household is in definite order."

The earl exhaled, waiting for the pain. After a moment he breathed deeply again, relieved that no pain came this time with the tightening in his chest. "Good," he said, forcing himself to calm down. The pains seemed to come when someone aggravated him. "I'm glad to hear it. Now bring my supper and then you are dismissed. I shall entertain myself this evening and will not need you again."

"Yes, my lord." Higgins began to back away.

"Oh, and Higgins . . ."

He turned back to look at Percival standing in the lighted doorway of the library. "Should I have a body to dispose of . . ."

The man immediately lowered his gaze. "I would take care of it discreetly, my lord."

"Excellent, because were I to need such services, there would be a reward."

Higgins looked up, licking his lips. A reward, sir?"

"Have you seen the young girl that lives with the old midwife?"

Higgins touched his periwig. "The blonde with the blue eyes? Oh, yes, my lord."

"Would you like her?"

Higgins lowered his gaze, his lust obvious in his shark-gray eyes. "I would, my lord."

"Aye. I thought so, you sick bastard. So go with you and I'll call you, should your service be needed."

"Yes, my lord." Higgins backed into the shadows. "Thank you, my lord."

Percival smiled his crooked smile as he turned away, already anticipating his own evening's distraction. Perhaps a trip home was just what he needed to pick up his spirits afterall.

Kincaid lay in bed, his boots on the white counterpane, staring dismally at the rain that hit the window. Cradled on his chest was a bowl of calf liver stew only half eaten, in his hand, a pottle of wine he drank straight from the container.

Meg never let him drink from the bottle. It always had to be from a glass. Even when he told her he'd always drank that way at home, she'd said not in her home. She wouldn't let him eat in the bed, either. Crumbs.

He picked up a cold muffin from the plate on the side table and flung it onto the bed, watching the crumbs fly. He stared at his muddy boots and at the place on the counterpane where they'd left their mark. No dirty boots were allowed in Meg's house, either.

"So how do you like that, Miss Neatness?" he said to the empty room. "I can eat where I want. Drink when I want. Just like the good old days before I had a woman to drag me down."

No one answered him of course, because there was no one there. Monti was dead. Friends had claimed his body and it was being prepared for burial right now. Kincaid had seen to the matter on his way home from Saity's.

And of course Meg was gone.

Meg . . . his sweet Meg, his light in the darkness. How the hell had this happened? Why hadn't he seen it coming?

He shoved the bowl of stew onto the table and got out of bed. And what was he going to do now that she was gone? He felt so empty inside without her.

He groaned. She'd killed his father, damn it! How could he still feel this way about her? Why did he still physically ache for her, knowing the horrible truth of what she'd done. What was wrong with him? God's bowels, she was his step-mother and she'd killed his father!

He took a slug of the wine, resting the bottle on his shoulder the way the men had done in his drinking days in Paris. But for some reason it wasn't fun like it had been then. And without Meg here to tease, it seemed silly. Juvenile.

He set down the wine. Because it was juvenile. His whole reaction to this mess had been childish. His intention when he left Saity's had been to get drunk. Really drunk. Drunk like he hadn't been but a few times in his life. But the thought quickly lost its appeal. No matter how much he drank, he knew Meg would still be gone.

She'd left him. Not really loved him, he guessed. Wasn't that what his father had told him? That no one would ever love him? Could love him?

"Oh, Meg, why didn't you tell me?" he whispered. "Why didn't you tell me the truth?"

And then, it happened again. Just like it had in the Rutledge nursery. He could almost hear her voice in his head.

Because you would have hated me, she whispered in his head.

"No, I wouldn't have," he said aloud.

Because I would have hurt you . . .

Kincaid stood in the middle of the room, his head hung so that his chin touched his chest. "Because you loved me," he whispered to the empty room. "Of course. I see your reasoning. You left me because you loved me enough to sacrifice yourself and the happiness you so well deserved."

He wiped his nose with the back of his hand, his eyes clouding with tears.

He had to find her. He had to tell her how he honestly felt. What he really thought. Hell, the truth was that if he'd had the chance, perhaps he'd have killed his bastard father, as well. He knew what a cruel man his father had been. How could he blame her without hearing from her what had happened that night in their bedchamber? Knowing Meg as he did and knowing Philip Randall, he knew logically Philip was probably the guilty party and Meg the innocent.

So, what was he going to do now? How was he going to find his Meg? How was he going to tell her that he still loved her, despite the blood on her hands?

Saity, of course, was his only hope. Saity had to know where she'd gone. The trick would be getting her to tell him after he'd been so nasty to her.

He stared out the window at the pouring rain, deciding that the best way to endear himself to the laundress was not to wake her in the middle of the night.

He sighed, running his hands through his black hair, pushing it over the crown of his head. He'd go to Saity tomorrow. That was what he'd do. And he'd take one hell of an apology with him when he went.

Twenty-eight

Kincaid stood in Saity's doorway, several cloth sacks and boxes in his hands. "I come bearing gifts and a humble apology," he told her sheepishly.

Saity lifted up on her tiptoes to peek inside one of the sacks. "You got chocolate in there?"

He smiled a little. "And an orange."

Saity's eyes grew wide with excitement. "Orange? Bring yourself into my humble shop, my lord." She led the way. "I don't know how long I'm willin' to let ye stay, but at least long enough to let me get a taste of that orange."

Kincaid laughed. "I do owe you an apology, Saity." He dropped the boxes and bags on her worktable that was piled high with laundry. "I was an ass yesterday. I was mad and I was hurt and you were the only one around I could take it out on." He looked up at her, feeling awkward, but glad the apology was over.

Saity stared at him until finally Kincaid lifted his hand. "What? You want more groveling?"

She shook her head, her forehead wrinkled. "No. I'm just tryin' to figure out what you are, cause I know you ain't no man. Men don't ever say they're sorry. Never admit to being wrong, either."

He frowned. "Well, I was wrong to come in here knocking furniture around and shouting at you. There's no excuse for ill behavior like that in front of a lady."

Saity burst into a fit of giggles, covering her face with her damp apron. "A lady! Me! Come now, you knew me back in Mother Godwin's. You know what I done to turn a coin. It's only by luck ye didn't have a piece of my peppered tail."

Kincaid smiled, glad she could look at herself and her past and make light of it. "It's not what title a woman carries or what she does that makes her a lady, it's here." He tapped his chest over his heart. "It's what's in here that makes you a lady, Saity. And you are a lady."

Grinning shyly, she reached into one of the boxes and pulled out a wheel of cheese wrapped in cloth. "So now ye flattered me shamelessly and brought me presents. I know what ye want, ye sly weasel."

"Please, Saity." He clasped his hands. "I was up all night. I've thought long and hard on this. I can't live without Meg. I don't care what she's done. My father was a cruel bastard. I would guess Meg killed him in self-defense and that it was not murder as my uncle claimed. Saity, the man deserved it. I forgive her. I just want her back."

Saity stared at the orange in her hand. "I told her to jest tell you the truth. I told her you loved her enough to let it go." She frowned. "But she wouldn't hear of it. She thought that if she left, you'd never know the truth and get hurt by it."

Kincaid removed his hat and tossed it on the table. "I understand why she did it. I just want her back. I want a life with her. My days on the highway are done. I have no life without her."

Saity tugged on a lock of her blond hair. "Well, the thing is, we got a problem."

"What problem? Just tell me where she's gone. I'll find her. I'll tell her I love her. I'll take her to the colonies where she wants to go, far from Rutledge, and we'll have that life we dreamed of."

"You don't understand. I promised."

"Promised what?"

"That I wouldn't tell where she's gone. I swore that even if you tortured me I wouldn't tell."

"Tortured you?" Kincaid made a face. "What kind of man do you think I am?"

Saity sat down on a stool, her orange still in her hand. "I think you really do love Meg and that you belong together like the moon and the stars. But I gave my word, and what else have I got but my word."

Kincaid began to pace. "All right. All right. We can work something out here. Can you take me there?"

"Don't know where it is."

He looked up, fearing what she implied. "Please don't tell me she's sailed for the American colonies alone."

Saity grimaced. "Not yet, she ain't."

"But she says she's going there?"

"I ain't supposed to say."

Kincaid groaned, frustrated. He walked back and forth behind Saity's chair. "All right. Meg's going to America, but she hasn't left yet, right?"

"Right." She pointed. "But I didn't say that. You guessed it yourself, you sly devil."

He smiled. "All right. So she's hiding out, from me and from my uncle since both of us are looking for her. Yes?" He lifted a brow, waiting for confirmation.

She sniffed the orange. "Seems like it would make sense . . ."

"So where would she hide, Saity? Not here. Not here, because you knew I'd come here first."

"Well, she ain't just hiding. She had something to do before she went."

"Something to do?" He hit his forehead with the heel of his hand. "Something to do before she left England. Think, Kincaid. Think like Meg would. What would be important to her?" He looked up at Saity. "She didn't go back to Mother Godwin's or Newgate, did she?"

Saity made a face that indicated he was correct.

He shook his fist. "Damn. Where would she go? She doesn't know anyone here in London. Her husband is dead. Her family is all dead. She had no one else." He looked up suddenly, a bolt of lightning going through his head. He remembered the tiny grave outside the Rutledge churchyard where he'd left the apple blossom. "Ah, hell, Saity. She had no one else . . . but the baby." He took a step toward her. "Please don't tell me she went back to Rutledge Castle to the baby's grave."

Saity lifted her palms. "I didn't say nothin', mind you. You was so smart, you figured it out on your own." She pointed. "And I expect ye to tell Meg that when ye settle matters between yourselves. I don't want her thinkin' I didn't stick to my word."

"Hell." He grabbed his hat off the table and dropped it onto his head. "I was hoping I'd never have to set foot on that land again."

Saity followed him to the door. "You gonna go get her? Sweep her up in them big strong arms of yours and kiss her?"

"I'm going to go talk to her." He went down the steps. "Tell her how I feel. And if she's willing, I'm going to marry her, today."

Saity leaned over the rail of her stoop, watching him climb onto his horse. "You bring her back here 'afore you sail off to Injun country, you hear me? She's already got a ticket paid for."

Kincaid shook his head as he lifted his reins to back up his horse. Meg's capabilities never failed to surprise him. How a woman who had lived such a sheltered, abused life up until a few months ago had managed to book herself passage to the colonies, and gotten away so cleanly, he didn't know. But the one thing he did know was that if they could fix this, if she would marry him, their life together would be long and happy. As long as they lived, she would always be full of surprises.

Kincaid raised his hand as he started off down the street. "Enjoy your orange, Saity, and thanks again."

She just stood on the stoop, smiling and peeling her orange.

Meg walked up the hill toward the churchyard with Annie skipping along beside her. At first Meg had hesitated at the idea of Annie coming along. A part of her wanted to go alone, to be alone at her son's grave. But then she realized that perhaps it would be better if she didn't go alone. Having the child with her might actually help her deal with her feelings.

When Meg had questioned Annie as to whether it would be all right for her to leave the cottage without her grandmother knowing it, the child insisted her grandmother had already given her permission last night. Annie said her grandmother had said she would try to make it back by morning, but it depended on how quickly the next babe entered the world. If Mavis didn't make it by morning, Annie said they were to go on without her.

As Meg and Annie walked toward the church, they stopped to pick wildflowers in the tall, swaying grass along the road. The sun shone on their faces and a light wind carried off the trees. Annie sang, lightening Meg's heart.

As she walked toward the castle that loomed on the hill ahead, memories washed over Meg—memories she'd just as soon forget. But they were tempered by more recent memories that made her smile bittersweetly.

Meg knew in her heart that the night Kincaid had picked her up on this highway, he had truly saved her life. Not just her physical body, but the life inside her. Kincaid's love had given her the will to live, to survive despite her horrid past. And now, even though they could never be together again, his child would give her another kind of happiness she yearned for. Again, Kincaid was giving her possibilities she had never known existed. And for that, she would forever be grateful.

They reached the place in the road where the church was,

and Annie skipped down the unmowed path toward the dilapidated building. "This way. Been here before with Grandmama. She tends the graves, you know."

Meg stared at the church. "Why hasn't anyone fixed the door?" she asked. She had forgotten how run-down the church was.

"Don't have service no more. Not since . . ." Annie looked over her shoulder "Not since you left."

"And the vicar? Has he left."

"No." She lifted a shoulder. "Grandmama says he spends most of his time in the ordinary in his cups."

Meg frowned. "I see."

Annie reached the iron fence that marked off the churchyard and skirted it. She picked up a stick and ran it along the top spikes, making repetitive clanking sound. "This way."

Meg stopped at the gate. "It . . . it's inside the churchyard?"

"Nope. The earl wouldn't 'llow it, Grandmama said."

Meg gripped the flowers in her hand tightly. "Bastard," she muttered under her breath.

"Here it is." She stopped at a tiny wooden cross on the outside of the fence.

Meg took a deep breath. She remembered the pain she had suffered to give her son life and the joy she had felt the moment she heard his first cry. Then the sadness had crept in. Such a perfect child, but for his twisted little mouth.

Meg wouldn't allow herself to think beyond those first few minutes when Mavis put her baby in her arms. It was just too painful to remember what happened after Philip came into their bedchamber. The ranting . . . the raving . .

Annie went down on her knees, lifting the skirt of her blue homespun dress. "Look, someone's left an apple blossom for your baby." She twirled it between her fingers before returning it to the grave.

Meg came to stand at the foot of the grave that was so small. "Your grandmother, I suppose."

"I guess." Annie bounced up. "I'm gonna go see if there's any honey in the comb that hangs on the back of the church." She skipped away. "Grandmama loves honey on her biscuits."

Meg watched the little girl dance through the churchyard gate and disappear around the back of the old church. Finally Meg's gaze came to rest on the grave at her feet again. "John," she whispered, smiling, close to tears. "My sweet Johnny."

Meg knelt in the warm grass and gently laid the flowers she and Annie had picked beside the apple blossom. She stared at the cross, her eyes filling with tears. "I'm sorry it took me so long to come back," she whispered to her first born. "Only your mother's had quite an adventure."

She laughed, wiping at her tears with the back of her. "I know, Margaret Randall having an adventure, what a joke. But I'm not Margaret anymore, Johnny. I'm Meg. The Meg my grandmother loved. The Meg who's not afraid to stand up for herself or those she loves."

She began to arrange the flowers on the grave. "That evil is gone, Johnny. Your father. Rotting in hell, I hope." She sniffed. "But you must forgive him. It's a sickness with these Randall men, you know. They're just evil."

Then she smiled. "Well, not all of them. There's Kincaid . . . James Randall. He . . . He's your half-brother, but also . . ." Meg looked away, fighting her tears. "Also Mama's true love. I know it's confusing, but . . . but I'm going to have his baby. Your brother or sister."

"Only now I have to go away from England, a place far from here." Meg sighed, looking over the wooden cross that bore no name. "That's why I had to come, John. To tell you goodbye. Mama has to go because there's a bad man after her. In a place called America Mama will be safe."

She wiped at her eyes. "I won't be able to see you again, not here. But we'll meet in heaven and then Mama will hold you—"

"Oddsfish . . . how touching."

Meg looked up, the sound of the voice sending a shiver of terror down her spine. "Rutledge!"

"Who else?"

Meg scrambled to her feet. Where had he come from? Why hadn't she heard him or seen him? He had her pinned against the rusty iron fence.

"I knew I would find you." He chuckled, his disfigured mouth turning up. "But it never occurred to me you'd be such a fool, Margaret, as to deliver yourself into my hands."

"Get away from me," Meg said between clenched teeth.

"You thought you could run from me, did you little Margaret?" He pointed with his gold-tipped walking cane. "But of course you couldn't. Here I was, taking an early morning ride, and God delivered you into my hands. And who says the Randalls are cursed?"

Meg noticed for the first time the horse tied to a tree near the church door. Rutledge had ridden right up to her and she'd been so lost in her thoughts that she'd never heard him.

She pressed her back against the fence, the iron bars biting into her flesh. "Let me go, Percival."

"Let you go? But I've spent months looking for you, darling."

"It was self-defense, Percival. I killed Philip because after he killed the baby, he turned on me." She stared the mean bastard in the eyes, less afraid than she thought she should have been. "You know it's true. You know I'd not have harmed him otherwise. I'll tell my story in court. I'll find witnesses to attest to his character. Anyone who knew him knew he was capable of killing his wife. He probably killed the others."

Percival sighed, shaking his head. "Margaret, Margaret, ever the naïve one." He leaned on his stick. "Of course he killed the others. Apparently it took but a few stabs to take care of both Mary and Anne. And everyone thought the blood was from childbirth."

Meg stared at Rutledge in horror. He killed them? Kincaid's mother? Timid Anne, the young woman who'd brought sweets to the nursery for Meg? "He killed them," she whispered. "And he really was going to kill me."

"My brother wanted another perfect child like that snot-nosed James. If one wife couldn't provide, he assumed the next could," Rutledge explained coldly.

Meg shook her head in horror. "And you allowed the murders in your household?" she dared. "That makes you as guilty as he."

Rutledge sighed. "I told him it wasn't wise. I warned him that eventually someone would become suspicious and not marry off his daughter to him. But they all wanted their daughters to marry into a wealthy, titled family. Your grandmother wanted that for you, didn't she?"

As he spoke, Meg slid along the fence, edging away from him so slowly that she prayed he wouldn't see her motion. "She didn't know the truth. If she'd known, she'd not have—"

Percival burst into laughter. "She'd what? She'd have given you to Philip anyway. You meant nothing to her. You've never meant anything to anyone, Margaret, dear."

Meg stared at him, her eyes narrowed in anger. If she'd had a knife in her hand at this moment she'd have done him in the same way she had Philip. "So what are you going to do with me?" she asked boldly. As she spoke, she moved her foot a hair's-breadth to the left. "Call the authorities? Have me arrested and thrown into prison?"

"I considered that, but thought I might deal with you on my own. Afterall, it was my brother you murdered. I should think I would have a right to seek my vengeance."

His words made her skin crawl. "He killed my baby," she said venomously.

"His right as the father. As your husband, madame."

Out of the corner of her eye, Meg caught a glimpse of Annie's blue dress whipping around the corner of the lime-washed church. Please, Meg prayed silently. Run and get help, Annie. Run into the village. Of course who would help her there? Who would go against the earl to save her?

"What do you think you're doing?"

Meg's head snapped around to look straight into Rutledge's eyes. They were the same color brown as Kincaid's and yet they held none of the warmth, none of the humanness of Kincaid's. Rutledge was cold, a cold, unfeeling son of a bitch.

"I said what do you think you're doing?" He struck the fence beside her with his cane.

Meg forced herself not to flinch. She knew this game of intimidation all too well. She'd played it too long. But no longer.

"I'm not doing anything," she snapped. "Except for trying to save my own life."

He laughed, taking a step closer to her.

Annie was gone. Meg could no longer see her.

"Goodness, we've become forward haven't we, Margaret? All those months in that wicked city of London, I suppose. Makes a woman forget her place." His crooked mouth tugged back in a wicked grin. "But I know ways to make a woman remember her place. Learned a few new tricks, I have."

Meg realized then that there was no reasoning with the earl. She also knew her life was in danger. Something told her that she would never reach the authorities. Percival was serious when he said he intended to seek retribution on his own.

That left Meg with no choice but to attempt to escape . . . and now.

Without taking time to consider her choices, Meg bolted, hoping she would take Percival by surprise. Surely he'd not expect the Margaret he had known to try to run.

She dodged left and he swung at her with his walking stick.

"Come back here you little bitch!" he shouted, trampling the baby's grave. "How dare you run from me!"

Meg grabbed her skirts, lifting them up to her knees as she darted across the grassy knoll that led to the road. She could hear Rutledge's footfall behind her.

"Come back here!" he shouted. "Do you hear me? Don't make me angry, Margaret." She could hear him chasing her down, gaining on her. "You'll be punished all the more severely for making me angry!"

Meg ran as fast as she could. "Help me! Help!" she screamed. Her lungs burning, she knew she couldn't run fast enough. She felt the cane strike the back of her head and tumbled forward into the sweet summer grass. "Kincaid . . ." she whispered as the world dissolved into darkness.

"Oh, dear." Rutledge made a clicking sound between his teeth. He stood near the road looking down at Margaret, unconscious. "I told you not to run, and now look what's happened."

He panted, touching his hand to his breast. The ache ran up his arm and radiated through his chest cavity. "You've winded me." He leaned over, resting against the head of the cane, fighting the dizziness that came over him.

After a moment, the pain passed once again and he straightened his posture, smoothing his wrinkled waistcoat. "That's better. Now, let's get you more comfortable."

He tucked his cane under his armpit and grasped her by her hands. "What a silly girl to think you could escape," he chastised, dragging her through the grass to his horse that waited nearby. "And who did you think would help you? Who do you think would care what I did to you?" he finished with a snarl.

Dropping the cane, he grabbed her around the waist and flung her over his saddle, face down. Convinced she would remain on the horse long enough to make it up the hill, he picked up his cane and the horse's reins and started back up the road toward Rutledge Castle.

"Who would care?" he repeated. "No one, you stupid little bitch. No one in the world."

Meg woke slowly, disoriented. . . . Her head pounded and her vision was poor. Why was it so dark? Where was she? Then she remembered being at the baby's grave and Rutledge appearing out of nowhere. How had he gotten here? He was supposed to have been in London?

Meg blinked in the darkness, trying to make an assessment of where she was. Wherever it was, it was dark and cold and clammy.

She tried to move her hands and heard the clink of chains. She felt the weight of the cold metal on her wrists. She was seated, chained to the wall she leaned against. There wasn't even enough chain to allow her to stand.

"Bastard," she whispered in the darkness. As her eyes adjusted she saw the stone walls of her prison. Rutledge had locked her up somewhere, but where?

The castle dungeon she guessed. She'd only been down here a few times in all the years she lived at the castle. "Not a place fit for females," Philip had grumbled.

She stared at the cold stone walls. For once, Philip had been right. This wasn't a place fit for females, nor males, nor any living creature . . .

It was all Meg could do not to panic. She was cold and afraid of what might come out of the darkness.

What was even more frightening was the thought of why Percival had put her here. What did he intend to do with her . . . to her?

She shifted on the hard, cold floor scattered with straw. The one thing that she did know was that she wouldn't give up. She had too much to live for in the child in her womb. She wouldn't let the Randall family win. They'd not conquered Kincaid and they'd not conquer her.

A sound at the wall behind her head startled her. Was something down here? She listened without moving. It was a steady sound, like two stones clicking together. Had the earl incarcerated some other poor soul here in the bowels of the castle?

"Hello?" Meg cried cautiously, her cheek pressed against the wall. "Is someone there?"

The rhythmic clicking stopped immediately.

Meg waited and then after a moment called again, this time a little louder. "I said, is someone there?"

After a moment there was one distinct click. Like a stone hitting the stone of the wall.

"Can you hear me?" Meg asked.

One click.

"Yes? That means yes, one tap?"

Another singular tap.

"Are you trapped here, too?"

One click.

Meg's voice was shaky. The thought that Percival might have left someone else in this prison turned her stomach. "The Earl of Rutledge?"

Again a click, this time harder.

Meg laid her cheek against the cold stone, the chains on her wrists clinking as she shifted her position where she sat on the floor. "Can . . . you speak?"

There was a pause. Then two clicks.

If one click meant yes, two had to mean no.

"So you can't speak," she whispered to herself, closing her eyes. "You poor soul." Then louder. "Are you a woman?"

One click.

Meg exhaled softly. She was afraid to ask how long she'd been here.

"Don't worry," Meg said after a moment. "We're going to get out of here, you and I. We're going to outsmart the earl. Do you understand?"

There was no answer. Then the steady clicking began again.

With a sigh Meg rested her head against the wall, staring into the darkness. "We're going to get out of here," she repeated with determination. "We're going to escape."

Then she thought of Kincaid. By now he had been to Saity's. Saity had sworn she wouldn't tell him where Meg had gone. But what if she had? What if Kincaid had persuaded her in some way?

She smiled in the darkness. Kincaid could be very persuasive when he wanted to be. Perhaps he threatened and she told. But a better guess was that he'd sweet-talked her into giving him the information. Kincaid had always been a sweet talker.

If Kincaid knew she had gone to Rutledge, he would come after her. If for nothing else, to kill her himself . . .

Twenty-nine

Kincaid rode down the center of the highway, headed toward the meager town of Rutledge that lay at the foot of the hill from the castle. *I've got to do something about this,* he thought to himself as he passed the cottars along the road. They all toiled in their stump-filled fields, their movements only half-hearted. *What kind of existence is this for a man and his family?* He wondered.

After he found Meg, after he made everything right between them, be damned if he wasn't going to deal with his uncle concerning the poverty of the cottars. Even if it took most of his inheritance, he was going to help these people, to force his uncle to help them. After all, if the Earl of Rutledge didn't have any children, and he doubted he would at his age, then the cottars were really Kincaid's responsibility, weren't they?

As Kincaid passed a man walking through a field with his hoe on his shoulder, Kincaid waved. The man immediately glanced behind him, looking to see who Kincaid waved to. Then, realizing who it was, the farmer lifted his hand in astonishment, smiling hesitantly.

Kincaid tipped his hat and went on. The road was flanked with thatch and lime-washed cottages all in various stages of decline. The children that peeked through the doorways and from behind moldy haystacks appeared thin, their eyes dull.

"What a crime," Kincaid muttered. "To allow families to live like this."

"My lord?"

Kincaid looked over to see an old, hunchbacked woman coming out of one of the cottages. "My lord!"

He pulled back on the reins, recognizing the peasant. "Mavis."

She hurried toward him, dragging a girl in a blue dress along after her. The girl appeared frightened. "My lord, something's about in the castle."

Kincaid glanced up the road at the monstrous stone structure at the top of the hill. "What are you talking about? I haven't time. I'm looking for someone. A woman. Perhaps she even passed through here."

"Aye. Seen a woman." The midwife looked up at Kincaid. "My granddaughter, she did." She gave the girl a push. "Tell 'is lordship what ye know, child. Hurry and be out with it. It could mean a life."

Kincaid swung out of his saddle so as not to intimidate the girl any further. *What was Mavis babbling about? Whose life?* "You saw a woman with brown hair, green eyes?" he asked the little girl. "Are you saying she passed through here? You saw her?"

"Lady Surrey," the child whispered, wide eyed, in awe of Kincaid. "Slept in my bed last night beside me. We shared bread and tea this morning."

"Meg," Kincaid whispered. He took the girl gently by the shoulders, stooping so that he could look her in the eyes. "And where did Lady Surrey go this morning? Where did she say she was going after she left you?"

When the girl didn't answer immediately, he looked at Mavis. "What's her name?"

"Annie."

"Annie." He looked back at the girl. "This is very important. I must know where Lady Surrey said she was going."

"The churchyard."

"Of course." He looked up in the direction of the church. But she wouldn't still be there. It wouldn't make sense. She couldn't still be there. It was already after noon.

"I seen many an evil thing in that house," Mavis muttered. "Many an evil. Said he'd cut my tongue out if I told, but what do I need a tongue for?"

Kincaid stood, looking at Mavis. "Mavis, I'm in a hurry. What do you speak of? What evil? Who's going to cut your tongue out?"

"Let him." She spat on the ground. "I seen enough. No more. I won't stand silent 'nother day."

Kincaid grew impatient. "Mavis, make sense. Do you know what happened to Lady Surrey? Do you know where she's gone, or who might know?"

The midwife looked down at the girl, prodding her. "Tell 'is lordship what you seen when you was hidin' behind the church." She laid her hand on the little girl's head. "Tell 'im."

Annie turned to Kincaid. "He . . . he hit her."

Kincaid's mouth went dry. He would kill him, whoever *he* was. "Someone hit Lady Surrey?"

Annie nodded solemnly. "The one with the ugly face. The earl."

Kincaid swore a French oath under his breath. How the hell had his uncle gotten back here from London so quickly? Had he somehow known Meg was coming? "When? Where? I must have the details if I'm going to find her."

"This morning." She stared at him with her clear blue eyes. "We went to the baby's grave and I was playing. Only then the earl came and I was afraid, so I hid."

"That was smart," Kincaid said softly. "You're a smart girl. Now tell me what happened to Lady Surrey."

"He shouted at her. She hollered back. I couldn't hear what they was saying, but she was awful mad. It was somethin' about the baby."

Kincaid would have smiled at the thought of Meg standing up to Percival if the situation hadn't been so dire. "Go on," he urged. "Tell me what happened then, Annie."

"Then she ran. That's when he hit her with his walking

stick and she fell over in the grass. Then she didn't move anymore."

Kincaid stood up, so angry he couldn't see clearly. He took a deep breath, careful not to scare the child. He didn't want her to think she'd done anything wrong. "And what did he do then?"

She pointed toward the castle. "Put her on his horse and took her up the hill."

Kincaid grabbed his horse's reins. "He took her to Rutledge Castle? Not somewhere else. You're sure of that?"

She nodded solemnly. "I watched him lead his horse up the hill and then I ran down to find Grandmother and tell her. She was deliverin' a baby, but I found her."

"You did the right thing, Annie." He climbed into his saddle. "Thank you," he said, as he lifted his reins. "Bless you." Then he sunk his heels into the horse's flanks and barreled up the hill to the place he swore he would never return.

Please, God, he prayed as he rode uphill. *Don't let her be dead. Please, don't let him have already killed her.*

Kincaid pushed open the front door and stepped into the hallway. "Rutledge?" he called. He was so angry that his voice came low and laced with steel. "Where the hell are you?"

He heard footsteps and the servant Sam appeared. "M . . . my Lord Surrey. It . . . it's good to see you again so . . . so soon. We . . . weren't expecting you again."

"Where is she?" He took a step toward the man. "Lady Surrey."

Sam cringed, obviously thinking Kincaid was going to strike him. "L . . . lady Surrey?" He looked confused. "G . . . gone. Gone, of course."

Kincaid grabbed Sam's sleeve. "She's not here? You've not seen her?"

"N . . . not since that d . . . day, my lord. She went up . . . upstairs for the lying-in." The servant's entire body shook with fear. "And . . . and we never saw her again. N . . . none of us saw her leave after . . . after she k . . . killed him, my lord."

Kincaid tried to be patient. This man had nothing to do with any of this. He knew that. He just wanted to be certain Sam hadn't seen Meg. "Look, Sam, calm yourself. I'm not going to strike you. It's just that I have reason to believe Lady Surrey returned here to Rutledge. Last night. This morning she was seen at the churchyard."

"And . . . and you think she might 'ave come here?" Sam asked, wide eyed. "That . . . that wouldn't make much sense, would it m'lord. You . . . you and his lordship lookin' for her . . ."

"I'm not saying it makes any sense. I'm just telling you she was seen in the village last night and at the churchyard this morning. She didn't just disappear into the air, Sam. She's got to be here somewhere."

He clasped his hands. "Well, I . . . I 'aven't seen 'er, I can tell you that my lord."

Kincaid brushed past him, going down the hall. "Where's my uncle? His library?"

Sam ran after him. I think so, my lord. Only . . . only he said he wasn't to be disturbed."

They reached his uncle's closed door and Kincaid opened it without a knock.

"I told you I didn't want to be disturbed, Higgins!" Rutledge shrieked from inside.

Sam took a step back into the hall, covering his ears.

"Where the hell is she?" Kincaid strode into the library with an air of authority.

Percival looked up from his desk where he had been writing correspondence. "So good you could return, nephew. We weren't expecting you to return, but it's a pleasant surprise." He set down his quill. "Now where is who?"

"You know who. Meg." He exhaled. *"Margaret.* My father's wife."

Kincaid could have sworn his uncle blanched.

"Where is Lady Surrey?" Rutledge said after barely a second's hesitation. "Where, indeed?" He appeared to recover quickly. "I thought that was what you and I were trying to find out back in London."

Kincaid walked to his uncle's desk and leaned on it so that his face was only inches from Percival's. "This isn't going to work. You were seen."

The earl pulled back a little, at least slightly intimidated. "I was seen where? You're not making sense, nephew." He looked up. "Close the futtering door!" he shouted.

The door slammed shut from outside, closed by Sam who was obviously trying to make himself invisible.

"I'm making perfect sense and you damned well know it," Kincaid didn't allow his uncle to break eye contact this time. "She was here, at the churchyard," he went on evenly, "and you were seen arguing with her."

Rutledge gave a little laugh. "If I had seen the chit, I'd have had her detained and arrested." He laughed again, but this time his voice was even less convincing. "Surely you don't think—"

Kincaid slammed his hand down hard on the desk, silencing the earl in mid-sentence. "If you've killed her, so help me, I swear on my mother's grave, your life is forfeit, uncle."

Then Kincaid spun around and strode out of the library. He'd not waste his time mincing words with his uncle another minute. He'd find Meg himself.

The earl followed Kincaid close behind. "What is your sudden interest in Margaret?"

Kincaid headed straight for the twisting grand staircase. Perhaps he had locked her in one of the rooms. He'd search the entire house top to bottom, and if she wasn't inside he'd look outside. She had to be here.

He only prayed he'd find her soon enough.

"I said what is your interest? What would make you think she was here?"

At the top of the stairs Kincaid began opening and closing doors, moving down the hallway in a systematic fashion. If she was here, he would find her. "Meg! Meg are you here?" he shouted, his voice echoing off the gray stone walls. "Meg!"

"And why are you calling Margaret Meg? I believe you owe me an explanation."

Kincaid looked inside a door and then slammed it shut, moving on to the next. "I don't owe you jack shit." He cupped his hand around his mouth. "Meg! Meg, answer me if you can. I'm here! I've come for you, sweetheart."

Rutledge hurried after Kincaid, sometimes being forced to run to catch up. "Sweetheart? You call your father's murderess sweetheart? Do you know her?" Now he seemed genuinely concerned. "Please, James, tell me you've not become involved with your stepmother!"

"Meg? Meg?" Kincaid reached the end of the hall and turned back. For a moment he stood in indecision, knowing it was important that he not panic. She was here, he knew she was. He just hadn't located her yet. He had to think logically. She wasn't in the east wing. He'd check the west next.

He started in that direction. Perhaps his uncle locked her up in the nursery. That was a remote part of the castle. It would make sense to put her there.

"James!" The earl put himself in front of Kincaid, forcing him to halt halfway to the nursery. "I demand that you stop this nonsense this moment! I want an explanation and I want one this instant." He stomped his foot like a disobedient child.

Kincaid wanted to punch him in the face. It was all he could do to contain himself, but what mattered right now was Meg. Kincaid couldn't let anything get in the way of finding her. Meg was who was important, not the earl, not himself. Meg.

Kincaid pushed his way past his uncle. "Meg!" he started shouting again. "Meg, where are you?"

He found the nursery door unlocked and his heart sank. He checked the rooms just to be sure, but she wasn't there, either. He went back down the hallway, headed for the central staircase.

"There, are you satisfied, James?" The earl was sweating profusely. He was obviously nervous. To Kincaid, he looked guilty as hell. "She's not here. The little slut is not in my household. Now stop this nonsense and tell me how you know the jade."

Kincaid spun around, feeling as if he might explode. He knotted his fists, holding them to his sides, fearing he was going to lose his temper and strike the pathetic man down. "Don't say that again," he threatened. "Else I warn you, you'll regret it the rest of your days."

"You're crazy," Percival shrieked, throwing up his arms. "As crazy as Margaret."

Kincaid turned and grasped his uncle's arm. *"As crazy as Margaret?* You say that as if you've seen her. As if you've spoken to her."

"I said nothing of the kind!" Percival back-pedaled. "I only meant—"

"You meant—"

The sound of a woman's voice downstairs brought the conversation to an abrupt halt.

"My lord! My lord. I know where she is! My Lord Surrey, are you there?"

"Mavis?"

Kincaid rushed toward the landing. From the open landing he saw below the old woman running toward the stairs with Higgins in pursuit.

"Stop her!" Percival shouted from behind Kincaid. "Stop her, Higgins! Shut her up!"

The old woman reached the staircase and started up, moving rather agilely for a woman her age. "The bastard!" she shouted. "He's got her. Got 'er just like I said!"

Higgins grabbed Mavis's black skirt and began to drag the old woman down, but Mavis managed to detach herself and moved up the stairs again.

Kincaid started down the staircase, but she was still a full level below him. "Let her go, Higgins!" he shouted. "Else it'll be your head!"

"Stop her!" The earl ran behind Kincaid, holding his hand to his chest. "Shut her up, Higgins. Do you hear me? Shut the witch up! She'll ruin everything. She'll ruin it all!"

"She's there, my lord," Mavis called up to Kincaid. "I seen him goin' to check on her, the eel."

Kincaid raced down the steps. "Where, Mavis? Where is she?"

Just then, Higgins caught Mavis around the waist and pulled a knife from his coat.

Kincaid heard the old woman cry out in pain. He turned on the center landing, out of view of her for an instant. By the time he came around on the landing he saw Higgins rolling down the stairs. Mavis stood on her own two feet, bleeding from the arm, but with the knife clutched in her own hands.

"Take that!" she cackled, waving the knife. "And see what ye can do with it, Higgins."

"Stop her," Percival shouted, still behind Kincaid, limping down the stairs. "Stop that crazy old woman, James. She's mad. Everyone knows she's mad and can't be trusted." He thrust out his hand. "Look, she's killed my manservant."

Kincaid reached Mavis and put his arms out to her. "Are you all right?"

"No thanks to 'im!" She pointed to Higgins's body that had come to rest at the bottom of the stairs. The servant stared at the ceiling, his gaze lifeless.

"Where is she?" Kincaid said softly. "Where's my Meg? Please tell me she's not dead."

"Don't know if she's still 'live or not." Mavis wiped the blood from the blade on her skirt. "Only know where 'e put her."

Kincaid held his breath. "Where?"

"The dungeons."

Kincaid started down the steps again, taking them two at

a time. "You son of a bitch," he shouted over his shoulder. "You'll pay for this, uncle!"

"Wait, wait, James." Percival stumbled down the steps, past Mavis. He was out of breath, his deformed face pale. "Wait," he called in a pitiful voice. "Let me explain. You don't understand, nephew. Let me explain!"

Kincaid burst out the front door, dropping into a dead run. *His Meg in the dungeon?* What kind of animal was his uncle?

"Meg! I'm coming," he shouted as he raced toward the entrance to the cellar at the kitchen wing. "I'm coming, Meg."

Just please still be alive.

Thirty

Meg closed her eyes, leaning her head against the cold, rough stone of the wall. Her legs were stiff from sitting so long and the metal of the chains bit into the flesh of her wrists and ankles. Time passed so slowly that it had seemed to stop. Here in the dark, isolated from sight and sound, it was easy to let her mind wander, to take her places she didn't want to go. It was all she could manage to fight the panic in her chest that threatened her ability to think rationally.

Earlier, the cell door had opened and Higgins had brought water. She had always hated the man, trusting him even less than she trusted the earl. When she'd begged Higgins to help her, to send for help if he was too afraid of Rutledge, he had only laughed. When she tried to question him about the woman in the next cell over, he had slapped her across the face and told her she needed to worry about herself.

Despite how much she despised Higgins, Meg had hated to see him go. At least when he came there had been the light from his lantern and a breath of air. He'd only stayed long enough to check the security of her chains and give her the water. Then he closed the wooden door and dropped the latch and Meg was in darkness again, in tears.

Her tears had long dried up. That had been at least an hour ago, perhaps two. She was done feeling sorry for herself. Now she was ready to do something about her situation. She'd told Higgins to send that bastard Rutledge down, hinting that someone would be here soon looking for her.

Meg was expecting Rutledge anytime. She didn't know what she was going to do or say when he got there. She didn't know how she was going to get out of this mess, only that she would. She had to.

When Meg heard the echo of a door opening somewhere in the cellar, she tapped on the wall. It had been a long time since the woman in the other cell had responded. "Can you hear me?" she called. "He's coming. I'm going to talk to him. I'm going to figure out a way to get us out of here. Do you hear me?"

She waited and was rewarded by a single tap.

Meg smiled in the darkness. "I will get us out of here," she said softly, brushing her hand against her abdomen. "I swear I will."

Then Meg heard footsteps. Someone running. *Running?*

The door to her cell swung open and she squinted in the bright light of the lantern. "Who . . . who's there? Percival?" She tried to see who it was.

"Sh . . . shut up." A hand grasped her arm and yanked her to her feet.

"Who is it?" she demanded.

He was unlocking the chains that bound her to the wall. Then her feet. "Thank you, thank you," she whispered.

Then she realized it was Sam, one of the earl's servants. "Sam? Sam? You're letting me go?" Sam had never taken the initiative in anything in his life. He was petrified of the earl. Maybe he was taking her to him . . .

"Sam, answer me!"

"L . . . let's go." He grabbed her by the arm and when she didn't move fast enough, he dragged her.

"Sam! What the hell do you think you're doing?" She struggled to get away, beating him with her fist. "I want you to let that other woman out of there! Do you hear me?"

Then Meg felt the cold barrel of a pistol pressed against her cheek. She immediately ceased struggling. She stared at the pistol and then Sam.

"You . . . you m . . . move a . . . long and k . . . keep quiet. You . . . you understand me?"

"Where are you taking me?" Meg stared at his face. She didn't know what was happening, but realized something wasn't right.

Then, coming as brightly as a light in the darkness, she heard a familiar voice.

"Meg?"

She stumbled. Sam was leading her deeper into the catacombs of the cellar—away from Kincaid. "Kincaid!" she screamed. "Help me! I'm here, Kincaid. Help me!"

"L . . . Let's go," Sam said in her ear, dragging her when she lost her footing. "C . . . can't disappoint the . . . the earl. C . . . can't. He'll . . . he'll k . . . kill me for sure."

"Kincaid!" Meg screamed. "He's taking me away." She jumped up and down, making as much noise as possible, betting Sam wouldn't have the guts to shoot her.

She heard Kincaid running. She heard him calling her name. "Where are you?" he shouted. "Meg!"

"Here! Here!" she sobbed. She fell on the dirt floor and thrust her feet up in the air, kicking Sam as hard as she could. Sam tripped and fell and the pistol went off in a flash of light. The lantern flew through the air and hit the ground several feet from her, casting ugly, warped shadows on the gray wall.

"Here, Kincaid!"

Suddenly he burst into the light and she felt his arms around her.

"Meg, Meg." He went down on one knee, pulling her against him, stroking her hair. "Are you all right? Tell me you're all right. He didn't hurt you?"

Meg was close to tears. "I'm sorry," was all she could say over and over again. "I'm sorry. I'm sorry I murdered him. I didn't want to kill him, only defend myself."

"No, no." He pushed her tangled hair from her face so that he could look her in the eyes. "Don't say it. Don't ever say it. It was self-defense. That's not murder."

She rested her head on Kincaid's sturdy chest, tears now running freely down her cheeks. He believed her! He truly believed her!

"He killed my baby, Kincaid. He wasn't born dead like they all said. Mavis saw him alive, ask her," she sobbed. "Philip . . . he slit his throat because he . . . he had a harelip and he said he couldn't stand the ugliness."

"Meg, Meg," Kincaid's voice cracked. "I'm so sorry." He rocked her in his arms.

"Goodness, isn't this cozy?" The Earl of Rutledge appeared in the circle of light with Mavis just behind him. "So the two of you are acquainted." He leaned against the wall. His left arm hung limply and he was clutching his left breast, obviously ill. His face was bright red and appeared bloated. Sweat trickled down his temples. "Don't tell me you know this woman, this murderess, *intimately.*"

"You sick bastard," Kincaid whispered. He would have stood, but Meg wouldn't let go of him. She couldn't. Not yet.

"I don't know how this came about!" the earl flung in a tirade. "Did you help her escape that night? Did you cuckold your father, aid in the murder, and then help our Margaret escape? Have you fornicated with your stepmother?" he screeched, spittle running from his twisted mouth.

"Not his stepmother at all," Mavis injected.

"Shut up." Percival whipped around, flinging a hand to slap her, but the old woman was too quick for him.

She stepped closer to Kincaid and Meg, further into the light. "Time he heard the truth," she cackled, obviously taunting Rutledge in his state of incapacitation. "Cut my tongue if you like. Been threatenin' me all these years, do it! But the midwife knows, doesn't she? The midwife always knows the truth behind the family bloodlines."

Kincaid stood, lifting Meg to her feet, holding her against him in his arms. "Know what truth? Whose bloodlines?" He looked at his uncle. "What's she talking about?"

"Tell him who he is," the old woman chanted. "Tell the boy. Tell 'im. Tell 'im. Tell 'im."

"Shut up!" Percival covered his hands with his ears. "Shut up! Shut up!" Then suddenly he doubled over in pain. His wig fell off his head and he kicked it with the toe of his shoe as he caught himself against the wall. "Shut up! Shut up or I'll—"

"You'll what? I know, cut out my tongue? Ye haven't the strength old man!" Mavis threw back her head in crackling laughter. "It looks like yer own curse will send you to the grave, eh? Look at you, your heart tears as you speak. It's yer evilness eatin' you up."

The earl tried to take a step toward Mavis and went down on his knees. He was a pitiful sight with sprouts of white hair on his bald head. His shirt and cravat were wet with his own spittle.

Out of the darkness, Sam crawled. "My lord, my lord are you all right? Should I send for your surgeon or take you to bed?" The servant was desperate. "A drink. Brandy? Your brandy always helps."

"Get back," Kincaid ordered Sam in a tone that indicated he was in control of the situation. He stared at his uncle with hatred in his eyes. "We'll send for your surgeon, but first you must tell me what the midwife speaks of. Is this the babbling of a mad woman, or is there truth in her words?"

"No," Rutledge sobbed. "It's not true. None of it. Whatever she says. A lie. A lie conceived by that slut bitch mother of yours. That's why your father had to do away with her."

Meg felt Kincaid stiffen beside her. "My father killed my mother!"

"Not your father," Mavis offered gleefully. "Not your father at all, eh, Rutledge? Eh, dying Earl of Nothing! Here is where this bloodline ends. Here in the dirt where it belongs. This man," she pointed to Kincaid, "he will lead the Randalls back to the honor they once held."

Kincaid looked to Mavis. "What *are* you talking about. Did my father kill my mother or he didn't?"

"Aye, Philip killed your mother, but 'e weren't your father." She laughed. "Why do you think you escaped the curse? Not a Randall at all."

Kincaid brushed his lips against Meg's cheek and then carefully disengaged himself from her. He went down on his knees in front of his uncle who now lay on the dirt floor. "Tell me," Kincaid insisted.

"Lies. Lies," Percival blubbered. "A surgeon. I must have a surgeon. A letting of blood is what I need. Call for the leech!"

Kincaid looked at Sam who sat against the wall, huddled to protect himself. "Go. Do as he says. Fetch the surgeon." He gave the trembling man a push. "Hurry."

When Sam finally scrambled to his feet, Meg caught a whiff of fresh urine. Sam took off down the corridor toward the exit.

Kincaid looked back at his uncle and then up at the midwife. Meg hung back, realizing Mavis wasn't just babbling. She was trying to tell Kincaid something very important.

"Tell us, Mavis," she said.

"Please tell me," Kincaid repeated. "Tell me what you speak of. If I'm not my father's child, whose am I?" He pointed at Percival. "Not his?"

She snickered. "Not a Randall at all, I said, boy. Listen, listen. Blue runs in your blood."

"Not a Randall?" Meg whispered, utterly confused. "If he's not Philip's and not Percival's, whose is he?"

Mavis rubbed her wrinkled hands together with pleasure. "A Stuart, of course!" She grinned. "A Stuart."

Meg knew her mouth must have dropped as she stared incredulously. "A Stuart?"

"Brother to our present lord and king, Charles II. Born on the wrong side of the sheets to the first Charles. A bastard, James be, but a Stuart no less."

Kincaid rose slowly, staring at the midwife. He spoke haltingly, as if it took time for the words to sink in. "My father was the King of England?"

"Aye. Lord Surrey knew it from the first. Took the royal leavings as 'is own, 'e did. Took the king's gold to give the child the Randall name. But 'e hated ye. Always hated ye," she told Kincaid.

Kincaid looked at his uncle for confirmation. The idea was absurd. Mavis was mad. And yet the idea was so ridiculous that it could have been possible. "Is it true, Rutledge? Am I not a Randall at all?"

"Not fair," Percival moaned, his eyelids fluttering. "It was never fair. You were so perfect. That's why you were so perfect. Not one of us . . . never one of us. But not hard enough. We tried. We tried."

Meg stared at Percival, lying so pitifully on the floor. The man disgusted her, and yet a tiny part of her almost felt sorry for him.

As she came toward him, the earl rolled his head back and gasped for air. His chest rose and fell with a wheezing sound. His entire body convulsed and then he was still.

Kincaid crouched over him, pressing his hand to the earl's neck. "Dead," he whispered. Then he straightened, reaching for Meg's hand. "His heart, I think. My grandfather, *his father,*" he corrected, "went the same way."

Meg threw her arms around Kincaid, holding him tightly. "You came for me," she whispered. "You found out the truth and you still came."

He kissed her cheek where it was damp from her tears. "We'll talk about this later. Let's just get out of here," he whispered against her hair. "As far from here as possible."

Meg nodded in agreement, then looked up, suddenly remembering the other prisoner. "There's someone else," she whispered. "Another woman."

Kincaid looked into her eyes. "Another woman where, Meg? What are you talking about?"

Meg let go of Kincaid and grabbed the lantern, stepping around the earl's body. She ran back down the corridor, not even certain which door it was. "I don't know who she is. A woman. She's here somewhere. I heard her. Rutledge was keeping her prisoner here, too."

Meg turned the corner, passing the open door to the cell where she'd been held. "Here!" She tried to open the door, but it wouldn't budge. Locked. She banged on the door with her fist. "We're here," she shouted. "We've come for you!"

Kincaid came up behind Meg. He tried the door with a hand. "Stand back," he said.

Meg stepped behind him and lifted the lantern to give him more light. She watched as he lifted his boot and kicked the door. It took three kicks for him to shatter the frame. When the door popped open, a muffled, whining sound came from within.

Mavis stepped through the doorway and stopped.

Meg raised the lantern high to cast light into the ill-smelling cell.

In the back, in the corner lay someone, something that resembled a human.

Meg closed her eyes, so dizzy she feared she would faint. It was a woman near to starving, so thin her ribs could be counted. She was completely nude, but a leather hood was pulled over her head that did not allow her to see or speak.

Mavis reached out to the woman, and she shrank back, making the animal sounds.

"It's all right, sweet thing," Mavis cooed. "Come to Mavis."

Meg watched in horror as the midwife gathered the woman into her arms like an infant. She unlaced the hood and pulled it off her head. The woman just lay in Mavis's arms, helpless.

"Oh my God," Kincaid whispered, pressing his hand to Meg's back.

"You know her?" Meg whispered.

Kincaid took the lantern from Meg's hand and set it on the

ground. "I'll send help down, Mavis," he said. "You stay with her."

Kincaid took Meg by the shoulders and led her toward the staircase where the light came pouring down.

"Who is it?" Meg whispered, holding tightly to him, shaking.

"Mary Mummford," he answered. "The Baron Mummford's daughter." He led her up the staircase and into the sunlight. "She's been missing for months. Presumed dead."

Meg rested her head against Kincaid's shoulder as they stepped out of the cellar and into the grass. "I'm glad he's dead," she said softly. "Heaven help me, may the Earl of Rutledge rot in hell."

The song ended with the final gay note of the fiddle and Saity burst into laughter, flinging herself into the lap of her new husband.

"Again, again!" Clancy shouted, wrapping his arms around her and clapping his hands as the fiddler began the next tune.

Breathless, Saity planted a kiss on his lips. "No, not . . . not again! I'm done too tired out fer another. It'll have to be Meg that dances this next piece!"

Meg stood beside Kincaid in the public room of Mother Godwin's House for Girls. It was a wedding celebration. Saity and Clancy had been married this afternoon and Kincaid had insisted he throw them a party. The room was filled with Saity's old friends and their customers. The idea that a girl could leave a whorehouse and find happiness was cause for great celebration among those who had not yet been so lucky. Meg found it gave them hope. She could see it in their smiles and hear it in their laughter.

"Meg! Meg! Meg!" Mary Theresa and Maria chanted. They were dressed alike tonight in pink taffeta dresses cut down to their rouged nipples, the skirts hemmed above their knees. In their hair they wore pink ribbons.

"Dance for us!" Maria encouraged, her cheeks flushed from the good wine Kincaid had ordered. "Dance for us, Maiden of Honor."

Meg looked up at Kincaid. His brown eyes were sparkling with green flecks of light. "Should I?" she murmured.

"Why not? Dance well enough and I'll buy you one of those gowns to match Maria's and Mary's." He winked at her.

She laughed and lifted up on her toes to kiss him. When she did, she parted her lips to tickle him with her tongue.

He tried to catch her by the waist, but she was too fast for him. "I thought you wanted to see me dance," she teased, slipping out of his arms.

"I'd prefer something else!" he called after her.

The crowd burst into bawdy laughter as Meg lifted her skirts and joined the other women in the country dance. As she whirled and dipped, copying their steps, she was watching Kincaid.

He clapped to the lively tune, tapping his foot, watching her watch him.

"I love you," she mouthed as she whirled by him, her loose hair flowing over her shoulders the way he liked it.

"Love you forever," he mouthed back.

The dance ended and Meg returned to Kincaid's arms, breathless and laughing. It felt so good to laugh. The burden of her past had lifted and for the first time in fifteen years she felt like she could truly breathe. She finally felt like she had the right to be happy.

"Ready to go home?" Kincaid whispered in her ear.

She leaned against him, facing the crowd. Saity and her new husband were dancing, the others clapping as they sang a lusty song meant for newlyweds.

"I think so." She exhaled, feigning fatigue. "I'm ready for bed. It's been a long day and tomorrow will be even longer. Our ship sets sail at noon and I've still that last crate of dishes to pack."

He put his arms around her and kissed her bare shoulder.

"If you're tired I can take you home now and tuck you into bed." His tone was filled with concern.

She looked over her shoulder at him. "Whoever said anything about sleeping?" She smiled a saucy smile. "I had something better in mind, husband."

He made a growling sound in his throat and kissed her soundly. "You mean you're still interested now that the dashing Captain Scarlet is gone, his duty done?"

"Mmm hmmmm."

"And James Kincaid is gone, too. His last poem written. Gone off to France, I hear. Won't you miss him?"

She shook her head. "No."

"As for James Randall, we know he wasn't truly real, either. His castle is sold to a nice duke, his holdings dissolved. All of his cottars are living in new cottages with meat on their tables and tools in their sheds."

She smiled. "But the money is in his pocket, is it not? The spoils of a secret no one will ever know, but you and I and the midwife who delivered you."

"Is it right though, my taking the Randall fortune not really due me?"

"There are no other heirs, Kincaid. The holdings would revert to the king. The way I see it, you deserve the comfort your father's and uncle's holdings will bring you. Besides, to tell the truth would defame your good mother's name."

"I suppose." He rested his head on her shoulder. "So who am I now? A Randall? I'm certainly not the king's brother." He sighed. "I've spent a lifetime being so many men. I'm not sure who it is I should be."

She turned in his arms to face him, looping her arms around his neck. "Let's see. Who are you? You're a tobacco planter on some river in a place called the Maryland Colony. You're Meg's husband." She lifted her hand and rested it on her abdomen that in the last few weeks had begun to swell. "And you're the father of this child."

He smiled, stroking her cheek tenderly with his knuckles. "What else could a man ask for?"

"What else, indeed?"

Meg and Kincaid kissed again, a slow passionate kiss of mended hearts and pasts finally laid to rest. Then, hand in hand, they walked toward the door that would lead them to a new life, new identities, and a new-found happiness.

Epilogue

Maryland Colony
Fifteen years later

Meg lifted the sleeping infant from her breast to rest him on her shoulder. "Where's your father?" She rose from her rocking chair near the hearth, patting the baby's bottom rhythmically.

Meg's and Kincaid's eldest daughter, Rachel, who was almost fifteen, closed the cover on the book she was reading. "I saw him heading down toward the river." She got out of her chair and opened her arms to take the fifth Randall child, Meg's and Kincaid's third boy. "You know how he gets in the fall when the geese begin to fly. He hates the thought of winter coming and having to spend all that time cooped up with all these women." She rolled her eyes. "Men."

Meg laughed at her daughter, so proud she had become such a bright, beautiful young woman. "I think I'll go find him." She indicated the long trestle table in the center of the parlor where the Randall children took their studies in the late afternoon. Three small heads were bent over their books. "Could you make sure they finish up today's lessons?" She glanced at the English case clock on the mantel. "Ten more minutes and they may all be dismissed."

Young James, twelve and full of vinegar, turned in his chair. "Then may I dig for my private treasure on the beach, Mama? May I?"

"It's nearly dark, James. I don't think—"

"Father said I could take a lantern if I did my Latin right the first time."

Montigue, only seven, jumped out of his chair. "I'll go with James. I'll protect him!" He raised an imaginary firearm to his shoulder. "I'll take Papa's musket!"

Meg's eyes widened. "You'll do no such thing, Montigue Kern Randall! Musket, indeed." She looked to her eldest son. "You may go with a lantern *if* you take your brother."

"Oh, Mother!" James moaned. "He's a pain in the arse."

Meg's eyes widened.

"Neck," James conceded.

"You may take your brother with you, James, or you may stay here with me and tackle tomorrow's Latin lesson."

James looked as if he were going to comment, but seeing the look on Meg's face, he gave up. The boy seemed to know his mother could always be more stubborn than he.

"I don't think it's fair." Little Saity, with her blonde curls, turned in her chair. "They get to go dig pirate treasure and I don't?" She thrust out her lower lip in a pout. "That's because I'm a girl, isn't it, Mama?"

"No, Saity, it isn't." Meg dropped her hand on her hip. "You may not go dig for treasure because you, *young lady*, are still in trouble for cutting the cat's whiskers." She twirled her finger. "Now turn around, all of you, and back to your studies. You still have ten minutes by my calculations."

Obediently the children returned to their lessons.

"I'll fetch your father and be back shortly," Meg told her eldest daughter who was putting the baby to bed in his cradle near the fire.

"All right, Mother."

Humming softly to herself, Meg picked up her cloak off a peg in the front hallway and tossed it over her shoulders. She stepped out into the crisp autumn air.

Standing on the porch steps, she tied the tie at her neck,

choosing to leave her hood down and let her dark hair blow in the salty wind.

From the top step of the Georgian brick house's front porch, Meg could look down the lawn that ran a quarter of a mile to the riverside. A dock used for ships to load tobacco stretched out into the water. On the end of the dock, she spotted a lone figure. The man was dressed in dark breeches and a white linen shirt with high black boots. His black hair, that had been brushed neatly and tied back in a queue this morning, flowed freely down his back.

Meg smiled to herself as she crossed the lawn, walking downhill toward the dock. The years were slipping by so quickly that she could barely remember the life she had once had. Rutledge Castle, Philip, the Earl of Rutledge . . . they were nothing but distant memories that sometimes didn't seem real at all anymore.

What Meg remembered of the past was Kincaid. Only Kincaid. He was her savior. Her lover. Forever, secretly, her masked highwayman.

Just then Kincaid turned to face the house. Seeing her, he waved. He met her halfway down the dock.

"I'm sorry, sweet. Were you calling me for supper?" He lifted her hood to cover her head. "You should have sent one of the children. There's no need for you to be out in the wind."

She kissed him lightly on the lips. "I just came to find you. Can't a woman occasionally speak with her husband alone without spilt milk and a thousand interruptions?"

He laughed, his husky voice sending trills of pleasure through her. Even after all these years of married life she still loved to hear him laugh. "Good point." He took her hand, squeezing. "So what would you like to talk about? He led her toward the end of the dock to a bench.

Both sat down to look west into the setting sun.

"Nothing in particular." Beside him, she snuggled in his arm. "I just like to be alone with you, that's all. The new baby's taken so much of my time that I've missed you."

He hugged her. "Missed you, too."

She watched the sun's rays dance across the smooth water of the river. "So was our tobacco crop a good one?"

"Excellent. Better than last year. Much better than Harper's down the river."

She glanced into his dark eyes, speckled with green. "You've made a good planter, Kincaid. Surprised us both, I think."

He lifted a shoulder in a shrug. "I like the hard work. Seeing the results."

"So you don't miss the highway, Captain Scarlet?" She lifted an eyebrow, a twinkle in her green eyes.

"Miss it? Not the robbery, no. All that danger, saddle sores. Nah. But the women." He shook his finger. "Now the women I miss. Kissing all those innocent young females . . ."

She burst into laughter, sinking her elbow into his side. "I don't know why I ask you anything! You can never be serious."

With one smooth motion, he set her on his lap. "There's one thing I can be serious about and that's my love for you."

She smiled. "It's a good life, isn't it? I don't miss England one bit." She looked down at him. "Do you?"

"Too many bad memories there." he murmured, tenderly tucking a stray lock of her hair beneath her hood. Then once again he looked out into the setting sun. "Here we've started anew. The Randall family has a fresh beginning far from the frigid walls of Rutledge."

"Just like Mavis said," Meg whispered. "The honor has been restored."

"Thanks to you."

She looked at him. "Me?"

"Yes, you." He prodded her with his finger. "You had the courage to fight back. I want our daughters to have the same courage."

"And our sons," she added.

They were both quiet for a moment, content to be together.

Then Meg looped her arm around her husband's neck to stare into his smiling eyes. "Shall we go see about supper and then perhaps an early bedtime?"

His smile turned to a broad, masculine grin. "Madame, is that a proposition?"

"No. But this is." She whispered provocatively in his ear and both of them burst into husky laughter.

Hand in hand, Meg and Kincaid walked up the hill to their home and their beloved children, knowing that love truly could conquer the past.

About the Author

Colleen Faulkner lives with her family in southern Delaware. She is the author of sixteen Zebra historical romances, including DESTINED TO BE MINE, O'BRIAN'S BRIDE, CAPTIVE, FOREVER HIS, FLAMES OF LOVE, SWEET DECEPTION and SAVAGE SURRENDER. Colleen's newest historical romance, FIRE DANCER, will be published in November 1997. Colleen loves hearing from her readers and you may write to her c/o Zebra Books. Please include a self-addressed stamped envelope if you wish a response.

Please turn the page for
an exciting sneak preview of
Colleen Faulkner's
newest historical romance
FIRE DANCER
coming from Zebra Books
in November 1997

One

August 1759
Somewhere in Penn's Colony

Mackenzie Daniels stared up into the tree limbs overhead, fascinated by the patterns of light and dark that poured through the dense foliage and swirled on the forest floor in a kaleidoscope of colors and textures. The warm wind blew in her face, and the smell of honeysuckle was strong in her nostrils.

Her horse moved rhythmically beneath her at an easy pace. In front and behind her rode a dozen English soldiers, her escort to Fort Belvadere. Her father, Franklin, brought up the rear in his wagon filled with trading goods and her precious art supplies.

"We can stop and rest if you're tired, Mackenzie." Joshua Watkins met her gaze with those cow-brown eyes of his.

She loosened the reins in her gloved hands, encouraging her mount to pick up the pace.

She sat astride a man's saddle, rather than sidesaddle because Major Albertson, the commander of Fort Belvadere, had ordered it so. He had warned her father that it would be easier for her to escape in case of Indian attack.

Indian attack. She shuddered at the thought.

"Mackenzie? Did you hear me? I said that if you're fatigued—"

"I'm not tired." Mackenzie met Josh's gaze again. She'd completely forgotten him. "I'm fine."

Rather than being flattered by his attention, as her father suggested she should be, she was annoyed. She didn't care if Joshua was the only man interested in her. She didn't want a man. What did she need a husband for when she could ride, shoot, fish, chop wood, and skin out her own deer? "I told you I was fine half an hour ago, Josh," she continued. "And I told you an hour ago."

"I . . . I know. I was just checking. It's been a hard journey."

She frowned. He was just trying to make her feel *womanly* again, as if she was his delicate flower. Glancing at her clothing, she snickered at the thought. She wore a blue tick skirt and her father's shirt with a pair of men's leather riding boots made by the saddler. In clothes like these, she wasn't exactly a picture of femininity.

"Oh, it has not been hard. It's been nothing like you and Father tried to warn me." She tugged off her straw bonnet by its flat ribbon and shook her mane of auburn hair. Then she looped the reins over the pommel and passed the hat to Josh to hold while she swept loose strands from her face and secured them in a ribbon at the nape of her neck. "I've quite enjoyed the journey. I've seen none of the dangers you warned of."

She held the ribbon in her teeth as she tugged on the unruly handfuls of hair. "The birds, the deer, those foxes we saw yesterday. The rivers, the clouds, the moon at night. It's all grand, Josh, just as I imagined. I haven't seen a single redskin since we left the Chesapeake." She caught a stray lock of hair that blew in the breeze. "I swear, I'm beginning to think you men made up this whole story of hostile Indians so that you could traipse off into the forest with your guns and sit around at night and drink and spit and scratch."

"You might not believe it now, but just you wait 'til we

reach the fort," he responded anxiously. "The soldiers say the place is swarming with the devils."

"I'm not afraid of Indians." She lied. She was afraid. Her father's whispers behind her back had made her afraid.

"Which is just why I don't think you belong here, Mackenzie. With the fighting all over the colonies, it's too dangerous. You don't know enough to realize when you're in danger."

"My first commissioned portraits," she scoffed, "and you think I should have turned Major Albertson down because a few scalps have been taken?" She drew the ribbon from her teeth and wrapped it around the thick pony-tail of hair. "That's just why it will never work between you and me, Josh. This is a perfect example of why I could never marry you."

He looked behind them to see if anyone had heard her. "Shhhh." He lowered his voice. "I thought we weren't going to talk about that. I thought we were just going to see how things went on this journey."

She took her bonnet from his hands and slapped it on top of her head. "You and Father made those plans, not me. I already gave you my answer, Josh." She whipped the ribbons through her fingers to tie the hat down. "I'm not marrying you. I'm not marrying anyone. I just want to—"

Gunfire erupted from the forest and her horse shied and danced in place.

"Indians!" a soldier shouted.

Mackenzie grabbed her reins tightly, keeping control of her horse. The soldiers immediately formed a tight circle around her. She crouched and stared up into the trees waiting for the Indian attack.

Joshua drew his musket from his leather saddlebag, his face pasty with fear. "Oh, God. Oh, Jesus God. I knew we were going to be massacred." He shook. "I knew it."

"Get ahold of yourself, Josh," Mackenzie snapped. She jerked her mount around and faced the nearest soldier. "What's happening? Are we under attack?"

"Don't know, ma'am." The soldier checked the prime on his pistol. "It's Lieutenant Burrow's weapon that discharged up ahead. He must have come upon something, but I don't 'ear Indians. They usually hoot and holler on the attack."

Mackenzie glanced over her shoulder, craning her neck to see her father. He was still pulling up the rear in his wagon, but his musket now lay across his lap.

"Lieutenant?" one of the soldiers called into the forest. "You all right, sir?"

"I've got him," came a shout out of the trees. "I got the bloody, horse-thieving bastard!"

Mackenzie's heart pounded and her hands were sweating inside the calfskin gloves as she and the soldiers rounded a bend in the road. *Were they under attack or not?*

She spotted Lieutenant Burrow holding his musket on a red man. She took a second look. The Indian was just a boy.

"He the only one?" one of the English soldiers called as he looked up into the trees suspiciously.

The other soldiers dismounted and ran toward the prisoner, their muskets pointed at him.

"I believe so," the lieutenant answered, his perfectly pronounced speech seeming out of place here in the colonial wilderness. "I caught him riding out with Major Albertson's horse. I believe we ought to hang him right here. Cassidy, get me a rope."

"Hang him?" Mackenzie jumped down from her mount.

The Indian was less than five feet tall, dressed in buckskins with seashells tied into his long ebony braids. He looked to be about ten, the same age as Josh's younger brother. The Indian boy appeared frightened, yet he was brave enough to glare at the lieutenant with defiance in his black eyes.

"Mackenzie, come back here!" Joshua shouted. "He's dangerous."

"Dangerous?" She gave a little laugh, though she was still shaking from the scare. "Dangerous? He's a boy." She left her mount's reins dangling and marched toward the child.

One of the men grabbed the boy by a hank of his hair and shoved him onto his knees.

She walked right through the middle of the soldiers. "You men afraid of this little boy?" she dared, irate at their handling of him. "You ought to be ashamed of yourselves."

"I must ask you to stand back, Miss Daniels. My men and I are trained to," the lieutenant cleared his throat, "deal with the enemy."

"Leaping apes in hell! He's a boy." She lifted her hand. "Children can't be enemies." Then she spotted blood on the sleeve of the boy's buckskin tunic. She stared at Lieutenant Burrow. "You shot him?"

"He stole the major's horse. He was trying to get away."

Mackenzie glanced at the bay casually nibbling on a bush. It was bridled with rough leather straps and saddled with a deerhide blanket. There were Indian symbols painted across its haunches in red ochre. It didn't look like a soldier's stolen horse to her.

She turned back to the Indian and reached for his arm, but he pulled back, saying something in his foreign tongue.

Mackenzie looked into his eyes, speaking slowly. "It's all right," she murmured. "I won't hurt you. I just want to look at your arm."

He relaxed a little, his gaze locked onto hers.

"That's right," she soothed. "I only want to look." She peeled back the blood-soaked leather of his sleeve. To her relief, the suntanned skin had only been grazed. It was an ugly, bloody wound, but clean, with no lead embedded in the flesh.

She called over her shoulder. "How do you know he stole Major Albertson's horse?"

"That's Major Albertson's horse, indeed." Burrow nodded. "I would know it anywhere. It has the white star on its forehead."

She snatched a water can from a soldier's saddle, opened the lid, and poured some of the water on the boy's arm. She hiked up her cotton tick skirt and knelt in the deep leaves to get a better look at the wound. "The major's horse is missing and you're certain this is it?"

"It's missing now, isn't it, Miss Daniels?" The lieutenant's tone was sharp and belittling. "Now please, if you will just step back and—"

"This man did not steal," the Indian boy said so softly that Mackenzie wasn't certain she heard him.

She looked up at his face, startled by the thickly accented English. "What did you say? You spoke English. I heard you."

He stared right into her face. "This man no steal English horse. Uncle's."

She blinked. "You didn't steal the horse?"

He stared at her with his black eyes. Her father had taught her to fear the redman. To avoid him. Now up close, the Indian boy seemed no different to her than a white boy. His blood ran the same color red. She saw the same fears as white men in his eyes.

"This man not steal," the boy repeated softly. "Take horse to fort. Uncle's horse."

"All right," she whispered so that only the boy could hear her. "I won't let them kill you. I swear it." Mackenzie reached under her skirt to tear a strip of muslin from the hem of her shift. She tied the muslin strip tightly around the boy's arm, speaking loudly. "Which way was he headed, Lieutenant?"

"Miss?"

She rose from her knees and whipped around to face the English officer. "The question was simple enough."

"Mackenzie, please. It's not our place to interfere," her father warned as he pushed his way through the crowd of soldiers.

She had done it again. She'd stepped over the line of female propriety. She could hear it in her father's voice. Yet she didn't care—not when she was all that stood between the boy and death. Mackenzie ignored him. "Lieutenant, I want to know which direction the boy was headed when you came upon him. Was he headed north toward the fort, or south toward us?"

The lieutenant avoided eye contact with her. "You do not know these scurvy red rats like I do, Miss Daniels. They can be rather crafty."

"I see." She swept off her bonnet to wipe the sweat from her forehead. "They're so crafty, these Indian boys, that they can be riding one way, but make it look like they're going another?" Her sarcasm was so thick that several of the soldiers snickered.

Lieutenant Burrow flushed. "Miss Daniels—"

A soldier approached them. "I got that rope ye asked for, Lieutenant. You want us to string 'im up right here on the road so the other redskins can see we're serious when it comes to horse thievin'?"

Mackenzie took a big step backwards putting herself between the Indian boy still on his knees and the soldier with the rope. Her bonnet fell to the ground, but she left it where it lay. "You hang this child, and I'll have you stand trial for murder," she threatened.

The soldier glanced at the lieutenant. The lieutenant looked at Franklin Daniels as if to ask why he couldn't control his own daughter.

Franklin cleared his throat. "Mackenzie, honey, step back and let the soldiers do their job."

"Do you hear yourself, Father? You sound just like them." She pointed at him. "We don't know if this horse is Major Albertson's or not."

"Mackenzie, I'm certain that Lieutenant Burrow has more experience with these matters than you or I do. He's lived in these woods. He's dealt with these hostiles."

"You always taught me to stand up for what I believe, Father." She stared him down. "I won't let them kill this boy for theft without a trial. We don't even know if that is the major's horse!"

She grabbed the Indian boy's hand and backed away while

still remaining between him and the soldiers. "There's no reason why the lieutenant can't wait until we reach the fort to sort this matter out. Major Albertson can witness for himself if this is his horse. If so, then I agree the *boy* must be punished, but I doubt our friend would agree to hanging a *child*, Father."

Franklin studied her for a moment, then reluctantly turned to the lieutenant. "Ed, she's right. We'll be at the fort in a few hours. If he stole the horse, what's the difference if you hang him now or at sunset?"

The soldiers waited for the officer to respond.

The lieutenant frowned, silent for a moment. "Cassidy," he shouted. "Tie the redskin up to your saddle. Let him trot a few hours. We'll give our major the satisfaction of hanging the little bastard himself." He walked away.

Mackenzie let out a sigh of relief. "They're not going to hang you," she told the boy quietly. "They're going to take you to the fort. Do you understand me?"

The soldier called Cassidy pulled the boy roughly to his feet and bound his hands together in front of him.

The boy looked at her, his ebony eyes filled with fear and relief and gratitude. "My uncle will speak the truth. *His* horse. Gift from English *manake* soldier many moons. This man no take the horse."

She smiled grimly. "We'll get to the bottom of this, I swear we will." She gave Cassidy a rough push on the shoulder. "Easy there. That's tight enough. You'll cut the blood off to his hands if you make those knots any tighter."

"Mackenzie," Joshua called as he led her horse toward her. "You'd best mount up." He kept his gaze lowered as if he were embarrassed by her forward behavior.

Not that she gave two snaps.

"I'm not riding." She snatched her hat up off the ground and beat off the leaves clinging to the straw.

"N . . . Not riding?"

She shook her head. "No. The boy walks. I walk. If I don't,

you know they'll move too quickly. They'll be dragging him behind a horse in less than an hour's time." She walked away before he had time to think of an answer.

As she approached Fort Belvadere Mackenzie could smell raw sewage and unwashed bodies.

The fort itself seemed rather unimposing here in the middle of such a grand wilderness. The fifteen-foot palisade walls were cut from nearby gum and sassafras trees. As big around as a man's forearm, the tree trunks had been sunk into the ground with the bark still attached and sharpened to points on the top.

A lookout high on the wall cried a warning and the gates swung open to allow the group inside. Mackenzie walked beside the Indian boy, her eyes and mind taking in all she saw and smelled and heard.

Inside the walls, one large, two-story log building ran east to west, its rear wall attached to the palisade. Smaller, even cruder buildings were scattered in the muddy yard.

Men in red uniforms hurried back and forth through the filthy compound. Pigs and geese ran freely, turning the entire yard into a slop pit. She nearly gagged at the smell of refuse that was piled everywhere: rotten cabbage, rancid meat, bean shells all just tossed into the yard on top of animal droppings. Yet she was fascinated at the same time.

Her father's tavern and trading post saw some activity during the traveling months, but there were never more than a dozen people there at a time. Here there had to be nearly one hundred soldiers, all milling about, most appearing bored.

Mackenzie felt trapped as the gates of the fort swung shut behind them. She understood the walls were for protection against the warring Indians, but she wasn't sure they made her feel any safer.

"Franklin! You're here at last. Mackenzie, dear." Major Al-

bertson rushed across the compound, his arms outstretched to
hug her.

Instead of looking at the major's familiar face, her gaze
was immediately drawn to the man who strode beside him.

A red man.

A savage.

The most glorious man she had ever laid eyes on.

LOOK FOR THESE REGENCY ROMANCES

ROMANCE FROM JANELLE TAYLOR

ANYTHING FOR LOVE   (0-8217-4992-7, $5.99)

DESTINY MINE   (0-8217-5185-9, $5.99)

CHASE THE WIND   (0-8217-4740-1, $5.99)

MIDNIGHT SECRETS   (0-8217-5280-4, $5.99)

MOONBEAMS AND MAGIC   (0-8217-0184-4, $5.99)

SWEET SAVAGE HEART   (0-8217-5276-6, $5.99)